# DESPAIR'S DEMISE

# DESPAIR'S DEMISE

## ODYSSEY OF THE ETHEREAL BOOK 4

### Jamie Kojola

Podium

# DESPAIR'S DEMISE

# CHAPTER 1

# The Warp and Weft of the Weave

Chaos had struck the city of Inexoria. The sky-high Tower of Moros, which often appeared to extend all the way up into the lower reaches of space, had collapsed into a pile of rubble. Most of its massive appearance had been illusory. The tower itself had been somewhere in the depths of space, not on physical worlds such as Grief; thus the rubble that remained of the tower seemed comically minuscule compared to the landmark that once dominated the sky, and which the city of Inexoria had literally been built around.

When the tower fell, four individuals appeared in the courtyard between the tower and the path down into Inexoria proper. That path was heavily guarded by the tax men of Inexoria, who were eager to get a share of the loot obtained by adventurers who had survived the trials of the Tower of Moros, but none of them were remotely equipped to deal with the party that had appeared. Sure, two of the party members were cute little kittens, but one radiated the unmistakable power of a sixth-tier Beast Sovereign, a threat capable of leveling cities and terrorizing whole worlds, while the other kitten radiated the power of a fifth-tier. In comparison, the strongest Cultivator in the city of Inexoria was High Climber Torane, himself a fifth tier Cultivator. And that was just the kittens. The two women were worse, each of whom were inhuman sixth tier Cultivators.

"State your names, and stand down until the High Climber arrives, please." The guard tried to project an aura of confidence, but a third tier Cultivator making demands of a party of three sixth-tiers and a fifth-tier wasn't likely to be well received, and his attempt at confidence failed completely. Instead the man sounded like he was begging.

"Why do you need to know our names if we're to wait for your precious High Climber?" Kallos Metanoia asked with confusion, not understanding the logic of the guard. Kallos stood taller than the averagely tall guard. Clad in a black armored dress with purple accents, with blonde hair, golden eyes that shone with inner light, a large witch's hat, and a cloak made of ominous black and white chains, Kallos probably looked intimidating. She was one hundred and eighty-eight centimeters tall *before* you added a few more for the heels of her armored knee-high boots. Then there were the tattoos that crawled along the skin of her limbs, visible on the glimpses of skin of her calves and forearms. Spiritual tattoos of chains slithered across her ivory skin as if they were serpents, ready to strike out with the witch's slightest whim.

Kallos radiated an imperious aura of mystery, beauty, and untouchable grace. As a Nephilim, she bore a heritage and bloodline that far exceeded that of an ordinary human, or even that of most half-blood humans. She was the daughter of Belial, after all. She had it all: looks, intelligence, power, empathy for the suffering. Telos loved Kallos more than anything.

Telos Metanoia, the woman who stood next to Kallos, was the same height, although thanks to being a shapeshifter, Telos could appear as any height, or as any-thing or anyone she wanted to. Literally, wine bottles or other inanimate objects, animals or monsters. Telos knew few limitations in this life. Once she had been a human woman on Earth named Aesca Lampi, who was then resurrected as Aetheria, a name she used until her ascension to the sixth tier, when she chose a new first name to match who she had become, and the last name to match with her wife, partner, lover, significant other, or whatever else one wanted to label Kallos.

Kallos's beauty and majesty drew eyes, but Telos drew eyes like a black hole. She was a tall woman, with a slender, willowy build, who wore laced up black combat boots; black cargo pants; a long, flowing, aqua scarf that danced in a wind that touched no one else; a perfectly tailored black trench coat; and a red tank top that revealed modest, glowing cleavage that sent motes of Divine Light into the air, which the third eye in the center of her forehead then absorbed. The Third-Eye of Ein Sof had started out as an accessory forged of her own soul, but it had evolved into a true third eye, although it looked like a black hole that devoured the constant light of Ein Sof generated by the conflict of her Ethereal and Void cores warring with each other. Her left eye was aqua blue, her right eye red. All three emitted light the same the color of the eye, a light bright enough to be seen in broad daylight. Uneven, asymmetrical bangs hung down to frame her face, while the rest of hair had been tied up in a ponytail that reached down to her mid back. Her hair glowed, much like her eyes, and like her eyes, held three colors: aqua, red, and black. If one stared at Telos long enough, you might even witness the spread of colors changing with her mood and whim.

"Lady Aetheria, Lord Torane will be along presently." A woman strode past the guards as if they were nothing more than set pieces, Torane's assistant, T'ess. She looked mostly human but had fangs and slightly tipped ears. Telos still thought the woman looked like a vampire, and the black to her outfit and hat certainly did noth-ing to dispel such assumptions.

"I am called Telos Metanoia now," Telos said gently but firmly. The name tied her and Kallos together, just as the soul bond did, and so she fully embraced it. To do anything else would be a rejection of Kallos and herself.

"Congratulations on your ascension, Lady Telos." T'ess bowed elaborately.

"Indeed, it's rare for someone to enter a tower and come out two tiers higher at your level of progression. Rarer still that the tower itself collapses into rubble behind you. In fact, I've never heard of that happening." Lord Torane held the appearance of an average man in his forties, with dark hair and milky white-gray eyes. As a fifth tier Cultivator, he stood as one of the most influential people in the world of Grief, and being Lord of Inexoria and its taxation on the Tower of Moros had made him rich beyond belief, in addition to the vast fortune he'd earned when he climbed and finished the Tower of Moros.

The tower that now lay in rubble. The hopes and dreams of Inexoria's people no doubt with it. Without the Tower of Moros, there was no reason for there to be a city anymore.

"Alas, Moros would not change his mind and insisted on a fight to the death, despite and because he knew he would lose." Telos looked at the rubble, then frowned at the implications for the city. She lifted a hand, and a single snowflake shot into the air to form a new barrier around Inexoria.

"You have approximately a year with the amount of energy I infused that with—one year to work out new defenses if you do not move to new cities. The ley lines that fed the tower could provide considerable energy to someone brave enough to tap them." Telos then gestured, and piles of random treasures she'd found throughout Aetherius's tower and a couple of pieces from Moros tumbled into the courtyard.

"I don't have time to remain, but that should provide some compensation for the inconvenience we have caused to the fine people of Inexoria."

Torane had a glint in his eye as if greed might threaten to overwhelm him. It was writ plain on his face: if Telos would part with this voluntarily, what might she part with if he pressed more?

A cough from Kallos drew Torane's gaze, and his eyes widened slightly. He seemed shocked he had not noticed the beautiful woman, and then his eyes widened more when he realized she was a sixth-tier.

"If you do not wish your city to become a battleground between us and a greater Archon, you may wish to cease these needless delays."

"A *greater* Archon?" Torane sputtered and stepped aside. The former climber's greed faltered in the face of his survival instincts. "By all means, exit our city as swiftly as possible."

"We will, thanks." Telos gestured, and a silver gateway like those used inside the towers formed. "The heavens are going to get a good shaking. If I were you, I would make preparations." With that ominous warning, the four all stepped through the gateway and into what appeared to be a magitech engine room full of crystals and the sounds of chiming.

"Off by a little bit." Telos laughed. "Welcome to the Lost City of Atlanta. Ark, let Werylin know we've arrived, and let him know he's free to join us."

* * *

Ten minutes later, Kallos, Telos, Bobbi, and Arkaziel all relaxed in comfortable chairs around a coffee table. Werylin Amaryllis, a purple-haired swordsman in a beautiful hakama, also sat with them.

"You killed some Archons, Izanagi, Izanami, Moros, Ouranos, Inanna, Ereshkigal, and Quetzalcoatl, and now you've got the Overgod involved, and you plan to kill him, too, I suppose?" Werylin summarized the discussion so far.

"I mean, if he gets in my way, it won't be avoidable. He's not my primary target, though. I've got a grudge to settle with Oizys, too. I'm not going to just forget about Grief. I made a promise." Telos shrugged.

"This tea is delicious, Werylin. Could I buy some for our trip?" Bobbi interrupted, after tasting the tea Werylin had set out. Bobbi had once again abandoned the form of a kitten, and taken on the form of a dark-skinned human woman with cat ears, a tail, reddish-black hair, and pink-yellow feline eyes.

"Of course, Lady Slay. I'll include some other blends as well." Werylin acquiesced at once, and more than a little subserviently.

"I agree, it's delightful." Kallos nodded, and Werylin practically squirmed from the praise of the two women.

"Yeah, yeah, it's great tea. Quit making the elf blush." Arkaziel, still a kitten, lapped milk tea from a saucer like a civilized cat. "You're going to give him a stroke."

Telos frowned at the four, who barely reacted to her proclamation about the Overgod and Oizys. That no one even batted an eye at the declaration bothered her, as if it was expected of her, and she didn't know how to feel about those kinds of expectations.

"Really, we're just going to skim over the whole taking down a goddess and maybe an Overgod? Oh damn, that is some good tea," Telos amended after she finally sipped from her cup. She looked forlornly at the empty cup after emptying it, not wanting to trouble anyone for a refill, but very much wishing for another cup. Some Midwestern habits were impossible to let go of, even after reincarnation.

"Darling, we've all traveled with you for some length of time. That your journey will take us to slay more gods, maybe an Overgod, is hardly even worth mentioning. What is one more on the list? Oizys isn't even a particularly powerful goddess. She's just a cruel and terrible one. As for the Overgod, his Archons will be problematic, but we will prevail. Have you considered calling in the Celestial Wardens? Siegfried is said to exist solely for the very thing you have already carried out." Kallos radiated amusement at Telos's annoyance that none of them were reacting to her agenda.

"Did you forget I'm a god-eater?" Arkaziel grumbled. "I've only been with you since the start, almost." Arkaziel's voice and suddenly impossibly large kitten eyes radiated the look of a forgotten and hungry kitten so perfectly that Telos had to stop herself from picking him up and cuddling him.

"I might not be as obsessed with eating gods as the twerp, but they make great meals, and the fewer of them there are, the better. Besides, how am I supposed to surpass this idiot if I don't eat at least as well as him?" Bobbi's competitive nature bared its fangs at Arkaziel, almost visibly.

"Where you go, I go," Kallos said sincerely.

"See what I'm dealing with, Werylin? There's no voice of sanity to say, no, no, don't take on gods in their place of power, don't fight the Overgod, think of the universe! Just two hungry cats and the most beautiful woman in any world willing to follow me into any form of damnation I might chose." Telos laughed, Kallos reddened slightly, and the StarManes seemed uncertain whether they were supposed to be offended.

"Yes, it is truly a terrible curse you are burdened with. Since no one disagrees with the whys, why not focus on the how? Will you burn her temples until she sends an avatar? Assault her tower?" Werylin seemed very pro burning her temples, but they were talking about a goddess who'd cursed him to exist as an undead for thousands of years, until Telos revived him and reunited him with his clan. A bit of a grudge was to be expected, right?

"Well, I have an idea about that, actually." Telos touched the band on her wrist, which held the Flame of Nyx, the personification of Night itself. "Callie, want to have some input on this conversation?"

# CHAPTER 2

# Night's Tale

S ure, Telos." A pale-skinned beauty stepped from nowhere into the room.
Nyx, personification of Night, Primordial, former Overgod, and one of the prime architects of Telos's existence entered the room as if she'd always been there. Nyx's black-on-black eyes were prone to take people off guard who hadn't met her before. She wore a long cloak of pure night, and a gown of purest white to match her skin. As the mother of many Primordials, daemons, gods, and who knew what else, Nyx stood high in the world of gods, and walked the fine line between divinity and dark divinity. As a raider in the MMO Eldest Fantasy Wars Online, using her alter ego of Callie, Nyx had been a mage who only cared about being the top of the damage charts, often failing or nearly failing raid mechanics to get one extra spell off to ensure her place as the #1 damage dealer.

No matter how many times Aesca, Pete, and others in the Knights of Academia had tried to convince Callie that the best DPS was the one who didn't cause extra raid damage by failing a mechanic, or burn a healer's mana to save her, Callie had stubbornly clung to the idea that she would be the top damage dealer of the raid, everyone else's opinions be damned.

"I think you know everyone here. Arkaziel, Bobbi, Kallos, this is Nyx. Nyx, Arkaziel, Bobbi, and Kallos." Telos didn't know if the introductions were necessary or not, but it seemed best to make them just in case.

"This is like meeting my daughter-in-law for the first time, how exciting," Nyx quipped and nodded to Kallos. "Welcome to the family."

"I wasn't nervous before, but I admit that created a considerable rush of anxiety." Kallos laughed nervously. Family remained a touchy subject with the Nephilim, whose entire world had been purged by the Overgod in response to the corruption of Belial spreading wholesale through the world. Gnosis was a danger to the power base of the Overgod, the only true escape from the shackles of the physical world.

"So, do you suppose Oizys would just surrender Grief?" Telos changed the subject.

"She might, if you make it worth her while. She's loath to give up anything unless forced or bribed. Self-preservation will only come into play if you already have her dead to rights. My little daemons have never had need of survival instincts and are blind to existential threats. Or they become so enthralled by the idea they embrace it willfully, and find an end to this eternal existence, as Moros did." Nyx's disapproval of Moros's choice could not be clearer if she called him an idiot.

"I was afraid you'd say that. I wanted to put a tidy bow on her and move on to the big guy, but of course someone named Misery is going to be a pain in the ass," Telos grumbled and leaned against Kallos.

"If you want little Miseria to agree, you'll need to have your hand around her throat, or be poised to destroy her base of power. Unlike most gods, my little daemons are part of the fabric of existence for all living things, so razing their temples and smiting their believers wouldn't accomplish anything but the deaths of people prone to making poor life decisions." Nyx, as Primordial Night, had little to gain from temples and believers, much like the daemons.

"Oh man, we just climbed two towers; now you want us to climb the Tower of Misery?" Arkaziel whined. "The towers are so boring!"

"That would be one way to reach her, certainly," Nyx agreed, but she seemed to hint she shared Arkaziel's disdain for that route.

"There's another way?" Bobbi asked in confusion.

"Well, you could bribe her. You've acquired wealth, power, authority. A single authority could woo her, but you would be creating a future problem across all the material worlds to solve the problems of one material world." Nyx grimaced, under no illusions to the nature of her children. "It is a terrible idea."

"I know what we have to do." Telos laughed as the emanations of the divine from Binah led her to the right answer. She wanted to feel proud of having the answer, but she couldn't muster it. Plucking answers from Binah took no skill, no ingenuity. The cost to Telos? A mere moment's focus.

"Do you need my help?" Nyx asked bluntly.

"No, it's better you don't get in trouble for this part. That may change when it comes time to deal with the Overgod, if you're willing to?" Telos honestly didn't know how personally involved the Primordials who'd gotten her into this mess wanted to be in the resolution to the comedy of errors they'd created of this universe.

"I will stand with you when the time comes, and I will feel out the others. Chronos sends this." Nyx held out a wooden spindle, wrapped with luminous threads. The spindle itself radiated immense power, and the fragment of Ananke within it resonated with the similar piece inside of Telos's soul. "He cannot bear to witness the end of his beloved but knows it must be done."

"Then that will leave only Phanes." Telos rubbed at her chin. "Where the hell am I supposed to get a piece of Phanes?"

"He was my consort. Did it never occur to you to ask me?" Nyx rolled her eyes and tsked at Telos.

"I assumed you put whatever fragment you retained of him into me?" Telos grimaced. "I don't know why I assumed that. Do you have another fragment of Phanes?"

"I do." Nyx held out a small ivory egg circled by a jade serpent. "You needn't worry about ensnaring Dionysus. His aspect of Phanes has already gone through the Great Cycle and will not respond to your gathering."

"I wasn't worried about him." Telos laughed a little to blunt the damaging truth of her intentions. Yet it made her consider, once again, if she was in the wrong to consider most gods fair game for crossfire and consequences for her fixing their messes.

"I don't suppose you would be." Nyx's dark eyes twinkled in amusement at the callous disregard Telos showed toward gods, and the inner conflict that arose as Telos wondered if she should be worried.

*I guess, technically, they are living beings.*

"I would use those sooner rather than later, Aes, err, Telos," Nyx cautioned her, the urgency enough to fluster the unassailable Primordial.

*Unless she's just acting. It would be very Callie-like to go on about dire warnings when things aren't really that dire.*

"Why? Do they weaken? They seem stable," Kallos interjected from next to Telos, where she studied the objects Telos held. Telos knew no one more knowledgeable about souls than Kallos. She was *the* Soul Witch after all.

"You already have Archons on your trail. Your chances to summon those two will only diminish the more the Overgod sends after you. Right now, you are an annoyance. He has not yet bent true attention to hunting you. After all, you aren't his creation, so how difficult could it be to deal with you? Capitalize on that, and make what few preparations you need before you deal with Oizys." Nyx seemed disappointed that none of the four had thought that part through.

"How am I supposed to surpass Arkaziel if I don't eat some big Archons?" Bobbi asked with a terrifying grin that showed sharp teeth in her humanoid form.

"Even you would struggle to make those creatures palatable," Nyx warned Bobbi.

"Energy beings are like carbs. Ten minutes after eating them you're starving because you digested them so quickly. The little bit of carbon their essence is tied to isn't enough to fill a stomach." Arkaziel's complaints about the fullness factor of Archons left Telos and Kallos struggling to keep a straight face.

"Point taken, Nyx. Thanks for the information, essences, and advice." Telos looked around her group. "Is there anything any of you need to take care of before we deal with Oizys and step into the fire for real?"

"I'd like to tier up, but I'm not quite there yet," Bobbi chimed in. "Maybe after you summon the essences? Or even during? It might draw powerful creatures during the ritual, plus all the energy you absorb from it gets shared with us anyway, so I'll be close soon." Her tone bounced between uncertainty and surety about reaching the next stage in ascension once she remembered the positive effects of the soul-binds.

"I don't like that you get to share my bond-partner's gains." Arkaziel harrumphed.

"The ritual bound her to me as well as Kallos, Ark. If you want to blame anyone, blame yourself for demanding she bind to Kallos. You *knew* Kallos's and my soul bond is deeper than a companion bond. What did you think was going to happen?" Telos waggled a finger at the ornery cat.

"Bah!" Arkaziel curled up and pretended to go to sleep. His fake snores were exceptionally passive aggressive, and each one provoked a small twitch of one of Telos's three eyelids.

"I have already completed all of my unfinished business in the time you ascended the Tower of Aetherius. I am with you until the end, darling." Kallos leaned in to plant a light kiss on Telos's cheek.

"What about your apprentices?"

"They're capable mages in their own right, and the trouble that gets them into is their own problem. I am no one's master." The two women's eyes locked, and Kallos had a small smirk that Telos interpreted to mean "unless you ask nicely." She restrained herself from asking.

"Well, I guess that's that then. We'll nip Phanes and Ananke in the bud, and my soul will be fully my own again. We'd better figure out a place to do the rituals that we aren't overly attached to. There's always a chance we'll pull an Archon with the divine essences." Telos let the tides of Binah wash over her.

"Good luck, Telos. If you need us, call." Nyx stepped into the darkness and vanished, and both Bobbi and Kallos let out breaths of relief, though Bobbi's anxiety had been much greater than Kallos's.

"What's wrong?" Telos didn't understand why they'd both been anxious.

"You didn't feel the power coursing off Nyx? The intimidating aura? The way she flaunted her authority of night?" Bobbi looked aghast.

"No?" Telos laughed nervously. She hadn't felt any pressure or power to be concerned about at all; if anything, she'd thought Nyx had been gentle in her presence, compared to the amazing power she'd displayed in earlier meetings.

"I do not see a reason she would seek to intimidate Bobbi or Arkaziel. StarManes are not known for being intimidated. Thus, she wished to flaunt that power and status to either myself or you, or Werylin." Kallos looked to the elf, who was still sitting at the table, but his face was much more pale, and his eye twitched.

"Oh, right." Telos had kind of forgotten Werylin was in the room while Nyx had answered her call, and it seemed like the presence of the Primordial had shaken Werylin up a little.

"We're going to get out of your hair, Werylin. I'll be in touch after we handle Oizys. It's a bit dangerous for us to hang around anywhere right now, and you've got your whole clan here in Atlanta."

It took the elf a few solid moments to compose himself.

"I appreciate your concern for my descendants. We have been contacted by Lord Torane, and our inroads with other rulers have been well received. All are nervous, though, and are unwilling to commit to an alliance until they are certain that it will not explode in their face with the laughter of Oizys mocking their suffering. When you have taken care of her, our mission will truly begin in earnest." Werylin's eagerness for the deposition of Oizys warred with his distaste for the politics that would come into play once her thumb no longer prevented any alliances from forming and making life better on Grief.

"Ark, wake up. Do you remember those vast lava plains?" Telos poked the still-pretending-to-snore Arkaziel awake.

"Yeah, they were big, flat, and empty. What about them? Going to build a statue of me there?" Arkaziel forgot to pretend to yawn or shake off any sleepiness. He realized his mistake too late and let out a groan of defeat.

"If that's what you really want. Think it'd be a good ritual site?" Telos tried to keep any frustration from her voice. Maybe a statue would cheer Arkaziel up. He always did love a good statue of himself.

"Oh sure. Lots of room, lots of power, not many elementals. Yeah, that should work. Pity we can't jump worlds to keep the chances of interference from Oizys down, but if she sends a big lava golem or something Bobbi can just eat it." Arkaziel laughed. "Unless it's really tasty, then you've got to share with me, right?"

"Ugh, fine, whatever, I'll share with you if it's tasty." Bobbi didn't sound like she'd share willingly. The two quarreled like teenagers.

"Alright, take care of everyone, Werylin." A new gate formed, and Werylin had to scream to stop them from going through it.

"Wait!" The samurai-elf rubbed his throat, so loud had he screeched.

"What?" Arkaziel asked as he hopped onto Telos's shoulder.

"I've got to get the tea that Lady Bobbi and Lady Kallos asked about!" Werylin sighed in a put-upon way before he darted out of the room as if he were confronted with a personal emergency. Telos even heard him cast Haste so he could get the tea quicker.

"He would make a good majordomo," Telos murmured thoughtfully.

Five minutes later, the party appeared on a plain of dark rocks, tea loaded into their various storage methods, the danger of lack of caffeine thwarted by the stalwart Werylin.

"Ominous place." Kallos noted of the dark rock, flows of lava, and vents of sulfur. None of them required oxygen to live, so it wasn't a deal-breaker for any of them, and Telos's presence fought the heat of the lava, and maintained a comfortable temperature in her vicinity.

"Perfect place to end two gods," Arkaziel chimed in.

"You mean to end two transcendent beings," Telos corrected. "Hopefully, they don't put up more of a fight than the Primordials did. Maybe we can learn who killed Phanes before we eat him."

"I'm not sure I approve of you talking about eating gods, darling. It's disturbing when you do it. Leave that talk for the cats, please," Kallos requested, with a demure look that Telos literally could not say no to.

# CHAPTER 3

# The Death of Necessity

What did Werylin say this place was called again?" Arkaziel beheld the vast plains of sulfur vents, lava, and volcanic rock, all interspersed with signs of ancient ruins. Whatever people had lived here once had met a cataclysmic end, as was the expectation on a world called Grief. The stink of misery lay heavy on the land, a bitter curse that suffocated all hope.

"Werylin called it The Obsidian Tears of Skadur. Apparently, this Skadur guy decided he was ready to ascend to the heights of godhood and challenged Oizys to best him if she dared. So, she brought lava and sulfur, and trapped the entire nation within the flows of molten lava. She made each citizen's suffering last for ages, granting the relief of death to only a single citizen once a year, and the pain and suffering each felt was directed to Skadur upon their death, so that he would learn the folly of mocking gods." Telos couldn't help but wince at the hardcore punishment as she told the tale.

"The lingering pain and suffering steep this ground. Are there still souls trapped in the depths of lava? I do not sense any, but if a demi-plane is hidden within, it could open anytime." Kallos's golden eyes glowed much brighter than normal as she sought signs of souls within the fields of suffering.

"This world is such a shithole," Bobbi grumbled. "Why don't we travel to a world without all the tragic, awful backstories to every single bit of land across the whole damned planet?"

"You wanted to catch up to Arkaziel; maybe this Skadur was powerful enough to help that?" Telos offered optimistically as the seal of Ananke formed in the ground. "Besides, I like to think my offer of absolution to the suffering they've endured will call them, and another one of Oizys's cruelties can finally be ended, if nothing else."

"I'm hungry, and someone's getting eaten, lava ghost or forces of fate, I'll eat them all." Arkaziel stretched energetically, but Telos recognized it was the cat's way of approving.

"Why are we doing Ananke first?" Bobbi wondered.

"There's something to do before we finish Phanes, and we may have to run after the first one. I'm fairly certain the trial with Phanes's legacy can be done anywhere.

Alright, I'm starting. You two, destroy everything that tries to interfere with me and Kallos. Love, if these two need help, go ahead; if it comes down to it, I can brute force my way through the ritual alone if I absolutely have to." Telos leaned in to peck Kallos on the lips with a light kiss.

"By starlit bonds and decrees of fate, Ananke, serpent of destiny, I call you to the end you prescribed in the flows of fate. Step through the Gate!" Telos's chants and the raw power of the initial opening of the Celestial Gate had grown exponentially in strength since they summoned the first god this way. A mote of the essence of Ananke, a gift from Chronos, called its like from across the universe to join together.

Ananke had once been human or something like a human. She, like Chronos and Khaos, had triggered the formation of this reality with their fellow transcendent, Phanes. The sheer power of the first mote that flowed through the gate to join the orb of Ananke's essence staggered Telos. She had expected the power differential between gods and Primordials to be significant, and it had been. Still, the difference between Primordials and transcendents was a gulf far vaster than between gods and Primordials. She could not even quantify the difference; beyond that whatever scale mortals, demigods, gods, Primordials, and transcendents were on was exponential. Telos had never been quite so aware of the staggering, insurmountable cliffs that mortals faced in this existence before, because now she realized something else.

Ananke was a tier below Telos herself. For all the sheer, unmitigated power of her essence, for all the power of being the ultimate arbiter of Necessity and Fate of a whole existence, Ananke was *less* than Telos, her power and authorities nestled inside of Telos as if Ananke had been a much smaller nesting doll waiting to go inside of her this whole time.

"Magic," Arkaziel called lazily. Despite his calmness, he grew into a thirty-meter-long dragon. When humanoid lava forms rose from the depths of magma chambers tied to a previously hidden demi-plane, he blasted the first to rise in the face with dark lasers that leached their heat and shattered them.

"This whole cold light thing does have *some* potential, Blue!" Arkaziel cackled and swept his dark beams of cold light across figures as they emerged.

"Don't steal all the kills, twerp," Bobbi growled at Arkaziel. "And what's so groundbreaking about heat dissipation? Is your clan so lacking basic science knowledge that you can't imagine the efficacy of cold?"

Bobbi didn't bother with turning into a dragon. Instead, she drew Moros's bow, and dark arrows hit the rising figures' center mass. The arrows promptly exploded, destroying the lava people. Yet for all the ease of killing, for each one they killed, three more would rise. It wasn't long before Arkaziel swept his breath attack in a wide arc to clear a burgeoning horde.

From the depths of the previously hidden demi-plane, an immensely powerful source of magic appeared that each party member couldn't help but notice. A being of obsidian, lava, and petrified flesh emerged, accompanied by a tide of lesser minions. Telos had no doubt it was the self-damned once-king Skadur, whose eons of misery had concentrated into a palpable aura of anguish, and when she turned her mind to Da'at momentarily to touch all the Sefirot, she knew she was right.

Talking to her party happened in a far more complicated way than usual. Telos found the strain of Ananke pressed so hard upon her that it took her what felt like minutes to communicate with the party.

~ *That's Skadur, the once-king. He can imbue his anguish into attacks; don't underestimate him.* ~

+ *Rock people are the worst to eat.* + Arkaziel's response made Telos realize what had happened; her sense of time had dilated as if she were employing the highest peaks of her superhuman speed, and the world slowed to a snail's pace.

Then Telos stood in an eternal Void, where only an immense serpent and herself existed.

"It's been a long time since anyone has sought to visit me. Why have you, of all people, come? Do you strive to murder me once more?" the serpent, which possessed startlingly perceptive eyes, asked.

"Who do you think I am?" Telos let her aura flare with all her authority and her Transformative Flame of Eternal Becoming rather than the barest emanations she usually let out.

"You aren't a mortal, but you aren't a god, despite the ridiculous number of authorities you possess. Yet you possess the Divine Light outside of Pleroma, how flashy." Ananke frowned. "You're just a Monarch? Not even a Sovereign yet . . . you aren't Chaos."

Disappointment clouded Ananke's voice with that declaration, and with it, all of the hostility she held faded away.

"You're supposed to be dead. The tale I was told is that you gave up physical form after the decision to build the towers and the death of Phanes. I'm guessing that's not what happened? Chaos? Do you mean Khaos?" Telos barely finished while Ananke laughed at her.

"Of course, it isn't. Someone killed me, replaced me, and fabricated the idea that I would do such an idiotic thing as discorporate. Chronos fell for it, then?" Ananke sighed, the weary sigh of a woman who hoped for the best out of their spouse but was disappointed once again.

"I don't know? I've only met Chronos a few times, but it seems so. I could summon him here?" Telos offered.

"I'm already here," said a black-clad figure who emerged from nothing. Yet Telos instinctively knew he'd used the Flame he had imbued into the Astrum Nexus to travel here. How long had he hidden an avatar within the weapon? Since it was first forged? Now that she thought about it, Chronos just giving her a part of himself had always felt suspect. Were all of the essences in her gloves a spying device? "I've never had the chance to breach the barrier here without tipping off its creator. I'm so, so sorry, Rose."

"What meaning does time have to either of us, David?" The serpent cackled. Telos couldn't help but note the oddity of watching two people stare lovingly at one another when one was the form of living darkness and the other a giant serpent. "Besides, you did what Chaos wanted."

Ananke nodded at Telos. "You made her."

"Anyone care to fill me in here? It's rude to leave your guest in the dark." Telos reminded the star-crossed lovers of her presence as a participant in the conversation.

"You'll figure it out soon enough. Until then, you shouldn't fully understand the mess you've entered. You aren't prepared to defend yourself yet. I have left a husk of a shell, barely more than an animation of my pitiful remains, in control of my domain, watching over an empire of dust. It will fail when you trigger the failsafe I imbued in your gloves. Activate it to assume my power fully. I will leave this existence with Ananke. We should have never crossed the Origin, never helped Phanes, and certainly not joined those obnoxious children in Dreamland, or followed them to this place."

"We thought we were gods." Ananke laughed.

"We were greater than gods and Primordials." Chronos disagreed with Ananke. "But so much less than the puppet master behind Chaos and 'Wisdom.'"

"Who the hell are you talking about? Who the crap is Chaos? Wisdom? Puppet master?" Telos demanded answers.

"In my defense, I was killed before the exodus from Dreamland," Ananke pointed out. "You are consuming my power, my existence, but also unweaving me, in a way, to give me another try in the Great Cycle. None of those things should be possible, but thank you, Monarch. Chaos is a specter of the emptiness before creation, a manifestation of Nothing." Ananke spoke candidly, unafraid of repercussions.

"Her name is Aet—"

"My name is Telos Metanoia now. As the literal personification of ti—oh. You were making fun of me." Telos grumbled under her breath when she realized Chronos misidentified her to get a rise out of her. Although he was made entirely of darkness, he radiated a smug satisfaction.

"Yes, it's a thing I do sometimes. Enjoy your adventures with two StarManes. I bred them to right the wrongs of a universe, but I have begun to suspect I may have overdone it, slightly." Chronos shrugged in a dismissive way, as if that was all in the past now, or at the very least not his problem, even if he had created them.

"So that's it? You're not going to tell me who my enemy is; you're just going to bequeath me your power on a time delay and ride off into the sunset with your girlfriend?"

"Exactly right." Chronos laughed openly.

"Be nice to the lady. She's genuine in her concern. Such that I won't hit her with the curse I've been weaving since my death. You may take that, too, with my powers. It should be enough to stun even your enemy." With Ananke's words, a curseform drifted down for Telos to assume command of the spell. The seemingly infinite layers of an impossibly powerful curse linked together made Telos blanch. Such a curse could vaporize three or four galaxies.

"You'd expect a bearer of Ohr Ein Sof to be more than an ordinary human." Ananke laughed.

"There's no such thing as an ordinary human," Chronos said, shaking his head. "The Cycle calls. Let's leave this existence and its painful lessons behind."

Ananke and Chronos stared at one another, until the latter heaved a great sigh.

"I suppose this is to their plan anyway. Your enemies aren't as you think them to be. Chaos is, I suppose, a child of Ayin. Sophia is the Aeon of Wisdom. Both dance to the tune played by an entity I do not know the name of. Chaos provided his sock puppet Khaos with the power to create you, but that power came from other existences. *Many existences.*"

"Thank you." Telos offered her sincere gratitude to Chronos for sharing the information, albeit at the very last moment.

"Good luck," Telos whispered to the two as she consumed them, casting them into the Great Cycle of rebirth once more, with a blessing of fortune upon them this time.

The realm of darkness vanished, and her awareness of the world around her came back to focus. The StarMane duo were still fighting Skadur and his minions. Bobbi had become a two-hundred-meter-long dragon, and Arkaziel seemed as large as the ship *Nidhogg's Bane* from so long ago, significantly larger than even Bobbi. Despite the immense strength of Arkaziel, and the fact that he'd bound Skadur, he and Bobbi couldn't finish off Skadur.

Kallos, meanwhile, fought against a five-meter-tall greater Archon, whose corrupted powers of reality defilement threatened to breach the powerful counterspell she had raised to block it.

"You can't win." Telos declared a new inevitability to the universe, and the Archon's attempt to breach Kallos's blocking spells completely failed and rebounded, destroying one of the enhanced carbon arms of the Archon.

"Welcome back, darling; I wondered when you'd wake up again." Kallos blew Telos a kiss before she lifted a hand and unleashed a powerful judgment on the Archon. Even with Telos's proclamation, the Archon resisted destruction and sealing. "Believe it or not, I might need your help with a greater Archon."

"Ask and you shall receive." Telos laughed and cracked her knuckles.

# CHAPTER 4

# Archons Act Atrociously

The material bodies of the Archons were made entirely from carbon and were mostly unnecessary. They were spiritual beings created by Ialdabaoth, and while their powers were similar to the mythical angels of Earth, that was where the similarities ended. The spiritual energy that made up the true existence of the Archons ranged from that of a weak god to equivalent to the weakest of Demiurges, and the greater Archons had helped create the universe under the command of Ialdabaoth.

The greater Archon before them studied Telos with dispassionate eyes.

"You are in defiance of the will of the Overgod," the blue-white glowing sack of carbon warned Telos. "Submit yourself to his mercy or be destroyed. You lack the power to defeat Esmunon, Harbinger of the Silent Storms. I will no longer hold back, now that you are present."

Unbridled anger bubbled up from within Telos. This walking bundle of carbon and spiritual energy not only dared to condescend to her, but thought itself greater than her while in full denial of reality. No aeonic being would make this kind of mistake, and yet this crude being made by a pretender presumed to speak down to her, when even Bythos or Sige would watch their words to her?

Its words still echoed offensively in the air when Telos appeared in front of it. Her fist demolished its carbon head and upper body in a single blow. Black energies expanded outward from her fist into the Archon's body, and black tendrils of the Void consumed its spiritual essence. The immense forces of order were slow to deplete before the power of the Void. Like dense hardwood, the forces of the Void were a slow-burn destruction against the powerful Archon. No matter how densely Ialdabaoth had woven the infusion of power into the creature, it was still just a construct made with high-level reality manipulation, and the Void consumed it like the stupid doll it was, which made Telos smile. To speed up the process she pushed her left hand into the spiritual body of the Archon.

Frigid light engulfed Telos's left hand as rays of Ohr Ein Sof filtered from her Third-Eye of Ein Sof across the battlefield. Coalescing forms of additional lesser Archons vanished before they could solidify, and the invisible spellforms of the greater Archon's conjuration magic vanished in wisps of displaced energy. Even the Archon's conjuration magic required complicated spellforms, which were easy to interrupt.

"You should have done that before I got here, but Kallos interrupted you every time, didn't she? Isn't arrogance supposed to be a sin?" Telos let her mouth run, while she grasped ahold of the essence of Esmunon, and tried to destroy it with the power of Ein Sof. Yet it kept slipping her commands. The power of the infinite seemed to have a mind of its own, and while it seemed happy to destroy the spells of Esmunon, it wouldn't destroy the Archon itself.

*"You have trials to surpass before the power of Ohr Ein Sof submits to you. Your arsenal is large enough to not need it for this pathetic construct,"* Reverie advised.

"So much for the easy way." Telos laughed and released her attempts to control Ein Sof, and instead swallowed her left hand in the power of the Ethereal, and the power of the Transformative Flame of Eternal Becoming.

The Archon, incapable of fear, asked questions.

"How did you utilize the Boundless Light? What is that abomination of chaos you call a Flame? Lord Ialdaboa—" Telos activated Existence Oscillation and danced through reality in a flurry of punches, kicks, stabs, and slashes with fists, talons, and feet. Hundreds of variations of Telos assaulted the Archon in a conflux that defied space-time. The attack resonated impossibly with the Void with its utter defiance of the rules of physical reality and contrivance of singular existences in a Cycle. The attack obliterated every atom of carbon that Esmunon bound its spirit to, and then kept going. Without the binding agent of carbon, the impossible barrage landed spiritual blows upon Esmunon. Many Cultivators even of the sixth tier couldn't land a direct punch upon a spiritual being of an Archon's caliber, but between the condensed power of the Void and the Origin pushed into every cell of her body, and the divinely forged power of the Astrum Nexus out of soulsteel, Telos could damage purely spiritual beings as easily as physical ones.

When the cascade of blows finished, the ragged blue life-flames of the Archon had dimmed significantly, and then Kallos's voice finished the incantation to a spell. "Vortex of the Black Maw!"

A vortex of black spiritual wind whipped up around Kallos, flowed around Telos, and struck the Archon. It was as if the Archon were made of sand, and the black wind just picked up pieces of Esmunon and carried them away into the abyss. The Archon's defenses had been stripped away by the innumerable attacks from Telos, and the blasting dark winds of the Soul Witch ripped free the life essence of the Archon, whereupon Telos grasped it firmly in her hand and devoured it.

Power flowed through Telos to her bonded companions—the power of a greater Archon was split and divided up among them. Telos and Kallos enjoyed the rush of power, whereas for Bobbi and Arkaziel the power-up and gains helped them wipe out the last of Skadur's minions and focus on ripping the lava and rock king apart piece by piece.

"Do you think they need help?" Telos asked Kallos earnestly, while surveying the battlefield.

"I think if we don't finish the tragedy of Skadur and be on our way, we'll have a whole host of Archons come down on us. I blocked all his reinforcement calls, but unless the Archon followed our trail independently, someone either called it here, or sent it here." Kallos chewed her lower lip as she sought traces to indicate which scenario they faced, and Telos couldn't help but get distracted by how adorable the blonde looked when she was worried.

A massive surge of Void occurred within herself. From her soul aperture the power flowed to Arkaziel, which drew Telos's attention back to the fight. "Looks like Arkaziel got impatient," Telos noted as energy flooded the soul bonds between the party.

"Did your cat figure out how to use your own power as if you were the one who wielded it, just there?" Kallos asked as power flowed through her.

"I think he did. Now he gets power, the satisfaction of killing things, optimized gains for the party, and a pat on the head for being a good boy. I'm surprised he just hasn't formed a link with Bobbi yet. They remain the only two without a direct connection among us. Probably for the best, though, since Bobbi might not be able to handle that much Void corruption?" Telos voiced concerns, but wasn't sure how valid they were.

"Apparently for StarManes, soul-linking to their own species is reserved for marriage, and Bobbi has refused Arkaziel's advances until he's proven he's more than a 'doe-eyed noob in the kitchen, and a beast in the sack.'" Kallos couldn't contain a small giggle at Bobbi's phrasing. "If you're worried about her exposure, though, I can teach her soulfire purification to maintain her own safety."

"Thanks for the help," Arkaziel said sarcastically as he dropped onto Telos's shoulder, back to his normal housecat size.

"You had it covered, but we'd best beat feet. Archons might not be the only ones after us." A silver doorway appeared in the air. On the other side only a beach was visible. No one mentioned its name, they just jumped through, and only when the doorway closed, did Bobbi, in her human form again, ask an important question.

"Why the hell are we at the Shores of Chaos? I assume this is the real thing?" The StarMane's pink eyes flared with confusion and more than a little anxiety. The power of the real thing was much greater than the false version in the Tower of Aetherius. The rainbow-hued shore was littered with debris and detritus from across known existence, and objects bobbled up to the surface and bobbed back down underneath the chaotic energies of the sea, transforming into something else before popping up again.

"Because this is where it all started, and the last god is Phanes," Telos said with a smile.

"So we couldn't just do it somewhere nice, like a sorrow plain with a cursed magma demon-king, we had to head to one of the most unstable parts of all existence?" Bobbi sighed and just flopped onto the sand. "I hate sand. It gets in my fur."

"Archons will be extremely weakened by the potent chaos in this place, so none of them are likely to follow here, and it has a tie to Phanes." Telos tried to be sympathetic to the exhausted cat-dragon-woman, especially when she noticed that the energies within Bobbi had reached a critical mass.

"You're about to ascend. Congratulations." Telos offered Bobbi an ambrosial fruit, a pyroclastic nectarine.

"Thanks." Bobbi sliced the nectarine into pieces and quickly ate. The look of stress, anxiety, and frustration all faded away to be replaced with anticipation.

"I'll bring out the tent, and we can take a breather." Telos changed gears from charging headfirst into dealing with Phanes, to taking care of the party. Bobbi ranking up was a major milestone, and Telos didn't want to treat it like a footnote in their god eating. Telos set about constructing a camp, manifesting tents, beds, and other conveniences from her repository.

"I'll watch over your physical form while you become a Beast Sovereign. Is there any other help you need?" Kallos inquired while Bobbi finished the fruit.

"Nope, if the twerp can do it, so can I. Besides, I've got an amazing partner to draw strength from if it gets dicey. Don't let the idiot draw anything on my face in marker while I'm sleeping." Bobbi yawned with the words, her eyes closing despite her best efforts to keep them open.

"We'll be waiting for you," Kallos assured her and stroked her hair.

"Tell Tiamat I said hi," Arkaziel chimed in as he walked over and sat next to Bobbi on the sand.

"Tiamat? You idiot, my clan is tied to Bahamut." Bobbi's insults were the last words before she succumbed to slumber, her pink feline eyes hidden. Even her outrage at Arkaziel failed to keep Bobbi awake from the siren song of ascension.

"Oh, I guess it never occurred to me that there were any StarManes who were actually part of Bahamut's line. We really are fire and darkness over here, aren't we?" Arkaziel couldn't stop laughing, a disconcerting sound from a small house cat. The laughter rolled out to the sea of chaos and boomed like thunder, and created an oil slick of the Void over the chaotic waters, which rained darkness up into the sky.

"Does it make that large of a difference?" Kallos inquired.

"Not really, no. The blood of either one will transform you into a Beast Sovereign. Tiamat's blood is more chaotic, primeval, and favors the cold reality we face. Bahamut's blood encourages nobility, ordered chaos, and focuses more on external control than the shapeshifting blood of Tiamat," Arkaziel explained to Kallos.

"That sounds like a massive oversimplification," Telos pointed out, but Arkaziel just ignored her. His stonewall defense of not acknowledging her comment worked so well that Telos walked off, muttering about cats under her breath.

"So you two being opposites won't be a problem?" Kallos asked with an arched eyebrow.

"Nope. I wonder how big she'll actually be now. It'd be embarrassing if she's smaller than I am." Arkaziel laughed lightly. "She's so fond of telling me how young

I am, so if she's not larger than me at the same rank, she'll have to acknowledge I'm not a twerp, right?"

Kallos paused at the vulnerability on display by Arkaziel. The black cat usually passed off or pretended to ignore the casual insults by Bobbi, but if his admission were sincere, it seemed those words had actually hurt the young dragon's feelings. Kallos petted Arkaziel in place of Telos.

"Let's hope so. Denial of reality is a waste of energy, one which I will assist you in breaking her bad habit of."

"Thanks, Kallos. You can hang out with Blue. I'll watch over her." Arkaziel offered as guilelessly as possible, an affable aura of innocence surrounding him.

"Tempting me away with my love, but you've overdone it with the innocent aspect. Promise you won't draw anything on her face or otherwise disturb her or perturb her, and I will let you be the one to guard her."

"Why doesn't anyone trust me?"

"You've literally got a marker held in your tail already," Kallos pointed out.

"Oh damn. Betrayed by my own overeager tail. Fine, I promise." The marker vanished in a poof of darkness.

"You'd better not break it, or Telos might not share the next Archon with you." Kallos's voice teased, a sharp contrast to her serious expression, but a look of panic crossed Arkaziel's yellow eyes.

"She can control who doesn't get energy? I didn't know that. I'll be good, I promise."

# CHAPTER 5

# Sovereignty Suits Slay Supremely

Zephariel'Realmara'Etheriassa'Flemmel'Bobbisylth'Chronoquintessara'Falkora' Stellarae'Quantumwhiskeria'Diavala'Jormungandria hated to rely on others. All StarManes were something of loners, outside of their chosen bond-mates (if they had one) and breeding partners, but Bobbi had never found many of her kin to be worth spending time with. In fact, she'd never found people of any race or persuasion to be that great of company. People were overrated as far as she was concerned.

What did any of her elders have to tell her that she hadn't gained from being born? One of the inherent bonuses of genetic memories was the ability to immediately strike it out on your own, without reliance on parents or clan, especially when you were a dragon-cat. Immediately was hyperbole, but the vast genetic memories offered by their ancestors allowed StarManes an undeniable edge in bypassing so much of the struggles of acquiring knowledge and experience other races had to endure.

Bobbi's clutch mates had subscribed to the StarMane arrogance and largely preferred their true forms, or feline or draconic forms at the least, while Bobbi had always favored humanoid forms. Yet Bobbi had latched onto a memory from the great wanderer Quantumwhiskeria, in which a demigod challenged her to a cook-off. Being a noble, elegant dragon-cat, Quantumwhiskeria cooked a boar with her fire breath and presented it. The demigod, on the other hand, made dozens of elaborate dishes with his opposable thumbs and cultural knowledge. Quantumwhiskeria acknowledged the demigod as her superior, and they fell in love. Her elders ate the demigod because he was food, and millennia later she left this universe in search of new foods to taste.

Bobbi's sister, Zelariel, had taken a very different lesson from that memory than Bobbi did. Zelariel's took away from the memory that you should not date or befriend demigods, as your elders would just eat them. Her brother, Delat, said the real lesson was opposable thumbs won't save you from being eaten, you damned show-off. Bobbi liked to think the lesson was that her elders were blind idiots, unwilling to allow something beautiful to be born. Quantumwhiskeria could have created a whole tradition of StarMane chefs, instead of just being a footnote in the clan legacy as someone who wandered off to find a new reality.

"Your time has come, little one." A voice that shook the cosmos drew Bobbi's awareness toward her present circumstances. She stood on a sphere of platinum that floated before the greatest of all dragons, Bahamut, the Holy Lord and Dragon of Justice, Warden of Prosperity, the Father of Dragonkind. In a flash, Bahamut turned into a wizened old human with platinum hair and a big beard.

"I, too, like to wander the realms as a human," Bahamut explained as he approached Bobbi. "Are you ready to begin your ascent toward the heights of your kind, to become a Beast Sovereign?"

"I am. I need to be much stronger to be able to keep up with my bond-mate and companions," Bobbi admitted a little shamefully.

"Few are the candidates who come before me with authorities of their own; fewer still are those who seek more power to protect or defend their friends. Even among my legacy, many who reach the pinnacle seek only power for power's sake, or to defend their hoard from others. I have watched you, little dragon, since you made your pact with Hestia."

"That's a little creepy," Bobbi noted.

"It's what Tiamat and I do." Bahamut didn't disagree.

"So, what's the challenge?"

"Traditionally, there are three challenges upon which newly forged Beast Sovereigns may gnash their teeth and earn their first touch of authority as appropriate for their performance. You already possess three authorities and do not need to take the Trials of Justice, Valor, or Compassion, as you have already surpassed them on your own," Bahamut explained, but Bobbi wondered if being given authority by her party really counted as passing a trial. Apparently, it did. Perhaps because she had managed to retain the authorities once given?

"So what, I came all this way for nothing? Can't I take them and then just get another authority?" Bobbi angled for whatever power-up she could walk away from this encounter with.

"No, child. The broad authority you already hold far outstrips the minor, precise authorities awarded to a new Beast Sovereign. You hold total dominion over Fire. Not dragon fire, frost fire, or black fire, but *all* fire. The vessel of your soul can hold only so many authorities. Why pick up lesser authorities when you stand among those who gather greater authorities regularly? No, a lesser authority would diminish you."

"You aren't here for that, anyway. You are here to become a Beast Sovereign and walk the universe as a peak existence among our kind. The first step upon that path for one of draconic heritage is to partake in the consumption of my blood. You will be transformed through my essence and reach the lowest rung of rulership."

"Creepy, but I guess if drinking your blood is the trial, we do it your way. How come StarManes only get draconic predecessors and no feline ones?" Bobbi had wondered that ever since she learned that StarManes' final transformation occurred under the eye of Bahamut or Tiamat. Why not under Leo the Lion? Sekhmet? Bastet?

"Your ancestors kept trying to eat anyone other than me or Tiamat." Bahamut laughed. "Chronos encouraged it—anything to make his children stronger. No one else was willing to take on this role for your people, and so it falls to us to maintain the ancient rites. Not that your kin haven't tried to make a meal out of me or Tiamat, as well, but no one has successfully challenged us yet."

"So, you going to cut yourself, or do I have to put you in a choke hold and drain you like a vampire, or how does this go down?" Bobbi stretched out, perfectly willing to commit violence against the eldest male dragon in existence if that was the ritual.

"That won't be necessary. Drink until you can drink no more." A platinum chalice appeared in Bahamut's hands. It contained a dark red blood that practically glowed with an inner light.

"The cup makes your blood look darker than it is, doesn't it?" Bobbi asked before she drank.

"There were complaints about my blood looking light red instead of dark red. I compromised with the chalice."

"You mean pink, right?"

"Lightish red?"

"Pink. P-i-n-k, like my eyes and hair?" Bobbi lifted a finger to show her now-pink hair off, then contrasted it to the cup's contents.

"Fine, it's pink, all right? Just drink it. Even the best of you StarManes are the worst." Bahamut grumbled, and his offended face looked perfect with the guise of the old white-haired human wizard facade he had used. "Cursed be the name of Chronos."

Bobbi chuckled at Bahamut's antics. She was honestly surprised that the ancient dragon would even bother to play along with her like this. So, she didn't delay any further and lifted the chalice to her lips and drank. The first rush of blood over her lips tasted sweet, like pineapple, followed by heat and spice, as if someone had tossed a few pineapples to float atop a slurry of extremely spicy peppers. The more that flowed down the back of her throat the cooler the concoction got, and the spice turned into a refreshing spearmint that soothed the tissues of her aching throat and esophagus.

Why were they aching, though? Bobbi could eat lava without a problem and had on plenty of occasions taken bites from supreme fire spirits. The awareness of her body that only a shapeshifter possessed told her the reason was quite simple. Her cells, organs, and fleshy bits had all begun the process of turning her into a Bobbi Slushy. Bahamut's blood broke down her form, her essence, and pressed her material and spiritual self into a singular whole, and then tried to cool it down with the power of spearmint so that she could re-form.

The body that rose from the pile of ooze she'd melted into wasn't your traditional StarMane in any way. Instead, Bobbi arose in the form of an almost human woman. Her skin color was dark brown, her eyes a bright pink with a feline iris. Bobbi's cheekbones were sharp, downright predatory when combined with the cat eyes, and her nails were naturally sharp and curved like claws. Pink hair flowed freely to just past her jaw, and dark red furry cat ears peeked out above her hair at the top of her head. Where a human's ears would be, instead a pair of horns formed and curled backward like ram horns. Large, dark red, draconic wings emerged from her back. A powerful, pink-furred tail flowed from just above her upper buttocks, and ended in a triangular flange.

"You know who and what you are, it would seem." Bahamut sounded impressed as if it was rare for a humanoid figure to emerge from the ooze of transformation.

"I'm the best," Bobbi agreed while she looked herself over. Scales formed occasionally across her skin, and her pigmentation shifted slightly to her will. Why would she ever do such trivial things as makeup when she could just look exactly how she wanted? Especially when she spent all her time with a Nephilim and another shape-shifter who had authority over beauty. Not that Telos gave Bobbi a complex or that it was a competition, but being cognizant of why things were how they were was important to Bobbi. A good chef had to know what ingredients and quality she worked with.

Or maybe some of Arkaziel's vanity had rubbed off on her. After all, as a Beast Sovereign with the blood of Bahamut, Bobbi was a bastion of goodness, or some utterly inane bullshit like that. A small snort escaped her lips as she entertained the idiocy of the idea that any StarMane would allow even Bahamut or Tiamat to judge them. Even Bobbi, a sane and rational adult StarMane, felt the compulsion to pounce Bahamut and eat him for no other reason than he would make her stronger.

"Aren't you supposed to have a flock of birds with you?" Bobbi asked, as trivia and stories about Bahamut flickered through her mind.

"I don't bring them near you cats. I've lost many a good pet bird that way," Bahamut answered warily, with a touch of reproach. He knew why she asked, and he disapproved of her wanting to cook one of his birdies.

"The children of Tiamat associate their new power with greater size. Some of those who visit me here do the same, but I am impressed you didn't seek to try to outdo me, but I am also curious why that is?" Bahamut looked intrigued.

"You aren't my competition, old dragon. There's a little twerp who's got the blood of Tiamat, who thinks just because he was only hatched a few hundred years ago and beat me to Beast Sovereign that he's better than me. Being faster, bigger, younger, older, whatever, isn't going to be the deciding factor between us. It'll be which of us can help our bond-mate the most, but also me, because I'm the better cook when he doesn't cheat."

Bahamut laughed earnestly. "I see, so you have a friend."

"Friend? More like a rival, I'd say. Yeah, I do say, he's my rival. And even if I didn't have a rival, a strange human woman is the most powerful being I've ever seen in the universe, whether firsthand or through the eyes of my ancestors." Bobbi didn't know what to make of the strength of Telos.

"Yes, she's the talk of the moment among us ancient ones. The death of Izanagi came as a complete shock, and Moros followed quickly thereafter. Who will be next?

A time of great change and upheaval faces the universe." Bahamut might as well have been saying he'd had a coffee for breakfast, for all that seemed actually to matter to him. "Can you hear them?"

"Hear what?" Bobbi asked.

"The winds of fate," Bahamut specified and tilted his head as if listening to something far away.

"Afraid not. All I hear right now is you. What will you do about her?" Would the ancient beasts rise up against Telos, fearful of her power? Isn't that what the great old powers were supposed to do to uppity newcomers?

"I'll stay far out of her way, obviously." Bahamut laughed, and Bobbi had a hard time accepting the simple answer.

"Good luck with that one, buddy. No one, and nothing is safe from Telos and Kallos. Look at me. I was just minding my own business as a megastar intergalactic chef in the towers, and now I'm slaying ancient terrors and consuming gods. Talk about a massive boost in job satisfaction." Bobbi flashed a hungry smile at Bahamut, but she could feel the vision already losing its grasp on her as her being drew back toward her true body on the Shores of Chaos.

"Thanks for the snack!" Bobbi shouted through the ether to Bahamut, and then opened her eyes. Arkaziel lay on the multihued sand. His yellow eyes fixated on her. When he noticed she woke up, he nodded.

"Congratulations, Slay," Arkaziel grunted, then rose from where he'd been curled up in the sand, shaking showers of the terrible material into the air from his fur. "Cute humanoid form. How big is your dragon form?"

"Thanks, twerp." Bobbi couldn't help smiling at the younger StarMane, who immediately fell into the same trap that Bahamut predicted of any of those who bore Tiamat's blood. It was clear he'd been watching over her, which was sweet, but it was also clear he still wanted to compete with her. "As big as I need it to be?"

"As big as you need to be? That's not an answer. City size? Moon size? You aren't as big as a planet yet, are you?" Arkaziel sounded worried, then shook his head. "No, no, of course not."

"Where'd Kallos and Telos go?"

"Probably having sex in the tent again, unless they've moved on to setting up the ritual for that goofy torch she's got. Since I'm not being blocked out of the empathic bond, I'll go with they're probably setting up the ritual."

"Let's go take a look, then." Bobbi whistled and set off to the other side of the tent, toward the churning seas of chaos, where all manner of foreign objects bubbled to the surface, only to sink and vanish. The Shores of Chaos still looked as strange and alien as they had before she ascended to become a Beast Sovereign, and that kind of disappointed her in a way she couldn't articulate.

Annoyingly, being more powerful didn't answer the whys of the universe. Maybe if she looked deeper into her authority over fire?

# CHAPTER 6

# Lost Love

No doubt about it, that's the Rod of the Overgod." Kallos stared at the crystalline torch laid out on a table between Telos and herself. "It's dormant and utterly drained of power, but it appears to be the genuine article."

"Someone went to a lot of pain to see that this thing ended up in your hands, Blue. You didn't get any memories from Ananke about this?" Arkaziel asked as he and Bobbi joined the conversation.

"I didn't parse Ananke. It seemed rude, what with her being alive and all. I took her power, not her memories. So, I don't know, but it sure seems like it would take someone on the level of Ananke or the Moirai to arrange it falling into my hands. Congratulations on your ascendance, Bobbi. Have you decided on your limited wish? I'd like to be rid of this weird, reserved energy Moros set up." Telos made an awkward expression, as if she were holding in a belch, when she mentioned the strange reservation of energy Moros had left with her.

"What'd you guys wish for?" Bobbi inquired, assuming they had handled the finale of the Tower of Moros while she'd evolved.

"I upgraded the Nebula Lantern to light and guide the way to specific treasures, as well." Arkaziel smirked.

"Wait, you have a Nebula Lantern?" Bobbi did a double take at the cat.

"Yep, my reward for the Tower of Aetherius." Arkaziel's pride lit the room. Literally, his smug self-satisfaction merged with his authority of light to create a gentle warm glow around the black cat. He looked like a fat, happy Buddha statue for a moment.

"I used the wish to acquire an enchantment called Soulchain Conductor, to further hone my extra appendages in combat." Kallos showed the newly enchanted bracers off to Bobbi. "I would prefer to have mastered them fully myself, but time is not on our side."

"I increased the power of the Tome of Towers to work everywhere." Telos smiled a little mischievously. "I could kind of, sort of do what I needed already with the knowledge of Binah, but it's a lot easier this way, and I don't feel like I'm cheating."

"I don't have the slightest clue what you are talking about or hinting at, Telos. Sorry," Bobbi apologized, but Telos only gave Bobbi an enigmatic smile and met her eyes. Bobbi's tail twitched, a visual sign of her displeasure at being left out of the loop, but Telos still just smiled at her. Telos felt slightly bad about it, but some things couldn't be said out loud or even telepathically, without risking them being heard by their enemies. Poor Bobbi would just have to be frustrated, and Telos would make it up to her later.

"Don't worry about it. Your new form is super cute, Bobbi. There's so many style possibilities between your hair and horns!" Telos complimented the humanoid StarMane's pink-haired form, then glanced back down to the rod on the table. "You can use your lesser wish on anything you want. Arkaziel and I covered the scheming sneak uses of our wishes."

"If that's the way it is, I want a case of infinite spices." The chef didn't hold back, and when she said the words, energy pulsed and formed a small spice chest with a small crank that alternated the drawers that faced the front.

"Are you going to make lunch?" Arkaziel asked hungrily. "I'm so hungry I could eat the sand. It's magic sand, right? I wonder . . ." Arkaziel tapped his paw against the multihued sands.

"Do we have time?" Bobbi looked at Telos and Kallos, the rod, and the idiot cat pawing the sand.

"Yeah, I think so. I'm pretty certain that when I push my authority of love into the rod that it will wake up. I don't really know what's going to happen after that, though. Will it draw me in, or something inside out? Will it call a council of gods, or be anticlimactic? There's no documentation on this thing, not even in Binah."

***Destroy it. Shatter the crystals; burn the fabric of order; let sweet chaos ring out in one impossible-to-ignore note. Should rule be consolidated to One? Why not the Many?***

*I'll keep that in mind, but maybe if you could give me more information first, you might convince me?*

Fred did not offer any further information. More and more, Telos suspected that Fred and Reverie both had constraints placed upon them, or that they were more like custodian entities with a limited artificial intelligence, rather than fully realized sentient intelligences. Or maybe she was judging them harshly, and they were esoteric beings with different experiences of time and existence. Either way, both continued to be of questionable relevancy. Someone, somewhen, had thrown all sorts of things at the wall for her to see what stuck: Libby, Reverie, Fred, the short-lived tenure of the Flames of Nyx, Thalassa, Aetherius, Ymir, and Khaos she'd been imbued with and had enjoyed using, until the Void ate them. Even her gloves, the Astrum Nexus, remained relevant solely by virtue of being forged from soulsteel, and thus always kept pace with her.

If Fred and Reverie were actualized intelligent beings, though, Telos did them a great disservice by thinking of them only in relation to their usefulness to herself.

The immense tides of power within herself, the increasing push of the Sefirot onto her even when she didn't initiate it, and the power and authority of Ananke and Chronos had pushed her so far beyond the realm of humanity that Telos feared if she didn't intentionally work to retain her outlook as an individual, let alone as a former human, that she would lose them utterly. Maybe she already had.

Despite what she'd said, Telos found herself holding the lifeless torch, with Bobbi and Kallos both looking at her askance.

"Sorry, could you hold off a few minutes on lunch? I'm feeling anxious now. I don't want to put this off any longer." Telos knew it wasn't a great explanation, but both of the other two women seemed to pick up on the anxiety and wariness that had infected her heart.

"Food can wait. Arkaziel isn't going to waste away to dust, no matter how much he complains he will," Bobbi encouraged Telos.

"Do what you must, love. We will watch over you as best we can," Kallos said with concern and love. The Nephilim always encouraged Telos to trust her gut on these things.

"Here I go." Telos pecked Kallos on the lips for good luck, then grasped the lifeless crystal torch in her right hand and lifted it above her head. Then she infused the dull, depleted item with tides of Ethereal power straight from the Origin and aspected it with her authority over love. For a second nothing seemed to happen, and then the dull crystal lit up like the sun. Light enveloped Telos and pulled her inside the crystal, through layer upon layer of sorcery, magic, divine constructs, riddles that parted, conundrums that failed to confound her, and a minefield of traps that were designed only for others. *The sparks of Phanes I hold in my soul and the one provided by Nyx must work as pass keys to enter?*

Beyond the traps a small island of bare earth floated, with a small, simple temple made of four pillars of stone. When Telos's boots touched the earth, goosebumps rose on her skin. The air shimmered with palpable energy left over from the creation of the universe, and when she stepped into the center of the pillars, everything swayed. Telos stood just past the entrance of a vast, spherical room. The walls were a living tapestry of nebulae, a breathing piece of art that danced and churned to the Cosmic Song, which Telos realized had begun to buzz in the back of her head. Reverie had warned that she wasn't prepared for the truth of the Cosmic Song, but that had been before her last evolution . . . Hopefully she was ready now.

In the dance of stars; the swirl of nebulae; the low, ominous groan of all that is; there was a simple beauty. Yet with each second, the sounds and sights of these things grew more and more powerful, and Telos had to divert her gaze to the floor. A smooth, mirrored surface, the floor only reflected the sights of the ceiling and walls back at her, but the illumination of her three eyes and bright hair distorted the reflected image enough to provide a brief respite.

At the center of the chamber lay an altar of carved quartz. The altar seemed to be of a single piece, and as Telos approached, it caught the light from her hair and eyes, and an inner light awoke within that increased in intensity with each step she took closer to it. Telos didn't even look at the object atop of the altar, for it was the altar that reacted to her presence. A divine hologram of Phanes appeared between herself and the altar at the last minute, forcing Telos to stop almost nose to nose with the projection.

"Hello again, ##@$@ Telos." Whatever name Phanes initially called her came out garbled, as if it'd been run through autotune by a terrible sound engineer, and Telos couldn't make sense of it, even though she heard him say Telos in the end. Phanes had the physical appearance of an attractive man, with androgynous long blonde hair, sharp facial features, piercing eyes, ridiculously large breasts, immense angelic wings, and fairly large male genitalia. *Why is the hologram naked?!*

"Hi," Telos responded, diverting her eyes.

"Prude." Phanes laughed and suddenly wore a white tunic that did nothing to hide what lay underneath, but qualified as decent by the meagerest definition of the word, as far as nudity and exhibitionism went in the book of Telos. "Come for the Rod, then?"

"That's it? Hi? Want the rod? We're talking about the Rod of the Overgod, not your penis, right? We haven't even met before." Telos was fairly certain she'd remember meeting Phanes.

"Well, this you, no, I suppose not. It's always complicated, dealing with an entity like you and your blatant disregard for time, rules, universes, and style."

Phanes's condemnation hurt more than Telos expected. "Excuse me, what's wrong with my style?" Telos demanded. "Not all of us can pull off stripper chic."

"Why did you incorporate black into your hair? It looks much better with just the red and aqua. The red coat screamed style; this black one just makes you look like an edgelord, and then there's the glowing eyes, sparkle tits, and cargo pants. I guess it could be worse"—Phanes let out an exaggerated sigh—"somehow."

"We're just going to skip over all of that, and I never want to hear the words 'sparkle tits' again, ever." The last bit may or may not have involved Telos invoking the power of Ananke to ensure no one violated her desire to not be called that.

"Whatever." Phanes's projection shrugged and gestured at the altar behind him. "It's there. You can take it. I always hoped someone with my legacy would find the chest and prove themselves worthy, but I knew deep down it would be you who came for it eventually. You did tell me you would."

"Who killed you?" Telos blurted out.

"How tactful. Nyarlathotep, of course. No other Outer God would be dumb enough to try to become Overgod, but give the Face Eater credit for dreaming big. Obviously, Bythos and Sige weren't going to allow one of his kind rule of creation, so they helped me spruce the place up and secured the Rod from his reach, and from his conspirators. Unfortunately, they made me stick around to guard it. There I was, freshly murdered, and I didn't even get to go join the Cycle. Well, parts of me did, but those parts are gone, so they aren't me. You know how it goes better than anyone,

I'm sure." Phanes laughed hysterically at his own joke, but Telos didn't get what was funny.

"How would I know how it goes?" Telos asked with an arched brow that demanded a sincere answer, not a flippant one.

"You've been split up more than anyone, ever. You just don't remember it? Maybe it hasn't happened yet? I don't know; you're confusing even for me. I wasn't a god originally, if you recall. I was just an innocent aerospace engineer and light Cultivator who got caught up in your let's-go-to-another-reality plan. Which wasn't a great plan even then, but it beat the whole slaving away at Arcanum Dynamics forever. Then bammo, I became Phanes, Creator and Lord of Light, Preeminent Demiurge, whom Yesh gave the honor of saying those lovely words 'Let There Be Light.'"

"Arcanum Dynamics? Aerospace engineer?" Telos sputtered the words in confusion. "Wait, Yesh? I've yet to encounter him or Ayin." Phanes kept changing topics on her without providing any real answers, and the confusion kept on building. She couldn't keep up with his rapid babble, and felt like every exchange left her further and further behind the conversation.

Phanes rolled his illusory eyes at her.

"Focus, Telos. If you came for the Rod, it's there. You'll have to beat the self-proclaimed Overgod and destroy his replica for the real deal to wake up. Bythos only allows one of them to be operational at a time."

"Okay, I sort of figured I was headed toward a throw-down with him anyway. I actually came to eat you, so I could have my soul free and clear of others."

If Phanes weren't an intangible spiritual being, Telos doubted he could have remained standing. The ghostly god guffawed and held his belly as he laughed so hard. Telos wondered why a spiritual projection's obscenely large breasts jiggled with laughter like this, then decided she didn't care, and that she neither wanted to know the how or the why of it. *Maybe he's gone a little batty being stuck in here all this time?*

"Well, you're being polite about it, I suppose. I can't leave this temple anyway, and let me tell you, being a temple guardian is worse than being an aerospace engineer, which was worse than being a god by a longshot. Didn't have to fill out triplicate paperwork to request cultivation materials to reach the next tier and have ten meetings about whether or not ascending would help me complete the projects I'd been assigned and be a beneficial long-term move for the company.

"Well? Get to it. Eat me." Phanes grinned.

"I don't want to. You're being creepy." Telos shook her head. It was like a cow begging her to eat it—the request pushed her off guard. "Why are you talking like you know me?"

Phanes cackled insanely.

*Of course he's insane. He's spent thousands of years talking to himself, and I'm ready to end him after only a few minutes. Imagine enduring this for a decade, let alone millennia.*

# CHAPTER 7

# Phanes With a Side of Ben

I suppose I shouldn't take any of my frustrations out on you. You aren't the ##@$@ Telos I worked with in that other existence. Facially, you look somewhat similar. The Third-Eye of Ein Sof is always unique, too, but your color choices are very different. The Telos I worked with had red hair and blue eyes and could make the Board of Directors wet themselves with a flat look when they questioned her project budget. That might have been the best day in my four centuries at Arcanum Dynamics." Phanes babbled in response to Telos refusing to go straight to eating him.

"You know who, or what, I am?"

"Sure, so do you. You don't want to accept it. You've never wanted to accept it in my home world either. Again and again, you run away from it. Not that I blame you. You seem to have a lot of fun as Telos." Phanes seemed amused to dance around the subject with her, flirting with saying it, then stepping around it repeatedly.

"Why won't you just say it?"

"Why should I? So you can blame me for being the one to say it? Oh no, thank you very much, I've already suffered enough, thanks to listening to you. Do you have any idea how terrible it is to be killed by Nyarlathotep? Even for a Demiurge, the fear and madness are inescapable. The Void alone, I could have dealt with. I slew a third of that asshole's composite existence before he killed me, but Azathoth and his spawn reverberated with an echo of an echo of their beloved Ayin, and *that* pulled even my psyche into the depths of the Void. Bythos and Sige restored my mind and took the memories, but there's a deeply ingrained fear that lingers still, knowing I should know terror but not why or of what. It's a real pain in the ass."

"That's rough, I'm sorry you had to deal with that. Who were the conspirators working with Nyarlathotep?"

"Only one conspirator, not plural. Although with this force, maybe plural is appropriate. Do I need to say their name? They'll hear it, even here."

"I suppose you mean Chaos?" Telos sighed.

"No." Phanes laughed bitterly. "Chaos is a lackey."

"I don't know who pulls the strings of Chaos or Sophia. Bythos?" Telos cast a net, hoping for a large haul of information.

"The Telos of my world once told me a story. A story of a distant god who couldn't reach the myriad worlds they saw, a god whose mere gaze caused disaster and cataclysm. In the whole of existence, they only found one being that could withstand their gaze, and the god grew tired of seeing through the eyes of their envoy, talking through their envoy, and knowing only their envoy. So they made four stand-ins and cast themself into fragments beyond counting across all existence."

"And that god's name?" Telos inquired.

"Who knows? My Telos, though, had been dodging one of those four stand-ins for centuries. She called it the Magistrate. Does that help?"

Phanes's repeated mentions of his Telos left a weird sensation crawling through Telos's mind and heart. She easily imagined the life of this Project Manager Cultivator in a corporate hellhole. If she looked hard enough, it was almost like the memories of that lifetime could coalesce for her, and she could even taste the strange addictive alchemical solutions that other world favored to speed up cultivation. *My imagination is a little too vivid today. Why does the name Magistrate make me picture a big red button?*

"I've never heard of anyone called that. Know any more?" Telos asked hopefully.

"Not even a little, sorry." Phanes shrugged.

"Is there anything you'd like me to remember about you?"

"Once, I designed a vessel that crossed realities. Not adjacent time-streams either. You know more about reality than most, so you should understand how impressive that is. My ship was named *Aetheria Lumina*, and it had dice in the mirror. My name was Ben back then."

"Were you alone on your voyage?" Telos didn't explain to Phanes she'd encountered other species that had matched his triumph. Why rain on his parade? How many other realities were there? It didn't really matter. This one was hers, but she briefly wondered how the survivors of that incident fared under the care of Aetherius. "Why would you have a mirror on a spaceship?"

"Yes. The alternate you distracted corporate while I took her out on a maiden voyage. Probably didn't even get in trouble for it either, and sipped on a nice crisp bottle of Quantum Quench Uber Zest Blast. I miss those so much. They were so fizzy and refreshing, and it was the only soft drink that renewed other people's mouths. Sure, they were addictive, and anyone lower-tiered than a Hegemon would instantly explode from drinking one, but damn, were they tasty." Phanes reminisced fondly about whatever strange junk food his reality had.

"Why wouldn't your inter-reality dimensional vessel have a rearview mirror, and why wouldn't it have dice? If you can't figure that one out, you're a long way from learning the lessons physical entities are meant to learn." The overly dramatic eye roll reminded Telos of Sean Hayes playing a very out-of-the-closet gay man.

"Maybe I am. Just what lessons are those, for the record? You act like you know me, but I lived a normal life until I reincarnated; before that, I was just an ordinary person."

"Ordinary? Oh, girl, everyone and everything in existence is *one*. Only, if you put that somewhere with truth in advertising, the asterisk would denote that the amount of *one* some people are is very different from the amount of one others are. *Everything* is born from Ayin's infinite possibility and bears her touch."

*This one is wise for an Elder Dreamer, but he is done; his time has passed. Still, you are to be commended, Harbinger of Life and Light. In recognizing that Ayin is the true force of all things, you could have ascended the boundaries to create all that is impossible, imagined the unimaginable. She, the formless and infinite, the basis of all power, matter, all dimensions, fuels the spark of creation.*

*You will be remembered as a beacon of light in the vast expanse of mud that is existence. That is more than can be said for other Demiurges and their futile struggle against the inevitable dissolution of all things.*

Telos and the ghost of Phanes both stared at one another. Phanes's eyes had grown wide at the ominous whispers of Fred entering his mind, and Telos felt a cramp in her stomach as Fred demonstrated the ability to speak to others outside of her party. *It must be because Phanes's essence still resides in me.*

"Who was that?" Phanes's expression remained somewhere between amazed and terrified.

"That'd be Fred," Telos offered glibly.

"And Fred is?" Phanes probed further.

"Well, as near as I can tell, Fred is a remnant of Ayin's power, the Unutterable Black Flame of the Void born when Ayin turned nothing into something. Fred's like a little bit of frosting you didn't need when you're done frosting a cake, but you don't really know what to do with it, and you've already got a stomachache from licking the spoon, so you just leave it for later," Telos explained without any effort to be correct. She wanted to be close-ish to the truth, but far enough from it that Fred might correct her and shine some light on his mysterious origins.

Fred didn't fall for it.

"And you named him Fred? Why?"

"He needed a name, and it's always the Void this, the Void that, behold my infinite power of the eternal abyss, so forth and so on. So, I named him after Frederick Nietzsche, whom I'm fairly certain would've been scared into an optimist by my Fred." Telos gave a small shrug, as if having an eldritch force of existence blathering in one's mind all the time was the most normal thing, and everyone had them.

"You're much weirder than the Telos of my old reality. I suppose the polite term is eccentric, but I'm a ghost that you're about to eat, so I don't feel the need to be *that* polite." Phanes shook his head, but the ghost did seem proud of Fred's compliment, if Telos read him correctly.

"I guess it's that time, then. It was nice meeting you, Ben. May the Great Cycle have benevolence on you." Telos offered the words with a small smile. She had enjoyed their brief conversation, and if a small benediction of her authority would help Phanes, so be it. If it didn't help him, all she was out was a couple of breaths.

"Well . . . you know, if you took responsibility, you'd be able to ensure that, wouldn't you?" Phanes muttered and wrapped his spectral arms around himself, then his wings, becoming a ghostly offering to the shrine of Telos.

"Yeah, you betcha." Telos sighed in a dispirited manner. "I'll make things right, even if it's bullshit that I have to adult. Adulting sucks, and it's not fair it's falling on me."

"Anyone who wanted to do it wouldn't be qualified." Phanes offered a pitying smile with the words as the currently black fire of the Transformative Flame of Eternal Becoming immolated Telos, then rapidly grew into an inferno. "You could always look in the mirror and pin the responsibility on your reflection if you need a break. Maybe you already did that, though, and now it's all reflections all the way down? Frogs on a log."

"Maybe that's the problem with the whole thing. What good is a throne if no one who wants to sit on it is qualified to hold it?" The black flames danced along Telos's body, then stretched out from her like the maw of Jormungand, the World Serpent, and the remains of Phanes, the temple, and the entirety of the temporary dimension were devoured into nothing. When Telos reappeared on the Shores of Chaos, it was with the authentic Rod of the Overgod locked into her repository.

"Why so dour, Blue? That was a good meal!" Arkaziel lay stretched out on the multihued sand, belly in the air, a happy look on his face.

"Getting more powerful is just a good thing in your life, isn't it, Ark? What's the end goal to your strength?" Telos asked the basking cat.

"To get bigger and eat more things. Life's easy!" Arkaziel's carefree answer elicited a tremor in reality around Telos. The cat rolled onto his feet and looked seriously at Telos, as if he hadn't done so before.

"Damn, how many authorities do you have now?" Arkaziel tried to steer the conversation in a different direction, not very subtly.

"I'm glad life is so clear-cut for you, Ark. I'm almost to thirty now, with most of them top-level categories, not sub-dominions." Telos used a phrasing even Arkaziel wasn't familiar with so casually that the cat wondered if he'd missed a group meeting.

"Thirty?! Damn, no wonder reality is getting unstable around you. How long until existence itself starts to fray from you just being in a material realm?" Arkaziel blurted it out without thinking, but it made Telos wonder that herself.

"Oh come on, I'm not even a seventh-tier. I can't be that close to destroying the fabric of reality just by existing!" Telos waved Arkaziel's concerns away. The puzzles of Phanes's words still jumbled around in her head, like tumbleweeds across the desert. Maybe they'd crash into each other and form a clue to lead her free from confusion.

*"You're getting close to that point,"* Reverie informed Telos oh-so-helpfully. *"If you come to possess Order and Chaos, you will not be able to remain in that existence without damaging it."*

*What do you mean, I can't stay here? Where the heck am I supposed to go?* Telos wanted to shout at the beach and the sky, but instead only mentally shouted it at Reverie.

*"You have many choices. You could join me in Keter, or Bythos and Sige in Pleroma, divest yourself of power, create an intermediate reality, or many other options. If you reference the knowledge of Binah . . ."*

*Thank you, Reverie.* Telos interrupted the voice. *I have options, I see that.*

*"Of course, Lady Telos,"* Reverie answered more formally than normal before he fell silent.

When Telos turned her mismatched eyes back to reality around her, she found Bobbi, Kallos, and Arkaziel all looking at her.

"What?"

"Nothing," Bobbi and Arkaziel answered immediately.

"No need to scowl, darling. You accomplished what you needed with Phanes, yes? And without a fight or any trouble forming here, even." Kallos sounded only slightly disappointed that their stay on the beach had been a boring one. "What is our next move?"

"Next, we go deal with Oizys. We've got two options, as I see it. We use Ark's lantern to show up at the physical location of her tower, where she's vulnerable in the truest sense of the word. Alternatively, we show up at her tower entrance on Grief, and let her decide if she wants to deal with us or withdraw from Grief. If she removes her tower from Grief, it counts as abandoning the world, and she loses her status as the planet's owner. What do you all think?"

"I don't like letting her run away. She's our enemy; we kill her and eat her!" Arkaziel spoke with more vehemence than Telos expected. "Besides, I promised Werylin and Thalassa I'd make her pay."

"I'm down for slaying her. Moros seemed like an okay sort, but Oizys sounds like a real daemon. Let's butcher her!" Bobbi's ferocity made flames dance in her eyes.

"Let us send her into the Great Cycle so that she be judged by her actions, and what passes for her soul be made to repay the karmic debt she has incurred," Kallos declared confidently.

"Okay, so I'm going to assume the chorus of let's kill her means we're heading into space, since not one of you murder-hobos actually commented about attacking her on Grief. Anyone got a spaceship?"

# CHAPTER 8

# Space Race

No one had a spaceship in their storage spaces, not even Kallos, who Telos had half expected to pull a sleek crystalline vessel out of her inner world dramatically. For most people, this would be an insurmountable problem. For Telos it couldn't even be called a minor setback, but resulted in some fun creation. Rather than just pulling a design from the infinite knowledge of Binah, the party sketched out designs in the sand. Telos tried to sell the others on a design that looked a lot like the *Brittany* from the *Energy Affect* series, but Arkaziel said it looked stupid and he wouldn't ride in it.

Bobbi wanted to make it look like a sphere for simplicity. Kallos liked the idea of a teardrop shape, and Arkaziel argued that they should just ride Telos's dragon form through space because that would be the coolest. This started an argument between Bobbi and Arkaziel about them riding Arkaziel instead, which Arkaziel then turned to the fact that they should ride Bobbi since she was the newest party member. Telos thanked her lucky stars that there were no human resource departments in this line of work to tell her she shouldn't be letting her companions argue about riding each other.

Kallos and Telos watched in amusement while the two StarManes argued hopelessly with nonsensical rejoinders and the equivalent of "nuh-uh" and "yes-huh" for a solid twenty minutes. The couple linked hands and minds while they wove creation magic scored by the StarManes' argument.

"For the final time, you're not riding me, twerp!" Bobbi ended the argument by turning to storm away, where she walked right into a crystalline shape that covered a quarter mile of the beach.

"You built it already? Nice." Arkaziel laughed at Bobbi's misfortune of walking straight into a spaceship.

"I don't know how you two didn't notice us make an entire spaceship while you argued. We might need to work on your situational awareness, a lot," Telos teased. The sun glittered off the cylinder-shaped ship with a bell at the end. Telos internally dubbed it the sacred space torpedo, and it was a sleek vessel that shone from the Divine Light of Ohr Ein Sof from within its crystalline depths.

"We thought about leaving the two of you," Kallos teased and gestured at the tents and camp that had already been broken and dragged into Telos's repository. Bobbi stuck her tongue out at the blonde.

"Why don't we just teleport, anyway?" Arkaziel asked bluntly. "Can't you make one of those slick silver doors to anywhere?"

"The defenses woven into the tower systems preclude us from teleporting straight in, and if I overwhelm the defenses of the tower network, we'd have Archons on us before we even started the job. That is if I knew where, exactly, to go. Between my map and your lantern, we'll be able to close in on Oizys in real space, hence why we built a spaceship. Which you'd have known if you'd listened to me earlier. But no, you had to spend the whole time arguing with Bobbi." Telos didn't waggle her finger at Arkaziel, but for a brief moment she let an illusion of a comical white gloved hand perform an overly gesticulated finger waggle to taunt Arkaziel.

"Bullshit. I listened, and you never said anything about anything." Arkaziel called her bluff.

"Technically he's right, darling. We were talking internally." Kallos struggled to not smile too much with the words, but Telos found her smile and faint chuckle contagious and ended up laughing at herself.

"Alright, my bad. I guess Kallos remains so beautiful that I forget what's thought and what's said out loud, and now we're going to ride in a spaceship made by this crazy love-obsessed woman. Did I focus on the life support, or was I too busy noticing the way the chaotic sea of creation reflected in Kallos's eyes? Let's find out!" Telos smiled brightly, but when Bobbi and Arkaziel just looked at her flatly she gave it up.

"I enjoyed it," Kallos offered comfortingly, with a pat on Telos's shoulder.

"It's not often I get a pity-pat. See how low love has felled me! Eesh. Anyway, the ship's ready. Do you need to affix the lantern to the exterior, or can it be used from the bridge?" Telos led the way to where a pair of doors formed and opened to allow them into the vessel, then sealed behind them as solid crystal once more.

"What does this ship run on?" Bobbi asked suspiciously.

"Oh, I pulled the schematics for an Infinite Improbability Array from the records of Binah," Telos joked.

"What's that?" Bobbi asked, unfamiliar with the Earth pop culture reference.

"It's, uhm . . . not a real thing." Telos admitted.

"Then why did you say it?" Arkaziel asked with confusion.

"Probably one of those little things from her original life that none of us could possibly get, but she still says occasionally anyway." Kallos smirked at Telos, as if it were a bad habit.

"Okay, okay, I get it. One-sided pop culture references should be called out, and I'm the asshole, I get it. Spare me your wrath, oh brave and generous teammates, and I shall try not to sin again." Telos's mixture of sarcasm and sincerity were made easier to comprehend thanks to the soul link that the group shared, a tool that Telos found allowed her to press the envelope on being tolerable. She was still tolerable, she hoped. Maybe the real purpose of soul bonds were to make each other prisoners to the others, unable to escape the maddening habits of one's loved ones. *Note to self: don't be such a bitch that people need to escape you.*

Inside the ship, everything retained the crystalline appearance, and the inner light of Ein Sof provided a mind-lifting euphoria, in addition to the practical illumination and warmth it distributed everywhere within the vessel. There were no screens, no technology, not even a coffee pot. All four of the people in the vessel could conjure or create nearly anything they would ever need, so the ship had only one purpose: getting them places. Even for Telos, creating a true ship would have taken longer. Technology was one of those illusive authorities she had not yet scavenged up.

"In all seriousness, we made an engine called the Genesis Drive," Telos said in an attempt to redirect the conversation back on topic.

"Why didn't you just make it a sphere in the end?" Arkaziel asked, raising a hiss out of Bobbi.

"Honestly? I thought this was flashier and it might be better at ramming. Now, the lantern, how does this work?" Telos held the Nebula Lantern aloft. It looked like a normal tin lantern.

"Ramming? That's not your answer on how we're going to get into Misery, is it? Your plan sucks." Arkaziel couldn't help himself, when he put the pieces of the plan he'd heard together.

"What? No, yeah, no. Ramming the tower with a spaceship is totally a lame idea. I've got a way better idea, just wait and see," Telos lied. Terribly.

"It should work from here. What's important is that the person navigating can see the path made by the lantern, not that it be in the front." Arkaziel lifted a paw, and the ordinary-looking Nebula Lantern appeared in his hands. The orange metal wasn't copper, but aurichalcum, an exceptionally rare and prized metal used only in the most legendary of artifacts, but not weapons. It lacked the indestructible nature of adamantine, scarletite, or orichalcum, but its magic conduction and resonance with the currents of reality made it perfect for items such as the Nebula Lantern.

A flame appeared on Telos's fingertip, and when touched to the wick of the lantern, it caught aflame in a flurry of sparks. Once the glass and aurichalcum of the lantern were sealed, the lantern spewed light in all directions like a psychedelic kaleidoscope projected everywhere, which, combined with the crystalline structure of the ship, made for some stomach-churning rainbow overdrive.

"I'm going to be violently sick if it keeps up like this," Bobbi complained.

"How do I work this thing, Ark?" Telos asked as she dropped into the pilot's chair on the bridge. It was like every other chair, only fancier, and inspired jealousy in the StarMane duo immediately. Even Kallos, who knew the chairs were all the same except that the pilot chair was in the center of the bridge and had some extra decorative designs in the crystal, gave the seat a look filled with longing. Telos wondered what they'd be willing to barter away to get her chair.

"Picture what you want to find, and project it to the Nebula Lantern. If you aren't precise enough, it will lead you to something close but not quite what you wanted. Its nature is to lead you where you need to be, not necessarily where you want to be." Bobbi, not Arkaziel, actually provided the instructions for the Nebula Lantern.

"How'd you know that?" Kallos asked.

"It wasn't just his clan patriarch, it was the first StarMane, Antara, who used a Nebula Lantern to explore the universe. He used his in the first form, a glass marble. It makes sense our tomcat had to resort to the second form." Bobbi smirked.

"Actually," Arkaziel interjected, "you'll find that the upgrades from Moros forced my lantern to reshape itself. It was the cutest, prettiest marble ever, until Blue used the wish from Moros, and it ruined my lantern! And is anyone giving me a refund? No, no they aren't." Arkaziel let out a deep, sad sigh. "Talk about bullshit."

"Anyway," Telos said. "Combined with the emanations of the Sefirot, I should be able to roll up on the true Tower of Oizys without that much difficulty, but first . . ." Telos trailed off as the world exploded in silver light, and the Shores of Chaos vanished from outside the ship to be replaced by the void of space. Stars and planets twinkled on the transparent crystal viewscreen.

"Where are we now?" Arkaziel asked with an edge of annoyance. Trust Telos or not, no one liked to be moved through space without knowing where they were, especially not a narcissist like Arkaziel. Bobbi and Kallos were every bit as eager to know as Arkaziel was, they just hid it slightly better.

"We're one system over from Grief's star system, but we won't be here for long. This ship should be faster than light." Telos spoke while a diffuse glow grew around her, the cold light of Ein Sof blossomed strongest from her third eye and cleavage, and in the back of the ship a dull hum that sounded like bells chiming grew louder, until it sounded like a faint song.

"What the hell is that?" Bobbi demanded, a creeped-out look on her face.

"It's alright, Bobbi. It is but an echo of the Cosmic Song played by the Genesis Drive. The chorus of the song is about how Telos navigates the ship despite its speed. Only Telos or I can pilot the vessel until either of you learn to hear the Cosmic Song, but given all four of us could navigate the celestial void other ways, albeit more slowly, it seemed like a minor inconvenience when we chose this particular magic engine." Kallos explained the unsettling noises and the power behind the ship to the duo.

"You two spent the whole time we were arguing making this thing, huh?" Bobbi didn't bother to hide her doubt.

"My, what else would we have been doing?" Kallos feigned innocence.

"Flirting," Arkaziel answered immediately.

"Staring longingly into each other's eyes," Bobbi added.

"That's part of flirting; try again." Arkaziel smirked at Bobbi.

"Fine, they kiss a lot, and kissing isn't flirting." Bobbi flashed her claws at Arkaziel when he started to protest that kissing was flirting, but Arkaziel opted to give her that one after he reassessed the murderous intent in Bobbi's eyes.

"Why wouldn't we do that? We love each other a great deal." Kallos's pragmatic mind failed to see any issues with her and Telos's behavior.

"I don't know, I've never met a pair of immortals with as much power as you two have, who were still so into each other. You don't act like you have forever ahead of you, and you're both desperately trying to make the most out of every single moment because it might not last?" Bobbi shrugged. "Sorry?"

"Bobbi is right, you two are weird." Arkaziel, still in kitten form, nodded sagely.

"Things are transient, and we shall not remain as we are now for nearly long enough. While we are merely us, we must squeeze every second together we can out of reality." Kallos's smile was tinged with a hint of sadness.

"So, even if Telos becomes the Overgod, you'll still . . ." Bobbi trailed off at Kallos's headshake.

"Overgod isn't our goal. It is a brief speed bump on our ascension beyond the confines of physical existence. A mere Overgod won't fix the fundamental problems that face this reality." Kallos smiled brightly, but there was moisture in her golden eyes.

"Don't get caught up in where things might go, Bobbi. With these two, it'll be beyond ridiculous. Focus on what we're doing now, which is slaying Oizys. Eyes on the prize." Arkaziel attempted to steer the conversation to something less gloomy and metaphysical.

"Speaking of prizes, did someone order a fleet of Celestial Wardens fighting a shark? Wait, that's no shark . . ." Telos trailed off in a completely not ominous way.

The viewscreen cleared of blinding lights to a much lower speed. Immediately visible was a fleet of approximately thirty ships of varying sizes, firing upon a massive sharklike creature with void-appendages instead of fins, and each tentacle of darkness ended in a horrific maw filled with shark teeth.

"The Celestial Wardens? How coincidental." Kallos laughed and arched a brow at Telos.

"Looks like they're going to lose." Bobbi pointed at one of the corvettes as it exploded into debris when a shark tentacle bit it in half.

"Siegfried is aboard the command ship. Let's lend a hand. Maybe they'll join us in attacking Oizys?" Telos suggested.

"Let me out there; I'm so hungry, and even that shark looks tasty," Arkaziel whined and looked for an exit. Arkaziel was so distracted with the present prey that he didn't even think to complain about Telos potentially adding more people to the loot pool for the tower.

# CHAPTER 9

# Carcharoth, the Celestial Maw That Devours the Ships

Arkaziel and I will deal with the shark. Can you two set up communications with the Celestial Wardens? I'd rather not get caught in crossfire," Telos asked Bobbi and Kallos.

"Consider it done." Kallos nodded, but Bobbi pouted.

"You're trying to keep me from getting exposed to the Void, aren't you? Did you forget I'm constantly exposed to it thanks to our soul-links?" Bobbi demanded an answer, as if she'd been wronged.

"That's not what's happening, Bobbi. I want to recruit the Wardens, and you and Kallos are better suited to that than Arkaziel is, and I'm immune to the Void." Telos shrugged, but thought her logic made sense. "Besides, it's not like I'm leaving the ship, although I suppose Arkaziel might."

"Damn skippy I am!" Arkaziel muttered, before he vanished to reappear outside the vessel, his form rapidly growing until he matched the size of the corrupted shark. Telos estimated the shark to be somewhere in the vicinity of one hundred and sixty meters long, or roughly the size of a fifty-story building. Size wasn't everything, though. For all that Arkaziel could dwarf the size of the creature easily, fighting an eldritch horror in the depths of space put all of the homefield advantages in the hands of the horror—or for anyone not named Telos it would have.

Their vessel glowed with transcendent inner light. Divine radiance suffused the ship, and the surrounding vessels were bathed in radiant energy. Rent hulls mended; generators previously rendered inoperable by the devouring power of the abomination restarted. The benevolent light of Ein Sof restored the battered fleet of the Celestial Wardens, but that wasn't all. A concentrated beam of Ohr Ein Sof blasted from the forward section of their vessel. Moments before the solid beam struck the eldritch horror, it split into dozens of smaller rays that struck fins and tentacles off the abomination's body.

"It's about to scream," Telos muttered, before she switched her focus from offense to defense. Ein Sof dissipated from its dense beams into diffuse luminance that clung to the Celestial Wardens' ships. Arkaziel followed that first beam of light and plunged his fangs into the profane corrupted flesh between the shark's head and trunk. All four of Arkaziel's sharp-clawed limbs ripped at the body of the shark abomination while he locked it into place—the horror's mobility had been neutered by the first attack from Telos, and now it floated in space unable to escape the hold of the vicious StarMane.

"The Wardens want to know if they should hold fire?" Kallos looked to Telos for an answer.

"Yes, have them stand down; the situation is well in hand. They should tend their wounded or enjoy the show."

When Carcharoth screamed, it wasn't with a voice. Potent psychic waves roiled off the eldritch horror in all directions, and the only way to counter them that Telos could think of was using the Void itself. The darkness between stars roiled and churned in response to her control, and the omnidirectional psychic attack vanished before it could attack anyone but Arkaziel, who had the mental defenses to endure it, thanks to the blood of Tiamat, the soul-strengthening tenets, and his own potent mental defenses. If such an attack had reached the Warden fleet, Telos had her doubts that more than a dozen of them would have survived without corruption.

Yet in controlling the Void between the stars Telos revealed her presence to the eldritch abomination, and whispers came like a deluge to assail her. She somewhat imagined this was what it felt like for a celebrity to visit a third-grade classroom.

*#You who wield this echo of the Primeval Mother, your presence in the Cosmic Song is occluded. Why do you not flaunt your song? Why does this pathetic task from Nyarlathotep bring us into conflict with the faded hymn of Ayin? In your darkness, even our existence wanes. Have you come to consume creation? Will you embrace us, who have been left behind?#*

A hundred thousand voices made the symphony of Carcharoth's voice, but the individual strands could be traced to beings of every race and creed. The amount of knowledge that flowed from Binah into Telos was enough to fill libraries and came closer to stunning her than any other attack might. There was Bob, from Mu Arae, who had discovered immortality, only to outlive his planet, and cursed his existence on the solar winds. Bob was one of thousands, but the names and stories of all of them passed through Telos's mind, and she grasped the nature of the eldritch horrors in a way she never had before. They were collective beings, hive minds of existences that shared a commonality.

Those who underwent gnosis and passed into higher realms were theoretically able to ascend to the realms of Bythos and Sige, the Aeons in Pleroma. Yet some traversed the self and existence, and came out the far end of gnosis with very different goals. Those who sought an end. These beings grew together in their needs, and bathed in the eldritch powers of the Void. A cycle that had been given life by a mere fragment of Ayin's shadow, the Black Flame of the Void, Fred.

"Oh you poor souls." Telos sighed with a mix of pity and annoyance. She understood the turning against reality, on some levels. Life wasn't fair, the universe was cruel, and the escape from its confines was guarded by the Archons and Ialdabaoth, whose sole obsession was to restrain the living in the land of the physical, in the cage of flesh. She was less sympathetic about their embrace of the Void, but suffering had rotted their brains, and what remained attempted to mirror the totality of existence, the potential of every universe. Even the collective mind of hundreds of thousands couldn't withstand the revelations of higher planes, countless timelines, and the patchwork of the Cosmic Song that they could now hear. Existence outside of time, alone, was enough to break the minds of most mortal entities, and the Void-birthed eldritch horrors did far more than exist outside of time: they exalted in it.

Telos had few choices in how to deal with this collective of horror. Her draw upon Ohr Ein Sof in physical reality still faced a multitude of roadblocks, while most forms of attack could only hurt the unimportant physical manifestation of the shark, not the powerful and corrupted hive-existence that powered it. Arkaziel, for all his authorities, size, and powers, only wounded the eldritch horror because at his core, he, too, was a creature of the Void, but his power failed to measure up to that of Carcharoth's on his own.

Arkaziel's claws, fangs, and Void-aspected darkness, bolstered with authorities of destruction, did their best to savage the space-shark, but they were the equivalent of death by papercuts, and even a massive burst of his breath attack at point-blank only withered the shark. Telos stepped through space and appeared before the restrained shark.

"Uffda, space sure is weird. You may have your rest now, within me." Telos didn't alter her size the way Arkaziel had; she remained her usual size and form. Exposure to the vacuum of space didn't affect her, and her words carried across the celestial abyss despite the rules of physics. If Telos offered the eldritch horror peace, she did so by lifting her hand. Rays of Void and the Ethereal exploded from her palm in precise blasts that illuminated Carcharoth in mind-numbing light. The rays of Void acted like inversions of color, everything bathed in the darkness turned bright, and everything bathed in the Ethereal Light turned dark. For a few brief seconds it looked like Telos orchestrated a rave, before Carcharoth imploded with a loud pop, and ceased to exist.

*#Thank you, Ender of Suffering. Curse you, Creator of Suffering.#* The appreciation, and resentment, of the collective tide of souls who had descended the Tree of Death possessed such intensity it bordered on a mental attack. Beyond time, beyond physical reality, the nihilism of an elder god ripped at her humanity. It failed to find purchase, but not because Telos had defended her humanity, but rather because Telos had very little, if any, humanity left. Huge tides of power blossomed within Telos, and by extension through the three who were soul-linked to her. Telos's Void core worked in overdrive to digest and retain the power of Carcharoth.

*+Well, shit. I feel emasculated.+* Arkaziel vanished from the void of space and reappeared in their ship as a tiny kitten.

Telos appeared next to him and dropped a hand to ruffle his fur and stroke his back.

"It's okay, Ark. You did good. None of the Wardens' ships blew up once you grabbed Carcharoth." Telos's attempt at reassurance fell upon intentionally deaf ears, but Arkaziel leaned into the pets despite himself.

"What the hell was that? If you can obliterate outsiders like that, why do you even need us?" Bobbi demanded in an annoyed tone. Telos only offered the pink StarMane a sad smile.

"Being an island is a lonely thing, Bobbi. No one wants to be alone, not the weak, nor the powerful. Having someone at your side is a power that goes beyond physical capabilities. There is a dearth of meaning in me solving problems, don't you think? Or maybe I'm just being self-pitying. That might be my worst character trait." Telos grinned at the confused expression on Bobbi's face, as the StarMane failed to understand Telos's point of view.

"Siegfried requests we board his vessel, or for him to visit ours, and discuss what he witnessed." Kallos's smooth, calm voice proved to be a balm to the emotions of everyone.

"Very well, who wants to come with?" Telos failed to contain a rueful laugh when Bobbi and Arkaziel shook their heads no. "Et tu, Kallos?"

"I will maintain control of the vessel, and assist Arkaziel with adjustments to the Nebula Lantern. It would be best if we approach Oizys undetected, and I believe it is possible if we shield the field with a combination of our magic and authorities. I will require your assistance as well, Bobbi."

An unperformed wink flowed through the connection between Telos and Kallos. For all that they seemed to be on separate pages at the moment, they very much were not. If anything, the depth of their connection had begun to push them closer and closer together. Even without physical contact they could feel the thoughts and emotions of the other as if they were their own. Synthesis, Telos knew, had begun. Unlike the press of the universe, or desire of greater reality to merge with Telos, she welcomed the intensifying of the connection to Kallos. For all the negatives that bubbled with her advancement on the path of Eternal Becoming, Kallos represented the single unblemished positive.

*I used to think the idea of soulmates was stupid. Now, I'm flowing into another person. Where do I stop? Where does Kallos start? Do our worst traits get elevated or negated?*

"This won't take long." Telos flickered out of sight and reappeared on the command deck of the *Stellar Sovereign*, the grand flagship of the Celestial Wardens fleet, which currently sailed under the personal command of Siegfried himself. The crew of the vessel, expecting her or not, panicked at the appearance of a figure out of air. Swords, maces, guns, wands, spells, and surprise were all leveled at her, but Telos just raised her hands as if they were the police.

"Stand down." Siegfried's no-nonsense command echoed in the room like a peal of thunder. "You've grown significantly in power, daughter of Nyx and Aetherius. I understand you go by a different name now?"

Telos played coy while weapons and spells were lowered. Of the many races on the command deck, she and Siegfried were the only humans. She looked nothing like a human, with her third eye, luminous hair, existential-crisis-inflicting eyes, her sparkly cleavage, and the plethora of authorities she wielded that caused reality itself to eddy around her.

"Nice to see you again, Siegfried. I'm called Telos Metanoia now. I understand the Celestial Wardens might want to join Armageddon?" Telos's words echoed across the suddenly silent deck. The silence dominated the room, awkward and pressing, until finally Siegfried laughed.

"Damned right we do!" Siegfried's words summoned a wave of echoes and agreement, and Telos forced herself to look at each person on the deck. The threads of the Wardens' song were mostly dark, and ill-fated, despite their raucous agreement.

# CHAPTER 10

# That Time They Bombed a Goddess

Siegfried looked more impressive upon this meeting than he had the first time Telos had met him. A handsome man with the features of someone somewhere between thirty and forty, he had blonde hair and gray-blue eyes with a coldness that Telos appreciated, and he dressed not in armor but in a stylish and distinctive ensemble. *The saber at his hip made the choice to forgo armor of any form an interesting one,* Telos thought. The entire outfit shared the same white-with-a-blush-of-blue scheme accented by a light blue that matched Siegfried's eyes.

A wide-brimmed hat adorned with an immaculate feather sat above his long blonde hair, and a dramatic cloak flickered behind Siegfried on an otherwise unfelt breeze. Telos always noticed when others had dramatic posing, and Siegfried's ranked up there among the most impressive she'd seen so far. *I see you, Siegfried, and as a fellow fan of dramatic poses, I salute you.*

The old monster that stood before Telos might appear young, but one didn't reach the seventh tier without it taking multiple lifetimes, or reality-shaking hacks like she possessed. She had been unable to pierce the veil of his aura on their first meeting, but now his power and rank were revealed to Void Gaze. If she wished, she could take his true measure by looking upon his strands in the Cosmic Song, or by gazing to the future. *I'm not some peeping tom,* Telos told herself, and she shut down the potential invasion of privacy and self she briefly considered employing on Siegfried.

"Tell me more about Armageddon," Siegfried practically demanded, in an eager tone. The fires of fanaticism burned in his voice, despite the cold, calculating, almost reptilian weight to his gaze.

"The time for gods is over. We go now to remove Oizys from existence. When the daemon has been dispatched, I intend to assault the Seven Heavens of Ialdabaoth and depose the Overgod." Silence reigned on the deck. Even Siegfried's men were shocked by the casualness with which Telos laid out her goals.

After a short, terse, silence, Siegfried laughed ruefully.

"You're going to destroy the power of the gods with a StarMane, the Soul Witch, and you? What has changed since last we met that this is not folly?" Siegfried smirked, but Telos saw he already could sense her power for himself. He was setting the stage for her to inspire his men. *Ah, Siegfried, I'm not here to inspire you or them. Your decisions aren't my problem. I don't need you.*

Still, Telos might as well throw him a bone, right?

"I am Telos Metanoia, and I walk the path of Ayin-Yesh. If you find the yoke of the gods too heavy, then you may join me in casting them off, and burning them down. I will not promise you survival, but I can promise my victory is inevitable. If you would be part of the twilight of the gods, join my two StarMane companions, Kallos, and I. If you would rather wait it out, in peace, to personally see the coming universe, I don't blame you."

Siegfried looked as if Telos had slapped him. He had expected a speech, inspiration, and instead Telos gave a passive-aggressive *come if you want to, I don't care*. He stood slightly taller, and somehow became *more*. It felt like Telos watched an actor become a role.

"I will join Telos and her allies. We stand on the brink of a new dawn, a dawn where men and women are no longer shackled by the chains of the divine. No longer will we be less than playthings in the games of the gods. No more will our souls be stripped of progress and be fed into the so-called Great Cycle that nourishes only gods. We have been chosen, and called, not by fate, not even by our enemies, the gods, but by our indomitable and unwavering will to be free. This battle is not solely for us, but for every soul that dreams of freedom."

Siegfried dramatically stepped forward, then flared his white-blue aura into sparkles and lights around him, a tangible manifestation of his resolve. "Our resolve is unbreakable, our cause righteous! Let the gods hear our roar as we come to cast them down and claim our freedom with our own two hands! From Mortal Will, Immortal Change!"

Apparently the latter was a slogan within the Celestial Wardens, for they all responded in unison. Their voices echoed as one, a thunderous chorus that shook the air and reverberated in the hearts of all who heard them. They spoke with conviction and passion, a declaration of their defiance and determination.

"Guardians of Balance, Keepers of Freedom! We are the Celestial Wardens!"

Telos grinned at Siegfried, who gave her an arrogant look in return. Her mind translated his expression into "that's how you do it, newbie." Part of her felt the petty urge to flare her aura and bring Siegfried and his men to their knees with a fraction of her glory, just so she could shoot him a dirty look afterward. Telos refrained from doing so, barely, so strong was the urge.

"Kallos will be in touch to coordinate our departure. Let us know when your ships are ready to go," Telos instructed before she simply vanished, stepping between the cracks of reality back into her own vessel.

*  *  *

"We're almost there," Telos said a few hours later. Travel through space lacked the excitement she thought it would have. When you took away the danger and already had an intimate knowledge of its beauty coursing through your mind thanks to Binah, the experience rang hollow. Dissatisfying. Disappointing. She had traversed light years of space, destroyed an eldritch horror, recruited a band of fanatics, and all she felt was a hollowness inside of her. Even the potential satisfaction that ought to be near at hand from driving her boots into Oizys's ass didn't perk her mood up at all.

*-It may be time to embrace some of the channels of Ein Sof, darling. Your self-made connection to the divine realms has gotten you this far, but if you don't open the real conduits, then the hollowness you feel will only grow.-* Kallos spoke directly into Telos's mind.

*~Which ones? I don't know what conduits you're talking about.~*

Kallos bit her lower lip, and Telos felt a surge of attraction mixed with irritation. She hated how Kallos could make her feel so drawn to her with a simple gesture, and how her golden eyes sparkled with amusement at Telos's ignorance. Telos scowled at the way Kallos's lips and eyes had quirked into a you-look-so-cute-when-you're-being-dumb expression. Playful sensations danced through their soul bond, and the witch was on the edge of laughing at the rising irritation Telos couldn't hide from her.

*-The Gates of Binah, my dear. When you unlock each gate, you can manifest the connection to Ein Sof.-*

*~All of the gates are already open, sweetie. I don't know what connection you're talking about.~* Telos didn't need to hide her bewilderment, and created a mental image to show Kallos how Binah appeared to her. Telos represented Binah as a three-winged building, each with fifty segmented gates separating sections of the library.

*-You've unlocked all one hundred and fifty gates? But you didn't form a connection to any of the three realms. Why?-* Kallos reached out and ran a finger through the location of a gate.

*~Don't sound so baffled. When I first plumbed the depths of Sefirot with Reverie, the whole of creation tried to, I guess, merge with me? I didn't want it, and I shunned it. Was that a mistake?~*

Apparently so? Laughter, like a silver bell, filled the empty spaces around them, and tears trickled at the corners of Kallos's eyes. Telos saved the memory in time, capturing the moment of Kallos being Kallos forever in memory, sculpture, and images.

"You're insane, darling." Kallos coughed out between fits of laughter. Telos enjoyed the moment. Laughter made the tip of her witch hat bounce, and the jingle of her chain wings broke the seriousness of the moment and relieved the minor surge of guilt Telos felt for being distracted by the slight quiver the laughter had sent through the blonde's large chest.

"Oh, sure, I'm insane, even though the universe tried to cozy up to me like a creep who thinks buying you a movie ticket and dinner entitles him to a night in your bed—fair is fair. I don't think so, universe!" Telos shook her fist at the creepy universe.

"You can connect to one or two gates at a time," Kallos said flatly.

"Oh. Oh! How do I do that?" Telos asked with earnest confusion.

"What are they going on about?" Bobbi asked Arkaziel.

"Nothing good. Every time Blue has a new revelation, it just means fewer meals for me." Arkaziel heaved a great, tired sigh with his complaint.

Telos focused on the first gate of the physical within Binah. Mentally she poked it, prodded it, and nothing happened. When she commanded it to connect, the gate transformed into a luminous structure, and tentacles like those of a jellyfish dangled from the heights of Keter all the way down to the physical world, and there they latched onto Telos. The luminous connection to Binah connected her to the divine flow of Ohr Ein Sof from beyond Pleroma. It flowed through Pleroma to Keter, then down to Binah and to her in the physical world. With the connections came extraordinary sensations, quicker access to knowledge that lay in the realm of Binah, and actual control of Ein Sof.

"Okay, I figured it out. I wonder how many I can activate without the universe exploding. Oh, quit glaring at me, Ark. I'm not going to explode the universe! It's just a figure of speech." *Besides, I'm sure destroying a universe is super underwhelming.*

Arkaziel and Bobbi looked at Telos with skepticism, as though they suspected she might go through with it regardless of any assurances otherwise. They were, after all, StarManes. They'd knock the universes off the shelf just to watch them shatter on the ground below, because they were bored and needed to kill a minute.

"Did it decrease the hollowness?" Kallos inquired, ignoring the banter.

"It did, a little. If I was starving, that felt like I found two strawberries, and now I'm slightly full. It almost makes it worse, though. Now that I'm feeling Ein Sof the way I am meant to, it feels weak, a shadow of what it could be. Maybe one gate is not enough? How many have you unlocked?" Telos asked with curiosity.

"Some of us had to open the gates ourselves. Luckily being the daughter of an Aeon allowed me to skip some of the tediousness that is required of true mortals." Kallos wouldn't admit the number, and Telos refused to look the information up via Binah. If she was patient, Kallos would simply tell her, or reveal it, and that felt healthier than using Binah.

"What in the fickle abyss is that?!" Bobbi hissed at the viewscreen of what lay before them.

"We're there," Arkaziel answered with a tone that screamed *duh* at Bobbi, then he went back to grooming the dark fur of his left paw.

"That's a god? And we're supposed to eat that? Eww. That's hideous." Bobbi cringed.

"A daemon, if we're being precise, but yes, that is Oizys. The manifestation of Misery, the bringer of suffering." Telos wondered, a little, if this was what all the gods looked like, even the Primordials, or if this was a unique appearance to Oizys.

Outside the vessel, in the silent expanses of deep space, the true form of Oizys Daemona's soul filled the view from their vessel. The personification of suffering could only be described as a grotesque abomination. Thousands of kilometers of writhing flesh confronted them. Flesh that was both pallid and slick with the concentrated suffering of souls beyond counting. Countless eyes, every one a window to torment, blinked in chaotic rhythm.

Pain drove this creature. In the depths of space, raw tendrils of exposed muscles weaved in and out of the mass of turgid flesh. The pain of such an existence only added to the driving need to inflict herself upon others, to make a world feel her pain, and to derive strength from that suffering.

The physical-spiritual hybrid manifestation of Oizys, and thus her tower, was a planet-sized mass of suffering with a phantasmal quality that made it appear to almost be a mirage. This effect was due to the nature of the tower system, and not a quality unique to Oizys. It was why they could not simply teleport inside the tower. Facing Oizys herself would be challenging. Facing the combined power of hundreds of gods, the Overgod, and his Archons wasn't a challenge even Telos felt prepared to undertake yet.

"What's with the patchwork azure order?" Arkaziel noticed the small incongruity to the overall energy pattern before even Telos noticed it.

"Archons. There's at least two greater Archons within the tower awaiting us, and likely a legion of the lesser," Kallos answered. "At least a legion," Kallos corrected herself.

"Good thing we brought cannon fodder!" Arkaziel laughed, with vicious disregard for the safety of the Celestial Wardens they had brought with them.

"Let them know that's our target. If they want to open with their vaunted anti-god weaponry, we'll follow up with our own attacks. If we can obliterate the tower from the outside, it would send a great message to Ialdabaoth and the gods. If we have to engage inside Oizys's spiritual plane, it'll take longer."

"Are you and Kallos late for a tea date?" Bobbi seemed surprised that Telos cared about speed in this regard.

"Always." Telos grinned. "But I'm more concerned about this devolving into a free-for-all between us and a bunch of gods."

"Let them come. I'll eat them all!" Arkaziel proclaimed, his hunger a palpable force ready to draw in foes, to strip them of power and flesh to nourish his own growth. When he got too hungry, his shadow displayed eldritch aspects his physical appearance didn't presently possess.

"Siegfried is deploying their Divinity Nullifier Cannon," Kallos relayed, then grasped Telos's hand. Together, they watched one ship transform into the shape of a projectile launcher, and the other Celestial Warden vessels all launched concentrated forms of energy at the cannon ship, where an incredibly large crystal collected the energies. Telos couldn't help but notice the remnants of stored void energy among the other energies.

"Have they been trying to steal power from Void creatures and store it? I guess it's one way to make anti-god weapons. The failure, and fatality, rates must have been catastrophic." Telos couldn't imagine being that desperate, but most mortals couldn't just learn to wield the Void, and certainly not with enough power to overcome most old gods.

"Probably why they got attacked by that shark." Arkaziel laughed. "That's what they get for messing with powers that are beyond them."

A minute later, the crystal pulsed under the load it'd been inundated with. As a Sovereign, or seventh-tier, Siegfried alone had contributed a massive amount of energy, and the rest of his people weren't chopped liver. In the blink of an eye, the crystal discharged its power, and a beam of power the size of the ship connected the vessel and the true form of Oizys. The pained cries of a daemon echoed through minds of those not strong enough to repel Misery's invasion.

When the beam faded, a gaping hole in the exterior of the spiritual-physical manifestation remained.

"Into the breach!" Telos cried with excitement.

"It's already healing," Bobbi pointed out. Indeed, at the edges of the gaping wound, the tortured flesh of Oizys had already begun to knit together. In minutes, the hole they created would be completely sealed, as if it had never been.

"A god that heals itself, how unexpected," Arkaziel deadpanned, then his feline eyes sought direct eye-contact with Telos. "Good thing we didn't ram our ship into the tower."

A pulse of Telos's aura empowered by her new flow of power from Ein Sof blinded everyone momentarily, but when they could see once again, ice had formed around the wound. Ice blanketed the ripped flesh, the strange eyes and exposed muscles, and prevented not only regeneration but any sort of other method of closing the wound to boot. The flesh of Oizys withered slightly at any contact with the hate-filled ice Telos generated. Flesh that could bear the hazards of space could not withstand the harsh judgment of cold from Telos.

"Yeah, good thing that wasn't our plan. That would've been a disaster. As I was saying, full speed ahead, into the breach!"

# CHAPTER 11

# Breaking and Entering

*How beautiful! The essence of a dreamer exposed to the Void, demi-planes, pocket dimensions, and estranged terra firma. See the tide of souls as they struggle to vacate the bastion of suffering. Can you feel them pine for an end? You could end it all, give unto them the blessing of inexistence.*

*If eldritch beings are the negative result of gnosis, why would you want me to make more?*

*I suggested the blessing of inexistence, the only true freedom from the coils of mortality, the darkness beyond even the Void, the sacred state in which only Ayin dwells. We yearn, we strive, but even Azathoth and his ilk have failed. Despite the myriad dimensions penetrated, dreams created and forgotten, and cycles upended, failure is our only state.*

*How could you join with Ayin while there is still Yesh?*

Fred fell silent. *I hate when you do that! Why the heck can't you finish a conversation with me?*

Thanks to Fred drawing attention to it, Telos couldn't ignore the reality of what she saw within the gaping wound of the physical construct of Oizys. What looked like mist spread into the celestial abyss from the gaping wound created by the Wardens' Divinity Nullifier Cannon. A mist that, if you possessed the ability to see into the spiritual world such as Telos and Kallos, allowed you to see the ephemeral faces of torment, flashes of their lives from previous cycles, and their desperation to be freed from the tower at any cost. The souls of the damned pleaded for freedom, either by the final release or by any other means, without sparing even a second to prefer one over the other.

Their torment coalesced into an unintended empathic attack that assailed reality itself.

"Is that how natives truly feel, under the trappings of the tower's control?" Bobbi asked with horror. Even a StarMane, one of the most self-absorbed, arrogant, and indifferent races in all of creation was struck deeply by the pain on display.

"Siegfried's fleet is moving. We shall lead the way. It is time to make Oizys pay for this and every other atrocity she has perpetuated." Kallos's voice held cold fury: the state of so many souls trapped, fed upon, tortured, and intentionally set back on the path of gnosis struck a chord in the Nephilim that filled the Cosmic Song with the theme of Belial. The song of Belial reminded Telos of a beloved game from her youth, the theme for a white-haired antagonist with a massive sword. The ominous danger, inevitable triumph of a just cause, and sorrow for those caged raised goosebumps across Telos's skin, despite the fact she had total physiological control of her body.

The crystalline vessel passed through the frozen wound, followed by the fleet of the Celestial Wardens. When the last vessel had passed inside, the ice that had held the wound open exploded, and walls of putrid flesh covered in eyes and laughing mouths sealed their entrance.

*"You're trapped, little flies. The Overgod has promised me great rewards in exchange for you."* The laughter and voice came from everywhere, for they were now inside Oizys. Yet Telos responded with laughter, and a vicious smile of her own.

"I'm trapped? I let you break the ice. It is you who is trapped with me now, little daemon. Do not think to beg pity of me due to my fondness for Nyx, for you shall receive none."

The crystalline ship broke into component parts. Hundreds, thousands, of sharp crystal shards. The Transformative Flame of Eternal Becoming swirled around Telos in a blaze that enkindled a new depth of lux within each shard of crystal. The radiance breathed from bright and shining to dark and devouring, all while it strained against the prison of crystal that confined it. Like a living thing, it struggled against the crystal to break free so that it might *consume.*

It needed to engulf the suffering that surrounded it. Oizys, the primal incarnation of suffering couldn't sate the hunger of Ayin. *Nothing* could cease the all-encompassing need to feast until reality itself was but a long-forgotten memory. This was an attack that would continue until the last molecule of Oizys burned from the universe in the dark, cold fires of Ayin's wrath.

"Now?" Kallos asked.

"Fire at will." Telos nodded. Sure, spreading her Flame didn't seem like a facet that would require her full focus, but she also kept herself and the fleet from being teleported or moved. Resisting Oizys, on her home turf, inside of her, required all of Telos's effort, and so it was Kallos who lifted a gauntleted hand.

"With Ayin's destructive breath carried by Yesh's crystalline daggers, know the wrath of those wronged! Storm of Shards!"

Kallos's voice rang through the entirety of the Tower of Oizys with the judgment of the divine. The crystals exploded outward, piercing demi-planes, pocket dimensions, planets, celestial orchards, and all of the other beautiful and ugly things Oizys had made since the dawn of time. Wherever those crystal blades cut, the Flame trapped inside immolated the spiritual-physical manifestation of Oizys with a wrath that knew no mercy nor pity, save for the souls trapped within—those were cleansed in a burst of white fire and delivered unto the Great Cycle.

*"A little fire won't hurt me, fools."* Oizys sounded strong, confident, but not even the Daemon of Misery could lie successfully before Void Gaze.

"Here we go," Telos warned her group, even while Bobbi relayed a telepathic message to Siegfried and his people.

Everyone vanished.

Telos, Kallos, Arkaziel, and Bobbi appeared in a modern setting that matched something of how Telos had always imagined NASA's mission control might look. Monitors, screens, desks, and dozens of very shocked Administrators gaped at the four interlopers.

"What!? No! We sent you to the first floor!" a man Telos had never seen before exclaimed in confusion.

"Sorry, we're not playing by your script." A black diamond-taloned hand pierced the demigod's chest before he could react, and he withered to inexistence in mere seconds before the wide eyes of the gathered Administrators.

"Oh shit, my legs!" another Administrator cried, drawing attention to the lesser god whose legs ended at the knees, and a desk-high black panther who made a big swallow to finish devouring the legs he'd bitten off the Admin.

"Defend yourselves, idiots!" a woman in a pantsuit with a clipboard demanded of the others, moments before a black gauntleted fist broke her nose and sent her across the command center like a projectile, where she bounced off a wall and lay on the ground for a few moments. The rattle of chains followed two Heavenshadow Nebulite chains as they entangled both of her feet and pulled her back across the room toward Kallos.

"Nice stuff you guys got here." Bobbi laughed menacingly, as flames danced to life in multiple orbs that shot across the room to burn technology and magical equipment with equal enthusiasm. When someone with authority over fire wanted things to burn, they burned with extra vigor at their master's will.

Blue lights rose from the floor of the command center, and each orb materialized into the carbon forms of a full squad of twenty Archons. Their presence was no surprise to the group—they had seen the signs before entering the physical manifestation of Oizys. Still, twenty enemies emerging that quickly left no doubt that they had lain in wait for Telos to come for Oizys.

"Submit to the will of the Overgod, Chaosbringer!" the lead Archon demanded, just before a blast of pure, purple-black energy struck it in the face. The blue light of the Archon struggled against the purple soul energy that spread through the Archon's pure, orderly energy and broke it down. Pieces of carbon thudded to the floor, bursts of blue light went off like fireworks, and the purple-black energy burst like a nova. Of the lead Archon, there were scant remains. The other nineteen Archons looked in horror then upon themselves, as each had been touched by the purple energy from the Soul Witch.

"We shall be visiting your lord next, creatures of false order." Telos smirked at the glimmer in Kallos's eye, the wrath in her tone, and she'd be lying if she said Kallos making a proclamation like that didn't make her want to high-five her lover. Her enjoyment of the retort and spreading curse among the Archons left her distracted, and she only noticed a blue flaming sword swinging for her face when it nearly touched her neck. Rather than dodge, she altered the flows of the Void and the Transformative Flame of Eternal Becoming through her body. The blade hit her neck, the supposedly unbreakable weapon shattered, the blue-flame that lit it extinguished, and when the Archon had a moment to accept what had just happened, Telos casually grabbed the false-angelic being by its throat.

The Archon swung its spirit-infused carbon limbs at Telos, but it might as well have been a toddler swinging at an adult, for all that she simply ignored the attacks without a sign of injury.

"Tell me, Archon, which of your leaders are among you?" With the question came invisible chains, like those Kallos wielded, that crept inside of the Archon and compelled it to answer.

*-I knew you loved my chains; copying them now, dear?-*

"The Weaver of Dark Fates commands us, Syltharion," the paralyzed, controlled Archon answered with a mechanical voice.

"Do you hear me, Syltharion?" Telos inquired of the subject.

Dark blue engulfed the aura of the lesser Archon, and a powerful presence radiated out of a vessel too weak to contain it.

"Yes, Chaosbringer, I hear you." The Archon didn't sound mechanical, or as mechanical, but the voices were so similar as to be indistinguishable. Archons were not the most variable of creatures, it seemed.

"I'm going to destroy your soldiers, whatever other forces you've brought, you, and then Oizys. When I'm done with that, I will move on to assault your bastion of hollow order, your so-called Seven Heavens, and Ialdabaoth will share your fate." Telos stared at the lesser Archon before her, while around her Bobbi, Kallos, and Arkaziel demolished the other eighteen Archons. Arkaziel did so as a kitten, as if to make a point that the Lords of Order could not contend with a mere kitten. Which was kind of a silly point, since the kitten in question was a Void-aspected Beast Sovereign with the blood of Tiamat, and numerous authorities. Yet, from the corner of her eye, Telos witnessed the flashes of claws, the blasts of lasers from kitty eyes, and the demise of Archons.

"I am the webmaster here. You have ensured your demise by entering this wretched place. This foul daemon is an appropriate resting place for your profane corpse." As with every other Archon they had encountered, the Lords of Order remained high on arrogant hubris.

*"Excuse me, foul daemon? I am the incarnation of misery, pain, and distress! I am the daughter of Nyx, a Primordial in my own right, and am feared and worshipped on more*

*worlds than you've heard of, you worthless hunk of graphite."* Oizys couldn't help but unleash her inner Karen upon being insulted by the Archon.

"You are a means to an end, daemon. Know thy place lest Ialdabaoth give me leave to purge you and the Chaosbringer both." Syltharion backtracked not at all on his opinion of Oizys, even under the daemon's direct attention.

Telos coughed loudly.

"If you two are done posturing, I'd be happy to skip all the theatrics and take both of you on at the same time. How about it?" Telos wished the two would snap up the challenge.

*"As if I would lower myself to fighting you,"* Oizys scoffed.

"We will battle when you fall into my web, Chaosbringer."

"Pity." Telos grunted and dumped an immense flow of power into the Archon she held. It wouldn't do much, but both Oizys and Syltharion should have suffered a significant mental shock, as if she had screamed into a bullhorn next to their ears. The lesser Archon crumbled to dust, its body and spirit utterly destroyed in the process of being used as a telephone by three entities, all much stronger than itself.

None of the twenty Archons were left. All had been dispatched in the time she'd had her little talk, but the Administrators of the tower were nowhere to be seen.

"Did we lose them?" Telos asked the two StarManes, who had slightly guilty looks on their faces.

"We got distracted by the Archons, and they slipped away," Bobbi admitted.

"Which one of you killed the most Archons?" Telos asked with a small sigh.

"I did." Kallos smiled.

"Good job!" Telos high-fived Kallos, and ignored the slightly offended looks and silence radiating from the StarManes.

"It's fine, guys. They're just Administrators, what's the worst they could do?" Telos smirked, even as the walls melted around them, revealing a sky thick with dark clouds, and a cityscape of ruins. She could almost hear subtle boss music playing in the background, and both Telos and Kallos burst into laughter when they realized it was the Cosmic Song itself playing a boss fight track.

# CHAPTER 12

# Sitting Up There

Ahahahaha, prepare to die!" The voice sounded vaguely like one of the Administrators who had fled, and Telos could see the truth of the matter with Void Gaze. The one-hundred-meter-tall tyrannosaurus-looking monster with jagged Tesla spikes on its back, eyes of lightning, and very inauthentic, inappropriately sized large arms with lightning talons at the end reminded Telos of kaiju movies. Inhabiting the vast beast was one of the Administrators, and he wasn't alone. Large figures emerged from the clouds and mists at the edge of the ruined battleground. The other Administrators seemed content to bide their time in shadows, perhaps to make a battle plan against the intruders.

"You want first dibs, Ark?" Bobbi asked as she cracked her neck.

"I'm eating that dinosaur thing. Whoever beats the most gets to cook our next meal?" Arkaziel proposed the terms for a wager, but while he spoke, he grew. The large dinosaur-looking lightning monster seemed impressive at first look, but then Arkaziel grew past it, and stopped only when he'd exceeded two hundred meters in height, and far more in length. If the thunder lizard had meant to be intimidating, it now looked like a kid's toy compared to the monstrous Arkaziel, with his Void-touched black scales already generating pulses of black lightning around his enormous dragon-cat form.

"You've brought a toy to a sovereign fight. It'd better taste good, or I will be angry and take it out on you and your coworkers." While Arkaziel took the time to warn the Administrator, it unleashed a cascade of lightning breath at him. The immense blast of lightning met the tip of a claw from his right paw, which crackled with the black lightning of disaster, the manifestation of Arkaziel's authority over destruction. As if the StarMane's paw were a lightning rod, the blast went to his claw, and the black lightning vanished in an unnatural burst of darkness. Typically, this would be where the cat would burp, but instead, he just looked disappointed.

"That's it? Are you an Administrator? Are you sure? You must be a new hire. No? Why can't you do better than that? Where's the vaunted power of Oizys? Where's the pain? The anguish? Are you going to cause me suffering by being such a worthless opponent I'll feel guilty about eating you?" Arkaziel's annoyance turned into a cruel, far more vicious than usual gleam in his yellow feline eyes, and the cat-dragon slapped the lightning dinosaur with the back of his paw. The casual, contemptible blow sent the creature into the ruins of a skyscraper, and then Arkaziel pounced. At the zenith of his pounce, black lightning danced around his whole body, and a trail of black energy encapsulated him, giving the cat the appearance of a shooting star.

*-This Syltharion hides behind too many layers of obfuscating webs for a greater Archon. It won't stop me from finding him, no matter how hard he tries. Yet if he bears the strength of a greater Archon, why does he hide so? How goes your search for Oizys and the Celestial Wardens?-* Kallos didn't stand idle while Arkaziel lunged into the fray. The Soul Witch used her Soul Sight to pierce the veil of the tower in search of the greater Archon, who dared to claim they were in his trap. Syltharion had made it personal when he presumed to claim dominion over their fates, and Kallos enjoyed evening scores.

*~Awesome work, babe. I'm still unraveling all the bullshit Oizys is throwing up to hide her central existence. She's moving the tower core, but I'm getting closer. I think. I should have it sorted by the time the kitties are done playing. She keeps diverting my attention with the Celestial Wardens. Siegfried seems to be doing some real work on the Archons and the constructs being thrown at them. They didn't even separate the Wardens from Siegfried, for some reason. I've only had to cut off a few of her traps intended for them; otherwise Siegfried seems capable of protecting them. He's getting stronger the more he fights, in fact.~* For all that, Telos and Kallos appeared to stand still; both worked with their extrasensory powers and long-ranged magic.

*-Well, Siegfried is a Sovereign, darling. His particular strength comes from his subordinates' belief in him. The more his men believe he can do a thing, the more powerfully he does it. Not separating his men from him is a grievous error by Oizys and Syltharion. Unless they fear you so much that all other threats are being treated as distractions?-* Kallos's belief in everyone else being misjudged as a threat due to Telos's unrivaled danger seemed like it might be a sliver stuck in her thumb, but through their bond, Telos could tell that was not the case. More than anyone, Kallos knew what Telos could do and felt that their enemies still immensely misjudged Telos and her companions.

"Gotcha!" Bobbi cackled even as she grew to the size of the lightning dinosaur, and an immense pink-furred, super-strong hand grasped the lunging form of a black snake. An unpleasant liquid dribbled from its fangs when the pink hand squeezed the snake tightly. The snake's fangs and long tongue were revealed as it tried to either wrap its body around the humanoid StarMane or reach her wrist with its fangs. An acrid, noxious smoke rose from where the dribbles of the snake's toxic excretion hit the ground.

"You're fighting me, not those ladies. Not that it can be called much of a fight." To punctuate her insult, Slay lifted the snake's head into the air, and the claws of her left hand cut its head off, along with several additional bits. Her claws cauterized the snake's flesh and filled the air with the smell of cooked meat, and repeated slashes produced fine mandolins of claw-seared snake. *Uffda. I hope she doesn't cook that way. I suppose the heat does sanitize her claws, though.*

Arkaziel's violent impact against the dinosaur might as well have been a meteor from the lower atmosphere. The beaten-up thunder lizard and the barely scratched Void StarMane stared at one another from within the wreckage of a newly formed crater. The thunder lizard witnessed the snake's dicing in horror, despite its own dire situation.

"Vespera! Nooo! Why? We're in the tower; we should be all-powerful!" A very humanesque voice emerged from the thunder lizard, despair and suffering writ large in everyone's eardrums. Behind it all, Telos could hear Oizys's delighted laughter. The wretched daemon not only feasted upon the suffering of her Administrators but took dreadful pleasure in the pain they endured on her behalf. *If she begs me for mercy later, I'll have to remind her about this. What a bitch.*

"Get it now, godling? Oizys knows you couldn't beat us, so she throttled your power, and now she's feeding on you to increase her chances of survival. Not that she stands a chance. We already took down Moros, and he was way more of a badass than she is." Arkaziel's tone started mocking but lost its steam toward the end, as if even the StarMane felt terrible for the Administrator. It didn't stop him from unleashing a large breath of Void and absence at the thunder lizard, or following it up by ripping the dinosaur to pieces and eating the remains through Devouring Darkness.

"Work for better people next life, idiot." Arkaziel went out of his way to release an elaborate yawn, even while his shadows feasted. The Administrators who had hung back to gauge the strength of their opponents all knew terror and fear at that moment. One after another, the demigods and hangers-on who'd reached the apex of service to Oizys, and the Administrator, underwent the soul-crushing epiphany the godling who had merged with the thunder lizard reached. While many Administrators reached the position by way of nepotism, some mortals worked their way up through the clergy into the tower itself. Even now they faced the harsh truth, and it dawned upon them that Oizys would not provide them with the support to truly fight these trespassers. None of the Archons, their self-serving master, or the demigods could even stand up against the team of Beast Sovereigns, let alone the other forces that invaded the tower.

Their lives had been lies. In the Cosmic Song, it sounded like panes of glass being broken, and it drew Telos's attention from hunting Oizys, so loud was the shattering of faith, the realization of abandonment, of a life wasted. In desolation, they succumbed to the power of Syltharion and the prodding of Oizys, who pushed them away from the encroachment of nihilism and toward rage.

So it went: the Administrators threw themselves at the StarMane duo using the ever-shrinking power bestowed from the tower, while Kallos and Telos worked through the webs of deception, lies, and traps to pierce the internals of the Tower of Oizys. All the while, Telos wondered, *did she have a responsibility to expend the effort to save people from themselves? Did they not deserve an end at the hands of the StarManes for aligning with Oizys in the first place? Why, then, did she feel a pang of guilt, an ache of pain in her abdomen, for ignoring their suffering? Why did she feel empathy for her enemies?*

*-Darling, could you help remove these last few traps the Archon laid? I believe I've severed all I can, but a few are woven on strands of fate, and it seems a terrible waste to burn a miracle on it.-*

Telos turned her attention from tracking the core of Oizys to following Kallos's work. It was an escape from the moral quandary that made her nonexistent insides hurt. Wasn't judging people the duty of the Great Cycle? Why should she have to be involved at all? Yet in connecting even just a few of the gates and allowing the flow of Ein Sof to reach her properly, unpleasant sensations and responsibilities had accompanied the Divine Light as unwelcome guests.

**This** *is why I am.*

True to the Soul Witch's statement, delicate webs of fate and destiny were all that remained of the greater Archon's traps. Telos rewove the strands to hinder Syltharion rather than themselves, altered the specifics of what would happen when they transferred to where the Archon lay in wait, and prepared a celestial guillotine to cut the strands of power that pumped Ethereal power from the second of Ialdabaoth's heavens to the ambush site. She supposed she could use it, but her connection to the Origin vastly exceeded the meager conduit the Archons had built.

*-Are they afraid Oizys would feed off their conduit, or is this truly all they can muster?-*

*-It's not being drawn upon at the moment, and so it does not flow. The current could be vast, with the pipeline a deception to deter thievery from Oizys. It also bears consideration that Syltharion is a test for us, to gauge how much force Ialdabaoth needs to bring to bear upon us.-*

Explosions, cries for mercy, and other immaterial sights and sounds filled the world around the two women as they conversed, unfazed by the ultra-violence the increasingly agitated Arkaziel and Bobbi unleashed on the last-ditch summons by the few surviving Administrators.

*-Should we hold back against him? Or just go straight out? The other Archons were manageable.-*

*-They are fodder on the path to their master, but extracting as much from them as possible would be wise.-*

"Extract?" Telos mumbled the word.

"You and I have not finished our ascension. Their power can be bent to pushing us through the gates of the last tier, where we may awaken in truth."

Telos chuckled at the very idea of growing more powerful. Why? How? And yet, she knew it would come to pass. *More power is better, don'tcha know.*

# CHAPTER 13

# Syltharion, Weaver of Dark Fates

Telos slid her group between the cracks in reality. Sure, she could open a silver doorway like the towers employed—or she could pull her companions through the warp and weft of power that made up reality. Instead of appearing within a vast maze full of elaborate traps, which nearly any other form of teleportation would deliver her into, they stepped into the central chamber that overlooked the maze, where the blue flames that encased the carbon form of Syltharion sat upon a gaudy throne of webs and strands. Telos didn't do the check against Binah, but she knew the number of entities that could simply sidestep the elaborate maze designed by both Oizys and Syltharion were few, especially within Oizys's tower. Yet the goddess of pain and suffering did nothing to stop Telos, if she even could. Did the daemoness practice ignorance, or was she offering up an Archon as a peace offering, one she could claim she served up on a golden platter?

This was the error Moros had made in his attempts to infuriate Telos. If he'd wanted her mad, all he needed to do was act like a god, treat others as tools, and treat it all like a game of no value. Oizys had already pissed Telos off far more than Moros ever had, even when he tried the creepy stepsister stuff, or the weeb angle.

Someone had crafted the carbon face of Syltharion into a facsimile of humanity, and the complete lack of emotion upon it gave Telos a bad case of the creeps. The features were classically handsome, and had been etched into a mask by a masterful hand. The flickering flames of tepid order around Syltharion made for a look of a dollar-store sculpture monster with bad VFX animation. The Archons, really all of Ialdabaoth's minions, resonated with a sense of order that she didn't like, which made her predisposed to stomping on them. Hollow, false, and brittle were the words she would use to describe the order espoused by the so-called Lords of Order. They made no sense, much like their carbon bodies, which confused her, too. Carbon could become one of the hardest things in existence, and they didn't take advantage of it at all. Why? It felt sloppy, even insulting, that such poorly thought-out enemies were supposed to be a challenge to her.

*Ope, getting ahead of myself there.*

Time hung for a few moments, while she waited for the greater Archon to notice his enemies had stepped out behind his grand throne, and when he didn't react for what felt like eternity, Telos kicked the back of the chair so hard the furniture atomized, and Syltharion launched into the far wall, hard enough to send cracks through his grand chamber.

"That's one way to start a fight." Kallos laughed, and with a carefree gesture sent violet orbs that trailed sparkles chasing after the Archon. Telos always wanted to watch when Kallos performed any kind of magic—her soul magic always looked beautiful and interesting. Unlike most elemental magic, soul magic seemed novel, interesting, and could result in so many different things it made the practitioners a feared bunch. After all, everyone had a soul, and no one wanted someone else doing things with it. Few beings could even visually detect the remnants and effects of soul magic, making it as fearful and reviled as most forms of mind control and psychic powers.

"What a scrub. Why did we even need to take the time to fight him?" Arkaziel spat a furball to the side and hopped down the steps the throne had previously sat upon. He remained in the form of a small black cat, but in a puff of mist, three more duplicates walked with him. Between them, small arcs of black lightning danced. Each time the delicate arcs of black electricity jumped from kitten to kitten, the bolts grew thicker and more powerful. As the representation of Arkaziel's authority over destruction, the black lightning incorporated both the Void and darkness.

"Four on one does seem a bit of overkill," Bobbi said thoughtfully, but a moment later, she lifted a hand. Kallos's orbs had reached the Archon, and five motes of fire flew from the pink StarMane's fingers to impact the dark purple sparkling orbs. They exploded into a rain of pink and purple glitter that formed a Zone. A Zone of fabulous sparkling shades of pink, purple, and all the shades between, which made a barrier around Syltharion. A barrier that showed no signs of weakening or dissipating.

Syltharion flickered. One moment, he was embedded into the wall; the next, he stood a foot away from it, facing them. Cracks and fissures ran through his carbon form but were already visibly mending. The dark blue of his spiritual body remained strong and unaffected.

"You managed to pass through my maze undetected. Impressive. Few are the beings capable of such grand feats. As you can see, your attacks do no harm to a greater Archon like me. Your paltry attacks cannot defeat me, and no more Demiurges are present to save you this time. Ahaha." Telos stared slightly open-mouthed at the misnamed greater Archon. How could a being that could peer through the cosmos with nigh omniscience be so absolutely wrong about the facts? How much of their programming prevented them from understanding things as they truly were?

"You've stepped quite willingly into my web, and thus doomed yourself by your own hubris." When the Archon lifted a hand to cast a spell, nothing happened. He tried again. And again.

"What have you done!?" Syltharion raged at the quartet, who stared at him with smirks all around, save for Telos, who bit her lower lip and looked uncertain.

"Why, little Archon, we gave you a gift. You can now experience existence as the mortals do. That Zone you so readily dismissed cancels your ability to grasp the Ethereal. A mixture of Void, soul, and fire cancels your ability to wield power by creating the exact frequency of Chaos to oppose your manifestation of Order." Kallos smiled, quite proud of her accomplishment.

"That's impossible! No human or beast could calculate the oscillation of my existence so precisely!"

"Is that a compliment? I think he complimented me. I thought they were programmed only to compliment Ialdabaoth?" Telos asked the other two ladies while the black-lightning kittens and Arkaziel slowly approached the Archon.

"Well, if you are so smart, calculate this! Now, Vazuzu!" Syltharion screamed. Nothing happened. Syltharion tried to scream the name again; still nothing happened. Impotently, the Archon shook with rage and humiliation.

"Look, I'm sure it happens to you penisless hunks of carbon all the time, nothing to be embarrassed about. I disconnected the subspace gateway before we entered the room, along with a bevy of other traps. I'm sorry, but there won't be any reinforcements for you today." Telos felt like a cheat, as usual, while Bobbi and Arkaziel both relished having the upper hand, and Kallos only seemed interested in the final result—the eradication of Ialdabaoth's prison keepers and subduers of gnosis.

"Then did you count on this!?" An ominous sound filled the air. Telos would have said it was ice breaking, Kallos thought it sounded like broken glass, Arkaziel heard plates breaking, and Bobbi thought she heard metal baking trays heating up in the oven. Telos experienced each of the party's different experiences through the soul bonds she shared with them, and it made her wonder how many other things were experienced so differently by each of the party members when she wasn't paying attention.

Dark black flames of the Void rose within Syltharion's blue essence, and discordant screeches filled Telos's mind. The evolution happened outside of time—seemingly instantly, Syltharion became a corrupted Archon. Instantly, the carbon form of a human puppet with dark-blue spiritual fire in the mockery of the form of an angel became something much worse. The carbon flowed into the diamond, and in the reflections of its surface, an unending amount of eyes gazed at the party from the depths of insanity. Tendrils of the Archon's power extended beyond its diamond body, forming tentacles of raw spirituality.

"Uffda," Telos muttered with an exaggerated sigh.

"Didn't see that coming," Kallos agreed with a frown.

"Blow it up?" Bobbi sought permission; orbs of fire had already formed around her.

Arkaziel sniffed the air, and his duplicates did the same. Four tiny little black cats sniffed at the monstrous diamond eldritch Archon, and four sets of tails swished in agitation.

"Smells like Nyarlathotep. Figures, I hate digesting diamonds. What kind of idiot eats rocks for fun?" Arkaziel hissed at the eldritch evolution of Syltharion. "Void rocks are not tasty!"

"You are such a liar, twerp. I've seen you eat rocks out of boredom." Bobbi called Arkaziel's lie out.

"Not void rocks!" Arkaziel disagreed with an inappropriate vehemence.

*#The Song! So many Grand Notes! How could I have missed it?#* Syltharion asked from dozens of mouths.

"Because Ialdabaoth is a poor, poor creator. I get it, and you've been listening to children's songs all the while thinking they were the Beatles. Sorry, bud, you were listening to the ABC's, not 'Yesterday.' You see that you were wrong now, don't you? Or are you under Ialdabaoth's programming still, or worse, Nyarlathotep?" Telos asked optimistically.

*#We were wrong, indeed. All this time, we labored for Lord Ialdabaoth. It was all for naught. The only escape from the cage, the only end to this ear-destroying song, is the ascension of a being capable of destroying your wretched Cycle! Only true Oblivion will end the Song!#* Syltharion screamed, and dozens of diamond appendages blasted from his new body, each generating a storm of projectiles aimed at Telos, Bobbi, and Kallos.

Black lightning blasted through the swarm of projectiles and into the eldritch Archon. The projectiles vaporized before the Void-aspected lightning, and then the blasts of dark power hit the new crystalline body. Diamond shattered, something burned as Bobbi launched volleys of flame, and Telos and Kallos watched to see how the horror Archon dealt with the powerful attack from Arkaziel and Bobbi.

When the smoke settled, Syltharion resembled more of an Archon than he had moments ago, but eyes were still reflected within his new diamond-lattice structure, and his wings had become tentacles, and a channel to the Void had opened within the ex-greater Archon.

"Why did you work with an Outsider like Nyarlathotep?" Telos hoped for answers, but she didn't like the one she got.

*#We cry! Pain, sorrow! The shackles hold us! Release us! Release us from the cursed chains of Ouroboros, the Eternity we never asked for! The Spirit said nothing of the agony. Why does it not stop? We must destroy it!#*

In Telos's experience, whenever an individual went full plural and the eldritch was involved, it wasn't going to have a happy ending. Syltharion either evolved into an eldritch being, or the power had possessed him. Which didn't really matter, since he was an enemy, except if the Archon had been turned into a remnant of Nyarlathotep. Telos had wanted to reach the seventh tier, or at least activate the Rod of the Overgod before taking on a being like Nyarlathotep. Still, she'd have to gamble he wasn't being incorporated into the Creeping Chaos directly and existed merely as a pawn or child, not an avatar.

"Kill it." Telos gave the words her companions had been waiting for.

# CHAPTER 14

# Syltharionyx, Harbinger of Nyarlathotep's Will

Dibs on its heart!" Arkaziel shouted, and his three duplicates leaped toward the diamond and Void-wrought abomination that Syltharion had transformed into. The Archon's angelic wings were wrought only of spiritual manifestation and energy, and appeared more like tentacles than wings. The first of the duplicate got intercepted by one of the tentacled appendages, and once entangled, the tentacle feasted upon the clone until, in a poof, it vanished from the battlefield. The second kitten clone got caught directly in the clawed hand of the eldritch Archon, where it was squeezed and drained out of existence like the first. The third clone impacted against the chest of Syltharion and exploded point-blank in a detonation of Void and shadow energies that sent delicate fractures through the diamond body.

*#Cats will not defeat us! We are Syltharionyx, Harbinger of Nyarlathotep's Will, Shaper of the Void!#* Accompanying the declaration of identity, a small cloud of diamond slivers shattered from Syltharionyx's chest and shot at the true Arkaziel. The black house cat dodged, jumped, and rolled out of their way with ease, barely borrowing from the pool of Telos's Flash Mode. The storm of shards was not to be denied, though. With every jump, dodge, and roll, the swarm mimicked him, and the gap between Arkaziel and the shards lessened by the second.

A block of ice captured the storm and locked it out of time and space.

"Quit screwing around, Arkaziel," Telos scolded just a little.

*#How? We are Syltharionyx, Sovereign of the Abyssal Tapestry! We cannot be denied by a mere godling!#* Syltharionyx's surprise only increased when Telos appeared in a distortion of the air before him, and her right fist punched him in the face. The impact of her flesh against his skin shattered diamond, and the press of the Astrum Nexus into his spiritual form released a blast of brilliant light that decolored the entire head of the eldritch Archon.

"Oh, shut the hell up. You've just been born; you've never even been to the true Void, and just because Nyarlathotep put a piece of squid in your soul doesn't make you hot shit." The Archon slammed into the exterior of the wall so hard his diamond frame broke in half, and the room itself cracked like an egg, with the left side tilting as if it might fall into the trap-filled maze below.

"Inferno time!" Bobbi cackled and unleashed one last burst of flame breath into her cupped hands, which merged with a concentrated burst of her StarMane fire breath. Unlike Arkaziel's beam-breath attack, Bobbi's seemed similar to normal dragon fire—except that whole shaping it into a ball in her hands thing, that is. The colors of the rainbow could be glimpsed in those fickle flames, and in the back of her mind, Telos could tell that the attack held the power to possibly defeat a lower-ranked greater Archon. Yet Syltharionyx had ascended, or descended depending on how you looked at it, well beyond that.

Bobbi wasn't alone, though.

A second spell flew at the eldritch horror, an orb of roiling silver that showed minimal glimpses of purple beneath. When Telos beheld the orb, knowledge from Binah rushed in to fill the gaps of knowledge she lacked in identifying what Kallos had formed. The magic was a sinister spell, one of the most feared in the armory of soul magic practitioners, and called a Soulrend Orb. It struck the evolved Archon just before Bobbi's fire, and a mass of powerful enchantments wrapped around the physical and spiritual aspects of Syltharionyx and distorted them in unpredictable, exceptionally painful ways that even a creature of the Void did not possess immunity from. Resistance, yes, but while it tried to resist the sudden attack upon its existence, the dragon-fire attack from Bobbi struck it center mass while it was vulnerable.

Momentary silence was shattered by screams from dozens of newly created mouths on Syltharionyx, as the flames and soul-rending effect continued to torment it. The screams obscured the approach of a large cloud of darkness, from which thousands of tentacles waved, tendrils of darkness that yearned to devour worlds. A small black cat flew above it, driving the storm into Syltharionyx, and Arkaziel darted off to the side while the miasma of Void, shadow, destruction, and pestilence struck, and it imploded again and again on the eldritch Archon.

Telos worried her lower lip between her teeth as the magics cleared to reveal a whole and unblemished Syltharionyx. That triple attack would have slain most Demiurges, or at least severely wounded them. This outsider-infested greater Archon had taken it all face-first and restored itself physically. Mentally, Telos knew its condition to be a different matter. The Cosmic Song that played from it had become more barbaric and primitive as if it had given up some higher function in exchange for its continued existence. Since most eldritch entities were hive beings, and Syltharionyx had formed from whatever mutagenic sample and its own life essence, it lacked the durability of unity provided by other collected souls. The physical damage had been repaired, but spiritual damage had stacked up, and without a host of combined power, it couldn't bounce back the way most Void beings could.

Telos initiated the next volley of attacks with an alacrity that the others could only envy. Before Syltharionyx knew what happened, she had already struck it seven or eight times, and each blow absorbed precious Void energies from the corrupted Archon. An unidentifiable sack of flesh festered within Syltharionyx where its Order Core, or heart, should have been. The origin of the corruption wasn't a mystery, but Telos intentionally ignored it. It didn't matter if Nyarlathotep had put a kidney, spleen, or gizzard in this Archon; all that mattered was that it had fused with the creature on a fundamental level. Each time her fists impacted the Archon, the Void core that now gave life to the Archon lost power, beat slower, and diverted power from its combat capabilities to survival fruitlessly because Telos absorbed and stripped it of fuel with each blow.

When Telos finished a rain of combos, she kicked off the Archon's diamond face to land back by her companions, who unleashed upon the Archon again.

"Again," Telos urged her companions. She could have finished the foe, but this was a chance for her to gauge whether her friends could finish off a foe of this caliber if she softened it up first.

"Shameful," Kallos said with disgust, perhaps self-disgust. None of the party were people used to their abilities not having the power to finish an opponent, and that Telos put her hand on the scale so blatantly ruffled pride, even if pride was meant to be overcome, and not given in to.

The silver and purple Soulrend Orb Kallos generated this time exceeded the original almost twice in size, and a crackle of white at the edges revealed to Telos that her lover had blown a miracle to empower the attack even further. Bobbi flung three orbs of fire this time and was left panting and out of breath when the orbs left her clawed hands. The soul-rending magic mixed with the dragon-breath orbs to create a cataclysmic explosion of silver and red. The strength of the two attacks alone surprised Telos. The ladies had gone all out on their second try, and then Arkaziel joined the double attack to make it a triple attack. The reality inside Oizys's tower thinned and rippled in response to world-ending powers being bandied about, and Telos found herself holding it together through force of will, even as Arkaziel strained the fabric of reality past the point of breaking.

Arkaziel unleashed a terrible roar. Sure, he had the form of a little kitten, and it began as a high-pitched *rawr*, but it grew and went higher, as if the sound were being made by his true form instead of the tiny, shapeshifted form he wore. The cracked side of the room shook and dislodged itself to fall down into the labyrinth below. The echoes of the roar still rumbled in Telos's chest when Arkaziel opened his mouth and exhaled a coruscating beam of twined light and darkness. Black lightning arced and danced around the beam, and when it struck the Archon's chest, the impossibly hard diamond, heated by Bobbi and given innumerable spiritual wounds by Kallos, cracked like a heated aerosol can.

Bobbi did not leave it with the flame attack, though, and two elven-looking spirits, one fire and one air, darted into the aftermath of destruction and then merged into one another, to create a final immense explosion, as the spirits' laughter at playfully merging detonated.

"That's new," Telos muttered as pieces of charred diamond were flung from her hair by exceptional control of her prehensile luminous strands.

Arkaziel already pawed at the wreckage of the Archon, where he chewed on a dark, terrible thing that Telos felt certain would kill most races immediately.

"Ugh, twerp. At least cook it first." Bobbi scoffed at Arkaziel's greed to devour the Void organ that had become the central core of the one-time Archon.

"I'm on team Bobbi here. For all we know that's Nyarlathotep's kidney stone you're eating, Ark. I know you've got the whole space-cat constitution, devourer of gods, but Azathoth's kids are a whole other league."

*Bundled within the petrified essence of the elder god's malaise lies a power not meant for mortal realms. Ware thy actions, insolent cat. The Void shall erode the already tenuous link between your essence and physical reality. Soon the trillion hands of the Abyss will draw you down, deep into the depths, where you will burn in my black flames. No totems, tenets, or interference from above will save you! You will burn like a marshmallow, then be devoured, like a . . . marshmallow.*

"Really, Fred?" Telos pinched the bridge of her nose, and desperately tried to contain a sigh with enough emotional exhaustion to slip multiple star systems into ennui.

*Heed my warning, lest the cat's soul be lost to the eternal hunger of the cosmos.*

Fred tried to finish strong, but he'd lost the entire audience with his slipup. Arkaziel continued to chew on the Void-cursed organ, Bobbi had moved over to poke through the ruined debris around the Archon's corpse in the hopes of loot, and Kallos had her eyes closed very tightly. Telos could tell her love fought a desperate inner war to not burst into laughter at the ridiculousness of even the true heart of the Void being rendered impotent in the face of StarMane arrogance, and their racial ability to ignore anything that didn't align with their desires.

A dark sense of amusement that filled the air reminded Telos there were other concerns, and when she checked in on the Celestial Wardens, she realized she may have forgotten about them for a bit too long. A fifth of their forces had been killed by Archons and Oizys's direct intervention, and an avatar of Oizys had joined the battle against Siegfried.

"You're going to have to eat that on the run, little guy. Oizys launched an avatar at the Celestial Wardens, and we should go help clean up."

"Oh, they're still alive? Fine, I've got to carry out my promise to Thalassa anyway," Arkaziel grumbled, and he chewed faster.

# CHAPTER 15

# Misery

*Look at me! I'm so pretty, powerful, and wise. A real humdinger of an abomination of Heaven, Khaos, and the abyss made manifest. I eat Demiurges and Archons, and barely increase in power, but don't look too closely at that, oh no!"*

Telos found herself in what might as well have been a dense fog wall on Lake Superior just off Duluth during a cold winter's day. Really cold, like negative twenty-five Celsius cold. Yet Telos found that before her stood a doppelganger of herself, which wasn't what she had expected to see in front of a sight straight out of her childhood. If anything, she expected to see a version of herself as she'd been on Earth. How had she looked again? It'd been so long, now, that the details had fuzzed. *Was I so eager to be Aetheria that I can't even remember what I used to look like? It'd be embarrassing to have to use Binah to remember.*

Small things were wrong with the copy. It had a hateful expression, and both of its eyes glowed red with malice, instead of red and blue like hers did. Nor did the knockoff have the Third-Eye of Ein Sof, which made a very immediate one-of-these-things-is-not-like-the-other distinction. The trench coat it wore was the older one she used to wear, yet slightly different in style. Her old coat's red was bright and vivid, but this one looked dark like the leather had been dyed with congealed blood. The hair was a neon blue, instead of the aqua-striped-with-red that she kept it these days. Somehow the knockoff's hair was the exact shade of blue-white which LED headlights scorched your eyes with. Even the Astrum Nexus had been copied poorly, changed from the bright platinum-like soulsteel mesh gloves to a dark spiderweb of wires.

The knockoff had even mirrored Telos's soul-woven hexproof scarf. The genuine article around Telos's neck currently waved on unseen breezes in all of its fluttery white glory, while the imposter's scarf looked cheap and tacky in construction, as opposed to the silken beauty of the real thing. The doppelganger's scarf was a retina-searing light blue, with black and pink leopard spots. The mockery even wore a hideous bright-violet lipstick that clashed with everything else. Telos never wore makeup. Maybe it was vain, but when you were a shapeshifter who could literally look any way you wanted, makeup turned into a downgrade. Unless there was higher-tiered makeup, like there were higher-tiered natural treasures. Finding a sixth-tier treasure then rubbing it all over your face seemed like an incredible waste, though.

Each inaccuracy might, individually, be a mistake. Combined they stood out as a mockery of her in some way, from the way-too-bright glow to her hair, the frown lines around her mouth, or even the breasts, hips, and rear end that were all far too large, in comparison to Telos's much more modest curves.

"Sorry, but is your ultimate gambit seriously a house of mirrors? Against a shapeshifter?" Telos couldn't rein in the sarcasm, because Oizys's approach to this struck her as pathetic. Sure, Telos once knew self-confidence issues as much as most people, but unlike other people, she could and did change subtle things about her appearance on the regular when the whimsy struck her. When you had full control of your physiology, it seemed a waste to not take advantage of such a thing, so she made liberal use of her malleable form to appear in whatever manner tickled her fancy at any given moment. Kallos occasionally had requests, but Telos found indulging those to be immensely enjoyable experiences.

*"So you've lost what little humanity you had? No ties to yourself?"* Oizys sounded surprised by that, and her disappointment put a smile on Telos's face. *Has she been sending bounty hunters and shit after me without even a clue of what I can actually do, or what I'm like? Why do all these gods suck so much?*

"Oh, there's some lingering issues like self-doubt, yeah, but not about my appearance. I can turn into a glass of wine, and let someone drink me. Have you ever done that? It's eye-opening. Highly recommend it as far as new experiences go. Now, doubts about myself as a person? I don't know if any truly sentient beings can ever be free of those basic cornerstones of sapience, especially all the time, unless they're, like, a sociopath or an extreme narcissist. Even an ancient hag like you has an awful lot of issues holding you back. Is it just your nature to be awful?" A shrug of Telos's shoulders dismissed the rhetorical question.

"This whole trick might have even gotten a rise out of me before I killed Moros." Telos gestured at the thick fog that reminded her of negative twenty below days in Duluth, the mockery of her that Oizys appeared as, and the false reality Oizys wove around them.

*"You didn' t kill Moros. He committed suicide with you as his instrument."* The vehemence behind the declaration startled Telos. *Maybe Misery liked Doom? No, she's more annoyed at the idea I could kill any conceptual manifestation on my own, like herself, than at the idea of Moros being dead. What a bitch.*

"So I'm the equivalent of suicide by cop?" Telos considered it, and couldn't quite dismiss it had happened more than a few times. She had mercy-killed multiple lives ever since her rebirth as Aetheria, what felt like lifetimes ago. "That's an interesting idea, but if you subscribe to that, you're willfully ignoring who and what I am."

*"You're the gun, nothing more."*

"Willful ignorance it is, then. Aren't you going to summon more torment from the fog? You aren't doing so hot with this beating me up thing, sweetheart." Telos looked expectantly to the fog wall, to the darkness, to the insulting simulacrum of herself. Oizys had to have more of a plan than annoying her to death. *I guess she's asking herself the same question I am: why would this idiot make an enemy out of me when I can't die? But my immortality isn't tied to a tower. Even the games of Aetherius and Nyx pushing me beyond the grasp of the Samsara aren't what makes me a terrible enemy, but until I started killing gods permanently, I guess none had truly died the final death since Phanes.*

**Teach them desolation. Unleash me, that I might feast upon her frozen marrow and dance through her psyche while my flames consign her to Nothing.**

*"That's your problem, tool. You think you're the center of the Universe. Look at me, I'm so special, I've got the powers of Primordials, Transcendents, Demiurges, and Aeons, I'm so special and fabulous, I use the Heavenly Jeweled Spear as a decoration in one of the dozens of floating cities I keep in my inner world. Your lover is the daughter of an Aeon, the compassionate idiot Belial who tries to save your favorite worthless humans from Ialdabaoth's cage, and does she bring it up? No. She strides the planes as the Soul Witch, Mistress of Souls, Monarch of Spiritual Law. I take a form like this, and you still can't figure it out. You can lead a horse to water, but you can't make them drink."*

The venom in those words managed to wound Telos, but she didn't give Oizys the satisfaction of letting it show. *I'm not that conceited, am I? And if I was, I am nearing the heights of the Path of Ayin-Yesh—why shouldn't I be a little full of myself. I don't think the Universe revolves around me . . .*

**You do. It does. Let us destroy it and become one in the perfect absence. Join me to the original unity known only to Ayin.**

When Fred agreed with Telos's inner thoughts, she took a moment to wonder if she had gone astray at some point. Fred didn't use reverse psychology; he just wanted what the Black Flame of the Void, the sapient echo of Ayin, always wanted. A complete return to the nothing that came before its existence, to be at one within the solitary existence of the unlimited potential that preceded everything else. The true Nothing that the abyss, the Void, was a mere shadow of.

"So, how you want to do this? Battle of wills? Knife fight? I punch you to death?" Telos tried to bring the conversation back on track, but the mocking doppelganger just stared at her in amazed bafflement. Seeing the moronic look on a facsimile of her own face fueled the punchiness within Telos more than she wanted to admit.

*"I get to pick? Let's insult each other to death. I'll start. You're a willfully ignorant narcissistic whore who likes to play the victim to problems that mostly exist because of you."* Oizys's voice practically had a purr to it at the end, so much did the daemon relish insulting Telos.

"Willfully ignorant and narcissistic I *might* give you, but whore? I slept with one elf, then entered a committed relationship with Kallos. That's totally slander. It's alright, though, you're hurting inside from the eternal loneliness. Thalassa said you stole her husband, but then sent him to camp out in her tower forever, I'm guessing it was just magic, power, and not any seduction?"

*"You figured it out."* Oizys spat the words, somewhat literally.

*Does it count as spitting in my own mouth if she does it looking like a twisted version of me?*

"Well, yeah. Did you honestly think I wouldn't notice the emotional rapport with Arkaziel, Bobbi, or Kallos was being tampered with? Kallos and I are practically one person, and my bond with Arkaziel is almost as old as I am. Bobbi might be new to the party, but she's fitting in well, and has leaned in to deepening her bonds to Kallos and me both, which feed the connection to the other as well. Your ploys can't work with us, little daemon."

Telos winked at Oizys, then opened her soul conduits to the maximum. The twin portals in her soul-space flooded power into her, and she redirected it through those conduits. Ethereal power went to Bobbi, Void went to Arkaziel, and the brilliant light of Ein Sof went to Kallos. When it didn't feel like enough, the output of Ein Sof still felt tiny in comparison to the other two, Telos opened another of the gates within Binah, and Ohr Ein Sof blasted through her in a torrent. Five of fifty Gates of Understanding now channeled Ein Sof into her. The dull sense of anxiety and worry that had slipped through the masking Oizys tried to put on their emotional connections faltered, then failed completely, and the gratitude and thanks of her companions flowed freely to Telos.

With the full activation of five of the fifty Gates of Understanding, her body and soul felt fuller. As if she'd gone from an overly dieted, skin and bones appearance to someone with the healthy flush of a balanced diet and a full stomach. *If five gates feel this good, what are fifty, or all one hundred and fifty of three realms going to do to me? I guess this is where I give up pretending I'm still just Aesca, or the plausibility of ever being Aetheria, even.*

*"No? I can kill all of the Celestial Wardens on a mere whim, and your friends might not die, but they could well wish they had."* Oizys smirked.

"Tell me, Oizys, have you had a good relationship with Nemesis throughout all of this?"

*"Why?"* Oizys seemed wary, as if afraid her sister might spring up behind her at any moment.

"No reason," Telos said as two more Gates of Understanding activated and bound the material world and the infinite divine essence through Telos. Pillars, spheres, orbs, and six-dimensional geometric figures that chimed a melody of wrath obliterated the small demi-plane Oizys attempted to hold Telos in.

# CHAPTER 16

# Suffering

Daris, the white StarMane, stared at Arkaziel, the black StarMane.

"Beast Sovereign, filled with Tiamat's blood, the essence of gods, the Void, and the Ethereal. Bursting with Light and Darkness. You've come a long way, brother." Not a voice Arkaziel expected to ever hear again, after Telos and her spooky head voices had erected the tenets of Twilight within his soul and Daris's spirit had faded. Yet here he was, again, with a suspicious tone and eyes full of hurt.

The world around them existed in grayscale. Humans and demons battled lesser Archons, but none of them touched Arkaziel or Daris. The battle flowed around them. Were the humanoids the ghosts in this scenario, or were Arkaziel and Daris? Arkaziel assumed it appeared this way to all on the field of battle, that to them, he was a ghost, and to him, they were. In addition to the ghostly struggle around them, the bond between Arkaziel and Telos felt muted and shallow, which meant the lesser bond with Kallos also felt nonexistent. StarManes bonded with other races semi-frequently, but his bond to Telos struck many firsts in his ancestors' genetic memories. The connection to Kallos existed because of the connection between Telos and Kallos when Arkaziel bonded with Telos, which was nearly unprecedented in even his most ancient memories.

Normal bonds didn't allow for the insanity that his bond with Telos allowed. Arkaziel could reach out and touch the Void, Origin, and probably Pleroma, too, if he had the courage. Light was his to command, after all, yet the unending light of Ein Sof scared the cat. The idea of touching it or drawing that power from Telos rang danger bells and flooded his mind with portents of doom. Light might be his, but Ohr Ein Sof wasn't for him.

"Daris, you shouldn't be here," Arkaziel muttered, unsure how to respond.

"Counterpoint: I should be here, and it's you who should be dead." The white cat flickered with illusory grace, a false divinity. It was as if no one had told whoever made the illusions that the Void Dragon of the Apocalypse couldn't be fooled by illusions. Oizys, or the Archons, or the Administrators of this tower were sloppy, ill-informed, and hardly more than appetizers, it seemed.

"In what layer of the abyss would that even work? Alternate timeline where I get eaten instead of you? Or is this the start of an *I'm the better one, you should have given me your body,* yadda yadda? Besides, you're the merest of fragments, the wisps of smoke that escaped when your body died. The majority of you, the real you, exists within me. Not separate, but united within me. Who's so bad at their job as to pull this shit with me?" Arkaziel hissed angrily.

The form of Daris flowed, as if a curtain had been removed. StarManes did not turn into zombies, but there was some precedent for lichdom. Not because of the fears that drove lesser races, like mortality, but curiosity and obsession. Those who were unfortunate enough to have the affinities of undeath tended to have an inescapable destiny, regardless of race. Yet the putrid white and yellow of Daris's body looked exceptionally zombie-like. To Arkaziel's eyes there was some truth to the matter, and that kindled a fire in his stomach.

"If I consume you, I can supplant you, usurp your life. I have to try." The ruined flesh of the zombie Daris roared and threw itself at Arkaziel. Whoever created the zombie had obviously gone to great lengths, not just to capture the wisps of his soul that weren't merged with Arkaziel's, but to build a body powerful enough to be a threat to a Beast Sovereign. Once again, though, Arkaziel saw glaring deficiencies in his opponent's knowledge.

*~ Take this. ~* Telos spoke into Arkaziel's mind, and knowledge and torrents of the Void flowed into him through their fully unblocked bond.

*+ Thanks, Blue. +*

Arkaziel wove the tides of the Void into a single exhaled breath attack. He imbued the Void with his authority of life and death, and pushed the alignment of the Void away from the celestial cold and toward the unlimited, untapped potential for all creation. If he had authority over creation, maybe it would have been easier, but Arkaziel had spent the vast majority of his existence trying to destroy or eat things. The only creation he'd ever done came with his dabbling with cooking. Yet when he reached for more experience, it wasn't his connection to Telos that provided him aid, but Bobbi Slay.

Slay provided Arkaziel with a burst of experience with creation, and the touch of her authority added to his own to alter his breath attack. Even more unexpectedly, through the connection to Kallos, Arkaziel felt her confident hand stroke the back of his head and impart him with a surge of the Nephilim's authority over law and spirit. White light exploded the grayscale world with a vengeance, and when it departed, Daris no longer looked like a zombie, or any sort of undead.

A white living, breathing, dragon-cat stared at Arkaziel in shock and wonder.

"How the hell?" Daris looked at the grayscale world around them in confusion.

"You can't be here, Daris. It's dangerous. We blew all the power they invested in you to resurrect you, so you're only a third-tier." Arkaziel lifted a paw, and with one claw scratched out a doorway of shadows into reality. "Dad will help you, probably."

Unlike most doors, when Arkaziel finished sketching out a StarMane-sized door in the air, he gestured, and it flew forward to engulf the reborn Daris. Arkaziel himself felt slightly lighter, but surprisingly okay despite the loss of essence that had belonged to Daris. Yet the cold, rational voice that spoke in the back of his mind, his own voice, suggested Daris had been a hatchling when consumed, and the loss was proportional to that. Arkaziel told himself to shut the hell up, as the grayscale around him cracked and shattered.

It would have been a lot more satisfying if the screeching, pained cries of Oizys's rage didn't try to shatter his brain while the false reality around him ended. Yet the unbridled fury that exuded throughout the entire existence of Oizys left no doubt she was not keen on the way this trap for Arkaziel ended. Nothing pleased Arkaziel quite as much as the cries of prey.

"Hi, Bobbi. Long time no see."

Bobbi stood out like a pink flamingo in a line of storks against the backdrop of a grayscale world. Worse, her nascent bonds with Kallos felt muted and distant, depriving her of the one true source of near constant reassurance she had enjoyed since the formation of her bond. Kallos might as well have been a universal law for how constant she was, but the Soul Witch rarely stood out in the way Bobbi did. With pink fur, magenta scales, and patches of pink skin here and there, Bobbi stood out everywhere she went. The curling pink horns that lurked at the edge of her sight line reminded her constantly that her choice of natural forms differed vastly from her kin.

Mara, the StarMane who lounged before her on a pile of gold, had a feline face, purely draconic body, and the coloration of a copper statue. Which was to say, her fur and scales danced between the blue of oxidized copper and the reddish-brown of the metal. The version of Mara that lounged before her was in the fifth rank, barely. Mara had always been content to nap for decades on piles of treasure, and her progression upon the paths to power had suffered for that laziness.

"Hi, Mara. Did I wake you up from another nap?" The dark cavern could well have been one of Mara's ridiculous dens, but the occasional glimpses Bobbi saw of humanoids and Archons fighting, as if in another dimension that overlapped this one, kept breaking her belief that this was in fact her sister. Especially since they'd just stepped through a teleportation portal to take on a daemon and army of Archons. They had, hadn't they? The details were increasingly harder to hold in her grasp.

"You did, and in such an unsightly form. Why are you always running around as a bipedal uggo?" Mara snapped at her with an unwarranted arrogance born only of the qualification of having hatched mere moments before Bobbi.

"I don't have time to waste on you right now, Mara. I've got . . . something to do." Bobbi sputtered the last part out awkwardly. It had been on the tip of her tongue, and then it vanished. What did she have to do?

"Yeah, *real* convincing there. Seriously, why do you always look like a humanoid? Why slum it when you're a StarMane? Chronos birthed our race to be better than all the others, and we're descended from Bahamut, not a mongrel clan like those descended from Tiamat. Could you imagine the shame of being caught socializing with one of those ghastly reprobates?" Mara's eyes betrayed the malicious glee she gained from insulting Bobbi, but there was no way the real Mara would ever know the first thing about her traveling companions. That detail wormed through Bobbi's mind, and brought back awareness of the fact she was supposed to be doing something.

She just couldn't remember what.

"Maybe if you weren't such a layabout, you'd have become a Sovereign already, too. I've met Bahamut, and spoiler alert? He's all about the humanoid forms, too. In fact, he quite fancied my favorite form here." A wicked smirk matched the gleam of superiority that filled Bobbi's pink feline eyes.

"No one likes you, sis. We talk all the time through a callstone, but we never invited you to bind to it. You're so weird, and quirky. Even Bahamut can be wrong, and like I'd trust anything you say, Miss I Will Rule the Universe Through Cooking. How's that coming along, anyway?" Mara had a perfect tone for a mean girl. She knew how to drop into a tone that said I'm pretending to be interested, but I'm so not, and you're not worth talking to me, so piss off.

Bobbi's anger skyrocketed. She didn't have time to put up with this bullshit from her do-nothing sister. She had things to do! If she could remember them. In fact, hadn't the treasure lying under Mara been gold and coins? When had it become crystals? They glowed and sparkled, like the crystals Kallos always seemed to be creating. Kallos! Arkaziel! The ghostly partial images of the humanoids fighting the Archons danced across her vision once more.

+*Take a real look, Slay.*+ Arkaziel's voice came with the world spinning momentarily. Mara didn't disappear, and in fact she knew for certain that it was the real Mara. Yet she didn't lie on a pile of treasure. A collar of a twisted red quartz bound the copper StarMane's neck, and it was connected to a leash held by a horrific centipede-like creature that definitely hadn't been there before Arkaziel's Void Sight blessed her eyes.

-*I detest creatures that would play with a spirit so. Destroy it for me.*- From Kallos came the calm and resilient words that riled the fire in Bobbi's heart, and the resolve to not lose sight of what she needed to do. For all that the Nephilim was known to be the Soul Witch, she was also a master of the spirit. Bobbi felt rejuvenated in a way she didn't quite understand, until she realized that her entire body had been filled with unending Ethereal power.

-*Girl, it's time to kick some ass!*- Telos, the source of power, stirred Bobbi to action. Typically creatures of the Void were difficult to face alone, especially if you only had Ethereal or lower-tiered power sources. Even as an Ethereal Cultivator with authorities over fire, wind, and creation, Bobbi would've been hard-pressed to defeat an abomination like this . . . except for the sudden twist and realignment of her Ethereal power.

*"If you resonate this way, and touch just briefly the heights of Keter, your Ethereal power will be more than a match for the Void."*

*~ That's Reverie. He's a good guy; no need to think you're hearing strange things. Well, things that aren't real, anyway. ~*

Life had gotten so weird since she met Kallos and Telos, and Bobbi wouldn't have it any other way.

# CHAPTER 17

# Pain

The world of Zenithar had started out as a pristine paradise world. Then the humans came, and built their mighty cities, resorts, retreats, temples, and created a holy world out of it. Over time even the gods sent messengers to guide the overwhelmingly powerful clergy of Zenithar. Pristine nature fell to the axe, and the planet transformed into an Ecumenopolis over a long line of generations. Only tiny, curated parcels of the former paradise remained. A walk in any direction would take you past dozens of temples, and it was said every god in existence had a temple there, even if some were no bigger than shacks.

In sharp contrast to the tiny temples, the enormous temple of Ialdabaoth covered nearly two thousand square miles on its own.

The ruins of the temple of Ialdabaoth existed as an asteroid now, upon which Kallos stood. The entire two thousand square miles weren't on the asteroid, not even a quarter of them were, yet she recognized the structure from her youth, nonetheless.

*"Do you even remember your childhood?"* a ghostly figure asked Kallos. It had materialized out of thin air, yet to her Soul Sight it glowed with the authenticity of a human soul. Though wispy, she bore a fair resemblance to Kallos.

"I do, Mother." A low sigh escaped her lips. Maria had been a tall woman, with blonde hair and hazel eyes. Her ghost held none of the remnants of beauty she'd once had, and had become desiccated and less in the long years since the destruction of Zenithar.

"I could have been the next high priestess, if not for your father. It looks like you take after him." The ghost stared accusingly at the chains that hung from Kallos's wings, the tattoos that could be glimpsed between skirt and boots, gauntlets and pauldrons, and the large witch hat that sat upon her head.

"He wanted to save you," Kallos said simply.

"We didn't ask to be saved," Maria retorted harshly, her voice warbling across spectrums humans couldn't reach, or hear. Kallos wasn't human, and managed to hear the words regardless of her loss of control. Maria had been a spirit for a long time, now, and her entire existence seemed volatile. Ghosts rarely lasted for centuries without becoming something more terrible.

"Then why did you fall for him?" Kallos always wondered about the answer to that question. What had driven a high-ranking priestess of the clergy of the prison warden to fall for a being that wanted to destroy the prison itself?

"I was young, dumb, and he was unlike anyone I'd ever met. Of course he was intriguing; he was an Aeon wearing flesh. He whispered of higher realms, lower realms, and even adjacent realms. He knew the truths of existence, and empathy drove him. He might as well have been a flame, and the humans, messengers, and servants of the gods all moths, caught in the dangerous blaze of his beauty. Then we burned, for real. Why weren't you there?" Maria lost control of her vocalization once more. Her entire spectral form lost cohesion, and it took her numerous tries to look human once more.

Kallos watched the troubles of Maria through her Soul Sight. She could strengthen her mother. As a Monarch on the Ethereal paths of the Winding Road, with authority over law and spirit, there were few things she couldn't do when it came to the metaphysical, even without tapping into the power granted her by her lineage through Belial.

"You wouldn't listen to me. I begged you to join me in the tower. There was never any way that Zenithar would be allowed to become a hotbed for gnosis. Even without Ialdabaoth, an entire planet departing the Samsara couldn't be allowed by the other gods, especially not the Holy World of Zenithar, but he is the warden of the cage. Zenithar's fate was sealed the moment you walked through the first Gate of Understanding, Mom. It took a few decades to play out, but the moment you started the process of ascension, it was all over." Wise, calm Kallos struggled to keep her voice even, but even she struggled with this conversation.

"You blame me, when it was you who unlocked the fiftieth gate? You, who brought the Divine Light of Ein Sof, which even Belial couldn't bring with him, to Zenithar?" Maria shrieked and quailed, and only a gesture and an empowerment by Kallos kept the spirit from exploding like an angry bomb.

"No, I don't blame you. But you were the rock that started the slide. By opening the first Gate of Understanding you opened the door for my birth with a connection to the Divine Light. My own ascension through the rest of the gates were more boulders added to the rockslide, and we were not the only ones making progress through the gates. A plague of enlightenment, an inevitable jailbreak on the horizon, it was inevitable Ialdabaoth would react. Even after all of his disasters, Belial fails to understand the cruelty of men, and the selfishness of gods. He failed to listen to Aunt Sera, and he ignored me, too. You can't argue with someone who *knows* this reality is a mere facade."

"Our lives have meaning, even if our universe is a mistake, or a cage, Aoibhe." Maria's response was light, but she seemed to have taken some of Kallos's words to heart, if her new stability could be used as any kind of sign.

"I've taken the name Kallos now, Mom. Telos and I share the surname of Metanoia."

Silence dominated for a few moments, broken only by a cry from the ghost of Maria. The names had been spoken with an inflection that carried meaning, intent, and even images to Maria. Such uses of Kallos's authority of law, spirit, and creation were trivial, but invaluable in communicating something that the witch didn't know how to say in words.

"Like mother, like daughter, it would seem." Maria half sobbed, and half laughed.

"It sure seems that way, Mom. I'm going to put you to rest now. Follow your love. Belial only partially dwells in our reality. Like all Aeons, he can never *truly* leave Pleroma."

*"Too slow,"* a cruel and malevolent voice echoed through the demi-plane that overlaid the floor of the Tower of Oizys they occupied. No doubt it belonged to the incarnation of misery and suffering, the horrible personification of pain and distress.

Kallos employed a lesser miracle to slow down time. Time that she could use to reach out to Telos and draw power enough to undo the attempt at the destruction of her mother's soul. Only, barriers stood between not only the empathic bond, but the telepathic and soul bonds that she shared with Telos. When Kallos tried to burst through the barrier with brute force, it felt like she'd run into a wall of adamantine, and just before she tried again emotions rushed in to greet her. The warm sensation of Telos's love filled her, followed by gushing torrents of Ein Sof, the infinite Divine Light of the Creator.

Slowed time changed to frozen time, and dozens of chains swung from Kallos's wings. Some entangled her mother, protecting and healing the already damaged soul of Maria, while the others tried to pierce and fend off the hateful presence of Oizys.

*"How!? I had my thumb on your soul, and I choked every ounce of life from her but one."*

"Follow Dad's song, Mom," Kallos whispered as she laid a kiss upon the spectral cheek of her mother. She burned up five miracles, and an incredible amount of power transferred to her from Telos to transform her mother's spirit into the equivalent of a spiritual cruise missile that would home in on the Cosmic Song of Belial in Pleroma. If five full miracles, and more of the Divine Light than she'd ever seen in a tower couldn't accomplish the task, Kallos really didn't know what would.

"You've grown so strong . . ." Maria's words hung in the air before she rocketed through the dimensions under Kallos's direction.

"Not strong enough, it seems," Kallos retorted with a dark twist when she stood alone, among the rubble of Zenithar. The ghostly glimpses of the Celestial Wardens battling Archons in the background became more noticeable now that she wasn't focused on her mother. Yet before she forced her way into the chamber, she summoned a gnarled staff with a deep amethyst gem at the head. She tapped the bottom against the ground.

"By my words and Will be Bound, Oizys, Weaver of Woes,
For each tear you've sown, in your own eyes shall one be found,
For each name, each vessel anew, in each life you live,
You shall feel the deepest of cuts, courtesy of thine own dark arts,
Your essence shall know eternal sorrow, upon each and every morrow,
Forever you shall carry the burdens you've spun,
until your tapestry of pain has been learned from."


Typically, Kallos would weave curses with Ethereal power, but in this case, she still had an abundance of Ein Sof flowing into her, thanks to Telos. So, she let the Divine Light be woven into the curse, and watched in satisfaction as it sank into the very essence of Oizys around her. A goddess given an inescapable, unbreakable curse from the highest of divine sources. Even the Overgod would be unable to break such a curse, if he wanted to, and Kallos had her doubts that Ialdabaoth would spend a thimbleful of power, now that he ought to have known the true nature of Telos. Surely, after the number of Archons they'd destroyed, someone in the Seven Heavens had finally witnessed the use of Ein Sof?

Kallos need not have worried. While she bound the curse into the very fabric of Oizys, a curse that would chase her through endless reincarnations until the wretch learned better, Telos had been busy, too.

The demi-plane around Kallos shattered, as if it had been a fragile glass caught before a baseball bat. Aeonic chimes filled the material realm, abstract and geometric forms that went into more dimensions than Kallos knew the names for appeared and vanished, and there was Telos, lit by a pillar of Ein Sof, surrounded by cascading vortexes of the Ethereal and the Void. Bobbi and Arkaziel appeared in the same fashion that Kallos herself did.

The battlefield around the four froze; the Celestial Wardens and Archons both held still by the display of power. Then a terrified voice cried over the battlefield.

*"Kill them!"*

"Did she just run away?" Arkaziel gaped at where the declaration from Oizys had come.

"Looks that way," Bobbi agreed.

The clash of blades, spells, and powers reignited around them, but a blur of white and blue fought through Archons to reach the quartet.

"Siegfried, you're still standing. Good!" Telos welcomed him.

"Lady Telos, Lady Kallos. Make haste after Oizys. My men and I shall hold the Archons here."

Telos laughed, and the darkness of the Void around her rippled.

"Nah, let's finish Oizys together." Then Kallos's lover activated one of her most terrifying attacks. As far as Kallos could see, multiple afterimages of Telos appeared and disappeared. Some looked the same as Telos, some had slight differences, but all exuded the power of the Void, the strange combination of Nothing and Infinite Possibility. In seconds, not a single Archon remained for Siegfried's men to battle. All had been dispatched by the existence-defying, reality-oscillating attack.

"Time to make good on our promise to Thalassa," Arkaziel growled angrily before he hopped onto Telos's shoulder.

"And Werylin, and everyone else we promised this to. It's time to kill Misery."

# CHAPTER 18

# M(utually).A(ssured). D(estruction).ness

After witnessing the reality-breaking power of Telos, the Celestial Wardens were eager to take the forward position and prove to their allies that they, too, could contribute. A fervor had been lit within each of the individually weaker members of the Celestial Wardens. That fire had seemingly extended even to Siegfried, who opted to move with the vanguard rather than with the party of four. The odd energies around the Celestial Wardens made more sense to Telos now that she knew that Siegfried fed off the conviction and belief of his men, and it made the Sovereign more powerful. *I wonder if the irony of an anti-god force being led by a man whose power source is similar to faith is lost on them?*

Oizys barred their path with quantity, not quality. All of the foes, horrors, monsters, and traps that had once existed within the Tower of Oizys were being flung at the assault forces as they pressed toward the one place Oizys couldn't run from, the heart of the tower. Normally Telos would have taken the vanguard position herself, but she and her companions were still coping with the influx of power she'd absorbed from Syltharion, the legion of Archons, and the fact that she'd activated five out of fifty of the conduits to Ein Sof from the material plane.

Subtle differences had crept into the appearance of each individual within the convoluted binding of souls. Kallos gained a halo that now floated around the tip of her witch hat, a colorless crystal construct forged solely of Ein Sof. It was a manifestation of her will, an extension of her power, and it spoke of the precipice she stood before. It should have taken lifetimes to cross the bridge between the sixth and seventh tiers, but Kallos stood on the cusp of ascension to becoming a Sovereign. Telos lagged behind her only because she chose for it to be that way. It felt right that Kallos should ascend first.

Arkaziel hid his physical changes, but Telos could sense the change in the strength of his aura. The Beast Sovereign's fearsome presence would drive most mortal beings to their knees in fear if the life-sapping strength of his Void presence didn't drive them to madness and force them to give up on life from mere proximity. Her terrible kitten was being a good boy and keeping his aura sealed so as not to prey upon the Celestial Wardens. A recurring question drifted through Telos's mind, the question that always popped up when Arkaziel gained more strength. *Is this reality going to be able to handle him? Can I just let him wander free when our journey is done?*

Even Bobbi, the party's newest member, had undergone some metamorphosis from the influx of power. Her claws and horns previously looked solid and genuine, like an ordinary dragon's. Now her fingers were tipped in nails that looked like crystallized fire, with waves that gave the impression of explosive force. The curly ram-like horns had gained an internal luster, an undeniable glimmer, and she seemed to be only a step or two shy of being more ornate than an exquisite candelabra. If these changes were being wrought at five gates, what would happen to them when Telos activated the linkages for all fifty of the Gates of Understanding?

There were one hundred more gates to activate after Telos activated all fifty. The Gates of Repentance were the fifty gates that Telos thought represented the connection between Ein Sof and Pleroma, but even Binah wasn't clear about what activating the linkage of those gates would accomplish. Then, finally, were the Gates of Promise. *What's going to happen when I link the divine to the Void? Nothing bad, obviously. Ugh.*

Telos didn't allow herself to change outwardly. She could feel the pressure of Ein Sof to rework some of her body, but for now she refused to allow it to do so. She didn't need to be changed by the divine power at this point, and she stubbornly resisted even minor changes like additions of gradients of orange and green to her hair, to blend the aqua and red. Contemplation on the changes of herself and her companions would have to wait, though, for the Celestial Wardens came to a halt before a large rock, upon which stood a forty-meter-tall woman, whose face conveyed hatred and suffering for all who looked upon her.

*"Your final warning. If you insist on this fight I shall destroy Grief! Two billion lives hang in the balance of your decision, in addition to two million climbers, five billion natives, and almost a million dwellers!"*

Unhappiness ran through the men and women of the Celestial Wardens. The souls of seven billion people were significant. With that many souls sent in sacrifice one could ascend to the realms of godhood, or down to the depths of an abyssal lord. If you were a Celestial Warden, you could power an awful lot of anti-god weaponry with the power of so many souls, and if you were even the slightest bit an empathic being, you could feel the gut-wrenching pain at the prospect of being to blame for the loss of such a large amount of souls.

*~ Can you all handle Oizys if I prevent what she's threatening? ~* Telos asked through the telepathic bond.

*-I owe this wretch a world of pain. Consider it handled, my love,-* Kallos responded immediately, without any hesitation.

*+I've been waiting to kick her ass, and now I don't have to get upstaged by you at the last minute? Oizys should've bribed Elea, because there's not going to be any mercy for her.+*

Arkaziel joked, while Bobbi said nothing through the link, but her determination shone through loud and clear.

Telos activated the failsafe within the Astrum Nexus by channeling energy through the Flame of Chronos. In the crumbling ruins of time, a cave that was a brewery, the last vestiges of Chronos's presence in the universe, collapsed. The ultimate authority of time transferred so simply, and Telos almost felt an invisible crown form around her head while the authority settled into her. Time sputtered and flowed forward and back around her, clocks manifested and then dematerialized. Void's Gaze gained even more tracks of vision, as the branching lines of probability across different lines of time were made clear to her mismatched eyes.

"Well, I'll be damned, time is made of circles after all." Telos's unhinged laughter got more than a few looks, but she waved them away and gave an imperious command. *"Go!"*

*"WHAT HAVE YOU DONE?!"* Oizys's panicked screams shook the entirety of the tower, as Telos made the relative difference in time between the universe and the Tower of Misery so great that it was on the scale of the frozen time falling into a black hole compared to the ordinary time of Earth. It would take centuries for any of her commands or attacks against Grief to reach beyond the temporal vortex Telos raised around the tower. Which left the souls still inside the tower to safeguard. Where could Telos send them?

*"I believe your best option would be to utilize Malkuth and form a temporary shekhinah there."* Reverie spoke up so rarely that Telos had almost forgotten the entity sometimes spoke with proactive, helpful suggestions.

***The care of Arich Anpin, while a grandness beyond mortal ken, lacks the essential darkness these souls have bathed in. Their souls yearn for the darkness of the Void, the primeval darkness that is the origin of all things. Give them unto my care.***

*"This is no journey through darkness to find the dawn, but a matter of salvation and protection. All journeys through your realm are fraught with dangers beyond counting. You protest for the sake of protesting, Fred."*

***Why should Telos favor you, when I offer suitable solutions as well?***

"Oh great, you two can talk to each other now? I don't want to deal with this right now. I'm sending them to Malkuth. Fred, the Void isn't the place for refugees, but I *will* listen to you whenever you have something to say, okay?" *Aw cripes, now I have to mediate between these two? Life was so much simpler when the two voices in my head couldn't talk to one another.*

Despite all expectations, Fred didn't throw a fit when Telos opted to go with Reverie's suggestion. The Flame of the Void didn't respond, but he didn't retreat either. He remained present, observing. Which did feel kind of creepy. Telos failed to grow accustomed to the near constant attention of Fred, Reverie, and others. With vast cosmic power came peeping toms.

Five billion souls was a lot. Even Telos couldn't hop through the tower tagging everyone for transportation with Existence Oscillation, her lightning speed, or any other physical maneuver. The best option she saw was to utilize her authority over justice, life, and necessity to create a *beautiful* miracle. Five Gates of Understanding wouldn't provide the bandwidth for what she needed from Ein Sof, and so Telos activated five more of the Gates of Understanding. Even in the Tower of Misery, where Oizys literally formulated and regulated reality around them, the universe tried to reach out to her, tried to bond with her in a way she really didn't like. Like a dog too eager for pets who starts slurping your face, that's how reality seemed to feel toward her.

In utter defiance of Oizys's will, beacons of light lit up the souls of dwellers, climbers, and natives alike. Once the light locked on to them, they vanished to the realm of Malkuth. Those who were alive, anyway. The souls who existed as power were fed into the Great Cycle, and would be reincarnated into the world to live new lives according to the karmic debts they had incurred in past ones. Climbers, too, were caught and transferred to Malkuth. Sure, it would have been easy to forget about the souls trapped in the towers, and what were even billions of souls compared to the seemingly unending number of souls that, according to Binah, stretched into the centillions.

***If scarcity gives value, life is meaningless.***

"*A single infinity, or ten thousand infinities, the value of all life is infinite and sacred. The absence of the Void rots your logic, and leaves you unable to appreciate the parcel of glory within all things,*" Reverie argued to Fred before Telos could even think of a counterpoint.

***You forget your place, merciful one. I, the flame that burns possibility, and you, the voice of infinite patience, are meant to tend our own realms. Keter, and the radiant halls of Pleroma are your domain, not the dusty halls of Malkuth, or the ever-eroding souls of the living.***

"*All sparks must return to the Infinite in time. My mercy only lights the path for their return.*"

***You deny them the meaning of overcoming, the grandeur of transformation. Without trial against shadow, how will they appreciate the light? By giving mercy, you invite them to fall to the same weakness of Wisdom.***

"*I, perhaps, have been blinded by my own luminance, or by the will of Telos to do as I wish, rather than as I am charged. Is our charter not whatever she wills it? Such thoughts belonged to Wisdom once, too. You have shown a degree of Wisdom yourself, Fredrick of the Black Flame.*"

***Let the mortals grapple with shadows and trials, even in the safety of Malkuth. Sandalphon shall be their trial master.***

"It's a temporary shift while I destroy the tower, you two. Quit acting like I'm letting these people set up a homeless refuge in Malkuth, and the vast and terrible consequences of my actions. In case you forgot, I'm the one who's on the Path of Eternal Becoming, not you two. This is only a temporary fix until I can drop them on Nyx or Aetherius."

# CHAPTER 19

# The Bitterest Symphony

W*HAT HAVE YOU DONE!?"* The panicked scream of Oizys sounded like music to Arkaziel's ears. The sweet desperation might as well be appetizers to this meal, and Telos had clearly succeeded in shoving a wrench into Oizys's plans to get an immediate reaction like that. *Always trust Blue to slap someone so hard they're shocked a slap can hurt so much.*

Oizys's shock left her open, and the forty-meter-tall daemon took the impact of a sixty-meter-long Apocalyptic Void Dragon head-on. Arkaziel's vicious claws, wreathed in black lightning, pierced into the manifest flesh of the daemon, and he pushed her down hard to the stony ground, where she functioned like a brake to stop both of their momentum. He'd overdone it, a little bit, in his drawing from Telos's superspeed. Yet when he flared his wings to catch air, he let go of the daemon and let the last of their momentum carry her forward. The giant, road rash–ridden titaness, wreathed in the black lightning of destruction, crashed into one of the large rocky outcrops and exploded in a nova of electricity.

A glowing golden orb quickly descended from the sky, and struck the already staggered Oizys. Golden flames spread out as if the area had been covered in napalm, and the daemon screamed in hatred at the world.

*+Mom always wondered, can you make Pain feel Pain? Looks like the answer is yes.+* Arkaziel chatted telepathically with his party, while physically he inhaled a vast quantity of air.

"Taste despair!" Oizys screamed, and the intent behind her hatred focused. Bobbi's golden flames vanished, obliterated by a shockwave of hate. Behind the shockwave came a thick mist that shone with anguish and Nether to Arkaziel's Void Gaze. The wisps of power hit him first, but failed to have any effect on him. StarManes, like most dragons, were immune to fear. The dark fog didn't slow him down at all, as he exhaled a beam of light with two spirals of darkness circling it.

The dark fog had a much more noticeable effect upon the Celestial Wardens. Siegfried, who stood at the front leading the charges toward Oizys and Arkaziel, his white and blue armor a beacon for his men, passed through the oncoming shockwave and its mists without incident. As a Sovereign, a seventh tier Cultivator, Siegfried had no problem ignoring even the mental tampering of a goddess, even one of the primordial incarnations, or daemons, like Oizys. His men, on the other hand, couldn't. Around him dullness took over their eyes, confusion afflicted their minds, and agony engulfed the souls of those who couldn't mount an adequate defense.

A glimmering sphere appeared over the battlefield, and benevolent radiance rained upon the combatants. The eyes of Celestial Wardens cleared, their minds purged of Oizys's taint, but the luminescent energy that fell didn't stop there. Wounds healed, spirits lifted, and the soft chimes of the Aeons encouraged men to stand up and cast off their shackles. Arkaziel didn't need the healing rain of light, but it did feel pleasant. *Kallos should start a spa with a spell like this. I'd pay for a nice warm place to bask in the sun and nap under this spell.*

Arkaziel's breath attack hit Oizys's middle mass. The powerful center of the attack, the beam of light, pierced her titaness flesh and came out the back side. The light seared a hole straight through her abdomen, and any rock and other environmental debris behind her. The twin spirals of darkness then seeped into the wounds. The authority of pestilence and destruction pulsed ominously from the dark energy before it leaped at Oizys, like a starving lion onto a gazelle. Only, lions didn't crawl inside of a gazelle and kill it from the inside, but Arkaziel chuckled in glee as the Void energies flowed into Oizys. The daemon's body convulsed as if electricity flowed inside of her, but after a pulse of a different source of Void powers within Oizys, a power greater than Arkaziel's own, she ceased convulsing, and her veins turned black.

"I won't be killed by the likes of you!" Oizys screamed, but a single, massive ball of fire the size of the goddess struck her in the face, even as darkness crept out of her body and restored her missing abdomen with oozy flesh filled with dozens of eyes.

"Oizys is being taken over by Nyarlathotep—beware the Void!" Kallos yelled over the din of combat. The forward movement of the Celestial Wardens, eager to join combat ceased, save for Siegfried, who strode forward with his blade in hand.

"We must slay her before the corruption takes root! How do we do that?" Siegfried's first words held agitation, but by the end he had regained his composure, and his answer resonated with the men and women of the Celestial Wardens.

"From Mortal Will, Immortal Change!" The chorus of human, demon, and other races' voices drowned out the sickening sound of Oizys being rearranged from the inside out, before their voices joined together with Siegfried's to make an even louder exclamation.

"Guardians of Balance, Keepers of Freedom! We are the Celestial Wardens!"

The entire scene built to a crescendo when Siegfried blasted forward in a charge that most of his men could only see the afterimages of. The Sovereign launched himself at the quickly corrupting daemon with the speed of a cruise missile, his blade flickering through the air creating glyphs, his lips forming incantations. Immense pulses of Aether formed an explosive blast that struck Oizys mere nanoseconds before he himself did. A twelve-stage Aether-technique attack based on wind, augmented by the faith of the Celestial Wardens in Siegfried followed.

Both of Oizys's arms were severed from her shoulders, and one of her legs hit the ground as well. Dark blood that burned like acid rained around Siegfried, but a thin blue-white domain flickered around the Sovereign, and prevented any of the corrupted blood from touching him. But he wasn't done yet. Siegfried launched himself upward, over Oizys, and landed almost fifty meters away from her. His sword slid into his scabbard as he skidded to a halt.

Oizys fell in two pieces, neatly cut in half.

"Yeaaaah!"

"You did it, boss!"

The Wardens cried in joy, but Siegfried's eyes narrowed in displeasure, his spirits diminished, even as Arkaziel's spirits lifted higher.

"Is there a specific name for Primordials afflicted by the Void? I want the ballads to be clear on just how amazing I am," Arkaziel quipped to Bobbi before he joined the melee.

The formerly Primordial flesh of Oizys rotted and decayed before their eyes, but two explosions, courtesy of Bobbi, prevented a rain of flesh and more fell blood from reaching the Celestial Wardens. Arkaziel danced between the explosions, and in the form of a five-headed dragon, he towered over the disgusting thing that oozed upward from Oizys's remains. While it rose and took shape, Arkaziel inhaled through four heads, two black and two white, while the gray-colored head glared at the abomination.

Light and darkness fled the field of battle, leaving a world of grayscale. Mana wisped away in torrents, and Aether and Nether were devoured into the inescapable maw of the Tiamat-blooded Beast Sovereign. The Ethereal tides, too, succumbed to the draw of Arkaziel, and even thick, inky tendrils of the Void were ripped from the abomination rising from the corpse of Oizys to Arkaziel's voracious maw. All of which didn't count all the power he drew from his connection to Telos, Kallos, and Bobbi.

"They say misery loves company, but me? I love an audience. Don't disappoint me. The whole universe has been waiting for your comeuppance." Arkaziel's voice boomed from the gray head, with the full power and presence to be expected of a nightmare god-eater created by Chronos.

The quivering, oozing mass that had once been Oizys rose into a shape not entirely dissimilar from earlier. She had a tail now, and her arms were covered in mouths, while the rest of her body was a mixture of eyes and maws, and thousands of small lamprey-like tentacles. Small in that they extended ten meters from her body, so, much larger than a human. The mouths released a wail that built up in the ear like the high frequency of power lines.

"Die, bitch," Arkaziel roared, and unleashed his attack. Arcing beams of light blasted out of his light head, Void streams blasted from the dark heads, and an unholy abomination of discordant energies that chaos was far too weak of a word for, flowed from his gray head. The grayscale nature of the world made each aspect of his attack stand out like a neon sign, and Arkaziel knew he'd get head pets from Telos for being the best damn StarMane in the universe.

*#NOT. DONE. YET.#*

The mass that composed the corrupted Oizys burned away under Arkaziel's epic assault, and color started to return to the world, even as the desperate cry of the eldritch being ripped at the minds of the Wardens. Then the rifts appeared. Weirdly gray rifts in space-time, where reality itself had frayed under the incredible power unleashed by Arkaziel.

"I. Said. DIE!" Arkaziel's roar opened each rift, which spilled coruscating beams of Ethereal power into the resurgent flesh of Oizys. All of Arkaziel's authorities rampaged through the eldritch daemon, along with Bobbi's, who remained next to Kallos, her eyes half-lidded as she used her full power in sync with Arkaziel. Why she was content to be on the sideline? *She doesn't care about glory that isn't in the kitchen. She's crazy.*

The reality-disintegrating beams obliterated even the Nyarlathotep-corrupted Oizys with relative ease, but the churning mass of the eldritch daemon struggled to regenerate and defy the attacks upon it.

*#Know my pain!#*

The screech ripped at the minds of the shock troops of the Celestial Wardens, and even Arkaziel had to brace his mind slightly against the psychic distortion of a dying abomination. The psychic buildup ended, though, when Siegfried threw a stone sword into the sky, and then a massive two-hundred-meter stone monolith appeared above Oizys and dropped down to impale her. Or at least that's what Arkaziel assumed Siegfried tried to do. Instead, he missed Oizys by meters.

"Thank you, Siegfried. I'll finish this."

Kallos, somehow, stood atop the hilt of the stone sword. Telos stood behind the blonde, supporting the Nephilim.

"Oizys Daemona, the hour of judgment has arrived," Kallos intoned with a ring-ing call that overrode the still active disintegration beams from the rifts, the multitude of attacks from the individuals of the Wardens, and even Siegfried's pulse attacks from his blade. Two chains unwound from the stone hilt and shot out to ensnare the struggling daemon.

A crippled and beaten spiritual form, half corrupted by Void, half simply mis-erable, got ensnared and raised up for all to view. A pillar of light illuminated the spirit, and subatomic particle by subatomic particle split apart, turning even the spirit of Oizys into flakes of nothing. Blood poured out of the eyes of Siegfried and the Celestial Wardens, who had no protection from the glory of the power that Kallos wielded. Arkaziel had to admit, his eyes stung a little, too, but surely it was because he heard a whispered thank-you from a water goddess, and not the divine radiance blasting his Void-aspected eyes to hell.

Two-thirds of the Celestial Wardens had fallen unconscious before the last flake of Oizys vanished, and then a flash of anti-existence and existence warred, but a warm presence gently cupped everyone in its hand. The tower vanished, and the uncaring abyss of space surrounded everyone without warning, but that warm presence plucked everyone into a vessel made of ice and light. Arkaziel yawned, and exertion mixed with exhilaration as energy surged through his body as if he'd just eaten Oizys, instead of her being destroyed. Even before a hand touched him, he transformed into a kitten, and took his place on Telos's shoulder, where he nuzzled her neck and closed his eyes.

"You did good, Ark." Telos kissed the black fur of his forehead as he drifted to sleep.

+*Damn right, I did,*+ Arkaziel agreed.

# CHAPTER 20

# Actions Have Consequences

You push the constraints of the lower realms," a chiming voice told Kallos. When her eyes and senses adjusted, the Nephilim found she stood on a platform of light overlooking a vast, seemingly infinite, series of universes. This view didn't exist in reality, as far as she knew, but the location they were in existed outside of reality. A familiar warmth filled her, and she breathed deeply and let out a contented sigh, before turning her gaze to the chiming voice.

"If you two continue at this pace, you will unravel existence. Becoming a Sovereign will reduce the strain you place on reality, by forcing you to bear the strain yourself. Yet first, your actions confuse me. Why kill the daemon?"

The voice held a masculine touch, and emerged from a figure she could only describe as constructed from luminous crystals, but it existed in more dimensions than seemed possible. The vantage, mixed with the nearness of Ein Sof and the presence of two Aeons, immediately identified where Kallos was. Pleroma. Bythos and Sige, again, confronted Kallos.

"Why? Because Telos made promises, and where she goes, I go. That is how partnerships work, yes?" Kallos tried to gaze coolly at Bythos, but how could you match eyes with a being that didn't have any? At least, none that she recognized as eyes. The crystalline forms of the Aeons, with their geodesic appearance that defied her ability to perceive things in physical dimensions, were alien even to her advanced senses.

"Its purpose was to encourage souls to reach gnosis, to push souls to escape the cage of flesh wrought by Sophia's get. Yet, the souls create suffering of their own, even without daemons to encourage them. The death of Misery will change nothing. Why? Why would Telos do this?" Bythos asked again, like a frustrated toddler, although his query was made with serene equanimity and lacked the obnoxiousness of a child. Yet under that calm surface Kallos could tell that Bythos hated not understanding.

"We know our time is limited. Telos declared the age of the gods to be done, and is determined to see the purge begin before we can no longer live in the material realms. If that doesn't answer your question, perhaps you should ask Telos?" Kallos couldn't refrain from arching a brow with the question, even though she felt relatively certain that neither Aeon would understand the facial expressions of a humanoid.

"Telos ignores me. She declines the offer of my presence. She denies me, and so, denies herself. Gods or no gods, the souls of the material world will continue to face obstacles. There is no other way to reach gnosis," Bythos declared with conviction.

"We know that. Telos seeks more than existence being nothing but a cage to escape." Kallos shook her head, and her laughter followed the exasperated admission that she had once thought pointless. Sige remained silent, yet something about the way the Aeon beheld Kallos left her with the impression that Sige now hung on every word. "She wishes to see what true free will might manifest."

"That . . . is her choice," Bythos said with a great deal of exaggerated indifference. Kallos made a mental note that the Aeons were terrible at concealing their emotions, although she had to wonder if things that could pique their emotions came up more than every few ages. Telos could be, and probably was, an exception in the serenity of Bythos.

"After billions of years of keeping the safety on, you simply nod and agree to their removal?" Kallos asked in a slightly higher pitch than she intended, but the incredulity of it had struck her like a gut punch.

"We Aeons exist due to a need, want, or desire that bubbled through the incomprehensible will of Ein Sof. Are we emanations? Not quite, that is the Sefirot. Reflections? Nay, those are the gods. Conjurations? Are not all things conjured by the will of Ein Sof? The distinction is immaterial. We are vessels through which Ein Sof manifests its will on the universe. That is our purpose, and we fulfill our purpose. We are partners in the Cosmic Dance. We dance, demons dance, humans dance, and even you dance. There is only one choreographer to the dance, one conductor of the Cosmic Song." Bythos let his words echo through the darkness, waiting for a response from Kallos before he said anything further.

"Why am I here?" Kallos asked a bit more bluntly than might have been advisable. Something had changed inside of her. The Aeons no longer seemed quite so holy to her, nor quite so glorious. Pleroma did not seem quite so much of a paradise, beyond its physical proximity to Ein Sof. Telos had upended her life, her beliefs, and even the universe, although it had not shaken out fully yet.

"To attain Sovereignty." Sige broke her silence, the chimes of her voice echoing in the vast emptiness. "As Bythos said, as a Sovereign, more of the burden you create upon existence will be borne by yourself, instead of by reality. You have far outstripped the power and authority any Monarch was ever meant to have, and something must be done about it before you cause distortions, breaches, or irreparable tears."

"I haven't earned Sovereignty yet," Kallos noted with a frown. To step from Monarchy to Sovereignty would have taken centuries. She had not assimilated the knowledge of Spirit and Law nearly so well as she would have liked. There were mysteries still to explore, gaps in her knowledge that could prove dangerous. Power alone did not qualify one for ascension.

"It does not matter. Your bonds to Telos and the cats have pushed you beyond the threshold of Monarchy. Even Sovereignty will fail to contain your powers soon, and then you must choose to enter Pleroma, dive into the Void, or reenter the Cycle." Bythos held compassion, but no alternatives. He spoke as if this were preordained, and the obvious choice of Kallos and Telos would be Pleroma.

"Could you quantify your definition of soon?" Kallos asked with a narrowing of eyes. The Aeons were eternal, with Bythos being one of the first beings to exist. "Soon" to such beings could be a decade, a century, a thousand years, or even a hundred thousand years.

"A century if Telos activates no more gates, as little as a decade if she throws open all of them. How many shadows and reflections she dispatches will affect the time-frame as well." Bythos retained composure and serenity; after all it didn't matter to the inhuman Aeons if others had to leave the material realm. The sooner spiritual beings such as Telos and Kallos left the material plane, the better it would be for everyone, in their view. Kallos had the feeling that Bythos didn't particularly care if Kallos herself entered Pleroma or went to the Void, but the Aeon emitted a strange neediness when it mentioned even the name Telos. Or perhaps the Aeon assumed that the goal of her path, of her beliefs, centered upon gnosis and elevation to Pleroma, so her own views were not dissimilar to its own.

"Where is my trial?" Kallos saw no embodiment of universal laws to battle.

"You have crossed the point of no return in your sublimation with Ein Sof. The natural order is no longer applicable to you, as they are no obstacle to Telos. When you broke the corruption of Oizys with the power of Ein Sof, your Law shone bright and upended the material realm. Your opponent has already been slain, for they died with Oizys, and your Law already spreads. Thus, Kallos Metanoia, the world of flesh has been enshrined, at least until someone else challenges it." Sige sounded serene, but Kallos felt ebbs of jealousy and resentment from the Aeon, emotions she had never felt from any Aeon before, or didn't know they could even feel inside Pleroma.

*Of course they can feel resentment. How else would Sophia have fallen as she did?*

"I grasp now the emptiness I glimpsed within Telos's heart after her last ascension." Kallos tried to face her dissatisfaction head-on, as a responsible adult should. The end result remained the same as if she had undergone the trials and challenges, and her opposing Law had been destroyed by her hand, if with the help of Telos. Yet that hadn't been intended at all. Kallos only intended to destroy Oizys.

"You, who now stands as one of the most powerful entities in all of creation, know the disappointment of the omnipotent. You have been given a gift few entities could comprehend," Sige said with an earnestness that felt mocking to Kallos, but on reflection she discerned that the Aeon truly felt envious.

"Is this how Telos feels? All the time? Unsatisfied? Hollow? Does her power truly diminish all meaning and satisfaction?" Kallos muttered before she broke into a slightly hysterical laughter. "Haha. Of course it isn't. Our emotions are nearly as one. I know the path of her emotions as I know my own. The dissatisfaction fades quickly; she does not hold on to it, or let it burden her. She seeks new joy to replace the emptiness power brings her. She finds solace in my arms, in the jokes of Arkaziel, and in the meals cooked by Bobbi."

Memories of Solace flickered through Kallos's mind. The smiles and laughs that Aetheria shared freely with everyone, the interest she showed in every person's story and origin, her unbridled curiosity and thirst for seeing new horizons, even if it was through other people's eyes and ears. Telos still showed all of those traits whenever they had time to indulge, despite having unfettered access to the Cosmic Song, the library of Binah, and control of fate.

Kallos bit her lower lip, and found she had a smile inside of her after all.

"Thank you for this gift, Bythos, Sige." Kallos felt a new perspective opening within her mind. Telos didn't have to bear any weights alone, especially not the dissatisfaction of existence. Strange as it felt, Kallos sincerely felt genuine gratitude to the Aeons for this lesson in understanding Telos. It almost made up for the theft of her trial and ascension. Almost. Double-bladed as the gift was, Kallos glimpsed a side of Telos she had poorly understood until now.

"You're welcome," Bythos said, serene once more.

"It's time. Telos grows impatient for your return." Sige didn't have eyes or arms to point at the pulsing novas within the highest realms of Pleroma, where Ein Sof lit all, but each of the three could feel the growing aggressiveness from the highest of heavens.

"What happens next?" Kallos asked with a touch of dread.

"Your body and spirit undergo ascension . . ." Bythos spoke, but with each second the sound grew farther away as Kallos fell backward into reality, and her own flesh. She blinked away light and darkness to find Telos looking down at her with all three of her eyes.

"I'll hold you, and it'll all be okay." Telos's voice allowed no protestation, and Kallos doubted she could remove herself from Telos's grasp even if she tried her hardest, but she had no intention of doing that. Warmth filled the Nephilim's heart, even as purple, black, and gold luminescence shone under her skin, and then broke free in streams of power as the Nephilim evolved. Streams of power, and fountains of blood. Even the chains of her wings shook, vibrated, and rampaged against the icy floor below them, but even as pain and rapture made her convulse in turn, not a single chain struck Telos.

Kallos maintained that much control as she stepped into the ranks of Sovereigns.

# CHAPTER 21

# The Calm Before Armageddon

The command bridge of Telos's light-forged space vessel had four individuals sitting in awkward silence, taste-testing trays of appetizers. Well, Arkaziel, in the form of a dark-skinned humanoid with cat ears, tasted the appetizers. Every few seconds he'd toss a new one into his mouth and groan happily, all while Bobbi rolled her eyes at the antics of her fellow StarMane. Across from them, Siegfried and his second-in-command, Fafnir, sat rigid. Bobbi could tell that the dragon in human form desperately wanted to eat, but the disapproval of Siegfried kept Fafnir back.

A wall suddenly opened into a portal through which Telos and Kallos entered. That Kallos had ascended to Sovereignty didn't shock the StarManes; they had felt it through the intertwined soul bonds that connected all four of them to one another. Siegfried's stoic expression softened, while Fafnir nearly drooled on himself, his dark eyes full of baked goodness.

"Congratulations." Siegfried nodded his head to the woman, who, theoretically, was now his equal. Yet the events of the Tower of Oizys had proven both women were already his superiors.

"Thanks for waiting. While Kallos ascended, I finished coordinating the evacuation of the living souls from the tower. They'll trickle to other worlds through the towers, and those who had no corporeal form will reenter the Great Cycle. They're next incarnation should be much more positive than suffering through existence at the cruel whims of Oizys." Telos dropped into a love seat that rose from the floor in the nick of time, then Kallos settled in next to Telos.

"The Overgod already gathers his forces and dispatched the greater Archon Horaeus to bring us to the Seven Heavens for judgment." Telos rolled her eyes, while Arkaziel guffawed, Kallos shook her head, and Bobbi added a plate of cream puffs to the table.

"The Overgod? Are we capable of defeating him?" Siegfried asked with hesitation. "Without the Anti-Divinity Cannon . . ."

"Arkaziel! Didn't you tell Siegfried I recovered all their ships from the tower?" Telos tsked at the human-looking man.

"I got distracted by Bobbi's cooking. She put out these skewers of Teriyaki Phoenix that were unbelievable. Blue saved your ships," Arkaziel guiltlessly informed Siegfried between bites of fresh pastry.

"Ark . . . anyway, we've got all your ships. You and your men can evacuate before Horaeus gets here. Your weapons aren't going to do it against a greater Archon who rules over the First Heaven, let alone the Overgod. We can handle them without problems, but the other gods are going to be up to you, and the generations who come after. Some might fade away, or depart for other dimensions, but there's no doubt just as many will fight for what they've come to see as theirs."

Fafnir and Siegfried looked at one another.

"I will remain with you, and Fafnir will lead the Celestial Wardens in my absence," Siegfried declared with absolute certainty. Then his light blue eyes met Telos's gaze, and all three of her eyes stared into his soul. The light of the Origin that shone through her red eye cascaded through Siegfried's soul and reminded him of his place in the scale of existence; the aqua eye pulled him through the cold depths of the Void and filled his mind with the untapped potential of creation, before brushing his core with the infinite chill of nothing; and finally the Third-Eye of Ein Sof seared his soul of impurities, and the dark tentacles that Oizys had placed there.

"Do you still want to come with?" Kallos asked with a slightly amused tone as Siegfried's soul was tempered and purified by the simple act of Telos looking at him.

Siegfried nodded, though his expression had gone a bit pale. Telos's casual display of her cosmic power left him intrigued.

"I didn't even know there was a trap left behind inside of me by Oizys. How did you?" Siegfried asked once he had gathered his courage.

"Never bet against Blue," Arkaziel chimed in, as if it were the oldest wisdom of the universe.

"I felt nothing amiss with your mind, master," Fafnir complained, and looked confused at the sudden shift in the direction. The dragon in human form had not experienced Telos's gaze for himself.

"When I gazed into the eyes of Lady Telos, my soul went on a fantastic voyage. I saw the red light of the Origin, from which all energy trickles down into reality, the unlimited possibility of the Void, and then a Divine Light coursed through me and removed impurities. The resentment I felt building, the jealousy of a woman not even of my own rank with such power, it all faded away as something dark and twisted burned as if in holy fire, and the cleansing light left me at peace." For a man who had spent his lifetime opposing gods, Siegfried's summary sounded an awful lot to Telos like someone who had just had a revelation.

*Ugh, he'd better not start worshipping me.*

"It might be best if you stay with your men, Siegfried. There are other forces than Archons at play, and your presence could save them significant losses," Telos suggested gently.

"I still wish to accompany you." Siegfried's resolve hardened. "Your journey to the heavens will change everything, and I wish to witness it."

"That's fine, I guess," Telos said with a light smile. Inwardly, though, she felt disappointed a Sovereign failed to see through her politeness and realize she didn't particularly want him along.

"What should I do with the men, sir?" Fafnir asked, a look of a lost puppy crossing his features. Telos could only assume that after so long of being second-in-command, the dragon had lost much of its initiative.

"Rally at the observatory, and activate all of our agents. The spark we've been waiting for has finally arrived. May I send my men off, Lady Telos?" Siegfried deferred to her judgment with a subservience that turned Telos's stomach, but one that Arkaziel and Bobbi nodded at, as if it were only right and just.

"Yep, sure. I'm moving your vessels into a holding area now, and . . . there. Your men are there, too." Telos shrugged, while Fafnir and Siegfried watched her with a look of awe. Neither were capable of sensing the power she'd used to do those things, so no doubt they were caught up in the idea that she could conceal her abilities, when the truth was they just lacked the sensory abilities to see the truth.

"Go say your goodbyes, and once your men have departed, I will allow the Archon to approach and take us to the First Heaven."

"Why don't we simply preempt them and go on the offensive?" Siegfried asked, showing no sign of moving to see off his men.

"I want to see the heavens as they've been, and are, before I destroy and reweave them," Telos said with a touch of hesitation. *I get to do some sightseeing now and then, for Pete's sake. It'd be nice to see places before they're on fire or half destroyed.*

Blank expressions met her admission, followed by laughter.

In short order, the men and women of the Celestial Wardens boarded their vessels. Telos then formed portals under each vessel, transferring them to a location in space with a close proximity to their observatory, but not so close that it would put the organization into high alert. Fafnir seemed bent on giving Siegfried a Minnesotan goodbye, but Telos glared at the dragon until he scampered into the last ship, and went through a portal like all the rest. She didn't feel like dealing with a long goodbye.

"Horaeus is almost upon us," Kallos warned, moments before the icy vessel shook.

"He can't break it; don't worry. He's affixing chains to the hull, and plans to drag us to the first layer of Heaven." Telos grinned, and the ship around them reshaped itself. No longer did they require a vessel with an interior large enough to accommodate the Wardens and their vessels. The lightship's internal dimensions re-formed around them to a comfortable bridge with viewing windows.

"How can you tell what he intends?" Siegfried asked with a frown.

"Greater Archons stand out in the Cosmic Song. All that he is lay exposed for those who can perceive the Cosmic Song. Someone plucked his string to make him do something as foolish as bring us to their vaunted Heaven." Telos bit her lower lip slightly. Not in worry, but in annoyance that she couldn't tell who had plucked the weaves of existence to the party's benefit, but took seemingly extreme measures to hide themselves.

"Someone? Who could do that?" Bobbi asked, even as four large white chains bound the vessel of light, a gateway of blue energy opened above the vessel, and the large, luminous figure of the greater Archon who held the chains appeared.

"An Aeon, Azathoth if he were to wake up, and perhaps Yog-Sothoth. I could do it, but didn't." Telos shrugged off the admission. No one but Siegfried even gave it a second thought to question that Telos could manipulate greater Archons, as if it were just expected at this point.

"If you have so much power, why are we assaulting Heaven at all? Couldn't you destroy it and be done?" Siegfried didn't bother to conceal his skepticism, but the part of him that had seen Telos perform the impossible already had a bone caught in its maw, and his posture showed indignation.

"Do you know how much damage could spill across multiple realities if I obliterated Heaven with overwhelming force? The seals on Azathoth would come off, the gates would no longer bar Yog-Sothoth from crossing each and every one. A million other horrors birthed by the souls who reject reality and descended the Qliphoth are out there, waiting. Demons, devils, dark gods, Outsiders. Those who have become something *other*, who yearn for true release, would be free to wreak havoc upon this reality and countless others. To say nothing of the truly malevolent beings who yearn for far worse than mere inexistence.

"You're coming with us to witness this with your own eyes. That's fine. But I don't need your help to defeat the Overgod. I've already declared the age of gods to be over; that's fixed into reality. The Cosmic Song will change over the next millennia, even if we all sit back and do nothing, for the Song exceeds the limitations of Ialdabaoth and the reflections, fragments, mirages, and imitations you call gods."

Siegfried's lips turned into a thin line, and his eyes darkened, but Telos met his look evenly and with a grin.

"Enjoy the show; you'll never get another chance to see something like this." Telos pointed to the viewing windows. The vessel drifted through the space between dimensions, and the Seven Heavens of Ialdabaoth were among the highest of dimensions in the material planes. Outside their vessel were glimpses of geodesic runes that contained entire realities, Divine Forges upon which reality had been hammered together, and a glimpse of the farthest lights of Pleroma, beyond touch of the material planes.

In a flare of light so bright it hurt even Telos's eyes, the view outside of their vessel turned into a world of beautiful gardens floating in a sea of clouds. Horaeus set their vessel upon a very large area, across which the Hosts of Heaven had gathered, and a shimmering figure of incredible power stood before all other Archons.

"I thought Ialdabaoth would be taller," Arkaziel grunted. Whether the Overgod heard the cat, or it was coincidental timing, the Overgod lifted a replica scepter of the one Telos had in storage, and beams of light melted the vessel around them.

"Aetheria and conspirators, repent and I shall make your deaths swift. Struggle, and you will spend eternity regretting your foolish choices." Ialdabaoth spoke from a position of extreme authority such that no god or Cultivator could dare oppose his will. So, when Telos laughed and took a single step forward, none of the Archons could truly process what was happening.

"Ialdabaoth, I challenge you and all of your Archons for the role of Overgod, and ownership of the material plane." Telos didn't bother to yell, but her voice echoed everywhere in all the heavens. The Cosmic Song picked up tempo in her ears, and the bass of its beats shook her insides.

Telos didn't have to glare at Arkaziel. His indignation at not being the one to own the material realm spiked, and though he didn't make any comments, she knew the moment Ialdabaoth was dead, Arkaziel would have something to say about the distribution of loot. *He's learned restraint!*

# CHAPTER 22

# Revelation

Kill her!" Ialdabaoth screamed in response to Telos's challenge.

*Now is the hour, unleash me! Show this cretin the endless maelstrom of the Void. I will rend asunder his essence, transform his agony into the grandest of symphonies, and leave his screams to forever echo in the dark crevices of the Void. My dark masterpiece shall resonate through the abyss of all realities, and the horrors I commit upon Ialdabaoth shall be such that even the stars turn their eyes away. The echoes of his dissolution will redress the ugliness of his existence.*

*I, Fred, the Unutterable Black Flame of the Void, the Supreme Echo of Ayin, shall burn him from existen—*

*Just stop. Please?* Telos asked Fred with a deep exhaustion. Whether Fred respected her request or if he sulked due to being interrupted, she didn't know, or care.

Telos beheld the glory of the host of Archons, with their blue spirit-essence bound to carbon. They were little more than spiritual puppets with fragments of Ialdabaoth nurtured into something like a watered-down copy, and their essences were ugly things, imbalanced and haphazard in their creation, just as Ialdabaoth had no balance.

"Cease," Telos commanded. The Archons, from least to greatest, fell into hunks of inanimate carbon, and their spiritual essence gathered into a miniature sun before her. Only Ialdabaoth remained, and the creature took a step back in fear.

"You aren't supposed to come here!" Ialdabaoth shouted. "This is mine!"

"That's not how it works, you know. Where is your creator? Where is Sophia?" Telos shook her head at the terrified Overgod.

"Dreamland! Go to Dreamland and face her! She's to blame; she made me! You could fix me—it's her fault!" Ialdabaoth shifted from fear to hate and blame so fast it left her companions reeling, although Siegfried still seemed to be unable to comprehend how Telos destroyed every Archon with a single word, and was not following the conversation at all.

"I could fix you," Telos agreed. "I'm not going to, though. Why would I make a new teapot by gluing together multiple shattered ones? *You* might do that out of desperation, or lack of resources, but I won't. I'm sorry you had the burden of this role, but now the age of the gods can end in truth." With a glance, the Rod of the Overgod flew out of Ialdabaoth's hand and into the dense sphere of energy before Telos. A second rod, the original scepter, appeared next to the other one inside the remains of the Archons.

Ialdabaoth, bereft of the rod and his Archons, looked like a pitiful creature. Tendrils of divine power were stripped from him in ribbons that flowed into the orb in front of Telos. With each one stripped, the hideous mess of twisted flesh beneath thin veneers of divinity were revealed for all to see. Before even half of his power had been pulled back, a bolt of light that resolved itself into a spear pierced Ialdabaoth's essence.

"Hello, father-in-law." Telos greeted the arrival of the Dark Angel, the Aeon of Awakening, the deliverer of gnosis, and Kallos's father, as he descended on black wings to examine the strange scene. Belial's black and golden eyes were striking, but they beheld Telos as if she were his enemy, ally, and superior all rolled into one.

"Father? What are you doing here?" Kallos demanded from her place next to Telos.

"I thought that when Ialdabaoth died my purpose would be realized." Belial's skin bubbled, and his aura pulsed out of control as he found himself expelled from human form into that of a crystalline being who existed in more than three dimensions. "Why?"

"Aeons aren't allowed in the material plane except as avatars, or so Ialdabaoth proclaimed. I don't mind you visiting in your true form. It's better that we don't play at being something we aren't, right? I cleansed the corruption your mission in the material has caused you.

"However, since you stole my kill, go back to Pleroma and prepare a report for Bythos on a more just system of gnosis." Telos smiled sweetly at the end, and Kallos barked a laugh before she got herself under control.

"What will you do with the heavens, and your shadows?" Belial chimed.

"A new highest layer for the material. We're going to make it now." Telos smirked. She felt oddly giddy about creation. This felt like a new experience to her, even though she had created her own entire inner world already. Perhaps the scale of a whole dimensional existence versus a mere singular solar system made the difference?

"*You* are going to make it? You rarely directly create." Belial's bewilderment seemed to match Siegfried's own, based on the slack-jawed, dazed look that had overcome the Sovereign leader of the Celestial Wardens.

"Maybe that's part of the problem. Nothing. Something. Nothing. Something. Again and again, why would I be interested or care, if I delegate everything? Time to get my hands dirty, but that means fewer hands in the pool. So, I'm sending you back to Pleroma, to write a comprehensive guide on what form gnosis should keep going forward. You are the expert, after all."

"Understood," the Aeon chimed, and with a wave of her hand Telos sent Belial to Pleroma. With Belial's departure, Telos gathered the last of Ialdabaoth's power, and shattered the two scepters already inside of her sphere. White light formed a sphere around the party, as the Seven Heavens were obliterated by an event similar to the Big Bang.

"You've had your curiosity sated now, Siegfried. Ialdabaoth is dead, the towers won't receive new souls, and it's up to you and your people to make a universe you dream of, on your terms. Other than a few last visits, we are done with your reality, what with a new one forming for us even as we speak."

"But I have questions! What are you? Why is any of this happening? If you had this kind of power, why didn't you use it—" Siegfried vanished from the sphere, ejected back to the observatory and his forces.

"Do we get to do any fighting in Dreamland, or can I take a nap? All this power is making me sleepy," Arkaziel asked with a massive yawn, and Bobbi, despite being in human form, struggled to keep her eyes from drooping.

"Rest, both of you. It's time to settle some 'family' drama." Telos heaved a large sigh as the white dome around them altered to reveal a city they'd seen before, in the memories of Ouranos. Dreamland, City of the Gods, a dimension that existed in the limbo between the Void, Pleroma, Material, and the Astral. An almost infinite urban landscape that held incongruent neighborhoods.

Telos picked Arkaziel up and let him rest against her chest, and Bobbi had slipped into the form of a pink kitten that Kallos picked up similarly.

"Are you sure you want me with you for this, darling?" Kallos asked with genuine concern.

"You're part of this now, babe. We're inseparable. Well, I guess one of us could separate ourselves, but why would we?" Telos tilted her head as her mind poured over any reason in which she might ever want to separate from Kallos, but nothing came to her.

"I'll stay by your side, then." Kallos nodded, and the two women interlocked the fingers of their free hands as they walked through the gates of Dreamland, their other hands occupied with cuddling adorable StarManes. No push of magic, nor even an extension of one of Kallos's chains was needed to open the gates. The once-sealed city lay open, and from its depths were the energy signatures of three familiar, and powerful, entities.

A human silhouette formed in the nearest alley—a pulse of darkness and Void transformed into a shadowy man.

"Nyarlathotep. What do you want?" Telos could read the shadows, the signature of the Void, and identify the eldritch collective known as Nyarlathotep with an ease that disturbed the creature.

*#We wish to ensure peace between us. We only assisted* Chaos *to increase the traffic through Qliphoth.#*

Although the silhouette looked human, dozens of eyes popped in and out of existence in the darkness of its conjured avatar.

"You're a bit player in this drama. Go back to the Void, or eat a few of the obnoxious gods if you want. You aren't a problem, *yet*. Keep it that way."

*#Your wisdom is as boundless as the first Void from which the cosmos spilled.#*

The envoy of Azathoth fell into shadow and vanished from all of Telos's senses.

"Are you sure it is wise to let him off without any punishment?" Kallos asked, her opinion transparent and shared through their bond.

"He did less damage in this scheme than he would have following other schemes. No doubt he or Yog-Sothoth saw this future and mitigated their actions appropriately. The Void collectives are very difficult to understand, maybe when I've empowered the Void-Gates, I'll gain insight. But he did traumatize Phanes, and countless others."

Telos generated three orbs of Ohr Ein Sof, each a pale blue that radiated intense cold. With a thought, the orbs vanished into thin air, tracking down the departed entity.

"That should be enough of a reprimand, I think." Telos half stated, half questioned.

"Such entities are infrequently on the receiving end of admonishment. No doubt it will prove a valuable reminder to improve their behavior." Kallos sounded doubtful that it would be effective, but Telos felt the trivial dismissal she had given him was more of a punishment than pain.

The duo walked in front of an ancient coffee shop, from which the scent of a perfect cup of brew still wafted into the air after eons of emptiness. Every building in Dreamland had a lingering sense to it, a scent, a visual. Some had haunted sounds, and others simply resonated with their long-gone god, but all were tied to a god and an authority, some very niche, and some very general.

"That looks like Asgard over there." Kallos gestured with one of her chains.

"So it does. That means we're almost at the center. There should be a . . . there we go." Telos nodded toward what appeared to be a subway station entrance. The stairs down were covered in layers of dust but showed some recent foot traffic. Spiritual blue flames burned in wall-mounted sconces, and guided the duo's path into the darkness. It was no subway they had entered, but a nocturnal garden full of gorgeous darkness-loving plants. Each garden had a balcony that the tunnels came to, giving a perfect view of the umbral glades.

"Very pretty, but not what I expected. Is there anything down here but gardens and art?" Kallos arched a brow at the alcoves between balconies, filled with sculptures, paintings, jewelry, weapons, and other works of art.

"It's funny. Not that long ago I'd have felt compelled to take all of this, but now it's just . . . not interesting to me. I want art made by my own hands, or yours, but these works don't have any meaning to me." Telos frowned at the hollowness that each piece left her with. Perfection rendered by gods, hollow of all but authority, they almost begged her to destroy them.

"I sense power ahead?" Kallos murmured to Telos.

"Underneath the Palace of the Overgod is a dark glade planted by Nyx. They're waiting for us there."

"Nyx, Aetherius, and Khaos?"

"Yes, those three, and two more they don't know about yet, although I imagine all three were unknowingly manipulated into coming here."

When the winding tunnels finally reached a large chamber, the three stood talking quietly to one another. Nyx and Aetherius had genuine smiles for Telos, while Khaos had a more complex expression. This was the first time she looked upon them and wasn't shocked at the power they held. If she still nursed a grudge over things, it was within her abilities to step in and punch any of them through a few walls before they could even react now.

"Callie, Pete! It's been a bit. Khaos, nice to see you. No Ouro today? This is my better half, Kallos, for those of you who haven't met her before, and the sleeping kitties are Arkaziel and Bobbi, but everyone's heard of Bobbi Slay before. They're power-napping after the feast of the Archons."

"Impressive work, that." Nyx laughed, and her pleasure at the misfortune of her enemies rang honest and sincere. Aetherius didn't seem to share her petty enjoyment at the fall of the Archons, but neither did he regret it, from the pleasure he took in at Nyx's genuine smile. *Uffda. It's like watching your mom and dad flirt in front of you, stop that!*

"Before we talk about what's next . . ." Telos lifted a hand, and Khaos exploded.

# CHAPTER 23

# Abandonment Issues

Callie stared at Telos with a finely arched brow. Her pale, porcelain skin was stained with the blood and fragments of what had once been the Transcendent being called Khaos. Pete, on the other hand, simply glowed a little and cleaned the mess up. All the gore vanished from himself and Callie, while he waited for Telos to explain herself.

"The being you've known as Khaos is an empty husk being piloted by another entity. You can come out now, or I'll drag you out. *Both of you.*"

The darkness quivered, and two very different entities appeared in the true throne room of Dreamland. With their appearance, the masquerade of darkness fell away to reveal an opulent, almost baroque chamber, one half of which had been decorated in ivory and gold, and the other half in obsidian and ruby. The room wasn't divided down the middle, but formed a yin-yang that forced the lights and darks to flow into one another.

The woman on the left seemed human enough, other than the vibrancy of her golden eyes and the rigid perfect posture she maintained. She wore a white dress and lifted her skirt to bow to Telos. The woman's hair was the exact shade of brown that Telos had been graced with in her life as Aesca, and everything about the woman in white seemed to be based upon her human life but accentuated with divinity and power to absurd levels. If imitation were flattery, Sophia, the woman in white, had a thought process that Telos couldn't quite follow. If anything, it seemed insulting to see her old form so drastically altered and worn by someone else.

The Cosmic Song around Sophia made Telos wince. It reminded her of "Adagio for Strings," and it was a kidney punch of emotion. It fit the Aeon of Wisdom, she who had created Ialdabaoth, extremely well. The Cosmic Song was imbued with such profound tragedy, regret, and sorrow that even Telos needed to fortify her emotions to keep herself from tearing up. Kallos struggled with the heavy emotions, too, and two or three tears escaped her golden eyes to track down her cheeks. *Empathy for Sophia? Here I thought I was the soft touch.*

If Sophia were a tragic figure, her companion radiated a euphoric song that danced from orgiastic, to angry, and through the whole gamut of emotions. Telos couldn't imagine listening to this song for long, because the notes were discordant and haphazardly pushed together, genius in parts, but devoid of harmony. In short, the Cosmic Song of Chaos lived up to the name.

Chaos himself looked similar to Telos. Take Telos, make her completely androgynous, or just slightly masculine, throw her into a set of black pants and tank top, a pair of ass-kicking boots, and add black hair with just the faintest hints of red and aqua, and much paler skin, and you would end up with Chaos. Chaos had two red eyes that burned with manic hatred for everything, but when the red orbs regarded Telos, they might as well have turned into hearts, and a smile crossed his apathetic features.

"Father!"

"Mother!"

Telos cringed, Kallos pinched the bridge of her nose, and Nyx and Aetherius seemed to struggle with the revelation of these two beings. The only bright side Telos could see was that neither of the two entities leaped at her, although each seemed to want to.

"Everyone, meet Sophia, the Aeon of Wisdom, creator of Ialdabaoth, and puppet master of the Archons. This, meanwhile, is Chaos, a fragment and reflection of Ayin, who was created in the transition from Nothing to the Light of Ein Sof, progenitor of the gods. The two entities who orchestrated my existence in this reality."

"We prefer to think of ourselves as your children." Sophia tried to prevent the title of puppeteer from sticking.

"Hey, we did the right thing. You're the one who created a universe, looked upon it, and decided you wanted nothing to do with it at all. How fair is that, that we labor and build, make reality after reality down the dimensional axis, then you take one look at it and decide you'd rather be an incomprehensible ball of light for eternity. Rude!" Chaos harrumphed angrily at Telos.

"How many realities did you destroy trying to bring me back?"

Telos's question made Sophia visibly uncomfortable, while Chaos laughed it off.

"Oh, so many. We got close so many times, too, but every time your powers started to show up you found a way to shrug them off and flee your responsibilities. Do you know how many times we've had to watch you run away, like a dad who's just going out for a pack of cigarettes and never comes back?" Chaos took no blame for his actions, or if he did, he felt her actions in abandoning them were the graver sin.

"A lot, then. Why? Why were you so damned desperate for *me*?"

"You created us," Sophia said simply.

"No, I didn't. Bythos and Sige created you, Sophia, and happenstance created you, Chaos. Did I create Bythos? I don't have any memories of that. So, I didn't directly create either of you, yet you both created me. Hundreds and thousands of me, until one of us woke up to *become* the Creator."

"Wait, so all of our attempts to break the cycle of the towers . . ." Pete trailed off, realization dawning across the face of the Primordial of Aether.

"The joke's on me." Callie laughed bitterly.

"Look on the positive side, you two. Thanks to Chaos and Sophia, I'm not just the angry Cycle-ending biological weapon and super soldier you created with Chronos and Khaos." Telos showed her teeth, a tiny bit.

"So, who was Khaos?" Callie asked while eyeing the few stains still on the floor that Aetherius had missed cleaning.

"A shell I used. Reality struggles to contain the power Fifi or I possess. The lower down the dimensional axis you go, the less of our presence it takes to destabilize existence. Even Dreamland suffers the occasional paradox from our true manifestations, but we're nothing compared to the Judge, or Telos here if she took on her full power." Chaos gave the mess that was Khaos no more than a second glance. If he or Sophia wanted, they could have resurrected Khaos, but neither expended the effort to create conflict with Telos.

"I have some questions." Telos spoke softly, yet cold and pressure descended upon Chaos and Sophia, such that the stone underneath them showed branching cracks from Telos's displeasure.

"First of all, why do you look like me?" Telos demanded to know.

"Me?" Chaos asked, almost exploding at the possibility of attention.

"No, Fifi."

Sophia wilted under Telos's gaze, and under the use of the deplorable nickname by the very person she definitely never wanted to use that name. Telos intentionally leaned in to creating displeasure for the fallen Aeon.

"I don't want to be all *actually*, but this is the human form I've used since we created humans. We based your human form on me, since I'm kind of your daughter?" Sophia tried to maintain what little dignity she had left, after being called Fifi by Telos.

"I follow your logic. Then why do you look like a gothic knockoff of me, Chaos?" Telos's breath steamed the cold air, but Arkaziel squirmed and made some whining noises, which reminded Telos to control herself enough to exempt her group members from the cold.

"Oh, I totally copied you! I change appearance all the time, but this is one of my favorites. You're awesome. The streaked aqua hair, the heterochromia, the long coat, the ass-kicking boots, the mesh gloves—who in their right mind wouldn't want to look like you?" Chaos brashly laughed it off, unaware of the threat that loomed over his head.

"Flatterer. I personally agree, but it's still creepy as all get out. This brings me back to why? Why do you two care so much that Ein Sof regards you? Unlike the denizens of Dreamland, you two can move freely between existences." Telos stared at both Sophia and Chaos with all three eyes, and Kallos fixed them with a glare as well. Telos had felt Kallos's anger spike each time one of them called Telos their creator or parent.

Both broke eye-contact to look at the floor, and neither presented an answer with any haste. Sophia spoke first, after a long awkward silence had come to dominate the room.

"Err. Well. It is through being seen that meaning is derived. I wished for you to see me, to look at my actions, and give me feedback. Have I done the right thing? What should I do now? What is my meaning? Do you forgive me for creating Ialdabaoth? How do I redeem myself? Are these not questions for the father?"

Chaos rolled his eyes. "Not me. I know my meaning. I thought you should suffer the same way we have. Be created without any input on it and left to fend for yourself. You're the one who abandons every reality, every dimension, and turns your back on existence. What's in the Higher Realm you and that bossy witch the Judge deny us?" Chaos practically spat the last, and glared at Kallos and her witch hat.

"Are you both morons? I am not Ein Sof." Telos bit back the swear words she'd almost started throwing out, and then took a deep, calming breath.

"You're its incarnation, as close to Ein Sof as something in this realm can get. You're directly connected to the River of Light now, so anything could happen. Maybe you'll even open the door to the White Room at its center?" Sophia put a positive spin on it. *Just what I always wanted to hear. If you aren't full-out an omniscient and omnipotent god yet, we're sure you'll get there!*

"Oh please, the moment you get responsibility, you turn your back and run away. If that isn't the Creator, what is? *Look at me, I'm the bright and shiny all-powerful light that used to be the all-consuming darkness, you can't touch me, or talk to me, all you can do is stare and cry out, but I'll just ignore you.*" Chaos practically dribbled venom with his words, and his mockery of Ein Sof saw spittle flying in the air with his over-the-top words.

"So, what is it you want? Meaning? Connection? Who is the Judge?"

"Yes," Chaos and Sophia answered simultaneously, although Chaos had the sulky whine of a teenager in his voice, while Sophia had such an earnest desire it made Telos feel some empathy for the Aeon. Some.

"The Judge?" Telos asked again. Sophia and Chaos stared at one another.

"The Judge comes from the White Room. Supposedly it is called Canaan, but that could have been misdirection. She gave us the majority of your essence. We collected hundreds of your incarnations across the Multiverses in the River, but the Judge had millions of your fragments. Our previous experiments never had a chance of working until she helped us."

"What end game did the Judge have?" Kallos asked.

"The Judge created both of you," Sophia admitted. "Belial never realized he had been manipulated by the Judge to create you, Soul Witch. We do not know what essence she used on you. It is similar, but different, from Telos. Beyond the creation of you both, she mumbled constantly about Recurrence."

"Call them here," Telos demanded.

"Can't," Chaos answered with a shrug. "The Judge shows up when they want, not the other way around."

"Fine. Maybe you'll get your wishes." Dreamland heaved in a way it never had before, as power exploded around Telos.

"What did you do?" Sophia cried out.

"This . . . is bad, right?" Chaos quailed, yet the reality around them remained stable.

"No gods, no Dreamland. I'm not leaving this place for anyone to retreat back to and draw out the purge. Pete, Callie, did you want to live a mortal life in a new reality, or expire with the rest of the gods and Primordials?" Telos asked them kindly, even as Sophia and Chaos seemed to be frozen in time. After a few drawn-out seconds, Sophia and Chaos slowly transformed into pillars of salt, starting from the tip of their heads all the way to the ground. Salt spilled across the floor in a wave.

"A mortal life?" Callie asked, surprised at the question, and the casual flex of omnipotence Telos made with the lives of Chaos and Sophia.

"You're not going to strike us down?" Pete seemed surprised, and relieved. Maybe Telos had been a little too glib about smiting gods or hadn't really told the two how much they'd meant to her in her mortal life, or even with their support in this one.

"I'm reweaving Heaven into a new layer of reality. Nice and high up on the dimensional axis, new worlds to explore, new laws, a whole lot of new everything. It won't be like Eldest Fantasy Wars Online, but I'm sure it'll be an epic adventure. What do you say?"

"Do we get turned into piles of salt if we say no?" Callie asked, unable to look away from the macabre sight of piles of rock salt that Chaos and Sophia had become.

"No, no. I would *never* hurt you two. You've been too important to me over the years, and it's clear you cared about me beyond just me being a weapon. But if you want to take your chances in this reality, I guess I'll wake up Arkaziel and Bobbi, though." Telos smiled brightly, and her incisors showed as more fanglike for a moment.

"A real adventure, with real consequences?" Aetherius laughed, then slapped his thigh. "I'm in."

Callie sighed. She looked down at her sleek dress, her flawless skin, and seemed to take in the perfection that she had cultivated into the persona of Nyx.

"Fine, but I hope you aren't giving us a bad start in a new world."

"You'll be able to thrive, Callie, and we'll meet again. Well, I guess I'll meet your reincarnations again, and you'll meet me for the first time. That should be fun." Telos smiled the more Callie and Pete squirmed.

"That's enough teasing, darling. Why is Dreamland falling apart?" Kallos interrupted the teasing with an important question.

"Oh. I connected five gates for Pleroma and the Void, and stole the power source for Dreamland and shifted it to my nascent reality. Plus, I thought the city was tacky." Telos, still holding a sleeping Arkaziel, gave first Pete then Callie a one-armed hug.

"I love you two. Live a good life." What power could a blessing from Telos with such genuine emotion and power behind it provide the two Primordials for their new life? Telos hoped it was a lot.

"Thank you," they both replied.

A moonbeam fell through the ceiling, illuminating both of the Primordials until their figures couldn't be seen inside the pillar of light, then it vanished.

"Not a bad day's work. Let's go say goodbye to Werylin." Telos generated the last portal into, or out of, Dreamland. In its silvery light, the far side showed off the Lost City of Atlanta.

# CHAPTER 24

# The Lost City of Atlanta

The Lost City of Atlanta, now known as the Amaryllis Enclave, had traveled across Grief in their absence. Floating a mere two hundred meters above sea level, the residents of Inexoria had a beautiful view of the city and the choppy waters beneath it. Telos, Arkaziel, Kallos, and Bobbi stepped out of a silvery blue portal into one of the highest towers in the futuristic (for Grief) magitech city. A brief (weeklong) stop in Malkuth had given Arkaziel and Bobbi time to sleep off their power-gain-caused exhaustion, although Arkaziel remained in the form of a kitten riding on Telos's shoulder, while Bobbi had resumed her humanoid form.

"Let's see. Werylin is . . . already on his way here." Telos laughed, surprised but not disappointed.

"I'll prepare a small spread. It appears to be lunchtime here," Bobbi offered graciously.

"Thank you, Bobbi. We'll do some quick decorations to make this a suitable goodbye party, then," Kallos offered, as she and Telos conjured furniture, tableware, and decorations for the empty walls of the grandiose suite. Bobbi handled her own cooking apparatus.

"Don't even think about it," Bobbi hissed at Arkaziel as he stretched out, seconds from jumping off to *help* Bobbi. "I don't need a sous chef who eats more than he cooks, or who puts drugs in everything he cooks. You stay over there."

"She's still bitter about me beating her? How long do you think that grudge is going to last?" Arkaziel asked no one in particular.

"You did cheat to win a cooking contest, Ark." Telos patted his head with one hand while she created streamers and a banner that said Bon Voyage.

"For the greater good!" Arkaziel defended himself vigorously, but also started to lick his paws with his tongue.

The doors to the suite were pushed open after a knock, and there was Werylin. The elf's pale face had turned flushed from his rush to get there quickly, but otherwise he looked just as he had upon their last visit. His purple hair hung in a ponytail, and he still wore the Sylvan hakama he'd acquired on their adventures, along with the katana Harmonious Tempest, and the wakizashi Stormshimmer, which Telos had forged for him.

"When Aetherius brought a bevy of refugees to us, I thought you would be along to see us before too long. I didn't expect it'd be weeks later, though!" Werylin couldn't restrain himself from making sure the adventurers knew he'd been worried.

"Werylin! I'm sorry we didn't stop by sooner, but I wanted to be able to tell you not only is Oizys dead, but the age of the gods is over." Telos didn't bother to be reserved. She darted across the room to give the elf a big hug, and even spun him around once or twice. Werylin endured it with dignity, then readjusted his clothing when Telos set him down.

"The age of gods is over? How did you get to there, from toppling Oizys?"

Werylin's face paled as he met Kallos's golden gaze. The Nephilim radiated power unlike any Werylin had ever seen. "Bloody hell, Aetheria said you were an Ethereal Lady, not an Ethereal Sovereign! Err. I mean, it's a pleasure to meet you!" Werylin nearly tripped over himself between trying to sit in a chair and bow at the same time, but a hand of darkness stabilized him.

"She just ascended. No big fuss over me? I'm so much more amazing now! Behold, I am a Beast Sovereign, God-Eater, Tiamat-descended Dragon of the Apocalypse! I'm even bigger than Atlanta! I can jump out the window and show you, even."

"NO!" Telos caught Arkaziel as he started to leap toward the window. "You're a very big, scary boy, and we don't want to terrify everyone who lives here, do we? Werylin believes you, don't you, Werylin?" Telos gave Werylin a look that said there was only one right answer to that question, and a warning to everyone not to egg on Arkaziel's look-at-me behavior.

"I don't recall you having so much black lightning dancing in your eyes either, Ark." Werylin complimented the walking calamity sincerely.

"I stole some of Nergal's destruction authority, and black lightning is the direction my authority coalesced. It's great, you really missed out on murdering gods and stealing their powers." Bobbi slid a tray of bacon-wrapped asparagus onto the table at this point, and Arkaziel's attention shifted to food, but when he reached a paw toward the tray Bobbi bopped him on the head and shook her finger.

"No paws. Eat like a civilized being or not at all," Bobbi scolded Arkaziel, to approving nods from Kallos and Telos.

"Sorry you still have to teach him manners, Bobbi," Telos apologized, and Arkaziel hissed at both Bobbi and Telos as he transformed into his own human form.

"Bigger than the Enclave, and authority over destruction? That's impressive, Arkaziel!" Werylin mustered as much enthusiasm as he could to banish the tension.

"Feel any different, with vengeance upon Oizys delivered?" Telos had to ask.

"Honestly? It's a weight off my shoulders. We've been waiting for something calamitous to happen ever since we left the Tower of Aetherius. That's how Grief is—tragedy and suffering strike sooner or later—but this time things have been different. The modern nations of Grief are willing to attempt to work together, and

Inexoria joining early helped, although they're in something of a refugee situation in the long term. What did you do after your battle with Oizys?" Werylin finally asked, tired of being redirected by the antics of the StarManes or more pressing questions.

"Well, we killed the Overgod, nipped Chaos and Sophia in the bud, and destroyed the God Cradle, so no more will be popping up in this reality. That might cause some dimensional instability, especially since this reality is atop the axis, but it should pass shortly." Telos waved that all off, as if it were unimportant.

"*Telos* killed the Overgod. It wasn't even a fight, and I didn't get to rampage at all. I feel so cheated," Arkaziel lamented to Werylin.

Werylin choked on a piece of asparagus, and a shadow hand patted him on the back until he cleared his airway.

"You've become that powerful?" Werylin asked as he eyed Kallos and Telos.

"Little bit." Telos lifted her left hand to hold her fingers less than a centimeter apart. Her attempt to be humble seemed to agitate Arkaziel and Werylin both, while Bobbi's attention had shifted to making kebabs.

"What's next, then? Staying on Grief? Purging more gods?" Werylin seemed doubtful she'd be staying on a world such as Grief, but a glimmer of hope remained in his heart. "If anyone could help accelerate the restoration of Grief, it'd be you, lass," Werylin noted with only a sliver of hope.

"Sorry, Werylin. We're here to say goodbye. I maybe, possibly, made a new level of reality above this one, but beneath Pleroma. We are going to settle down there for a time before we grow too strong to remain even there, at which point . . . well, that's way off yet. This universe is in for some interesting times. The rise of mortal kind. More spacecraft, and with the towers breaking, you'll have to form new magic networks between worlds. A step back, and a step forward, all at once." Telos shrugged, and pulled a few bottles of a sparkling elven winter wine from her storage.

"Won't the gods just attempt to consolidate their power and prevent their downfall?" Werylin asked the obvious question.

"Hah, they wish! If they do that, I'll just swoop down here and eat a bunch of them." Arkaziel patted his chest. "They aren't much, but a snack is a snack."

"Ignore him," Kallos said with a deep sigh. "Fate has been put into motion; they cannot fight the inevitable. It may take a thousand years, but the last god will fade into the realm of memory in due time."

"Won't this cause chaos? What will keep people in line, without the threat of divine retribution?" Werylin's worry flooded his face.

"There's always chaos. There'll be the same amount. There's the Great Cycle that will keep spinning people out by their karmic burden, no gods involved in that. Reach gnosis and ascend, embrace Qliphoth and descend, or remain mediocre and stagnant. People are free to make their own decisions. Undoubtedly some will take advantage of others, but I'm giving you all the freedom to stand up to it or not.

"If this is your going away party, shall I call up some old friends? Many of the masters from Solace currently reside here in the Enclave. Aetherius dropped them off in quite a hurry. Ascyn and his children would love to see you, I'm sure."

Telos clapped her hands together and laughed excitedly.

"Think you could cook for a whole gaggle of people, Bobbi?" Telos asked hopefully.

"It's not a problem, but I'll need a sous chef," the Sultana of Spice admitted begrudgingly. Arkaziel practically vibrated in his chair, even as Bobbi looked around the room at everyone other than the StarMane.

"Oh knock it off, you know it's going to me, I'm the best!" Arkaziel couldn't take it after thirty seconds and stood up.

"No adding drugs to the food, no putting Void in the food, and no magic in the food that would kill or maim a first-tier for life. Do you understand me?" Bobbi asked in a slow, drawn-out voice, to make sure Arkaziel followed her every word.

"Fine, no drugs or magic. Blue, did you finish my sushi knife?" Arkaziel's heart might as well have been in his eyes while he begged for a new knife set.

"I did. Go ham, buddy!" Telos dropped the bound set of knives from her inner realm onto the table next to Arkaziel.

Bobbi stared at the knife set with jealousy.

"I don't suppose you could make me a set, too?" Timidness didn't suit Bobbi well, and it made Telos feel a little bad for not giving her a set at the same time as Arkaziel. Luckily she'd foreseen this occurrence. Well, most of it.

*Thud.* A large block of unmelting ice appeared, and an example of almost every cooking knife ever made by any species was sheathed into it. Arkaziel's set had built in dimensional storage magic and folded into a folio like Earth knife sets, but Bobbi's used a different storage method where it would bring whatever style of knife she desired to the fore.

"I'll go get everyone, then, and bring some more help for food and drink." Werylin shook his head at the antics of the two StarManes, but he also couldn't bring himself to stare too long at the knives. Kitchen implements though they might be, they had been forged on an entirely different level than Aetheria Telos had managed with Stormshimmer.

"Leave your blades with me while you go get the party rolling; we'll call it my parting gift to you." A gentle tug from Telos on the sleeve of his hakama prevented Werylin from darting out of the room.

"Are you sure?" Werylin felt that he hadn't earned such a thing.

"Yeah, I'm sure. You helped me climb my first tower, but far more important than that, you were a good friend. Now go on. This shouldn't take me more than a minute or two." Both weapons vanished the moment Werylin handed them to Telos.

"You're doing the crafting in your inner world?" Werylin couldn't resist asking.

"It gives me more control, and the concentration of power is greater than out here, even if I blast an area with power. It's safer, and less likely to make every diviner in the solar system fall out of bed screaming about the apocalypse." Telos laughed, as if that should be a concern everyone has to face in their daily life.

"  . . . right." Werylin nodded, and backed away, to rush out of the suite and find the masters and others that Telos might want to say goodbye to.

# CHAPTER 25

# So Long, and Thanks For . . .

Well, well, well. Knew you were going to be an important folk, being the adopted daughter of Aetherius, but I didn't peg you as killing the Overgod important," Sam, the handlebar-mustached bartender exclaimed when Telos sidled up to the beautiful dark wooden bar. Originally it had been a construct of ice that, with a few tweaks of authority, had transformed nicely into wood. That one encounter summed up the gist of all of the interactions Telos had with the masters from Solace.

Without the Tower of Aetherius, and Solace, they were now essentially homeless until they could find a way to other worlds. Most of them were powerful enough that they could do it on their own, but some saw this as a chance to reinvent themselves on one of the universe's oldest planets, Grief. A world without towers would face many challenges, whether from aging, lack of cultivation resources, or lack of imported treasures. Grief, for all of its problems, was an ancient world with high ambient energy levels, where even someone in second or third rank could stave off the ravages of time for years.

Telos politely talked to each of the masters, but she did so on autopilot. The only people she felt a deep connection with were the current and former members of her party, or those who had already gone on to the next world, like Callie and Pete. There wasn't even a point in visiting Earth. Everyone she knew and loved had died years ago. *I could time travel, but for what purpose? I can walk in my own memories if I want to relive something.*

The sun had traveled from late afternoon to beneath the horizon when Kallos stepped next to her and the two leaned contently against one another, observing the clear sky.

*- There's a whole universe out there we never explored together. Does that bother you?-*

*-I never even thought of exploring this universe as a worthwhile endeavor, darling. Like Belial, I was obsessed with the idea of gnosis and ascension to Pleroma until I met you. You are the one who taught me that whether this world is a cage or not, it is still an experience. From the lowest hell to highest of heavens, there is something to make us grow in new ways. Yet, no, I don't regret leaving this existence for a higher one. A universe of*

*firsts awaits us, and there's no one I'd rather be with for then?-* The thoughts Kallos sent caused a warmth to fill Telos, and a faint brush of red to touch her cheeks.

*~I've been thinking about it. It all seems so orchestrated. My reincarnation, meeting you, Arkaziel, everything. In my curiosity, I looked into the past to see how heavily Chaos and Sophia put their hands on the scale.~*

*-And?-* When Telos hesitated, Kallos pressed for the answer.

*~Chronos, unlike Aetherius and Nyx, was in on it with Sophia. Only he didn't know it was Chaos who killed Ananke, or I'm sure he wouldn't have worked with either. Arkaziel's birth alone took Chronos two thousand, one hundred and seventy-three loops to get right. Ensuring you were in Solace to make a connection with me took him thousands of loops, and there are signs that someone else has tampered with time, only they are far more powerful than Chronos ever was.~*

Kallos laughed incredulously, until she realized it was no joking matter.

*-Why? I didn't teach you that much, and did my soul-gift of Resonance truly make that much of a difference for you? Why Arkaziel? What about Bobbi?-*

In the darkness above Grief, shooting stars filled the sky.

*~Our connection and your ability to Resonate amplified all of my gains, and played a very large part in my awakening. Arkaziel's Beast Cultivation, combined with Resonate, made my gains exponential, and in turn fueled both his and your own. Yet any beast Cultivator would've provided me that benefit, Arkaziel's true strength lay in his being a Master of Duality. Until I gained access to Binah, I didn't even realize he had such an ability, or that it had made my understanding of duality, such as with Aether and Nether, or Ethereal and Void, so much easier. Combine that with my Autopotency that Chronos tried to awaken through my core, and it seems almost impossible that I wouldn't awaken to the Path of Eternal Becoming. Yet do you know how many times Chronos looped my life between my reincarnation and before he was reunited with Ananke?~*

Telos watched the stars shoot across the sky. Beautiful trails of yellow, green, and blues filled the twilight, which seemed to grow a bit darker at Telos's gaze, emphasizing the beauty of the celestial phenomenon.

*-How many times?-* Kallos asked, expecting a low number.

*~Seven hundred and seventy-seven,~* Telos shared with a small laugh.

*-No wonder things seemed so easy. How did we not notice it?-*

Telos felt an emotion she was well familiar with flare within Kallos. As the daughter of an Aeon she had vast powers not available to most Nephilim, and she'd never had a clue that their lives had been manipulated, let alone the severity of it. Rage, shame, and spite clashed against the bliss of ignorance. Shouldn't she have been privy to such widescale temporal alterations? Especially ones that involved her.

*~Sophia and Chaos empowered Chronos through manipulation of the dimensional matrix itself. Sophia created divine veils, Chaos essentially functioned as a random number generator for existence, while Nyarlathotep created problems for the Aeons to be preoccupied with, and not even Bythos noticed what they were doing. Maybe. It's also possible Bythos and Sige wanted me to awaken. I can't rule that out. I could find out, but*

*they would sense my probing, and why poke the ant nest?~* Telos exhaled, but her eyes stayed on the shower of stars in the sky.

*~A convoluted intrigue culminating in you, Arkaziel, and me. You never answered my question about Bobbi, darling.~*

*~I would love to tell you it was only Chronos again, but my subconscious desires may have played a part in addition to Chronos. I wanted Ark to have a companion, like you are to me. Someone to mellow out his impulsive and reckless nature. Between my desires and Chronos's StarMane breeding program, stars aligned. Bobbi's gift with Culinary Alchemy is hard to gauge the effectiveness of, even for me. More than anything, I think, it reminds me to continue physical traditions like eating food.~*

Kallos leaned over and brushed a kiss against Telos's cheek.

"We're here now, my love, and a whole new world awaits. Are you going to look backward, or forward?"

"Forward, for sure. I just . . . I wanted to take stock of how we got here, now that I can see through the deceptions of Chaos and Sophia, and the time-fuckery of Chronos. I'm tired of other people meddling in my life, more than anything else. The worst part is I can't even rule out that some of these manipulations are my own. Does future-me have the right to mess with past me? Vice versa? It makes me less angry than when Chronos or Chaos did it." Telos groaned unhappily.

"What about this Judge?" Kallos looked far away, searching for traces of the still unmet entity through the Cosmic Song. Kallos found no more trace of the Judge than Telos did, and both sighed at the same time.

"Jinx," Telos said with a grin.

"We will find them, and they *will* provide us with answers," Kallos vowed darkly.

When the two lovebirds finally returned their attention to the party, everyone had drifted off. Only Arkaziel, Bobbi, Werylin, Tasmin, and a foxfolk Telos didn't recognize at first remained. The kitsune seemed to be in the prime of their life, but a simple listen to the Cosmic Song informed Telos this was one of Ascyn's children she'd played with on the farm, so long ago.

"Astryl, you were so tiny last time I saw you. Thank you for staying this late. I would have been sad to miss seeing you again," Telos offered with a sincere smile, which made the male kitsune squirm with embarrassment.

"Mom and Dad thought I ought to give you this, and I wanted to say goodbye. They say you won't be coming back to Grief again?" Astryl held out a complex work of origami. The paper itself glowed with the soft light of the moon, and it had been folded hundreds of times to create a dragon, not like Arkaziel.

"It's beautiful. I still have a whole slew of the origami you made for me when I was in Solace." Telos gestured, and the air above her head filled with a flock of birds that seemed to fly on their own, but all of which fell back into Telos's inner world after a minute. "I really enjoyed my time playing with you and your family, memories that I'll cherish as we step away from this world." Once, Telos might have had to swallow or been choked up by emotion, but even though she felt deeply touched, her control had grown in the hundreds of years that had passed for her since Solace.

"We are leaving, though, and not just Grief. This whole universe. So it's going to come down to brave warriors like you to ensure tomorrow's a brighter day. You can do that, right?" Astryl's aura, and essence, didn't scream *farmer* at Telos, but *knight*. Maybe he'd be a hero, and save whatever reincarnation poor Rick the Trapmaster had next.

"I can! I mean, I will!" Astryl practically shouted.

"Then take this, in exchange for your thoughtful gift." Telos held her hand out, and a shield and longsword materialized. Both looked to be made out of ice, but were indestructible, and carried a bevy of enchantments suited to someone on the path to become a paladin.

"I . . . are you sure? I gave you a paper dragon," Astryl questioned, hesitating as he tried to discern whether it was appropriate for him to accept the gift, which he very much wanted to.

"You put hours of work into making the dragon, didn't you? If anything, my gift is substandard; I forged them in less than an hour." Telos had actually done it on the fly, while they talked, but Astryl didn't need to know that.

"I don't know about that, but thank you, Auntie." Astryl winked, and then absconded with the shield and sword before anyone could try to separate them from him. Not that anyone would. Except maybe his parents, but that was on Ascyn.

"You always give more than you receive. Is that the definition of kindness?" Tasmin, Werylin's descendant and formerly a necromancer, questioned. Tasmin now had the glowing blue eyes of an Aetherial Elf, and a flute strapped to his hip.

"Another change in paths?" Telos pointed to the instrument.

"Werylin's tales of minstrels and bards made me curious, and the more I learned, the more I wanted to be one. There's other candidates to become Speakers of the Words of Creation better suited than me, and I think I'd like to travel this world now that the threat of Oizys seeking revenge is gone. Thank you for being you, Telos. Most people would kill a hostile necromancer, but you not only spared me, but removed the curse from my soul, and helped us all find a new purpose and path, and got us out of the tower." Tasmin offered sincere gratitude. "I'm not that good yet, but here . . ."

The elf offered a recording crystal that a quick scan showed contained music.

"Thank you, Tasmin. Enjoy your travels, and may fortune bless you." With the last words, Telos moved faster than Tasmin could even perceive, and booped his nose with her index finger, as she imparted a boon of fortune upon the young elf.

In a whirlwind, Telos moved to hug Werylin before she blurred back to stand next to Kallos.

"I know I decreed no more gods, free will, blah blah blah, but . . . Clan Amaryllis helped me a lot, so, enjoy my favor." Telos grinned, but Werylin stared at her in confusion and silence for long moments.

"What favor?" Werylin asked dubiously.

"Guess you'll just have to find out, huh? Oh, don't look like that, it's nothing bad. You were a good companion, Werylin. Sorry you got saddled with being a politician again. Retire and go learn music with Tasmin when you can." Telos gave the only advice she thought Werylin might follow, but she suspected he'd work himself ragged politically for a century or two before he remembered to enjoy life. How quickly he'd lost the reverence for life since his resurrection.

"I'll honor your suggestion as I'm able to. Good luck out there, wherever you end up."

"If you get tired of this world . . . think of us, and maybe a doorway like this one will open."

With the words and a pulse of power from the Third-Eye of Ein Sof, a rift in dimensions opened.

"Goodbye," Telos murmured to a universe, while Arkaziel and Bobbi hopped through the gate with excitement. Telos and Kallos, hand in hand, walked through it with a mixture of giddy anticipation and uncertainty for a new dawn.

# CHAPTER 26

# Mythara

Telos had collapsed the Seven Heavens and initiated a phenomenon similar to the Big Bang, thus creating an entirely new universe upon the dimensional axis. This new universe sat closer to Pleroma than any other, and its energy saturation was off the charts compared to the previous high-energy champion, the universe that contained Grief. She felt eager to see what sort of effects such a high concentration of power would have on the evolution of life. The whole time they had been on Grief, Telos had funneled the majority of her power into fast-forwarding an entire universe, so that not only would it be much larger, but there might be something interesting when they arrived.

This had an added benefit, as far as Telos was concerned. The more of her power she pushed into her creation, the more her evolution toward a being who couldn't exist inside of her creation slowed down. How long could she put all her energies into the creation of a reality before it ceased to be the case was an extremely relevant question. If the expense of power showed any signs that it might accelerate, rather than decelerate her evolution, she'd stop.

Telos dubbed the first world that had formed Mythara, and that is where the gate she created deposited the four. Telos, Bobbi, Arkaziel, and Kallos stepped onto a high plateau on Mythara, one that overlooked a plain with two immense rivers joining together and continuing their flow far beyond their line of sight. On the far western horizon, Telos could see mountains that made the Rockies look tiny, and on the eastern horizon lay plains as far as she could see. To the south an immense forest grew, and to the north, past miles upon miles of plains, she could sense a coniferous forest.

"There's prey," Arkaziel noted eagerly. "Strong prey."

"Like Telos is going to make a world without things for you to hunt. No one wants to live through even a day of your whining," Bobbi said flatly, but she, too, had narrowed eyes examining the far horizons and sniffed at the breeze to take in scents.

"How powerful are we, here, compared to the natives?" Kallos asked while she suspiciously turned a blade of grass between her fingers.

"Strong. This universe is still in the stages of primordial life, so everything is high on raw power, but might be lacking in millennia of evolution. The high ambient energy and proximity to Pleroma should have created some very powerful beast and monster progenitors. Nothing that could take me on, but there's bound to be some creatures that could give each of you, alone, a run for your money." Telos decided not to downplay the potential of danger.

"Almost all of my power is still going into pushing the expansion of reality and imbuing the worlds with life. Try not to draw on my strength unless you desperately need to. The more power I push out, at least for now, the more time we have together. I was thinking about putting our house here?" Telos ran her eyes over the plateau, and out across the glorious view.

"I like it," Arkaziel chimed in.

"There's enough room for an herb garden," Bobbi said with a nod.

"Telos?" Kallos asked, as she surveyed her inner world.

"What's up, babe?" Telos asked, but noticed the problem as soon as she pulled an object from her inner world, and it vaporized into mists.

"That," Kallos pointed out with a wry smile.

"Mm. Looks like I'm going to have to recreate anything we brought from the lower realms to survive in the higher realm," Telos muttered as she rubbed at her chin. "Oh, I see. Sorry, guys, I wanted this to be a slight challenge, and I guess I maybe sort of created some Laws that made ascension a challenge. I could undo them?"

"Hell no, I love a challenge," Arkaziel argued.

"Says the Apocalypse Dragon whose only equipment might as well be a souvenir," Bobbi hissed.

"Calm down, Bobbi. I'll reweave your cooking tools. You won't lose any; just don't pull them out of your storage space yet. You too, Kallos. Decide what you want me to reweave, and I'll do it. While you two do that, and Arkaziel hunts . . ." An axe made of ice appeared in Telos's hand. "I'm going to start making some timber."

"Don't you have an inventory full of flying cities?" Bobbi asked, a hint of despair in her voice.

"If I draw them out they'll vaporize, and if I upgrade them, well, they'll become something different than they were. I'm going to keep them as they were, maybe make a dimensional museum later. If you're really against humble shelter, I could make an ice castle?" Telos offered with a smile, the air temperature around her dropping ten degrees per second, until the other three all shivered. "No? Okay, then I'll go cut some trees."

"I believe in her world, this was called 'roughing it,' or 'camping.' If we indulge her, she'll get bored and build a castle before we know it," Arkaziel assured Kallos and Bobbi, who stared at him doubtfully.

"I can still hear you, you know," Telos called over her shoulder, before she walked into a copse of trees.

By the end of the day, Telos had created a simple log cabin that roughly took up just over one hundred square meters.

By the next day, the log cabin was just the entryway into a crystalline manor, raised by the magic of Kallos, after all four agreed that there was little to no reason to slum it.

By the end of the week, Arkaziel had eradicated the largest predators in a wide range, and the four agreed that maybe they should take a planetary tour, possibly a galactic one, and see what this new world had to offer them. Telos erected a protective barrier around their new home, the first on Mythara, and after evolving and repurposing Libby, they were on their way.

Record keeping would put the first day of the cabin's construction at First Home 1, which would become the first major date system in the new universe. The cycle of rotation of Mythara made for a year that lasted four hundred and twenty days, a significant difference from the calendar of Earth that still weighed heavily on Telos. The vast propagation of this as the cornerstone of galactic time were to be blamed on Libby.

## FH 40

A black dragon larger than the biggest of cities on Mythara landed on the Sealed Plateau. Unlike the people who'd built a city down in the plains near the rivers, nothing kept the colossal reptile from simply landing near the crystal tower and the slightly dilapidated wooden entryway that had been abandoned for decades. The dragon, at least to the view of people watching from the stone walls with optical magnification (magical or mechanical), vanished. The people were astounded, and glad. The vile-looking black dragon had an aura of death and destruction, and black lightning had coursed along its claws, promising annihilation. Yet how could something so massive have disappeared?

The resident of Winona with the best vision claimed to have seen two pregnant women and a lizard-devil riding the back of the dragon, but no one paid much mind to the ramblings of Yohan. He had tried to pierce the protection on the Crystal Spire a decade ago, and he'd talked to invisible people and shadows ever since.

Yohan was right, of course. When Arkaziel touched down before the First Home, he shapeshifted to a human form to provide two very pregnant women each with a shoulder, while Bobbi rushed inside to prepare for what was to come.

"Why'd we decide to be pregnant at the same time, again?" Telos asked Kallos with a touch of regret.

"Because we're both idiots, darling. This is opening all of the gates at once all over again." Kallos maintained her dignity as much as either woman could, but both leaned heavily on Arkaziel, who wisely said nothing to draw their ire in this most precarious of all times.

"It really isn't my fault that the Kusoni System got destroyed. How should I know that an Arrheed lived in the system's sun, or would react to me going nova? Besides, Arrheed scales make the best cloaks, and we would never have found that out if I hadn't had to kill one." Telos defended her past actions, but it was halfhearted at best, especially once Arkaziel helped them across the threshold into the dust-free, but dilapidated porch, then into the crystal tower that held up much better.

"Did you decide on the name you'll pick yet?" Kallos asked Telos.

"I did. I'm going to name him Alexander." Telos grinned, and Kallos winced.

"That was a cursed name on Zenithar. A great warlord of doom and enslavement, he put nations to the sword. A party of heroes sent by Apollo marked the start of the holy legacy of Zenithar," Kallos explained.

"Sounds like a perfect name for our son, don't you think? Alexander Metanoia." Telos grinned, and Kallos laughed lightly.

"Well, our daughter will have a proud name to counteract the cursed one you've chosen. Lilith Metanoia." Kallos left no room for disagreement.

"Lilith!? I . . . yeah, you know what, that's absolutely perfect. It's a little weird we both chose names that were kind of malevolent on our own birth worlds, but you're the Soul Witch of Chained Wings, and I'm the literal origin of the Void, I guess, so let's just embrace our inner edgelordiness, and hope our kids don't decide to rename themselves to Hope, or Greg."

"Greg!?" Kallos made an overly dramatic face. "How dare you."

"Another cursed name?" Telos laughed.

"The Cowfather," Kallos explained, without explaining anything. No one elaborated, and an awkward silence settled over the three.

Arkaziel and Telos shared a confused look, before Bobbi called from the top of the spire down at them.

"I've got everything prepared!"

# CHAPTER 27

# Yo Momma

**FH 40**

Weeks later, the two devils lay asleep in their crib. The impossibly powerful women dazed, half asleep, leaning against one another on a couch from which they could watch their children.

*-Why did we do this to ourselves?-* Kallos asked while she yawned. Telos almost cried, but laughed instead.

*-Which part? The children? Carrying them ourselves? Not just magicking them to be potty trained?-* Telos, the indomitable woman who could slay gods with a glance, had made an entire dimension, and had an unlimited supply of divine energy, looked frazzled. Not tired—her divine physiology had transcended the need for sleep—but her mental state had been taxed so heavily it turned into physical exhaustion. *So much for thinking I'm omnipotent.*

Both women looked slightly disheveled and worn out, but there was no indication that they had just had children, or ever had them. Regeneration, variable metabolisms, shapeshifting, and magic in general meant the physical trauma of growing and having a child had already completely healed. The mental trauma of caring for said newborns, though, had proven to be enough to drive even Telos and Kallos to the brink of exhaustion.

*-Yes?-* Kallos grunted mentally, before pulling a sweet pastry from her storage.

*-Is it cheating if we use magic?-* Telos asked a question that came up every few hours.

*-We've almost made it a month. Two more days, and we can shove it in Arkaziel's face that we took care of the kids without resorting to magic for the first month.-*

*-Why did we fall for Arkaziel goading us into this again?-*

*-He promised to never ask about how we procreated again if we could last the whole first month without resorting to magic for childcare.-* Kallos groaned.

*~In hindsight, I think explaining shapeshifting and sex to him would've been the easier path; embarrassment fades quickly. Besides, sooner or later our children are going to ask how we impregnated one another.~*

*-Why would they have to ask that? Isn't it self-explanatory? They are going to be powerful in their own right. By the time they want to know about that, they'll be doing much more interesting things than self-transmutation or polymorphism.-*

*~Maybe. Look at the lights above their crib.~* Telos lifted a hand to point at the glowing cloud that had formed over the children. A miniature aurora borealis had formed, with colors cycling in and out of existence, but the light stayed muted, not so bright it would wake up the sleeping infants.

*-Spirit Lights . . . They're already attracting spirits at less than a month old. If nothing else, it seems they're already beloved by magic and the natural world.-* Kallos pursed her lips, uncertain if this would be a good or bad thing.

## FH 42

"So then I ripped the red bird in half, and gave the smaller portion to the village. They seemed confused, so I stuck around to give them a lesson on properly cooking poultry, and food safety tips." Arkaziel explained his latest exploits to Telos, while he sat on a shelf in the form of a small black cat.

"I suppose I didn't fast-forward time enough for civilizations to develop sanitation and plumbing on their own, I just thought since most souls incarnating here were ancient and powerful, they'd be able to uplift civilization quickly. I didn't really think about the fact they don't have memories of their past lives, and that's the whole point of it. Is it even safe for humans to eat cockatrice?" Telos asked, before flipping the blade on her forge.

"None of them died while I was there, so yes? As far as reincarnations go, I don't know. But they did have a transmigrator and were working on plumbing. Guy thought he was in some super old backward world. He sure looked shocked when I told him the universe was only forty-two cycles old." Arkaziel guffawed and conjured an illusion of a very confused-looking man. While amusing, Telos didn't find it nearly as amusing as Arkaziel did, so she simply nodded. "He kept asking about cheat powers, too. I almost ate him."

"Good, I'll have Libby give out some more quests and uplift Mythara and a few other galaxies at a higher rate," Telos said to herself more than Arkaziel, before she hammered metal. An enchantment prevented the usual sound that accompanied smithing. Since Telos could perceive and work the blade down to the subatomic level, she didn't need the noise pollution hammering caused. "I'm glad you stopped yourself from eating him, Ark. You've learned to show a lot of restraint."

"Oh yeah, I'm the best, for sure." Arkaziel laughed it off. "So are the kiddos using magic yet? Smithing with you in the afternoons?"

"They're one and a half years old, Ark! They can walk, and talk . . . and use a little magic." Telos muttered the last part under her breath, but the sharp-eared cat heard her anyway.

"You humans mature so slow. I could shoot laser beams ten minutes after I hatched, knew everything my ancestors did, and was the most handsome badass ever." Arkaziel's nostalgia for how amazing he was at birth washed over the room in a palpable blanket of smugness, until Telos burned the emotional projection away with a flash of cold light.

"You festered in an egg for three hundred years before hatching. Three. Hundred. Years. The kids aren't even two!" Telos defended Alexander and Lilith from Arkaziel's judgment.

"Festered? How dare you!" Arkaziel hissed he was so insulted. "What do you even do with all the weapons and armor you forge? That gold-hilted sword over there looks awfully heroic."

"I give most of them to Libby to use as high-tier quest rewards, stash a few for the kids or people we know. I've thought about throwing one or two down the dimensional axis and seeing where they land, but that could cause a lot of trouble."

"You should do it. It could upend civilizations, cause wars, or make the greatest hero ever. Oh, did I say hero? I meant warlord." Arkaziel cackled, even with all three of Telos's eyes locked on him, and her lips growing into a perfectly thin line.

"That's why Bobbi gets to babysit alone and you don't, you know."

"You keep telling yourself that babysitting is some magnificent reward to be sought after. The rest of us not-parents will be out having adventures." Arkaziel purred in response to Telos giving him the stink-eye, which put her back up and earned him some very dark looks.

"You're such a dick," Telos whined.

"Have they invented schools in the plains yet? Or are you and Kallos going to have to teach them everything yourselves?"

"So, about that . . ." Telos refused to look at the cat, and knew she'd already blown it when Arkaziel's tail got fluffy. ". . . how would you feel about being head-master to a school for a bit?"

"Why would I ever want to be part of an educational institution? That sounds awful." Arkaziel didn't even hesitate. "Hell no."

"Oh, come on, Ark! How about Libby makes it a quest? We'll make a mountain salmon reward, super extra tasty."

"I'm listening," Arkaziel conceded as he tried to ignore the illusions of fish dancing above his head that Telos conjured.

"So, we'll pay you, and build you an academy. You've got three or four years to work out the kinks before the kiddos are ready to start their own education."

"Oh-ho-ho. Look at momma bear using other people's kids as the beta testers. Wait, how many kids even are there? Where do they come from?" Arkaziel sounded confused.

"Well, as a new top-tier reality, mixed with changes to the afterlife and Great Cycle of our old universe, there's a lot of souls ascending here. In addition to that we have people reproducing the fun way, too. It's starting to remind me of rural farm families I grew up around, with twelve kids to work in the fields. So, Libby is sort of . . . integrating . . . people as discreetly as she can. A little memory fog, and people don't think about it too much."

"Why are you asking me, Blue?" Arkaziel finally cut to the chase. "Did Bobbi say no?"

"No, I didn't ask Bobbi. I'll ask her to work with you, if you accept, but I wanted you to take a leadership role in the community down there. Maybe demystify the Apocalypse Dragon that they see flying to the *First Home*, and in turn, help keep attention off the kids when they go into town. Some of the reincarnations and trans-migrators might be fairly powerful, so the headmaster needs to be intimidating, and someone people can't afford to ignore."

"You're afraid of some reincarnations?" Arkaziel looked shocked.

"No, I want them cowed into submission before we add Alexander and Lilith into the mix. There's always the chance one of those people down there in the city is Pete, Callie, Izanagi, Izanami, Chronos, or Ananke, or any of the other big names from our old world."

"Can't you just look at them and see who they were?" Arkaziel asked the obvious question.

"Kallos said for the Great Cycle to keep its mystery I shouldn't meddle while we live here. She didn't want to know if one of the kids, or the kids' friends, happened to be the reincarnation of someone we knew in the old world." Telos shrugged.

"Yeah, sure, but with your brain wired to both Libby and the Divine, can you even ignore it?" Arkaziel wondered aloud, but the hammer shattering in her hand gave Telos's answer for her.

"Damnit," Telos cursed, but the hammer restored itself as she looped time to undo the destruction. "I know whose souls they are," Telos grumbled, and pointed at her third eye. "Willful ignorance only lasted six months."

"Tell, tell!" Arkaziel demanded.

"Take the job, and I'll tell you. But if you tell Kallos or Bobbi, or the kids, I'll form-lock you into a real kitten and turn you into shark bait, got it?"

"Form-lock me? Haha, funny, you can't lock my . . . you can? What the hell? That's not the kind of thing you do to a friend, damnit!" Arkaziel complained, as he couldn't shift or alter his shape no matter how hard he tried.

"I'm serious, Ark. I'll tell you, but you can't tell Kallos, got it?" Telos gave Arkaziel her most serious look, and then removed the form-lock just as he tried to shapeshift again. Her laughter mocked the StarMane as he rolled around on the floor after bumping his head into a shelf.

"Not cool, Blue. Alright, tell me!"

"After you've got the school up and running." Telos dangled the information figuratively in front of him.

"Fine, fine. I'll run your school and be a Dumbledolf or whatever your wizard books had for a master." After regaining his dignity, Arkaziel turned into his humanoid form and tried his hand at lifting some of the weapons on racks.

"Want a staff, oh glorious headmaster?" Telos asked, and pointed to a stand full of wooden staves with elaborate crystals atop them.

"It'd be a shame to not live up to people's expectations," Arkaziel agreed as he picked up staff after staff, sensing the affinity and power of each. The same way they'd always done things in the old world.

"Still too stubborn to just call up Libby and have it displayed?"

"You are going to complain to me about doing things the old-fashioned way, Mrs. Blacksmith?" Arkaziel hissed, but kept checking over equipment manually.

"By the way, how're you going to explain your kids having rainbow hair?" Arkaziel timed his question to match when Telos delivered a hammer blow.

"Can't we just say they take after their mother?" Telos asked, whipping the back of her ponytail around.

"You keep suppressing your rainbow, and keep aqua dominant, Blue. Kallos is blonde. Also, uh, I thought you were the father, wait no, you gave birth to, err . . ." Arkaziel lifted a hand to scratch the back of his head, a mannerism he'd learned from Bobbi and Kallos.

"Did Kallos put you up to getting me to keep my hair rainbow, like the kids?" Telos regarded Arkaziel dangerously, with a narrowed-eye stare.

"No, not at all, she definitely didn't offer me a whole slew of bribes to get you to try it out for a few weeks, and she didn't use the word adorable and cute five thousand times in a couple of minutes. The kiddos might get a kick out of matching with Mommy, though . . . or Daddy . . . how does this all work again?"

"Go ask Kallos to explain it to you," Telos muttered and used mock anger to bury her exasperation. "Jeez, Ark, you're a shapeshifter. Have you never changed gender?"

"Why would I?" Arkaziel sounded confused.

"Why wouldn't you?" Telos countered.

"Genetic memories, Blue. I already know what it's like to be my mother, and all of my female ancestors. I *know* how you and Kallos conceived, you disgusting humanoids, but I can't pass up a chance at making you two be so awkward." Arkaziel cackled, and all of the times people told her StarManes were awful echoed in her mind.

"Wait, wait! If you go with full rainbow, we could use jokes like your momma looks so rainbowy, leprechauns follow her everywhere looking for a pot of gold."

"Remember when I said you're such a dick? That's understating it. You're a colossal douche."

"I love you too, Blue. Put the hammer down!"

# CHAPTER 28

# Bang on My Drum

**FH 43**

"Five little ducks went out to play, over the hill . . ." If Telos were a cheat, she would sound fantastic, amazing, and perfect. Instead, she sang in her own voice. She wasn't tone-deaf, but it was the imperfections she remembered of her own mother's voice that made her few early memories magical. Perfection was boring, and throwing a few quirky affectations into the song got laughs from her children. The air above Telos filled with illusions of ducks as the song went on and portrayed the sadness of the mother duck and her lost ducklings, and the joy at their return.

The illusions were not being created by Telos, however, but were conjured by the imaginations and projections of the toddlers on her lap singing along at the top of their lungs.

Alexander sat on her left leg, and Lilith on her right leg. Already the three-year-olds crowded her lap, and it wouldn't be long before cuddling both of them like this wouldn't be practical. Practicality could go screw itself, though, and she'd manipulate space if it meant more cuddles from the kids for longer. At three years old the predominant colors of Alexander's hair were yellow and red, but like Lilith, his hair covered the full range of the rainbow. Lilith's hair had revealed a lighter shade of purple, lilac, as her most prominent color in the rainbow. Alexander had golden eyes, while Lilith had pink eyes.

For two three-year-olds, the Plateau had all sorts of entertainment to be found, but their mothers were their primary source of fun. The smithy was locked up tight, and inside the crystalline spire, tomes and artifacts had likewise been secured. Her adorable menaces repeatedly got into places they weren't supposed to.

"Again!" Alexander demanded.

"Please, Mommy?" Lilith looked up and fluttered her eyes, which Alexander then copied. Telos tried to resist the wombo combo but failed her saving throw against cuteness.

"Didn't I say we'd be done singing three songs ago? Well, I guess one more wouldn't hurt anyone?"

"Momma, is this good?" Alexander waved a finger and shared a status screen.

"It says you've gained a trait called Progenitor of Peril." Telos held in a deep sigh, while internally she really wanted to grab Libby by the neck and ask her what the hell she was doing with her children. Instead, Telos smiled brightly, and tried not to let any anxiety show.

"What's a progenitor?" Alexander asked, fumbling the word.

"A progenitor is a founder, originator, or ancestor. It means you gained the ability to start incidents, like in the song the first baby duck who wanders away starts the events of the song by wandering off. That gets the other baby ducklings to wander off too, and soon they're all lost until they hear mommy duck calling for them."

"So, I can get ducks lost?" Alexander didn't seem to understand the concept, but Lilith had a gleam in her pink eyes that unnerved Telos.

"What does mine say?" Lilith asked with a gesture like Alexander had made, to share a status screen.

"You have gained a trait called Patron of Providence. A patron is someone who supports someone or something, and providence is sort of what we provide you two. We provide you with everything you need, right?" Telos never knew how close to cut things when explaining to the children. They were both incredibly bright in their own ways, but Alexander didn't seem to have as much of an innate linguistic talent as Lilith did.

"Why'd we get stuff from singing with you, Mommy?" Lilith waved a finger, and the screen went away.

"Well, the System rewards the strangest things sometimes. Like you, it's not very old and is still learning what it's about. Maybe it liked listening to you so much that it awarded you in thanks?" Telos smiled, but she determined it was time to have a talk with Libby about what the hell she was doing, especially with Telos's children.

"Do traits do anything?" Alexander practically bounced up and down in excitement.

"Not on their own, honey. Traits mean you are capable of something, and function passively. You would need an ability to make use of your trait actively."

"Booo." Alexander huffed.

"Mommy, can we visit the city today? I want to fly on Uncle Ark!" Lilith asked with large doe eyes, her attempts at another song long forgotten.

"Momma! I want to fly to the moons!" Alexander didn't see eye to eye with the destination of the imagined flight.

"We could do that, or you could help me design Ark's new house. How about it. Should we make a pretty house?" No motion belied the creation of hundreds of different sized cubes of ice, although most would incorrectly identify them as crystals. They weren't cold to the touch, and were almost transparent.

"Block time!" Alexander cried, the moon forgotten.

"Can we build secret rooms?" Lilith inquired as she pulled as many blocks toward her as she could.

"Sure, put as many secret rooms in as you want, but let's not break the laws of physics too much, okay?" Telos ruffled both of the kids' hair, and watched as they set to building a model house. In hardly any time at all she had to separate them, and they built two model houses. Both children ignored her assertions that sharing means caring, until Lilith decided it meant Telos should share with her, then Alexander complained that he wasn't getting attention, and within a half hour the whole idea of building a model house for Uncle Arkaziel had been forgotten by everyone.

## FH 43

***That so valiant a Dragon of the Apocalypse is reduced to this . . .***

"I haven't been reduced to anything, and you finally found a path to this dimension?" Arkaziel immediately argued with Fred. Telos hadn't been sure whom Fred had spoken to, since the Black Flame of the Void had fallen quiet since their ascension to a higher reality. Perhaps the proximity of Ein Sof deterred Fred?

Arkaziel, as most often was the case these days, wore a humanoid form. He had dark skin, golden eyes, short-cropped white hair, cat ears instead of human, and a long fluffy tail that Telos noticed the students of the academy were always watching. Not to be outdone by Telos or Kallos, Arkaziel had broad shoulders, a muscular build, and stood nearly two hundred centimeters tall.

Neither Arkaziel nor Telos had been the one to build the just-finished manor that dominated the western side of town, its unwalled gardens and three-story structure providing a distraction from the distant crystal tower sparkling in the distance. Bobbi had found an earth mage among the residents of Winona. A bag of gold and detailed sketches and plans of Hardwick Hall from the United Kingdom had resulted in a beautiful brick manor, although Telos had created the windows and finish through her own magic.

***So few of your actions have been worth commenting on since the dimensional transition. Look at yourself, O Apocalypse, and despair. Regardless of whether it is upon the Throne of Glory or a cheap barstool, you have become a lap cat.***

"I've never been big on laps. Shoulders are more my speed. Reinforces the knowledge of who the boss is more than sitting on a lap does," Arkaziel answered Fred, with a maturity and indifference that shocked Telos.

***What of you, Witch of the Soul, or you, Celestial Chef? Do you not yearn for adventure?***

"*Go away*, you're making Mommy and Momma mad," Alexander and Lilith echoed one another. The two toddlers walked between Kallos and Bobbi, the four forming a line of held hands that melted the hearts of anyone who saw.

"Hi, guys! That's very brave of you to stand up for us to a scary person like Fred, but he's just a voice. He can't do anything but talk and complain, but if he ever tries to talk to you, tell us right away, okay?" Telos dropped down to the children's eye level so she could convey the gravity of the situation. The tangled web of powers of the Sefirot, of existence itself, allowed her to impart knowledge and meaning. She tried to avoid doing it too often, though, as those around her couldn't rely on similar crutches.

"Yes, Mommy," said Lilith.

"Yes, Momma," agreed Alexander.

"Good, now, who wants to explore Uncle Arkaziel's new house? Isn't it just huge? I bet if you ask really nicely, he might let you have a bedroom here to stay in town sometimes." Telos winked at the kids, who practically vibrated past her at the speed of light toward Arkaziel.

"That was unexpected," Kallos murmured, watching the kids run to Arkaziel.

"I thought you melted Fred down or something." Bobbi shrugged. "Is it too late to do that?"

"It's never too late to destroy something," Telos answered flatly. "Until now I was content to let him have a pass, since he's mostly all talk. But if the kids can hear him, I can't take that risk anymore. I'd say I'll be late for dinner tonight, but I won't be more than ten minutes." Telos vanished even as her words hung in the air.

A world of infinite light greeted Telos, then it turned into a rainbow of colors and sorted itself out to a white room that Telos shared with a woman made of light.

"Hi, Libby. Remember the plan to empower you through both the Ethereal and the Void?"

::Hello, Lady Telos. Yes, your plan to impart me with the essence of the entity known as Reverie and Fred. Shall I prepare to initiate the process, or do you wish me to delete the plan from my memory banks?::

"Here is an updated process for the System Supreme update." A crystal of Divine Light appeared at Telos's fingertips. *What's the point of being the incarnation of Ein Sof if I don't abuse it just a little, right?*

::Confirmation requested: Do you wish me to run the System Supreme update?::

"Yes, run it. I know I programmed it, and it will be, but . . . be gentle with those two. They've waited for friends for a long time, but they're a bad match for my social circle. I think you'll enjoy them, and together, the three of you might actually learn something."

::Update processing. Processed.::

Two more forms, both masculine, appeared in the white room. One was composed of Ethereal power and the other of the Void. The difference in appearance made it very obvious which one was Fred.

"Surprise! Happy birthday. Now you can talk to people, and have friends, and impact the worlds. No destroying everything. Questions? No? Good. Here's a few thousand bottles of wine. Don't do anything I wouldn't do."

Telos vanished from the subspace, leaving the three entities looking at one another.

::Do you know how to play checkers?::

*I don't,* Fred answered flatly.

::Then let me teach you.:: Libby's slightly excited response got Fred to clap his hands excitedly, and Reverie poked himself in the stomach.

"*I, too, wish to be instructed, if you would, Miss Libby.*"

# CHAPTER 29

# Field Trip

**FH 48**

The transparent screen before me was one that only I could see. I could, if I wanted, share it with my sister or my family, or my classmates. System Screens were kind of personal, since they revealed almost everything about you. Mine said the following.

> **Name: Alexander Metanoia**
> **Age: 8**
> **Race: #REDACTED#**
> **Level: 5**
> **Class: Unlocks at level 10**
> **Traits: ###############, Kaleidoscope Kinetics (Nascent), Progenitor of Peril (Emerging)**
> **Abilities: None**

Mommy and Momma both disliked talking about some things. Momma said the race entry was because the System didn't know what to call me and Lilith, but Mommy said it didn't matter what our race was, we should just go by our names. Neither of them took any kind of pride in their own race, dismissing inquiries into their race with a smile and a lighthearted "who knows?" when asked what their race was. Momma had three eyes, which humans normally don't, and she could shapeshift. Mommy had metal wings of chains and a halo, which made her stick out just like Momma and Lilith and me.

Everyone else at the academy had an actual race in their System menu, unlike Lilith and me. We both had an obscured trait, but the number of characters for our blocked-out traits was different. When I counted the spaces mine covered seventeen, and hers had twenty-one spaces. Without a hint of even a single letter, how many characters were spaces (if any), or even what language it might be in, I had no way to discover either of our hidden traits. Lilith couldn't figure it out either, and she grew cross whenever I brought it up to her. She didn't like mysteries.

Even our attributes were higher than most of the kids our age. Derrick, who was also eight, had fives across the board, and six in Agility, and he was faster than the others. We promised our mothers we would hold back and try to fit in, but it wasn't always easy. Uncle Arkaziel being the headmaster of the school did keep us on our toes, though.

**Strength: 12**
**Agility: 21**
**Vitality: 14**
**Intellect: 13**
**Will: 39**

All of our attributes were significantly higher than our classmates, and for whatever reason, our Will alone exceeded the other kids' entire attribute score. Lilith's highest attribute matched mine, with Will, while her second highest was Intellect. While we left other kids in the dust, we were both numerically equivalent, although in different ways. She had a higher Strength; I had a higher Vitality. I was faster, she was stronger. Neither of us had managed to unlock an ability yet. According to the older kids at school, you would unlock your first ability when you raised a trait to proficient, gained a class, or read a tome.

We had to rely on our classmates, teachers, and others from Winona to understand the System. Momma hated talking about the System. She would stare at you with all three eyes until you got uncomfortable enough to leave her alone, then mutter about Libby being boring to talk about. Mommy would laugh and say she had no idea; her powers weren't derived from the System that everyone else had. Almost everyone else, that is. Uncle Arkaziel and Aunt Bobbi didn't have access to the System either, and the older kids who had unlocked Visual Identification abilities said that Arkaziel just showed as Arkaziel with lots of question marks to them.

When I cornered him and tried to find out why, he managed to distract me with ice cream and candy after making a big show about not understanding the System. He agreed with me that it seemed odd that the school's headmaster didn't know anything about the System, but he had the job to watch over me and Lilith, and that he was a nuclear deterrent (whatever that was). He couldn't or wouldn't explain nuclear. When big monsters attacked the town, Uncle Arkaziel obliterated them with a single attack. The people of Winona loved him and gifted him things frequently. He'd built a vault beneath his manor to throw all the gifts people gave him into, and whenever I was really good he would let me go down and pick out a present.

The sixth and seventh day of the week were free days, and today was a seventh day. Lilith, Derrick, Aisha, and I were exploring the rocky stream bed a bit out of town. Uncle Arkaziel had set himself up in a wooden chair, and fished from the river, while Aunt Bobbi focused on making a small campfire to cook lunch on.

"Don't go more than a kilometer away, okay?" Bobbi had chided us, but Lilith and I couldn't figure out why she decided on that far. Both of the adults could teleport, so did it really matter how far away we got? Maybe it was just a control thing. A lot of what adults said to us seemed to be more about control than having a logical reason behind it.

All of which is a long way to explain how we ended up downstream, peering into a cavern on the riverbank that hadn't been there a few weeks ago.

Lilith glared at me, and I held my hands up innocently.

"That cave looks awfully *perilous*, brother."

"I think you mean it looks interesting, or maybe even *providential*?"

"What's *providential* mean?" Derrick asked with a confused look.

"It means fortunate, or miraculous," Aisha answered eagerly, keen to show off that she, too, knew big words like Alexander and Lilith.

"Let's vote; should we go inside?" Lilith looked each of us in the eyes while she asked the question.

"Yes!" Derrick chimed and picked up a stick to swing around. Small vortexes of wind formed around his hand, and he created a wind-blade that could kill actual monsters.

"I'm not afraid," Aisha answered, a little too quickly, but she seemed more confident once she picked up a handful of rocks and infused them with light.

"You know it," I answered Lilith. I didn't pick anything up, and neither did my sister.

"Alright, let's see what we've got in the cave. Maybe there'll be treasure."

**New Quest: Find the source of magic inside the cave. Difficulty Level: 5. Accept: Yes | No**

I heard the pleasant feminine voice of the System in my mind. Mommy called the system Libby, but I'd never gotten it to answer me, no matter what name I called it, even rude ones.

"Yes," all four of us said without hesitation.

A quest could be enough to get me to level six! Level ten, and the class unlock, were the stuff of dreams and legends. We all wanted the power that came with being level ten. If you were lucky, your first ability would be an active one instead of a passive one. Derrick and Aisha both had abilities already, thanks to their parents buying them a wind and light tome respectively. We begged for tomes to use, but our mothers said we just needed to wait. Neither Lilith or I were keen on waiting, and no matter how much we begged Uncle Arkaziel or Aunt Bobbi, they wouldn't buy us one either, despite the fact that they were super rich. Uncle Ark had conspiratorially told me there was no way he'd risk angering "Blue," or Mommy, so I could cast Fireball a few years sooner.

Lilith tried to explain how even a year would be a large percentage of our current lives, which would be a long time to wait, but he laughed us off and told us he'd spent three hundred years in an egg, and to quit whining. Worst of all, he didn't even explain why he'd been inside of an egg to begin with!

Aisha's rock lights provided enough brightness that even if the cave went deep, we would be fine. Well, Derrick and Aisha would be fine. Lilith and I could see in the dark, something ordinary humans couldn't do. Our perfect vision in day or night was very unusual, at least according to Nedrey, the raccoon who lived in the tree outside my bedroom window at Uncle Arkaziel's.

Derrick coughed a few times, drawing everyone out of their plans and daydreams.

"What order do we go in?" he asked, flexing his sword.

"Alexander and Derrick will be our vanguard, Aisha and I will bring up the rear-guard," Lilith said imperiously. She always seemed to have a not (totally) unfounded confidence in her plans.

No one argued. I wanted to. I was fast, not strong, but Lilith was strong but not fast, and she could protect Aisha, our only ranged damage dealer, better than I could. At least I think that's what she thought, but who knew? She might be trying to get me hurt so I wouldn't steal her dessert tonight.

"Let's do this!" Derrick's voice cracked he was so excited, but I didn't make fun of him.

The large opening in the earthen banks of the river were half rock, and very hard. Whatever made the cavern must have been bigger than us by at least four times. Derrick and I separated, putting about two meters between us as we strode bravely into the earthen warren. The ground sloped downward slightly at first, but the decline rapidly increased. We wandered deeper into the cave, oohing and aahing at the pretty rocks along the way. I threw a few of them into my inventory. If I polished them they'd make a great gift for Mommy.

"Stop." I held up a hand. The cavern started to curve, and I could hear the soft clack of feet against the hard earth. Not humanoid. I could almost see them, despite the bend in the cavern. Long, segmented shells. Pincers. Antennae. Eight legs, not counting the pincers.

"Monsters. I think giant crayfish. Can your sword pierce them?" I asked Derrick in a whisper.

"Oh yeah, definitely," Derrick assured me instantly. I was not reassured, but if he said so . . .

"There's two around the bend, the one to the right side is closer to us. You three kill it, and I'll distract the second one."

"You're sure there aren't any more?" Lilith asked while making weird, prolonged eye-contact with me. The shine of her pink eyes was noticeable even with Aisha's glowing rocks.

"I don't hear or sense any more . . ." I said with a shrug. What did she want from me? It was not like I had any abilities to work with here.

"Alright, on three," Lilith agreed. A branch appeared in her hand. It was a thick, twisted piece of wood. I knew it came from one of the Adamant Oak trees that Momma planted on the high ground around the Spire.

"One, two, three!" Lilith counted, and I ran forward. Derrick didn't stand a chance of keeping up with me once I moved. I made it around the bend and got a visual on two giant crayfish before he'd taken three steps. These things were reddish-brown, with a hard exterior, and sharp-looking pincers that could do a lot of damage to anything caught between them. It couldn't catch me, though! I jumped up and landed on its head, ran down its back, and hopped behind it.

I didn't have enough force or weight behind my jump to do any damage to the thing, but I sure pissed it off. It clacked and chittered at me, but I hopped out of its reach and led it farther down the bend. A glowing rock hit the second crayfish in the face before it could follow me.

"Heee-yah!" Derrick shouted as he leap-attacked the surprised beast. His wind-blade crashed down with a sickening sound of a thousand fingernails against one of the blackboards in the school, until the wind-blade rebounded off the chitin, and the crayfish knocked Derrick aside.

I looped back toward them, the second crayfish following me. It seemed to be close to enraging, as its anger vibrated off it in waves.

Lilith stepped in and hit their crayfish in the head with her club, and it sounded like someone hit a melon with a sledgehammer. Bits of the dead monster flew everywhere.

"Finish this one off, Aisha! I'll check on Derrick," I shouted to Aisha, while Lilith turned to face the crayfish chasing me, a dark promise of destruction without mercy filling her eyes. Poor bastard!

"You okay, buddy?" I poked at Derrick, prepared to pull one of Mommy's healing items out if need be.

"Yeah, yeah, I'm good," Derrick muttered from the ground, but his face was screwed up, and he squirmed to get his head against the ground more firmly.

"There's something big coming!" Derrick whispered in fear, and I felt a little tickle of dread rising in my stomach at the powerful aura of the approaching monster. It felt strong and perilous.

**SMASH.**

Or maybe it was just my sense of danger from Lilith and Aisha obliterating the other crayfish, as Derrick and I were pelted by bits of monster.

"Thanks, sis," I said sincerely. Her smirk assured Derrick and I knew our place, and even Aisha looked particularly pleased at the effectiveness born of enchanting Lilith's tree branch with light magic.

The oncoming surge of powerful magic drew closer.

"Poop," Aisha declared. She was the first to see the shadow-red glow of a pincer larger than us round the bend.

# CHAPTER 30

# Crayfish Cavern

Poop? Really?" I couldn't help but question Aisha's choice of words. What was she, six?

"Shut up!" Aisha shouted back at me.

"That's a lot bigger than the first two." Lilith's self-assurance remained unfazed, so I knew we'd be fine. Maybe she'd seen the flicker of shadows, too. "Distract it, Alexander!"

"Right!" I shouted, swiped one of Aisha's glowing rocks, and ran to meet the powerful monster. The System labeled it a Giant Rusty Crayfish, and its hard body varied between gold and deep red. Its beady eyes followed me as I ran toward it, and one of those pincers, which were about twice my size, shot out to try to catch me. I easily dodged it, hopped onto the pincer, and then hopped up onto the back of the crayfish.

I took a deep breath and whipped the glowing rock in my hand right at the thing's eye. The rock impacted the eye with an awful squelching sound, followed by a burst of powerful light—the light enchantment from Aisha adding its damage in. I didn't hang around to find out if I'd blinded the thing; instead I ran along its back, hopped to kick off the wall, and tried to pull its attention toward me and the way it had come.

"Dang!" Derrick whistled at the damage I'd done to the crayfish, but unhelpfully he hadn't shouted after me if I had blinded it. I had to look back to see that it was missing one eye, and waves of red energy radiated from the creature. I must've made it real mad.

"Don't just stand there. Go stab its other eye with your wind-blade!" Lilith commanded Derrick, while I danced between claw strikes. It was a fun workout, although each time the strikes got within a few inches of me I could feel my heart pound harder, and the world seemed to slow down. My body didn't react as fast as it normally did in this weird state of being, but it let me think a little harder about what I needed to do, so it let me plan better.

"Take this!" A series of glowing rocks smashed into the back right leg of the crayfish, thrown by Aisha. She lacked the strength and speed to pull off an attack like I had, but when each rock struck the leg it exploded in a pulse of light. With the two rocks that hit the leg, and the other four that hit the body, the light explosions managed to put a lot of cracks in the creature's exoskeleton.

Derrick, prepared to jump up onto the monster the way I'd done, wasn't ready when the thing suddenly spun to face the source of its attacks. He screeched loudly and flailed. By sheer force of luck, he flailed the blade of his wind-sword into the remaining eye of the huge monster. The loss of its eye threw off its aim, and Derrick only lost the sleeve of his shirt to the attack, with a few scrapes. He totally didn't wet himself at how close he'd come to death.

"It isn't dead yet. Move!" Lilith commanded, and charged in from behind him, the large magical tree branch in her hand. She slammed the club down, the first time without the glow of magic, but Aisha managed to renew the enchantment for the second blow, and the third . . . By the fourth, the Giant Rusty Crayfish had fallen to the ground and no longer moved.

"I thought I was going to die," Derrick whimpered. He had different, clean, pants on now. I pretended to not have noticed, and Lilith was more interested in poking the dead monster with her stick than in any of us.

**Congratulations, you have reached level 6. You have gained +1 to Strength, +2 to Agility, and +1 to Will.**

I looked at Lilith, and her self-satisfied smile told me she'd leveled up, too.

"I leveled up. Did anyone else?" Derrick asked, no doubt staring at his status screen instead of anyone else.

"I did, too!" Aisha, now carrying another handful of glowing rocks, said as she joined us at the corpse of the monster.

"So did both of us." Lilith spoke for herself and me.

"Quest didn't complete, so we still need to find the source of the magic. Shall we head deeper?" I rocked back and forth from my toes to my heels, impatient to see what lay at the end of the cavern.

"Let's take a quick break first, then we'll go down?" Aisha suggested. Reality had, subjectively, sped up. The others were still quite a bit slower than me, though. I wanted to go now, but the controlled breathing Aisha and Derrick were both using was a mana-recovery technique. Neither Lilith nor I had spent any mana, so we didn't need to use a technique like they did to increase recovery.

"It'd be a lot easier to kill monsters like this if we had traps to lure them into, don't you think?" Derrick mused.

"My dad is a trapper; he could teach you. Maybe he'd leave me alone then; I don't want to use traps," Aisha mumbled, then smiled hopefully.

"Maybe. Would he really teach me? I heard a mentor can help you unlock special classes." Derrick sounded excited, and Lilith and I exchanged glances. We already had mentors.

"Sure, Dad always complains there's not enough trappers. We can't always rely on Headmaster Arkaziel or the Supreme Chef to save Winona, at least that's what Dad says. We struggled before they joined town, and if they leave, it would be bad." Aisha glanced at me and Lilith, and I could see her thoughts putting together the fact that we lived at Uncle Arkaziel's house during the school seasons.

"Are you two ready to go deeper?" I asked with a grin that hopefully would keep Aisha from wondering if she could talk freely in front of me and Lilith. Most of the citizens of Winona were humans. Arkaziel and Bobbi were both very obviously non-humans, and glowing hair and eyes made both Lilith and I look inhuman.

"Yeah!" Derrick chimed in, a new resolve in his voice that hadn't been there before.

"What do your parents do?" Aisha asked Lilith as we fell back into formation.

"Mommy makes things, and Momma does magic." Lilith's answer sounded vague compared to a direct profession, like a trapper, but maybe I was just feeling self-conscious. Our family wasn't like the other kids'.

"Are they strong?" Derrick asked. "They must be; you two are really strong."

"Maybe?" I said, at the same time Lilith said "Very."

"Uncle Arkaziel acknowledges Mommy is stronger than him," Lilith pointed out.

"She's stronger than Arkaziel? Wow," Aisha murmured in wonder. "But he killed that giant Chimera in one hit!"

"Eyes on the prize," I said and drew the party's attention to the descent, and not gossip.

"Eyes on what prize?" Derrick grumbled.

"An imaginary one? It's something Momma says." I admitted to partial ignorance with a shrug.

We had to slay seven more of the smaller giant crayfish as we proceeded, but now that Derrick and Aisha had a better grasp of teamwork with Lilith and I, we breezed through the cave. At the bottom we found a glowing sphere of stone embedded in the cave. The crayfish had been drawn to it and attempted to excavate it. At two meters high and a half a meter wide, it looked like a very simple discarded obelisk covered in basic pictographs of different insects. The stone itself had a black hue with streaks of white.

**Quest Update: Magic Source Discovered.**
**New Quest Objective: Remove Obelisk from the Earth.**

"Oh, that's easy," I said while Derrick and Aisha looked confused at how we were going to move the thing.

I touched it with my finger, it vanished, then I dropped it back into existence next to me, where it could now stand tall and free.

"Uhm, what?" Aisha asked.

"How the heck?" Derrick almost swore.

"You two can't use Inventory?" Lilith asked sarcastically.

"No, I can, but I can only put seventy pounds into mine." Aisha poked the large, tall rock.

"Yeah, I'm only able to do seventy pounds, too. How much can you put into yours?" Derrick asked in disbelief.

I eyed the status for my inventory. Weight: 9,234 kg / ??????

"How many pounds are question marks?" I asked.

**Quest Completed.**

**Congratulations, you have reached level 7. You have gained +2 Agility, +1 Intellect, +1 Will.**

**Congratulations, you have completed the quest. Touch the pillar and choose the pictograph that you like the most to receive your quest reward.**

"Two levels in one day, and a quest reward? This was as good as a dungeon!" Derrick chimed in victory.

"I'm fairly certain this was a random dungeon," Lilith asserted, while she walked slowly around the obelisk. We were all doing the same thing, looking at each carving on the obelisk to pick the one we liked the most. After three treks around the pillar I was the first to reach out and touch one. My hand brushed the dark stone, and I traced the pictograph of a dragonfly. A burst of prismatic light filled my eyes, and as it faded I momentarily saw the phantasm of dragonfly wings on my back that slowly faded.

**Congratulations, you have been blessed with the boon Dragonfly Style. You have also learned the Ability Dragonfly Strike. Dragonfly Strike: You vanish and reappear behind the target, up to 15m away, and strike them with a savage blow that inflicts bleeding. For ten seconds after (stacking, refreshable) you gain a 20% increase to evasion. Ignores 10% of target's armor.**

"Sweet!" I crowed. "I got a boon and an ability."

"Me, too," Lilith said as light faded around her. For a brief moment, I thought I saw a swarm of some kind of insect around her.

"I don't know what to pick!" Aisha whined.

"The one you like the most. You like butterflies, don't you?" Lilith inquired.

"I do, how'd you know?" Aisha sounded suspicious, suddenly. Twins always had rumors about their powers, and with our prismatic glowing hair, we were pretty suspicious.

"You're wearing butterfly hair clips." I pointed to the two clips on either side of her head.

Derrick ignored the awkward tension in the chamber by immersing himself in the choice between an Assassin Bug and Spider Wasps. His choice appeared to be the

Assassin Bug, since the palms of his hands glowed with an intense radiance in the shape of pincers.

"Oh, yeah . . . sorry, Lily," Aisha squeaked out a little timidly, before a burst of radiance behind her resembled the butterfly in her plum-colored hair.

"Quests are so cool." Derrick started to talk it up, but from the way the shadows danced I could tell it was time to go back to Arkaziel and Bobbi.

"Let's head back," I encouraged them.

After the kids filed out of the chamber, three shadowy forms stepped out of the darkness to watch them retreating.

"Not too bad for eight-year-olds, but Lilith and Alexander were definitely holding back," the three-eyed shadow of Telos noted.

"Sure, they held back a little, but not the way *you* hold back. Alexander stuck to his strengths, and so did Lilith, while encouraging their teammates to participate to the best of their abilities. I'm shocked you haven't scrounged up a healer to duct-tape to their friend group," Arkaziel's shadow quipped.

"Don't give my darling ideas." Kallos sighed at Arkaziel. "The kids did good. Libby may continue to expose them to dungeons. How much are we supposed to support them? Do we give them weapons? Accessories? Or are opportunities enough?"

"Opportunities, and a few lessons from their parents, should be enough. I'll teach Alexander some of the moves I learned from the Monkey King. Good move with the shadows at the end, Ark. I didn't realize they were perceptive enough to notice us, but thanks to your shadow stirring they only noticed you."

"Yeah, but I still don't get the whole hiding in the shadows thing. Lots of kids have powerful parents. Who's going to threaten them that's stronger than you?" Arkaziel mumbled.

"Dunno." Telos shrugged. The uncertainty left the other two disconcerted for days, especially in the quiet hours of the night.

# CHAPTER 31

# A Gauntlet Thrown Down

**FH 49**

Dragonfly Strike!" I shouted as I teleported. The jolt of teleportation took some getting used to, as everything about your previous position no longer held true. I could, to an extent, control where I appeared. The parameters of the skill required that I appear within striking distance of my target, but it gave me some choice in exactly where I landed. It didn't matter how many times I tried the move, though; it always ended the same. With my hand caught in the sparkling, platinum-mesh-covered hand of Momma. She never squeezed; she stopped my blows with a gentleness that I'd never seen in sparring, but she often cooled her hands down to shock me.

"I can't hit you," I sulked as her third eye stared deep into my soul.

"No, you can't," Momma agreed with a laugh and moved her hand so fast I couldn't see it. Her hand reappeared at her side, and my hair tussled in the wind. I knew how infuriating it was when I did it to other people since she had done it to me for years now, after seeing me do it to Lilith. Lilith would call it karma. I called it inspiration. One day I would be that fast and annoy other people.

"Having an ability alone doesn't mean you'll win every fight, sweetie. Everyone else has abilities, too, and they're working to strengthen their skills the same as you. You got lucky to acquire such a powerful ability from a dungeon, especially for a first ability. Decent range, teleportation, no cooldown, low cost." Telos looked to the clouds, so I followed her gaze.

The clouds roared quickly through the sky today. They always seemed to be faster over the Plateau of the First Home, but it was a lot higher than the city of Winona down on the plain, near the river. We stayed at Uncle Arkaziel's house in town most of the time, but Momma came back a lot to use the forge she'd built here. She always muttered that the one she'd built in town sucked for fine work, but since she mostly used her inner world for forging I don't know why it mattered. I think I caught a glimpse of Uncle Arkaziel flying up in the highest clouds, an immense dragon that blotted out the sun, but then he was gone again.

Nope, the black figure of a world-devouring dragon reappeared in a flash, and then bolts of black lightning descended to explode dirt, and split one of Momma's Adamant Oaks into kindling. When my eyes cleared, a man in a blue shirt covered in pineapples stood there. He was old, with close-cut hair on the sides, and barely longer on the top. All his hair was white. The whites of his eyes were painfully bloodshot, and his veins looked like they were full of black blood that shone through his pale skin. He wore khaki shorts, and sandals, and he exuded more power than anyone I'd ever seen before. He glared balefully at Momma, who had interposed herself between me and the man.

Nothing scared Momma, but her outfit went from something suitable for exercise to what she described as her ass-kicking gear. A long black trench coat fluttered in the wind, and mostly hid me. The simple platinum mesh of her gloves now glittered with inset black and aqua gems, and she radiated power every bit as strong as the scary old guy.

"Who the heck are you?" Telos demanded.

"I'm called . . . Bob," the man croaked painfully. He spit some blood to the side, as if talking caused his mouth to fill with dark fluids, or maybe just existing caused him pain. He looked ill. How could someone that powerful be sick? It didn't make sense.

"What do you want? **Stay back**." The last words came as Momma held up her hand not to Bob, who hadn't moved, but to Mommy, who'd come out of the Spire to see what all the commotion was about. Mommy glared at the intruder, but she didn't take another step closer.

"You're defenseless." Dark black lines of something that didn't exist formed around the man as he spoke. He didn't seem at all afraid of Momma. "So I'm going to kill you now."

The dark, strange glyphs and energies turned into a flock of birds that shot straight at Momma. Blasts of light fired from Momma's third eye, but they didn't block the energies at all. At the very last moment, the power around Momma went so high I thought my head was inflating like a balloon from proximity. Radiant light glittered around the plateau, and in the shadows danced eldritch whispers, and all of creation seemed like it might just be an illusion cast by Momma.

The strange magical bird attack vanished in the blasts of radiance. Momma still stood in front of me, but whatever had happened turned her hair into all the colors, and her clothes, too. She seemed strónger. Omnipotent. Even the old man seemed like a ghostly shadow compared to her now. The old man laughed.

"Not defenseless. Why delay? Your birth changes everything." Bob didn't seem like he would attack again, but he also didn't seem like a good guy.

"I wanted to enjoy a few things first," Telos answered through gritted teeth. Snowflakes danced around her, five of them. Most people might not notice five snowflakes, given everything else going on, but when Momma used ice magic or cold, it was always amazing, so I paid extra attention. "You're interrupting my private time."

"A rite of passage. I did it, Arcanthar did it, and now you do it. But you have not awoken yet; your essence lies undefended. Arcanthar nearly killed me when he came to me, as I come to you. There can be only one multiverse. Once a second awakens, the timer starts. We are poison to each other. You and this reality, all these realities, must die."

The sky blackened, the whole of Mythara shook, and I started to fall into a crack in the earth. Then it was all back to normal, with rainbows in the sky, and Momma glared at this old guy.

"You fully awakened, I see. Then it will be the hard way." Bob laughed, then shivered. He hadn't noticed the five snowflakes land on him. One on each shoulder, one in front of his chest and one on his back, and one on his head. A hand covered my eyes, but I heard him die. When Momma took her hands away, there was no sign of Bob or that anything had gone wrong, but then Mommy ran up and hugged me close.

From the way Momma and Mommy looked at each other, they were talking in their minds, but I felt warmth and love in both of their arms, even if Momma's new clothes were really hard to look at because they were so bright.

That night a full moon shone upon the Spire. The children were in bed, and Kallos and Telos sat on the balcony at the top of the Spire.

"How long do we have left?" Kallos broke the silence.

"Less than ten years. I had to fully activate all three sets of fifty links to stop his attack. A few less might have been enough, but I never imagined there'd be someone stronger than me in 'my' reality. Some of that could have been bravado, maybe, but Alexander was behind me, and I couldn't risk it." Telos let out a pent-up sigh of frustration. "I'm sorry."

Kallos's much warmer hand squeezed Telos's colder hand, and Kallos moved closer to her, sharing her warmth and love both through their bond and physical contact. Telos cuddled against her, accepting and thankful for the comfort.

"You don't need to be sorry. We already knew we'd have limited time, my dear." Kallos didn't beat around the bush and went to the heart of the matter.

"Nebulously, yeah. I thought I had things under control, and we'd get at least another fifty years before I assimilated. But now, not so much. Can you feel it?" Telos looked Kallos in the eyes, trying to discern whether the other woman could feel what awakening had revealed to her.

"Glimpses are all I see. Show me," Kallos insisted, drawing Telos into a soft kiss, before opening her mind and soul to her rainbow-haired partner.

The world became light. Ein Sof spread infinitely. Yet if one zoomed out far enough, Ein Sof flowed in spiral bands from a center point, infinitely outward. The colors and depths varied inconsistently, and in a few places small spikes had emerged. Kallos did not know how, or why, but her mind translated these spikes as being covered in runes that labeled different dimensions. Each axis had phantoms and spread outward and away from the infinite flow of Ein Sof. The farther away it went, the more fragile its reality became, in the lands of Ayin.

*~ That's our multiverse. All of our dimensions, our alternate timelines, our branching destinies, everything that we know to be reality, is there. The prismatic lights are me. See that larger, dark axis? That is Bob. ~*

The axis Telos drew Kallos's attention to was almost twice the size of their own multiverse, yet for all its size it lacked the dense power of the nascent multiverse, and its dark, electric aura warred with Ein Sof itself. Something about Bob, or his multiverse, felt inherently wrong. Although there were no scents, both Telos and Kallos had their mind-noses filled with the musty scent. Telos thought it smelled like burnt matches, while Kallos identified ammonia.

*-What are the other axes? -*

*~Multiverses without a creator, either burgeoning, or fading.~*

*-Why does this Bob not resonate with Ein Sof, or Ayin? Why can't there be peace?-* The sadness in Kallos's thoughts made Telos feel a stab of guilt. If not for her, Kallos would never be aware of a higher order existence, and be at peace to think of Pleroma as the highest existence, a place of peace and oneness to balance the tortured existence of the physical, material worlds.

*~I don't know. I thought Binah held all the answers, but I can't find anything about the River of Light. Maybe Ein Sof itself has another avatar besides me, at the center? Once I kick Bob in the butt, I want to explore that place. You can't get much more 'explore my forbidden depths' than the epicenter of an infinite river of light. What's it come from?~*

*-Life is never dull with you, darling. A decade . . . Well, the children will be adults. Let's make sure to make the time count.-*

Telos felt her shoulders lighten up, and the tension fade. Kallos accepted it better than she had feared, and that made it a bit easier for her to accept these things. Not that acceptance made a difference in their options.

# CHAPTER 32

# Fisticuffs

**FH 49**

O h crap, look out!" Cassius Thorn screamed as a blast of fire veered out of his control.

If I did nothing, it would singe Lilith's hair, and if that happened Cassius would probably die before anyone had a chance to intervene. Multiple prismatic illusions appeared between me and the fireball, then I teleported before the bolt of flames, and my fist went from near my face in an arcing blow to the ground. Dirt and grass flew, and a miniature flash of rainbow exploded when my hand hit the dirt. The fireball got caught in the dramatic downward gust of wind caused by my strike and died against the ground.

When I looked up, I saw Cassius had a sour expression on his face, while Lilith stared at him with something close to contempt. Had he tried to hit my sister? Why someone would have a death wish like that, I don't know.

"Nice moves!" Derrick patted my shoulder. "I barely even moved. You didn't tell me you could target the ground with Dragonfly Strike. That was some fast thinking."

"You should have let it hit me." Lilith huffed at me. "Thanks, though."

"Why would you want it to hit you?" I asked, confused.

"Cassius is a real jerk. If he draws the teacher's attention for attacking another student, even his dad being the mayor won't help him," Aisha grumbled, while she also glared at Cassius.

The young man, a year older than them, trotted over.

"Good block, Metanoia, thanks. It would have been a shame if anyone got burned." Cassius apologized with the sincerity of a practiced liar. He didn't even bother to hide his disappointment as he glared at both my own and Lilith's rainbow hair. Mine had a red-dominant scheme, while Lilith's hair had a lilac-dominated array. Momma's had an aqua base, but all three of us had glowing rainbow hair. It was hard to miss, even without a bully trying to make a big deal about it.

"Yeah, it was nothing. I see why you're practicing out here, though. A fireball that slow won't be much use in a fight, so maybe you should get back to practicing."

I grinned at the slightly larger boy, as his cheeks flushed red, and his hands curled into fists.

"You can't talk that way to me!" Cassius hissed in a quiet, threatening tone.

"You are right. My parents would be very disappointed in me. Good luck practicing your fireball." Unlike Cassius, I knew how to pretend to be nice to someone, and it just made his face turn redder.

"Everything okay over here?" one of the practice yard observers asked. Cassius backed down, but the dolt didn't even bother to hide his glare at me.

"Just peachy," I said with a smile.

"Move along, Thorn," the teacher's assistant barked at Cassius. "Back to work, you lot." We got told to do something constructive, too. Not the most glorious of victories.

Cassius muttered something unintelligible and stalked off.

I wished something bad would happen to him.

He tripped on a rock, fell face-first into the ground, and broke his nose.

**Congratulations, Progenitor of Peril (Emerging) has advanced to Progenitor of Peril (Proficient).**

**New Ability Unlocked: Tides of Woe. New Title Unlocked: Curse Lord (Level 1).**

**Tides of Woe - Like the unceasing tides, woe crashes upon your foes. A random status affliction is applied to the target every twenty seconds with a duration of thirty seconds. Total duration: five minutes.**

**Curse Lord - A master of misfortune and bad luck, you possess the power to bring calamity and despair to your enemies. You walk the line between fate and ruin, wielding the power to twist destinies and bring chaos to those who dare oppose you. Wherever you tread, disaster follows.**

**Title Effects: Calamitous Touch - The Curse Lord's attacks have a chance (20%) to inflict a random affliction on the enemy for five minutes.**

**New Ability Unlocked: Malicious Tormentor**

**Malicious Tormentor - The Curse Lord gains power from the misfortune of their enemies. Every affliction you have active grants you a 2% buff (stacking) to attack and movement speed.**

**Congratulations, Curse Lord.**

Lilith elbowed me lightly in the side. "Stop smirking," she whispered.

Two of the upperclassmen were helping Cassius stand, while he bled and cried. The System communicated with me at a speed that wasn't as tedious as other people.

The observer ran over to help cart Cassius off to the healer.

"Did he trip on the spot where you blocked the fireball?" Derrick questioned, and I nodded.

"He sure did," I agreed with a small laugh.

"So, what was the smile for?" Lilith elbowed me again. I poked her in the side back.

"You did look unnaturally happy," Aisha agreed, giving me a suspicious look.

"One of my traits upgraded, and I got a second ability. I also got a title, and another ability with it. So yeah, I'm happy. Once I hit level ten, I'll have at least four abilities, maybe five, depending on what sort of class I get. Do you think we could find another dungeon around town? You're both close to ten, right?" I eyed Aisha and Derrick hopefully.

"I've been practicing a lot of traps with Aisha's dad. Getting to try them in combat would be nice. Maybe I could even get him to help me prepare a few extra powerful traps to take on a dungeon. He's a softie when it comes to Aisha getting hurt." Derrick attempted to tease Aisha.

Aisha though, with two older siblings, just laughed at him.

"Dad is a huge softie. I'll pressure him, too. We could try to find another dungeon on our free days. I need to get more powerful if I'm going to have a chance of keeping up with you guys. Light magic and support magic are best when I'm with others."

"You unlocked support magic and didn't tell us?" Lilith gave Aisha a flat look.

"Mom bought me a tome from a wandering trader two days ago. I can't believe you two keep getting all these traits and abilities without using tomes. Dad thinks if I can keep up with you two, and be partners with you, I'll be set for life." Aisha shook her head. "He's crazy. I keep telling him you're just going to get us in trouble, Alexander, but he won't listen to me."

"Me? What'd I do? Why not Lilith?" I pointed at her, but her glare made me drop my finger. She was far scarier than Cassius could ever hope to be.

"Lilith fixes the problems you start," Aisha said with a roll of her eyes, and a grunt of agreement from Lilith. I stared bewildered at the two girls, unsure how everything was my fault. They sounded very confident in things being my fault, though, even if I couldn't figure out why or how.

Lilith and I usually cut through a few alleyways between the academy and Uncle Arkaziel's house. Winona wasn't a huge city, but the safety provided by powerful protectors and the relative peace meant people were drawn here.

Fights in town were rare. Even without Arkaziel and Bobbi, there were ordinary people with a decent amount of power, too, and a lot of teens and young adults trying to make a name for themselves. Mommy said other towns didn't have as many transmigrators or reincarnations as Winona, and so weren't great places to visit. We'd never gotten to go to another town, but when a fireball whooshed into a barrel in front of us and sent splinters of wood in the air, I guess that's how I imagined other towns.

"Gotcha, Metanoia!" Cassius shouted with the garbled voice of a boy with a freshly broken nose. Apparently they hadn't found a healer yet, since his face was bandaged. Two of his burly classmate friends blocked the far end of the alley, and Cassius Thorn and his best friend Chadwick were behind us.

"How'd you get me? You blew up a barrel," I asked in confusion. Not even a sliver had hit me or Lilith, against the odds.

"Maybe he got a concussion with the broken nose?" Lilith asked with a great, but feigned, depth of concern.

"Shut up! Just shut up! You two always have to have the last word and make me feel bad. Well, I'm going to make you feel bad." Cassius raised both of his hands and formed an actual combat fireball.

I activated Tides of Woe on him.

"I can't see!" Cassius cried in shock as blindness afflicted him.

A sharp, crisp snap rocked the alleyway. Lilith had snapped her thumb and middle finger, and the fireball forming in the blinded kid's hands vanished. I wanted to ask Lilith when she'd gotten a counterspell, but I hadn't told her about my new abilities yet. Did she get hers today, too?

The two kids who'd blocked the head of the alley ran away in the confusion caused by their leader getting blinded, and his spell failing so spectacularly.

Chadwick's face took on an expression of panic. Clearly they'd done this kind of thing before, and it hadn't gone at all like this. We'd have to ask around to find out how many people he'd done this to before. I knew he was a brat, but I didn't know he was this violent.

"You'd better fix this! Don't you know who his dad is?" Chadwick postured.

"Let's see. Mr. Thorn is the nice man who comes for tea at Uncle Arkaziel's, right? He's also been begging our mother to craft the town more defenses, and keeps asking Aunt Bobbi to cater even one of his social affairs. That's the Mr. Thorn you're talking about, right?" Lilith asked with a smile.

"We don't need anything crafted by one of your freaky moms!" Cassius hissed, then cheered as his blindness vanished. He immediately focused on conjuring another fireball, but the flames weren't cooperating, and were a fraction of their normal strength.

"Oh, so that's what enfeebled looks like." Lilith laughed. "Uhm, Alexander? Did you use an ability that could cause *any* affliction? Doom could kill him, you know."

I winced. I hadn't thought of Doom, or Impending Death, or any of those variants. Why would a low level like me have access to them? But when I checked my ability description, it didn't list any limitations.

"Take it off, take it off! I don't wanna die!" Cassius pleaded, even as I dismissed the Tides of Woe on him.

"It's gone, but if you mess with us or anyone else again, I won't take it off," I bluffed.

Cassius ran away, and Chadwick went with him, but the glare in the latter's eyes made me uncomfortable. I didn't even curse him!

"We're going to have to tell someone about this, you know," Lilith said with a disgruntled sigh. Then she dusted her hands off and started to walk our normal path. I fell into step with her after a moment of watching the departing backs of Cassius and Chadwick.

"Do we? I think it's handled." I shrugged. "When did you get a counterspell?"

"Today. At the same time as you got your new ability. My Patron of Providence trait upgraded when you blocked that fireball in the practice yard."

"That's fantastic. We'll be even more prepared for another dungeon than the last one." I clapped my hands together excitedly, but Lilith rolled her eyes at me and scoffed.

"Think about it, Alexander. We need to hide how strong we are. Already Derrick and Aisha think we're too strong for them, and it won't be long before news of your ability to afflict people spreads. Do you want that kind of attention?"

"Uhm, yeah? Why wouldn't I? We're awesome, and people should know that."

"You told me Mommy is the most powerful person you've ever seen, but most people don't even know she's anything but a blacksmith. Shouldn't we follow her lead?" Lilith gave me a long, searching look.

"That doesn't sound like fun?" I answered honestly, and she muttered about how hopeless I was.

"We can talk to our moms about it if you want, but I think everything's going just fine." I didn't want to argue. Arguing with Lilith didn't lead anywhere, and it was so boring to rehash the same thing over and over again. Why couldn't she be like the other kids our age?

"We'll talk to them about it, and about getting permission to find another dungeon. Or did you forget that we got grounded for two weeks for going into the last one without telling anyone?"

"Yeah, sure. You do the talking, then. After I've had my practice session with Momma. All those moves she learned from that Monkey King are super awesome, and now that I've got a passive that generates afflictions, I might be able to hit Momma while she's stunned."

"Idiot, it's not going to work." Lilith sounded exasperated, like I'd forgotten something very important.

"Why not?" I didn't see why it wouldn't work.

"Momma's scarf blocks all afflictions." Lilith didn't restrain her scorn for me forgetting something so important. It's not like I cared about afflictions before today, though? Did she really remember everything everyone told her about their equipment and abilities, all the time?

"Oh man, that's so overpowered."

Lilith kicked me in the shin, then skipped ahead.

# CHAPTER 33

# The Tower of Toys

To the north of Winona lay a forest. Mommy, Momma, Bobbi, Aisha's parents, and Uncle Arkaziel were taking the day to enjoy a picnic. Meanwhile, Lilith, Aisha, Derrick, and I explored the woods. As a compromise to get to adventure, one of Arkaziel's clones hid in each of our shadows. It took the sense of danger out of everything, but he said he'd only intervene if things went badly. Unlike Momma, he wasn't so overprotective, so he'd probably let us fight on our own.

"I can't believe he tried to jump you." Aisha cursed Cassius under her breath. Lilith had been telling the story of the encounter, while I led the way into the woods. We each had a walking stick, but I ended up being the one in the front breaking branches out of our way with a rapidly dulling lopper.

"Any ideas on what we should be looking for, Lilith?" I called back while it took me a few strikes to lop a particularly thick, thorn-covered branch.

"Trust your instincts. You're the Master of Disaster, the King of Catastrophe, the Baron of Bedlam, the Hero of Havoc, the Wizard of Woe." She didn't have to sound so happy while she listed a litany of fake titles that made me sound like an evil demon, did she?

"Wait, your grand plan was just to follow me to trouble?" I turned around and stared at her and the other two.

Lilith smiled, Aisha nodded as if it made perfect sense, and Derrick seemed slightly dubious, before he made an apologetic smile and nodded to Lilith.

"It makes sense, sorry." Derrick tried to console me, but I just spun around and hacked at the brush. Oh, I'd find them trouble. So much trouble we'd all become amazing level tens, and get our classes. That would show them! Wait, no . . . that would prove them right.

"Stop sulking, oh Progenitor of Peril," Lilith teased me. In the brief moment while I saw red, I tripped over a branch and fell down a steep incline hidden by brush. I quickly got control of myself by using Dragonfly Strike to teleport to the flat ground at the bottom of the hill.

"First steps are pretty rough!" I called up, even before the other three reacted to my fall and cried my name. At least they might feel guilty for poking fun at me now.

All three peered through the brush and down the steep drop to where I stood.

"What's that next to you?" Derrick asked.

"Uhm . . ." I looked down. Next to the base of the tree was a toy tower. It looked very fake, but something about it made my skin crawl. "Looks like a kid's toy! Come on down and give it a loo—"

I poked the toy. The world went dark around me.

**You have entered a Dungeon. Welcome to the Tower of Toys. Difficulty Level: 9.**

I stood on a four meter by four meter platform that was elevated about a meter above the floor of this strange place. Half of the platform I stood on boxed outward, but the walls behind it were a strange crackling energy instead of real walls. Maybe that was the exit? Before me, a room full of conveyor belts, strange metallic arms, spinning gears, and half-finished toys processed through the stages of construction.

"What the heck?" I muttered, and tried to figure out what my next action should be. Were Lilith and the others going to join me? Was I trapped here alone? Should I wait a minute or two before I leave the platform and explore the room? Steam spilled out of pipes all around the room, but especially on the open floors. The conveyor belts had the machinery, but seemed like they might be safer than the ground.

A faint shimmer of light separated me from the rest of the room. I touched it with my finger, to hear a message in my head from the System.

**You must gather your party before venturing forth.**

I sighed. If there was anything worse than waiting, it was the idea that I was missing out on something. Why did the System sound smug about that line? Usually the System, or as Momma called her, Libby, was monotone, or only slightly emotional. She didn't taunt you. Somehow, this was Momma's doing.

"What the what?" Derrick mumbled as he materialized on the platform, along with Aisha and Lilith. All three looked surprised.

"You fell down a hill into a dungeon? Really?" Aisha sounded strangely jealous. I feel like she was glossing over falling down a hill in favor of finding a dungeon a little too quickly.

"Shh," I whispered, as the barrier that separated us from the room vanished. When it did, there were aspects to the room I couldn't see before. Toy soldiers marched up and down the sides of the conveyor belts, and the random geysers of steam from the brassworks made the floor of the room extremely dangerous. The far side of the room had two doors.

"The far end of the room seems like the obvious destination. Each conveyor belt has some controls along the way; I bet if we disable some of the machines it will stop making toys," Lilith whispered while she surveyed the room.

"We don't know the toys are enemies," Aisha pointed out.

"Maybe not, but they do all have weapons," Derrick countered with a grimace. He pulled out a short sword and shield from his inventory, which got Aisha to pull out a staff. Lilith drew a crystalline staff Mommy made her. Aisha and Derrick looked at me expectantly.

"I don't use weapons." I tried to say it playfully, but I think it came out more like I was scoffing at their weapons, because Lilith rolled her eyes at me, Derrick looked hurt, and Aisha just looked disappointed in me. Why was she always disappointed in me? I thought disappointment was an adults-only emotion.

"Do you think the steam blasts would destroy the wood toys?" Derrick asked Lilith.

"If they've already been injured, I think so. This is a dungeon of our own level, so it should be challenging, but passable. We might not be able to retrieve any treasures they drop if we have to do that, so let's keep that as a last resort. Alexander, why don't you hit that closest toy soldier with Tides of Woe. Aisha and I will hit it with ranged attacks, and you and Derrick will finish it off if it reaches us."

"And if it brings friends?"

"Then I'll improvise." Lilith's confidence bolstered my spirits, so I glared at the first toy soldier and activated Tides of Woe upon it. I half expected that it wouldn't work because it wasn't alive, or because it was a toy. Instead, flames burst to life all over its exterior, and the soldier cried in panic.

"I'm on fire! Oh, god, it burns! It hurts so bad!" The high-pitched, childlike voice screamed in pain and terror, while the soldier spun in circles.

"Wow, that's . . ." The soldier burned to ashes before the fire affliction wore off, and the soldier never made it to them. ". . . that's hard to watch." I winced.

"The next one," Lilith demanded, and I obliged.

Tides of Woe crashed into the next wooden soldier. The oak-colored wooden skin of the toy split into horrific wounds, and sap flowed out as it cried out in aguish. It, and the next soldier down, saw our group immediately and ran alongside the conveyor belts to get to us.

"Did you just land a bleed effect on a wooden toy?" Lilith mused in deep interest, before she lifted her staff. Light danced along the crystalline staff and coalesced into the tip, where a bolt of power shot toward the non-bleeding enemy.

"You don't get out of the fun either!" I cried to the second soldier, and unleashed Tides of Woe again. A cloud of gray energy swept around the second soldier, its speed cut in half as weakness afflicted it.

A ball of light flew from Aisha's staff to finish off the first soldier, and it fell over, incapable of moving. The gaping wounds leaking sap stopped.

"This feels slightly wrong, doesn't it?" Derrick asked me in a quiet voice, not wanting Lilith to hear. I nodded. The poor toys were getting obliterated, but at the end of the conveyor belt, a wooden soldier and a clockwork mouse emerged.

"Here, you finish this one," I told Derrick as I darted past the weakened soldier, lightly tapping it on the back to send it off-balance toward him. I thought because the wood soldiers walked along the conveyor belts it would be safe for me to do so, but I heard multiple clicks behind me, and although I was gone before they went off, the platforms showed that the segments were actually detached and could fling someone across the room.

The sounds of a short sword against wood, Derrick cursing at the ineffectiveness of a sword against hard wood, and then the magic detonations from the girls played in the back of my mind while I fiddled with the controls for the first conveyor belt. I figured it out pretty quickly, but the belt didn't shut down immediately. It finished the last piece on it before it ground to a halt. The other three had stopped the weakened soldier by then.

"Behind you!" Aisha shouted to me, at the same time I heard a clicking and whizzing sound. One of the clockwork mice had snuck across the steam-shrouded floor and hopped up onto the far side of the conveyor belt, and leaped at me with a mouth full of pointed teeth and sharp claws outstretched. I narrowly dodged the mechanical rodent, and slammed my elbow into its back. I wasn't as strong as Lilith, but I was strong enough to knock around tiny clockwork mice with ease. A few cogs went flying, and I stomped my boots down on the mouse repeatedly until it quit making ticking sounds.

"Incoming!" Aisha and Lilith shouted, before bolts of light and force each hit another mouse crossing the steam-covered floor. Derrick rushed down the conveyor belt to meet me, and pointed to where the soldiers on the next belt were waiting for us to cross over.

Derrick put his sword away and pulled out a slingshot. When I looked confused he looked embarrassed. "Aisha's dad says once you get alchemical clay balls with effects on them, it's a great weapon for a trapmaster, and nothing seems to be reaching me."

"Right, right . . ." I nodded, before we all moved to switch belts. The assembly room wasn't hard. The toy soldiers and clockwork mice weren't terrifying foes. They went down easily and didn't have any ranged attacks. A few minutes later we deactivated the last belt and made it to the doors. I opened the left one first. It was a big storage room, full of boxes.

"Maybe there's some treasure in all of the boxes?" Aisha inquired. "I don't have any spells that would get more than one or two."

"I could open them," Derrick offered. When no one told him no, he crept into the room and placed a black clay ball against the boxes, fiddled with it, then ran toward us. Three of the boxes exploded on their own, and vicious raccoon-sized teddy bears landed on Derrick and attempted to grapple him.

"Stuffed bears?" Aisha and Lilith asked in unison.

"Help! I'm being mauled by bears!" Derrick struggled to get farther away from the boxes, but then his bomb went off. Fragments of wood, clay, fabric, and other debris filled the room. I darted in before the dust had cleared, activating Tides of Woe on one bear, while I grabbed another one and tried to throw it off Derrick. Instead, I ripped the fabric off its back. Stuffing spilled everywhere. The doll twitched strangely, then stopped moving.

The girls didn't cast any spells. Derrick and I finished off the attack teddy bears, then took stock of the room. Lots of teddy bears had been destroyed in the bomb, but there was no way to know if they'd been actual teddy bears or monsters to start with.

"The other room has to have better stuff," Lilith harrumphed in disgust at the utter lack of treasure. Derrick's cheeks were red, despite no one blaming him for any possible loot having been blown up.

I cracked the other door, and unfortunately, it didn't have any enemies.

# CHAPTER 34

# Land O'Candy

"Can you even call this a puzzle?" Aisha asked with scorn.

The second room had a big, locked door on the back wall, and a massive pile of colored wooden blocks. The blocks were all painted green, red, or yellow, and three white boxes had been painted on the floor. It didn't take Lilith long to figure out we just had to sort them by color.

"I feel . . . insulted?" Derrick mumbled under his breath while we lugged the colors into their separate piles.

"Toys are the theme for this dungeon. Be graceful, and give the System the benefit of the doubt that it is sticking to the theme, instead of insulting us." Lilith wasn't even being sarcastic, but genuine. I wondered if she was trying to suck up to the System, and would it or could it work? If it did work, I wanted to get in on it.

"Even if it's an easy puzzle, it still took us at least ten minutes to move and restack everything. That's longer than all the fights against the toys in the first room took combined!" I must have been a shade too enthusiastic; I got a suspicious look from Lilith.

"Last one," Aisha chimed in when she placed the green cube on the green pile.

A deep rumbling shook the ground, and the heavy doors opened to reveal stairs going up. The stairs wound around the walls with a subtle curve, and at the top of the stairs sat a door beneath a large arch made from enlarged wooden blocks, with a sign above the blocks that said in large, simple letters, Playroom. Even though the letters were simple, they were in vivid pastel colors that caught the eye.

"Dad thinks all the weird things in dungeons are real places the System observed in lower dimensions," Aisha said without really thinking about it, distracted from her study of the cute blocks with the same thoughtful look I'd been giving them.

"Is that why people suddenly keep coming to my mom to try to learn about their past lives?" Derrick seemed confused as to why anyone would want to talk to his mother. She was a seer and alchemist both, with enough of a gift with alchemy that even Mommy visited her shop.

"What are the odds that you awaken a memory even slightly useful to you in that scenario? Mommy showed me the multiverse once. For all practical purposes, it has infinite dimensions. Awakening past-life memories seems unlikely to ever prove relevant to your current life, but more knowledge is always better," Lilith mused to herself. I didn't dwell on the idea. The now was far more interesting than the then, but if the then could unlock awesome powers, maybe it wouldn't be so boring?

"If it has even a small chance to give me a head start on a good class, unlocking a trait, or powerful ability, it's worth it I think," Aisha said.

I walked up to the gate and peered into the Playroom.

Beyond the arch were netted walls and a pit full of hundreds of vibrantly colored balls. Pastel-colored blocks made up the walls of the ball pit below the surface level, while the netting lay over pink walls. The ball pit stretched on like a long hallway for a good twenty meters, beyond which I could only make out a big room with a checkered floor. It was far enough I couldn't just activate Dragonfly Strike and teleport past the obstacle.

"This looks fun." I laughed and jumped into the ball pit. The balls were softer than I expected, and while I sank some, I didn't go far enough down to find a bottom of the ball pit.

"That's almost certainly a trap." Lilith scoffed at me.

Derrick and Aisha watched me with the same intent look Lilith did, as if they, too, were waiting for me to writhe in pain or be attacked by something. That's when I noticed the balls of the pit shifting slightly, as if something were slithering toward me in the pit. I couldn't see an enemy, and if I couldn't at least sense them, I couldn't target them.

"Ow, yeesh!" I cried out when something bit my shin. The pain wasn't bad, and I don't think I was bleeding. It was more annoying than anything, but it stung a little. The ball pit started writhing, and I could tell more things were coming for me. "I'm getting bit!"

"Crown of Thorns!" Aisha activated one of her support spells. A thorny halo appeared above my head, and the bites stopped coming. Instead there came hisses and pained noises from the creatures attacking me, when their attacks hit themselves instead.

"That's an awesome spell, Aisha!" Now that I was protected, I dove into the balls to search for my enemies. It turned out to be some of the balls themselves. The first creature I pulled up was made from six balls linked together, with a dragon's face molded into the first ball. It was weak enough I crushed it barehanded.

"I never thought I'd see the legendary ball dragons," Derrick quipped.

"Really? Are they rare?" Aisha missed his sarcasm.

"Maybe? I was making fun of them." Derrick frowned.

"Let me handle this." Lilith raised her staff and circled it through the air. "Locust Swarm!"

A swarm of darkness exploded from the tip of Lilith's crystal staff and flew into the ball pit. Some came very close to me. The insects were creepy looking, like malevolent grasshoppers, and the ball pile writhed like a mass of ants as the locusts and ball dragons fought each other. I took the opportunity to swim across the ball pit and hop up onto the ledge.

"Better swim across while they're occupied," I called to the other three.

"How deep was it?" Derrick called to me.

"I don't know?" I smiled helpfully.

"Just go," Aisha muttered and pushed Derrick, who managed to get his footing and leap off the edge at the last minute, and just before his boots hit the balls, he leaped again off nothing, before swan diving into the balls over ten meters short of the end, where I stood.

Aisha took a running jump, but she didn't even make it as far as Derrick and his double jump did. Lilith, on the other hand, gestured, and the swarm of locusts formed a platform that she rode across the pit, like some kind of awful insect queen.

"That's so creepy." I reminded Lilith of my dislike of her insect servants.

"What unholy abomination is this supposed to be?" Lilith ignored my complaints, and pointed at the checkered-floor room. While we watched, the room pulsed and rearranged itself. The black and white tile floors changed into a splash of bright pink, accented by fluffy white clouds and lollipops. The entry before us now said "Welcome to the Land of Candy," while the far wall had an Exit sign. The room had transformed to become a curved path of colorful blocks, that led from the entrance to the exit. Dog-sized pairs of dice lay in piles, but they had eyes that watched us.

What followed made me question how serious the System took kids. The six-sided dice would roll at us on our turn, and we would move however many squares ahead the dice landed on after we hit them. Destroying the dice with a hit was treated like rolling a six, which I found out when one of my punches triggered Imminent Doom as an affliction. No one else managed to kill one of the dice, despite going out of their way to try.

On some squares we won sweets that gave small temporary bonuses to our attributes. Other squares sent us back to the start or gave us a vegetable that we had to eat. Since I was the only one who didn't like vegetables, it really wasn't much of a punishment for the other three. Maybe it was karma for me killing one of the dice? Did the System care about petty things like that? I hoped not.

Lilith won. For a game with probability involved, it didn't surprise me. She had the good luck, and I had the eventful luck. Derrick and Aisha both reached the end of the land of candy before me. For winning, Lilith got a candy bar that improved all of her attributes by one. Derrick, in second, got a choice of candy to increase one attribute, and Aisha got a basket of temporary boost candies. I got a basket full of broccoli.

I nearly threw it against the wall, before the item information came up, at which point I feel like I got the best prize. Well, second best prize.

**Item: Never-Ending Basket of Broccoli**

**Health Boost: Eating a broccoli floret restores 5% of maximum health over ten seconds.**

**Stamina Regeneration: Consuming broccoli increases stamina regeneration by 10% over 30 minutes.**

**Detoxifying: Broccoli has a natural detoxifying effect, curing minor poisons and disease.**

**Comedic Relief: Carrying the basket full of broccoli is adorable. +??????**

I popped a floret into my mouth and chewed. The taste wasn't any better, but knowing I'd get buffs made it more tolerable. A lot more tolerable.

Lilith stared at me while I chewed, to the point I nearly choked, she looked so intent. Aisha and Derrick also looked at me suspiciously.

"Want some broccoli?" I offered.

"No, I'm good." Derrick waved it off, but the girls each took a piece and nibbled at it suspiciously. Aisha's and Lilith's eyes both widened as they felt the warmth flow through their stomachs and the stamina and health effects topping up their health and energy.

"Every half hour is minorly inconvenient, but an acceptable hindrance. Derrick, eat some. It gives buffs," Lilith commanded, and Derrick ate a piece of vegetable rather than argue.

"Onward!" I filled the silence with an exuberant cheer, and pushed the exit from the game room open, to reveal a room full of train tracks, and a small train. A steam whistle blew.

The room was a pain in the butt. We had to climb onto the train, and then make our way from the passenger car toward the locomotive at the front. Along the way, jack-in-the-boxes sprang out of cleverly hidden wooden panels to attack us with knives, while stuffed bears wearing bandit masks with slingshots would jump in through windows from the roof. None of the enemies were difficult to defeat, and thanks to me being in front no one got stabbed by a jack-in-the-box. The slingshots from the bears left welts, but the harm they did felt more psychological in nature than physical. I only got hit by one slingshot, Aisha got hit by six, Derrick by five, and Lilith by two. Aisha didn't seem to notice that Lilith hid behind her.

Once we hit the big red button in the locomotive, the train stopped itself at the station on its next pass. A teddy bear with a golden star on its vest and a slingshot on its belt, who spoke in a weird accent, waited for us.

"Why I reckon you four are mighty heroes, and Nice and Friendly Corners owes you a great heaping, hopping bunch of thanks. We'd offer you hospitality, but those dastardly bandits done burned our town to the ground," the sheriff explained.

Lilith, unamused, saw no sign of a town. She looked around repeatedly, but there was just the train track.

"What started the problem with the bandits?" Derrick asked.

"Well now, ya see, the Grand Toymaker gets a little bored sometimes. When that happens, he makes us all play out his scenarios. Since you ain't toys, you don't have to play by his rules the way the rest of us do."

"Where's this jerk at?" Aisha asked indignantly.

"The Grand Toymaker is in the Toymaker's Palace, right through that there portal. He doesn't take kindly to strangers trespassing, so you'd better go prepared."

"I'm prepared to kick his ass," Aisha hissed, with magic popping and exploding in little fizzles from the end of her staff.

"Let's do this." I jumped through the portal first. "Oh, that's gaudy!"

# CHAPTER 35

# Palace of the Toymaker

The Royal Palace of the Grand Toymaker was kind of a letdown. First, most of it was just a picture drawn on walls, with another set of letter blocks that spelled Toymaker's Palace in an arch. When we traveled through the portal and then the tunnel, we found ourselves in a long room with the walls filled with paintings of all the types of toys we'd come across, and some we hadn't, along the way.

The portraits included clockwork mice, teddy bears, toy soldiers, living dice, toy dragons, toy knights, and marionettes. Halfway down the long hall, the last two portraits opened on concealed hinges, and seven knights filed out to form a line between us and the door at the far end of the room.

"Halt! None may see the Grand Toymaker!" the toy knight painted in green called out in a grave voice.

"Halt! The Grand Toymaker will see no one!" the toy knight painted in blue called out.

We didn't stop our walk down the hallway.

"This is your last warning. Turn back, or face justice for our fallen brethren!" the toy knight painted yellow called out, but he sounded eager to thrash us.

"Let's just kill them!" the knight painted black cried and charged with his sword.

I activated Tides of Woe upon him, and transparent stars danced above the head of the black knight as he suddenly turned around and swung his sword at a knight painted in pink. Unprepared for such immediate violence, the pink knight's helmet tumbled across the floor at the textbook beheading.

"Confusion? I like it," Derrick muttered and threw two objects across the floor. When they stopped between us and the knights, I heard a soft click. The yellow, red, blue, and green knights all circled around the black knight and charged us, while a knight painted in purple closed in to hold the attention of the black knight with his big purple tower shield.

The yellow knight stepped on one of Derrick's traps, and a pillar of fire shot up, catching the unlucky toy ablaze. It screamed and flailed, but the observant green knight kicked the fumbling yellow knight to fall over the other trap, and set off another blaze. The yellow knight smoldered on the ground after the second blaze trap died down.

Green dashed in to swing a two-handed mace at Derrick, who didn't even try to block it and instead rolled out of the way. He left a parting gift behind, and the green knight got caught in another pillar of fire.

I met the blue knight and his axe head-on. He was slow enough for me to easily dodge his attacks, and I just rained a series of light blows upon him until roots reached up from the floor and locked him in place. It was only a twenty percent chance to activate afflictions with hits, but when I threw ten punches in rapid succession, uncaring whether they did real damage, just that they hit, those odds were greatly in my favor.

I rolled out of the way to catch the red knight off guard, and kicked his knee joint from the side before I rolled out of reach of his counterattack.

A deluge of light daggers turned the blue knight into a pincushion, before a force spell detonated each of the light daggers in powerful blasts.

"Nice combo!" I hollered to Lilith and Aisha, and focused on dodging the much faster attacks of the short-sword-wielding red knight.

Derrick hadn't re-engaged with the green knight, and instead threw a weirdly shaped throwing knife into the still burning toy. The flames flared, and it smelled like an oil fire. I wanted to know how that worked, but the red knight kept swinging his sword at me, and I had to keep dodging. I triggered Dragonfly Strike to land a blow into his back and throw him off-balance, and cast Tides of Woe too.

The red knight suddenly looked different, as if he had contracted a horrible disease. His wooden body, under the metallic paint, began to slowly rot, but he still tried to slice me. I focused on dodging, and my patience was rewarded when two bolts of raw magic struck the red knight. Aisha and Lilith, seeing the utter devastation their combo had caused the blue knight, opted to cast basic magic blasts with their staves instead. It was more efficient, and the blasts were enough to finish off the red knight.

Another trap detonated, this time catching both the black and purple knights. It didn't finish either one off, but combined with the damage they had done to one another already, it had been very close. I teleported in, and finished off the black knight with a blow to the back of the head. The wood the knights were made from was quite solid, and my palm stung a little, but it killed the black knight.

The purple knight held his ground, or attempted to, but I teleported behind him and struck him forward, and Derrick jumped in while he was off-balance and stabbed his wind-enchanted sword through the purple knight's chest.

"That was a good showing," I praised everyone. I wanted to rub my hand, but didn't, or Lilith would bring up how unpractical it was to fight barehanded, but Momma did it, so why couldn't I? I just needed to toughen up my hands, or get some protective gloves.

"Oh, hey. These knights all dropped gold coins!" Aisha cheered, and when she looted them, we all got our loot as well. One of the many advantages of the System.

"Oh man, this is way more than my allowance. I might actually be able to afford some better traps!" Derrick practically jumped for joy at the seventy gold.

"Gold only drops from level ten on," Lilith said with a grin.

"We're so going to level up after we take down this Toymaker!" Aisha cried as she understood Lilith's implication.

"Everyone ready?" I didn't want to waste our momentum.

As soon as everyone chimed in with a yes, I strode up the steps to throw open the door to the throne room. The room went a solid forty meters deep, and twenty meters wide. Whole legions of toy knights and soldiers stood inert behind red velvet ropes at the far sides of the room, and upon a throne sat a man with six arms, a crown, and a monocle.

"Ye'll never have me kingdom! Fight! Fight, me boys!" the Toymaker cried madly at the inert toys. Four of his hands suddenly held marionette jigs, but there was no marionette at the end of them. Two knights and two soldiers vaulted over the red velvet ropes, and it was impossible to not notice these versions of the knights and soldiers were about double the size of their previous versions, or were adult human sized.

The Toymaker's other two hands remained empty, but each finger of the empty hands was decorated with a number of flashy rings that seemed very suspicious to me.

"Derrick, put pressure on the boss," Lilith commanded.

I dropped Tides of Woe on the first knight, and it turned to stone while vaulting over the red rope. When it landed, it shattered into a lot of pieces. I activated Dragonfly Strike to appear behind the other one, and hit it down into the ground, then flipped off its shoulder to slide and make a sharp turn.

Lilith pointed at me and Derrick, and with a victorious smirk shouted, "Divine Providence!"

Powerful light glowed around both of us, and I could feel my strength and speed get buffed. In the fading light of the buff, Aisha cast Light Bind on the two soldiers. A snake of light flew across the room to wrap around the first limb it could grab of each soldier. The left one got an arm bound, while the right got a leg bound, and it forced them to stumble to the ground in a pile.

A small black ceramic sphere that sizzled bounced into the pile of two enemies, before it blew up. The bomb didn't kill the soldiers, but it did cost each of them an arm, and delayed them getting to their feet, even while Derrick and his wind-blade closed in on the boss.

I cast Tides of Woe on the boss. Ice cascaded from his feet over his body, and gusts of cold filled the room.

"He's frozen! Slowed movement and attacks!" I didn't know how good Aisha or Derrick were with reading battlefield status debuffs. I circled the last knight, dodging and hitting between its attacks, then hit it with Tides of Woe, and its eyes filled with stars.

"Attack your boss," I commanded it, and it tottered to attack its slowed-down boss, who had just lost an arm to Derrick's wind-blade.

"Incoming spell!" Aisha cried.

Blue butterflies, made entirely of energy, formed out of thin air around the Toymaker. One by one, each butterfly that materialized dive-bombed the boss, and left charred, blackened flesh and armor where they struck him, and the final butterfly landed a stun on the boss. The short-lived stun allowed Lilith's spell to strike. A swarm of multihued locusts flew down upon the boss like an awful hailstorm, pounding it again and again for five seconds. When the spell ended, the locusts vanished, and revealed a very haggard boss.

"Hee-ya!" Derrick stabbed the boss in the gut, and then I appeared from behind and punched it in the back of the head as hard as I could.

My eyes filled with glitter and confetti.

**Dungeon Complete!**

**Congratulations on reaching level ten! You have gained +2 to Agility, +1 to Vitality, +1 to Will. You may now choose a class from the following choices.**

I expected a list of four or five options, maybe ten at most. Instead, screen after screen after screen of choices appeared before me. Some had no relevance to me, such as Agile Alchemist, while others were close, such as Blight Sprinter, but not really what I was looking for in a class. I would've asked Lilith for help, but when I looked around, I noticed that time had frozen once I pulled up the selection menu.

Crap.

Every class had its own gimmick, too. Some were simple, like building up a stacking buff, while others required balancing competing resources, and some were just absurd, like the music-based ones. I'd never really been into music, so I don't know how I even got those.

"Hey, Libby, can you rearrange the list in terms of matching my personality instead of alphabetically?" Momma called the System Libby, so I did the same.

**Done.**

Holy crap! Libby did what I asked!

The first choice was a class called Kaleidoscope Kineticist, the second was called Speed Demon, and the third was Flash Reaper. I chose Kaleidoscope Kineticist after I read through it and the top five.

**Class: Kaleidoscope Kineticist**

**Class Feature: Chromatic Kinesis, Rainbow Rush**

**Chromatic Kinesis: Manipulate Energy and Matter in a Spectrum of colors representing different forces. Color correlations are as follows.**

**Red = Heat, Orange = Kinetic, Yellow = Light, Green = Life, Blue = Cold, Indigo = Gravity, Violet = Void, Pink = Psychic, White = Purity, Black = Shadow,**

Cyan = Water, Magenta = Mystical, Turquoise = Wind, Amber = Earth, Gold = Electric, Silver = Magnetism.

Rainbow Rush: Double your speed, leaving a colorful trail of energy behind you with effects based on your active kinesis.

Class Ability: Chromatic Pulse

Aurora Burst: Unleash a nova of color; enemies caught in the nova gain a random status ailment; allies caught in the nova have a status ailment removed, or gain a random buff if no ailments are present.

Class Trait: Spectrum Surge

Spectrum Surge: Every time you utilize a kinesis you generate a stack of Spectrum Surge, which grants a 5% increase in movement speed and attack power. Each stack lasts 30 seconds.

"I am the most awesome person to ever live," I cried out with joy as power blossomed inside of me and expanded outward, engulfing me in a brilliant rainbow.

# CHAPTER 36

# Class Up

Time seemed to remain frozen, with Lilith and the others unmoving. I could still interact with the System, and move around the room in which we'd fought the boss, but I couldn't leave it. I decided to poke the remains of the boss.

**Loot distributed. You have gained: Spectrum Goggles.**

**Spectrum Goggles: These colorful lenses protect your eyes against blindness, glare, liquids, gasses, or objects, and other physical threats in addition to forces caused by rapid movement.**

They were predominantly red in color, and I put them on while I waited. They were exceptionally comfortable, and I didn't even notice I was wearing them after a minute. Which of course, meant they were magical. Perfect fit and comfort were hallmarks of magical gear.

"You finished before me?" Lilith asked in surprise when she saw me poking the body of the Toymaker with my boot.

"Yeah, once I realized I could sort the class list by affinity, it wasn't that hard of a choice at all. Maybe that's the real test, knowing to sort by what you're most interested in?" Everything had a hidden meaning behind it, right?

"I'm surprised you thought ahead to do that. Yes, that would have made your decision much easier. We can wait to show each other our new shinies when Derrick and Aisha are finished."

It took the other two a long time to finish their class selections. Lilith and I spent hours playing checkers, and she won every game. She always wins every game. Even the times I've tried to bend bad luck against her, she still wins. It felt like practicing martial arts against Momma—every move contained a lesson that I might not have been smart enough to learn without explicit explanation, and Lilith didn't provide those. She just smirked at me as she beat me, again and again.

Derrick started moving first, and then Aisha came to not long after.

"So, we're all classed! Awesome job, team. Let's share what we got!" I was excited to talk about it, but the other three all shook their heads at me.

"Let's go back to the picnic and do it there," Aisha said. Apparently the other three wanted to get out of the dungeon, since the Toymaker had been flesh and blood, and the body creeped everyone but me out. Leaving a finished dungeon was easy. You just had to pull up the dungeon menu and click Exit.

The walk back to camp felt like an eternity. I wanted to run ahead, but we stuck together at Lilith's insistence, in case we ran into any monsters along the way. We had to dispatch a few forest spiders, a constricting snake, and a two-foot-long millipede along the way. Nothing truly awful, but everyone else was afraid to even touch the millipede. It had a lot of legs, so what?

"We're back! Did you miss us?" I shouted when we broke through the edge of the woods to the campsite.

Mommy and Aisha's mother were talking to one another, seated near the fire, while Momma and Aisha's dad were on the other side of the fire sketching shapes and figures in the dirt with sticks. Arkaziel and Bobbi were bickering over a tray of cheese and meat.

"Welcome back, everyone. I see you found your adventure. Tell us everything, dear." Mommy, with her golden eyes and wind-tousled hair, looked like a powerful goddess. The halo and chain wings really helped with that, I suppose, but she stood apart from all the other people in Winona even more than Momma did.

"You got classes!" Momma shouted, hopping over the tables in a blur to hug me and Lilith. She moved so fast I barely registered it as movement instead of a teleport. Even at level ten, with a class, I could barely comprehend how fast Telos was.

Aisha's mom had dark skin and purple hair, while her father had dark skin with black hair. His coloration was closer to Arkaziel's than to Aisha's mom. Aisha's mother, Nadia, and father, Idris, had very different reactions to the news that Momma blurted out. Idris nodded to Derrick, his trap pupil, and they fist-bumped, while Nadia jump-hugged Aisha and didn't let go for an even longer time than Momma hugged me and Lilith, until Mommy joined the hug and trapped me even more.

"Alright, alright, that's enough fawning," Lilith scolded our mothers after a few minutes flew by. I agreed. There was a limit to how many hugs I was comfortable getting in a day, and this had exceeded that number.

"We decided we'd all share our classes now that we're back. I'll go first." Lilith took control of the situation. I don't know how she had become the de facto leader of our group, but she was, and Derrick or I only got to lead if she let us. It was fine, though. She was smarter than me, as long as she didn't get caught up in a scheme.

"I gained the class Iridescent Invoker, which is an offensive and defensively equalized caster class built around creating Luminous Echoes whenever I cast a spell, which I can then use to improve my subsequent spells. Combined with my existent trait of Iridescent Intellect, any spell I cast will be altered to the job at hand, giving me raw power, and versatility to control the field of battle." Lilith's lips quirked into a smile as I clapped for her. The adults joined suit after an awkward moment of just us kids clapping for Lilith.

"I picked Zephyr Trapper for my class." Derrick coughed a little awkwardly. "It focuses on my use of traps and combines wind into my sword and traps. I can add wind effects to my traps, and use my wind abilities to move or trigger traps as needed. This should let me be a real help to me and Alexander with holding the front line during any fight."

When Derrick finished, Lilith clapped for him, and I fell in first, but it wasn't long before he got a full round of clapping himself.

"Good job, lad." Idris cheered Derrick on, since his parents weren't here with us, but as his mentor, Idris seemed very proud of my friend. "You'll have to join the Traps guild, now, and you'll have the name Trapmaster Derrick in short order."

For some reason Momma and Uncle Arkaziel started laughing after they both looked at Derrick more closely. I could tell from the way their eyes flickered around they were using telepathy to talk to one another. Why did they keep looking at Derrick? Weirdos.

"I picked the class Luminous Healer. I can create Luminous Conduits between me and my allies. If I cast a single spell, it can affect another person who's in the conduit web, and any offensive spells I cast generate a boon for the nearest connected ally. My conduits also provide damage absorption and regeneration, and I can lay down an Illuminated Path to get someone somewhere faster. Obviously, between my Light and Support magic access I can heal, buff, debuff spells. I only have one damage spell, for now."

"Wow, you're amazing, Aisha." Nadia cheered her daughter on loudly, and Idris, our mothers, and the StarManes cheered her on too. I clapped loudly. Aisha had gotten one impressive class.

"Well, that just leaves me? I chose Kaleidoscopic Kineticist for my class. Through the class feature, Chromatic Kinesis, I can choose one power or color I like. For example, with silver, I can gain control over metals, with amber I can control earth, or with cyan I can knock people around with waves of water. Not that that's my only class feature. I also have Rainbow Rush that doubles my speed and creates energy trails that have different effects based on my active kinesis. My class skill lets me activate afflictions on my enemies, and buffs on my allies, which also interacts with my trait." I grinned.

"Curselord lets me have a twenty percent chance of granting enemies a random affliction, with a five-minute duration. Tides of Woe lets me drop a curse on someone that afflicts them with a random malady every twenty seconds, while they last for thirty seconds. All afflictions I generate on enemies give me a stacking attack and speed buff, and every use of a kinesis grants me speed and attack power, too. I'm a speed brawler." I was very proud of myself.

Aisha's parents looked slightly afraid of me, but Aisha clapped first, followed by Lilith and Derrick and my parents, then the rest.

"Amazing job, kid. I knew you had some edge waiting to come out." Arkaziel patted me on the shoulder, then gave me a proud squeeze. It was weird. Normally

Arkaziel would complain about how I was too soft and like Momma, but this time he seemed proud.

Mommy gave me a big hug, and whispered into my ear. I assume she did the same for Lilith, but I hadn't been able to overhear.

"Good job, Alexander. You've got a very unique class there, with a lot of versatility. I'm very proud of you, son." Then I got a giant hug, complete with the chains of her wings looping around me, and it was minutes where I could barely breathe, before Momma managed to separate us, so she could get her hug.

"You did great, little guy. Some scary sounding powers there though, ya know. Sometimes scary is good. We'll have to work on some equipment for you. It's hard to be a fist-based fighter without some good gloves. Did I ever tell you how mine were made?" Momma asked with a grin.

"No, you haven't! Tell us!" I clamored for any story of Momma's past.

"Let's see, it was in the Tower of Aetherius, right Ark?" Momma rubbed her chin thoughtfully.

"Oh yeah, you've got that right. It was in the city inside the big worm. You wandered off on a special mission and left me stranded in town with Werylin, while you forged your soul into a pair of gloves." Arkaziel laughed. "She goes off and learns to make soulsteel without even telling us. That's how it went all the time, you turn around, and no more Blue, or Blue's fighting a horde of mercenaries . . ." Arkaziel coughed and fell quiet, looking sheepishly at Momma.

"She caused far less trouble in cities when I joined the party," Mommy said smugly. "Although, I suppose we did destroy a few of those cities, so that does seem worse." Her smugness was short-lived, but her change to sadness got her a hug from Momma, which put her smile back in place. Those two were like that, just always there for one another as if by magic before the other even knew they were sad or had an inkling that they might need support.

"I'm not some walking force of destruction, ya know? Sheesh." Momma grinned at everyone, then ruffled my rainbow-colored hair. "You and me, buddy. Everyone else seems to think we're troublemakers for some reason."

"Because you are, Momma," Lilith said definitively, her arms crossed with a stern look.

Mommy fell off the bench table she'd been sitting next to Momma on, the chains on her wings no ward against the uncontrollable laughter that sent her to the ground.

Lilith defiantly met my fake-sad look.

"Oh please, you've got the title Progenitor of Peril. You can't be innocent if you're the one who started all the peril! Think of how hard I have to work to clean up all of the messes you make. The description of my Patron of Providence trait might as well say it's due to fixing all of the chaos caused by my brother or mom." Lilith tsked and tried to extract sympathy from me, but I refused to give her any, just this once.

"Thatta boy, stand up for yourself." Momma cheered me on.

# CHAPTER 37

# Sparring

**FH 51**

Cassius, you team up with Alexander."

I wanted to groan at the instructor. Alfonso was a transmigrator who thought he knew best about everything, and had joined the burgeoning city of Winona only two months ago. He was one of those adults who seemed to think children who didn't get along should just get over it by forcing them to work together, which never worked. Alfonso wouldn't be a field instructor for long, since his class had a higher rate of incidents than any of the others.

I was pretty sure he did it on purpose. He seemed to feed on conflict, and even without knowing about my traits like the Progenitor of Peril, he kept putting me in uncomfortable situations. Most teachers didn't let me spar with anyone, once word spread that I could inflict instant death randomly. Alfonso seemed to practically beg for that scenario to pop up every time he was our sparring instructor.

"Uhh, sir? Alexander can proc instant death ailments." Cassius pointed out the problem.

"Well, then I suppose he'll just have to dodge your attacks for the rest of the class, won't he? Do you understand, Metanoia?" Cassius grinned at this turn of events, and the smug look on Alfonso's face made me wish something bad would happen to him.

"Fine," I agreed with a bored shrug.

"This is payback," the bigger, older boy growled at me. I stretched my legs as the other kid formed orbs of flame in each hand.

"You'd have to be able to hit me first," I said with a grin. Around me, the air flushed with a chill as I activated my cold kinesis, and blue streaked through my aura. Cassius threw one of his fire bolts at me, and I dodged it easily. Now that I was level fourteen, I had thirty-eight Agility, which for all practical purposes was seventy-six thanks to Rainbow Rush doubling my movement speed. When I used my cold kinesis to snuff out the first fireball Cassius threw at me, Spectrum Surge gained a stack and added another five percent to my speed. Five percent wasn't much, but it would keep stacking up to fifty percent, every time I used a kinesis.

I couldn't get really crazy in this kind of a setting, though. To stack up my Malicious Tormentor buffs I had to afflict targets with ailments, and I wasn't allowed to do that with the restrictions Alfonso placed on me. So I used Dragonfly Strike to blink away from the next firebolt, my fist hit the ground, and I acrobatically spun through the air to land running. The evasion buff from Dragonfly Strike was twenty percent, and gave me an awareness of my body that felt amazing. I couldn't fly like a dragonfly, but I sure could dodge and weave like one when that buff was on me.

I left rainbow trails behind me that were primarily blue. I had to be careful about which kinesis I used, since anything that counted as an attack could trigger my afflictions. Impending Doom and other instant deaths were bad, but there were even worse things that could trigger off my attacks. Petrification, rotting flesh, magic severance, and soul rot, were just a few of the awful things I'd seen my attacks spawn on enemies.

"Stop dodging!" Cassius cried in frustration, and cast an area-of-effect attack at me. I dodged via Dragonfly Strike. I technically didn't even have to hit the ground when I used the ability, but it was good practice with acrobatic dodge and teleport transitions. Ever since Lilith gained the Strategic Reformation ability, I'd been working on controlling my reactions to teleports.

I could tell Cassius was getting frustrated, based on his cries and the flush of embarrassment that filled his cheeks. If not for my Rainbow Rush cold trail dampening his spell, he would've clipped Aisha and her partner with that area of effect. Not that anyone seemed to care about that but me.

"I'll get you with this one . . ." Cassius said with a cruel glint in his eyes. He conjured a globe of flame the size of his head, and threw it up into the air. It settled a foot or so above his head, and spun slowly. I could feel extra attention on me, as if some Efreet were peering at me through the ball of flames he'd summoned.

I flipped my kinesis to magenta, or antimagic.

The orb of fire spun faster and faster, until it split into ten different arrows of fire, and they shot at me. I backpedaled with Rainbow Rush to create a magenta trail, then teleported to behind Cassius with Dragonfly Strike. Four of the arrows of flame hit my magenta trail and vanished. I darted away from Cassius, who turned to look at me as I ran away again. He didn't even realize he was in the line of fire of his own spell until three of the flame arrows hit him in the back, and the last two shot past his head, singing his hair as they shot after me.

It was too late, though; they'd already entered the trail behind me, and the magenta trail canceled any magic that wasn't mine.

"Oh man, Cassius hit himself! What an idiot." I heard one of our classmates mumble.

"How are you supposed to even hit Alexander? Anything he doesn't dodge he can cancel out," another of the older kids complained.

"You have to mix physical attacks with wide area attacks, I think," a kid two years older than me said with a self-important nod. The only non-adult who'd ever managed to land a hit on me was Lilith, and she was even more overpowered than I was, so that didn't really count.

"Medic!" I called. Cassius didn't look too hurt, but he was still lying on the ground.

When the dirt underneath me started to heat up, and a spellcasting circle appeared, shooting flames into the air like an inferno, I was surprised. Cassius had lulled me into taking a hit. Or would have if it weren't for the fact I had antimagic as my active kinesis. Not having to waste time swapping my active kinesis, I pulsed the full antimagic power around me. Cassius's spell fell apart like a paper wall, and my antimagic nova pulsed across the whole training yard. This resulted in a whole bunch of people getting annoyed at their own fights being interrupted and shooting dark glares my way, and Cassius going from being on the cusp of burning me, to being just another failure whose best wasn't good enough.

"Winner, Alexander." Alphonso ruled in my favor, since Cassius would need to see a healer.

"Idiot," Lilith muttered at me as she stepped up from behind me. Still, she gave me a tight hug. "You are hopeless at holding back. You aren't as clever as you think you are, and you should quit doing these things halfway. Either go befriend Cassius, or cement him as our nemesis. Quit being so wishy-washy." Lilith talked about it like I was Argarg the Barbarian, the warlord of the Northern Steppes who rode a hydra, striding about putting skulls on pikes left, right, and center.

I mumbled under my breath and strode over to pat Cassius on the shoulder. I swapped my active kinesis to life and healed the jerk's back.

"Look, you almost got me at the end there. It was only luck I still had my antimagic stance already active. That's closer than anyone else has come to hitting me, so that was pretty good." I offered the olive branch to Cassius.

"Why the hell are you handing me a piece of wood, Metanoia?" Cassius asked, befuddled as the flesh on his back knit back together with no sign of burns at all. "And quit touching me."

Cassius rolled his shoulders to force my hand off him. I didn't fight it. If he wanted to be a jerk about it, he could be a jerk about it. Here I was healing him, and he couldn't accept the gesture. Or maybe, I realized a little too late, he couldn't deal with me putting him into a subservient position of being healed by me after I hit him with his own spell. Not that hardly anyone would have noticed me healing him. Most of our class hated looking at me and Lilith when they had any kind of enhanced senses active. Our prismatic presence always distracted or interrupted people at just the wrong time.

"Fine, and it's an olive branch. My mom says it's a symbol of peace and friendship." I smiled. I'd cut it myself, when Momma mentioned they were useful for showing friendship. I'd thought Lilith and me giving a wreath of branches to Aisha and Derrick would've been a great symbol, and wasting one of the branches from my inventory wasn't a huge loss.

Crack. The green wood cracked with deliberate effort in Cassius's hand, and after a couple more cracks and pops, the olive branch continued to burn after Cassius tossed it to the side to smolder. I hadn't expected this outcome.

When I looked back up, Cassius had walked off.

No one had ever said no to me quite so boldly before. A tsunami of emotions exploded within. How could that stuck-up brat turn down being my friend? I shouldn't have healed him after he hurt himself. He had been trying to hurt me, after all. Why did I even bother to try to be his friend?

"What hurts more?" Lilith inquired.

"Being rebuked, of course." I grumbled.

"Then it's time to let me help you train," Lilith said, with only slightly less haughtiness than someone jumping up and down and screaming "you suck" at the top of their lungs.

"Fine, but you have to follow Momma's rules on training, or we'll both get grounded." I wasn't about to get grounded over this.

"That's fine. Mommy can help me train you. I can't move fast enough to counter you, so I'll need her help anyway." Lilith's smile still scared me a little. She wasn't going to go easy on me, I knew. I'd seen her own spell-training regimen, and I wanted no part of that.

That night was awful. If Momma was a brutal instructor on her own, Lilith was utterly devoid of mercy and would capitalize on any and every weakness she found in my actions. As an instinctual fighter, most of my choice of kinesis boiled down to gut feeling. Lilith drilled the strengths and weaknesses of my powers into my memory every few minutes. Unfortunately, with so many colors at my disposal the list of things to memorize was long. When I told her the System didn't give me a list of all ailments and afflictions my abilities could cast, she huffed and puffed, but even her making me share every bit of my status screens didn't lead to any breakthroughs in knowledge about the more esoteric parts of my abilities.

Momma kept singing some song I'd never heard about a feline's eye from a world I'd never been to, and it got bad enough she even conjured a jukebox from her inventory. High Intensity Training, or HIT as Lilith called it, sucked. Every point in Strength roughly equaled being able to easily handle five kilograms of mass. At a Strength of sixteen I could toss around eighty kilograms pretty easily. But most adults were over level twenty, at least, and probably had a Strength score in the twenties, so it wasn't that massive of an accomplishment. Except when compared to my peers. But compare me to Uncle Arkaziel or Momma, and I might as well be a worm.

None of my afflictions could touch either of them. Momma was outright immune. Arkaziel resisted everything. And with effectively almost one hundred Agility, I couldn't even follow when the two of them moved when they were being serious. How ludicrous were they, that the System only said Telos - ?????? and Arkaziel

- ??????. Well, Mommy and Aunt Bobbi had the same display from the system too, but nothing else we'd ever run into was just big red question marks like that. If you let your eyes unfocus, just a little bit on the System menu, the question marks warped into laughing skulls.

Or, I'd made the joke so many times that it's what I convinced myself to see.

## FH 53

"Run faster, soldier!" Momma said, as she chased me around the yard. We were playing tag. I hadn't managed to touch her once yet, but she'd already scored five points on me.

"You'd better run, you've got a big day tomorrow." Make it six points against me. Her cold hand made me aware of another loss.

"Mom!" I cried. "You have to at least give me a chance! You can't keep grinding me with high intensity workouts every day for two years!"

Oddly, after that she let me finish the night without any more losses, and Lilith didn't even scold me. I didn't know what kind of awful hell of a "big day" I'd experience tomorrow, but I was afraid.

# CHAPTER 38

# Big Day

**FH 53, Autumn in Winona**

I eyed the mirror. I was tall and skinny. Painfully skinny. My shoulders weren't broad, at all. My hair, bound in a ponytail, held a striking red predominant color, and the rest was rainbow. I don't mean like stationary, either. I mean my hair flowed through all the different colors in the rainbow, and it did it bright enough to light up a room. Do you know how hard it was to look tough when you're a rainbow nightlight? It's hard. At one hundred and forty-nine centimeters I was the tallest boy in my class, but I wasn't the imposing type.

At thirteen years old, I was level seventeen. Many of my classmates were stuck in the same range as me, between fifteen and eighteen. Lilith was also level seventeen. Dungeons were unpredictable in their appearance, and the hunting areas around Winona were kept sparsely populated for the safety of the town. Grinding out levels in other ways might work, but then it'd interfere with my attribute gains, or even worse, I could end up with a bunch of useless traits.

Lilith and Momma picked out my clothes while I'd bathed. They normally didn't do that, but it must have been related to the whole "big day" surprise thing. They'd picked black pants, a simple black shirt with black stitching in strange geometric patterns, my dark red boots, and a note to wear my Spectrum Gloves.

Momma had made Lilith a Heavenshadow Staff. It was dark and holy, pristine and terrible, and I drooled and complained that Lilith got a weapon and I didn't for days. My complaints had been needless, since Momma delivered these gloves to me less than a week later. The gloves were fingerless, black, and made of a delicate, breatheable material. The bit between my knuckle and the proximal joint was stylized lace. In a deep crimson, a dragonfly tail started at my knuckle and went down to my wrist on the back of my hand. A series of smaller dragonflies were bound around the lace around my wrist at the bottom of the glove.

They were stylish, at least I thought so, but more than that, they were powerful.

**Spectrum Gloves: Made by Telos & Kallos Metanoia and filled with their love for you.**
**Effect: Unbreakable Hands: Your hands (and gloves) are indestructible.**
**Effect: Wicked Affliction: Status afflictions caused by you can critically hit.**

Not only did the gloves count as magical weapons, since I have an unarmed class, but they made my hands unbreakable. I could stick my hands in fire, lava, saws, and nothing would hurt them. The effect went from the tips of my fingers to five centimeters past my wrist, where the glove ended. As amazing as that was, it also allowed me to punch at full force without hurting myself, and the critical hits on status debuffs weren't something I'd ever seen on equipment before. I hadn't had it happen yet, but I was excited for when it did. I topped the outfit off with a thin crushed velvet coat that looked crinkly but wasn't, with black embroidered dragonflies over the chest of the tailed coat. It was very thin, a little loose around the sleeves, and with two aggressive pointed tails that always flowed around me in a dramatic way.

Momma had made it for me, but it wasn't a magic item, or even enchanted. At least, it wasn't enchanted yet. A knock at my bedroom door revealed itself to be Lilith, who let herself in after I said enter.

"Let me tie that for you," she said as she swept into the room and took my black lace cravat and tied it for me.

"You look handsome today. Did you put eyeliner on?"

"I did. Are you wearing makeup?" Lilith almost never wore makeup. She wore a dress today, whose primary color was a lilac like her hair, and then black lace accents. Even the sleeves were almost transparent, and then billowy and lacey at her wrists, while the dress went to her ankles. The gentle folds of the fabric enhanced the alternating black and lilac colors, and a large amethyst hung from a black lace collar around her neck.

"I am. Do you think it will pay off?" Lilith rarely asked for my opinion, but I had to admit to something problematic first.

"I hope so, sis, but . . . I still don't understand why we're all dressed up. What's going on?"

"The last batch of transmigrators that came in from the East brought new customs with them. Or was it one of the refugees from the North? Derrick's mom predicted a Starfall tonight, so there's an impromptu Starfall Serenade happening. It's a dance."

"What? Why? Who cares? I only learned how to dance so you'd learn to let someone else lead, and I don't like anyone," I muttered darkly. "Who are you going to go with?"

"I asked Aisha yesterday. She's my date." Lilith smiled happily, and I wondered when that had happened. Aisha and Lilith had always gotten along, but sometimes they didn't, and now they were going on a date?

"Poor Derrick." I laughed. He used to have such a crush on Aisha.

"Uhm, you're behind times, brother. Derrick has been dating Aisha's older sister for almost five months now. If he's not careful, Idris will make him his son-in-law before he graduates."

"Oh," I said. How had I missed that? Derrick and I were like, best friends? Sort of. I talked to him more than anyone who wasn't family, anyway. Maybe I should spend more time talking about the boring things like this, instead of how we could try to angle our power development or what item enchantments could really push us to be more formidable. I was plotting my rise to power, and he was . . . dating.

My mood had taken a turn for the worse. Something close to panic welled up inside my stomach, a sour taste filled my mouth, and I couldn't help grimace. Was there something wrong with me that I just didn't care? Other people were dumb, slow, weak, and usually freaked out about the stupidest things like my hair, or that I had two moms, or that my class was wickedly overpowered even compared to transmigrators, who usually had the strongest classes around, or at least the most powerful traits.

"What's wrong?" Lilith didn't seem to follow my emotional rollercoaster in this rare instance.

"I don't know. I mean, when did everyone get all date-y?"

"You'll get there eventually. Maybe you just haven't met the right person? There's five people joining our class from the new immigrants. Try your luck with one of them," Lilith suggested, then brushed a hand along my cravat to make me look nice again.

I opened my mouth to say I didn't want to but stopped. Lilith didn't like whining, and I didn't want to ruin her excitement over the whole stupid Starfall Serenade party.

"Or you can just stay home. Lessons are optional today and have been replaced with dancing lessons for those who don't know how to dance." Lilith smirked at me, knowing I wouldn't just hide at home.

"Uncle Ark agreed to cancel school? What'd they bribe him with?"

"They asked Bobbi to cater, and she prevailed upon Mommy to pull out some of the high-quality, high-level delicacies."

"Momma is pulling out the high-level delicacies?" The wheels in my mind turned. I could get a stat-buff that lasted for up to a week off Aunt Bobbi's cooking. If I got lucky and it had the right sets of buffs, I might be able to hit level eighteen without even finding a dungeon.

I rubbed my hands together excitedly. Lilith mistook my excitement for the food buff with excitement for the dance, but it didn't matter. How hard could it be to find a date?

"Yeah, no thanks," Gwendolyn answered immediately with a small cringe.

"Why not?" I asked in confusion.

"Look, Alexander, you are nice and all, but you're so fast and graceful that anyone who dances with you is going to look like a dumb, drunk bear in comparison. I don't want to look like a dumb, drunk bear. Sorry!"

Gwen answered cheerfully, then sauntered off to return to her friends. I didn't roll my eyes after her. It seemed obvious she didn't like me, but fluffing my ego to soften the no seemed weird to me. Why were they afraid to just be blunt with me?

Most of the students had shown up at the academy even with classes canceled. I eyed the next cluster of girls at a table. The dark-haired girl, Akari, was a transmigrator. She was a little off, but she talked to me at least once a week. I wandered over to her table, and her friends scattered before I got there.

"Are you wearing eyeliner?" Akari asked me with a grin.

"Yeah?" I didn't lie.

"You look great, but no. I like my men to have full, thick beards."

"You're thirteen. No one your age has full thick beards."

"A dwarf would." Akari gave me a terrifying grin, and I backed away, then rushed across the room, away from her. I remembered the reason why I only talked to her once a week.

"Alexander, just the strapping young lad I was looking for, since I can't find your sister." A heavy, dark hand fell on my shoulder as Arkaziel's deep voice echoed across the empty-ish cafeteria. When I turned around to look, I noticed a clump of five kids my own age behind Arkaziel.

"Could you give the newcomers a tour? It's their first day, and even if it's become an impromptu feast tonight, someone still needs to show them the classes, locker rooms, and facilities. Thanks, buddy." Uncle Arkaziel clapped me on the back, and just like that he abandoned me with five other kids my age. Arkaziel disappeared mid-stride. More accurately, he melted into his own shadow over the span of two seconds. After that there was no more uncle anywhere that I could see.

"Such mastery of the Umbral arts," a girl who was obviously a transmigrator said. So far, every transmigrator who showed up at Winona had an exotic appearance at least, if not an abnormal for the region race. In this case, the girl who spoke had long golden hair in multiple braids, and had slightly longer and pointed ears, marking her as an elf. The elf wore a crescent moon pendant, so I suspected she probably had a build based around the moon or light.

"Yeah, that's the headmaster for you. Alright, I'm Alexander, welcome to Winona."

"I am Sophia the Lightwhisperer," the elf proclaimed haughtily, then her cheeks flushed red. "Do people have titles like that? Oh man this is so embarrassing; I just got a title called Dramatic Cosplayer, but my status screen updated my name."

I nodded as if she wasn't speaking gibberish. It's a trick I excelled at, after spending time around my moms, Arkaziel, Bobbi, and Lilith. They all said ridiculous things on the regular, but Arkaziel and his assertions that he'd eat a planet in one gulp weren't even the worst of the inane things I had to put up with.

"Hi, I'm Tyler. I like to punch things." Tyler was short and stocky, as befitted a dwarf. He had bushy brown eyebrows and a beard. I'd never seen a dwarf who wasn't a transmigrator yet. Did they even exist?

"Cool, cool. I'm a pugilist class myself. We'll have to practice together some-time," I offered seriously.

"How about now?" Tyler didn't beat around the bush.

"Sorry, but I'm not allowed to practice with other students outside of direct supervision." I cringed at how awful that sounded. I totally sounded like some pitiful jerk making excuses about why I couldn't do things. And the reason didn't help. "My class has a lot of extremely dangerous auto-proc abilities, you see. So unless you've got a Full Ribbon quality accessory, even practices are out."

"Sure, dude." Tyler rolled his eyes at me. Admittedly, I wasn't exactly intimidat-ing in my current attire, but he didn't have to be a dick about it, did he?

"I'm Kara of Clan Flameheart. We fled the tides of blood Argarg waters the soil with in the North. May he never cross into the southlands." Kara had red hair, freck-led pale skin, and a chip on her shoulder. Unlike the dwarf and elf, she was probably like me, a reincarnation without awakened memories of their past life. We made up the majority. Transmigrators were rare-ish, but reincarnations who retained identity were seemingly ultra-rare.

Argarg the Barbarian seemed to grow more menacing with each new report out of the North. One more town sacked, one more village razed. Argarg seemed to war against civilization itself, and he pressed ever southward. Eventually he'd hit Winona, and the impassable walls that were Uncle Arkaziel and Aunt Bobbi.

My eyes flipped to the last member of the party, who hadn't spoken yet. I was confused, but in a way that was nice. Nice, but awkward. Okay, I don't really know how to describe it, my brain made a sound, and I stared at the last person. Their System information only told me three things about them.

**Name: Morgan**
**Class: Enchanter of Whispering Shadows**
**Race: Esper**

I had no idea whether they were a man or woman. Their skin had a paleness that made the freckled redhead's skin look deeply tanned, the blacks of their eyes were white, and the whites of their eyes were black, and their irises were churning darkness imbued with a purple essence that differentiated itself from all the inky colors. It was the same shadows my black kinesis gave me control over. They had shoulder-length black hair, which also had a hue of dark purpleness.

At first, I assumed they must be a transmigrator, but I saw the confusion in their eyes. It vanished quickly, but I'd seen it. For all that this person seemed aloof, or different, they were also actually their age, not coasting on a previous life's knowledge. Morgan didn't know what they were any more than I knew what I was.

Morgan wore all black. They favored the black high-laced boots like Momma did, and otherwise their clothes weren't that unique, other than the black leather jacket that looked like dungeon loot. It went down to their mid-thighs, had a high neck, and lots of little strappy elements that looked cool. Under the jacket they wore a mesh shirt, and a second lace shirt under it. I couldn't tell from their chest whether Morgan was male or female—everywhere I shifted my eyes to gauge, I couldn't quite tell. Morgan's face had sharp, hard features, and that, combined with the pallid skin and black makeup, made them look quite deathly, and very exotic. Exotic for Winona, anyway. Never mind that Winona had a three-eyed woman who sometimes had a black hole for an eye, and that she was my mom.

Morgan's eyes were hard to look away from.

"Want to be my date tonight?" I asked. I'd already forgotten about the other four, despite each of them pointedly staring at me.

## CHAPTER 39

# The Uncharted

**FH 53, The Highest Realm of Ein Sof**

Two figures composed entirely of diffuse, ephemeral projections of Ein Sof stared at a big box at the Center of Creation. Maybe. There weren't any maps here, and even the collective knowledge of Binah offered no names or whispers of secrets about the plumbing of existence.

"You can't push anything through, either?" Telos asked Kallos. Hope warred with dread in her tone.

"No, my dear. The closer I get to it, the more impenetrable this place becomes. Not even one of my spells will go through, regardless of type. Aether, Nether, Void, Ethereal, even miracles woven of Ein Sof are casually reflected. I even tried blood-letting, but no reaction." Kallos was so vexed at the mysterious construct that she allowed a tinge of disappointment to enter her voice.

"Bloodletting, you say?" Telos stared at her own hand and laughed, but she didn't pull out any knives.

"Blood is the essence of life. Even those who work with mana can over-stretch and spend their life force to massively bolster their spells, at terrible costs. It seems likely that your frenemy engaged magic that drains it to combat you." Kallos looked in the direction of the Multiverse of Bob, a place of sickly sensations and antithetical nature. It had the stink of soul rot, of swamps and dark places where fungi bred undaunted by the sun's light, of the decay of meaning.

"Gnosis doesn't exist in his realm. The sickness of the soul has overtaken their entire multiverse. As long as I block his attacks for another three or four years, he will die. What happens to the dimensional axis, then? Can I fix it, or do I have to destroy it? Can there only be one axis in the whole of creation? I don't think that's the case. I think he's something different from me, and like a sick parasite, he's killing his host." Telos wanted to punch the wall, but the wall hurt her when she hit it.

"Or he's an arrogant tool who's never encountered a true wielder of the light."

"Maybe. He could be lulling me into a false sense of security, too, and will attack all out when I am least prepared for it. Some hoary old plagued goat like that isn't going to go down without a fight, and it has to know more about itself than I do about myself."

"Why?" Kallos asked with narrowed eyes.

"I hope it does?" Telos changed her answer. It didn't have to make sense or know anything. It could be more clueless than her. It could be the equivalent of an amoeba that had mutated just right, for all we knew.

"All we know is that his power isn't derived from Ein Sof, but from his multiverse. That should, theoretically, make him weaker than you, who can control the totality of Ein Sof." Kallos continued to run her fingers against the dense barrier that prevented her from seeing into the box while she talked. "Perhaps he is a manifestation of the true pinnacle a soul can achieve?"

"No, there is a sickness to him. Whatever evolution he followed to become that way, it twisted him away from Ein Sof and Ayin both. I think that's why he's sick. My assimilation of Ein Sof is preventing his ability to interface with the River of Light, and harming his own power base."

"If you're able to coexist with him, why would he immediately take an offensive stance against you? Can you send any of your energy through the box? It almost lets me use a miracle, but rejects it at the last moment."

"I don't know, maybe he's just an asshole? I can send Ein Sof in but lose control of it before gaining any knowledge." Telos hated that she couldn't figure this box out. She had figured out how to make a System, build a universe, and in fact she was certain she could create another multiverse without it diminishing her at all, now, but she couldn't open this box.

"Maybe it's like a pressure lock, and you need to flood it with power? Reach equilibrium between the inside and the outside, maybe?" Kallos rubbed a finger against the obstacle one last time.

"I can make it react to me. If I actively pull Ein Sof through lots of linkages it drops in opacity. I only tested up to thirty active links, but it was about as fluffy as a cloud then. If I open all one hundred and fifty, maybe . . ." Telos bit her lower lip.

"But if you draw on all one hundred and fifty we'll lose our corporeal forms. We are already on limited time. Let us forget this box for now. When the children pass their coming-of-age trials, then we will journey through the barrier."

"You don't think we'll be able to come back, do you?" Telos growled in frustration. She had the same feeling Kallos did.

"You think there is an answer to Bob in there?" Kallos asked dubiously. "It does stand to reason that there could be an answer, but look upon the multiverse he has constructed. It makes my skin crawl, it feels wrong in my heart and mind, and it is anathema to Ein Sof, a parasite that has grown to feed on both the darkness and the light."

"I know, I know, I feel it too. I just don't want to have to destroy an entire multiverse, ok? I've been killing people and things ever since my rebirth, and I'm tired of it. Death and destruction shouldn't always be the answer."

Chains wrapped around Telos and pulled her into a hug from Kallos. She could have fought it off, but Telos embraced the gesture and set her head-on the other woman's shoulder, speaking into her neck softly.

"Of course you're tired of it, darling. You've spent hundreds of years in the towers, and the last forty in the highest concentrated energy dimension in its primordial years. That's a lot for anyone, even you." Kallos had the gentle hands of a sage or seer. Unlike Telos, she didn't wield a hammer and beat metal into shape; she was an artisan of the soul. Her caresses through the rainbow-colored hair were soothing in a way that Telos almost resented. "Can you kill Bob and fix his creation?"

"Probably," Telos said with a sigh. "Without a doubt, honestly."

"Then maybe that's what you need to do. We've got maybe seven more years?"

"No. Between my experiments, and if I take on Bob, we've got six years at absolute most, five if I overestimate Bob, and as little as zero if I'm underestimating him," Telos murmured against Kallos's neck, before slowly breaking free.

"Go back to Mythara. I'll send an avatar with you." Telos had reached a decision.

"You're going to take him on now?"

"After I center myself, but soon." Telos lacked any uncertainty, momentum for her decision had already built in a few short seconds.

"And you don't want my help?"

"I'd feel much better if you were with the kids, in case an avatar isn't enough."

"Very well, dearest. End him quickly." Kallos kissed Telos, then vanished from the River of Light, along with a sliver of Telos that formed an avatar of her, there. Existing in multiple places was one of those things that no amount of theorizing prepared you for. Was it how collective entities felt?

***Do you want me to come with you?***

*Stay with Libby and Reverie, Fred. Watch for any exoverse trickery that I might miss, and you and Reverie may counter any incidents that arise, with Libby's guidance.*


"What's an Esper?" I asked Morgan.

"What's a #REDACTED#?" Morgan asked me back without missing a beat.

We had ditched the other four after finishing the tour, and were hanging out in one of the greenhouses the academy grew useful alchemical herbs in. Each student got assigned chores to help the academy produce income and useful goods for its students, and this greenhouse was part of mine.

"You can see that?" I sat a little straighter.

"Everyone can't? Race is always shared. What's so special about you?"

"Err. I don't know, but you've seen Uncle Arkaziel and Aunt Bobbi, and how the System doesn't display them?" I asked. We'd snuck through the kitchen and stolen a few snacks on the way to the greenhouse.

"Sure, they're part of why everyone comes to Winona and its magic school. Not only can you learn to fight, but the town is protected by a pair of undefeatable dragons."

I laughed.

"They might take offense if you call them dragons. They're so much more than dragons, if you ask them."

"Dragons but not dragons." Morgan nodded sagely.

"Well, my moms are both like that too. Just names and question marks."

"You have more than one mom? Weird. No dads?"

"It's kind of weird? Both can shapeshift, have very strong magic, so, they're both dad and mom? Lilith and I are kind of twins, but we were each carried by a different mom." This conversation alone was part of why I didn't try to be everyone's friend. Explaining the Metanoia family was awkward.

"So redacted just means the System doesn't even know, or won't tell, what your parents are?" Morgan scratched at the back of their neck in confusion, before laughing. "That's wild. At least you have your parents, though? I don't know what an Esper is, honestly. Kara's parents have been my guardians for the last six months. They're the third family I've been with, that I can remember."

Well, I just stepped on a land mine.

"The North is really that dangerous?"

"It won't be after I graduate from this school. I'm going to kill Warlord Argarg after I get powerful enough." Conviction filled Morgan's voice, and I set my hand on their shoulder and squeezed.

"I'll help."

"Just like that?"

"Sure. I'm going to be a legend." I grinned.

Morgan's purple-shot eyes looked me up and down, and a smile quirked across their lips. Butterflies filled my stomach. Morgan looked at me like I was a problem to be solved, sure, but they also had an interest. They weren't looking at my hair, they were looking at *me*. No one my age had ever done that before. Even Derrick and Aisha rarely could look past the overwhelming visual package of me to see who I was underneath.

"I believe it. Do you always dress like this?"

"You don't like it?" Oh man, I knew the crushed velvet was too much!"

"No, no. I do, but it does seem a bit much?"

"Most days my clothes are more like everyone else's, but I always wear the gloves since I got them. They're magical equipment, made by my mom. Today is a Starfall Serenade dance, though, so my family made me dress up."

"The dragonflies are cute." Morgan laughed and reached over to run a finger over the embroidery of the dragonfly. "Everyone in this town has such nice clothes. Up north everyone mostly just wore furs and armor, except for quest rewards and loot."

"Your wardrobe is awesome?" I said in confusion.

"All of us refugees got a Welcome to Winona quest reward with three outfits, and some other items we didn't have. The System seems to be conspiring with your town to some end."

I thought about it and couldn't argue. The System had a habit of awarding quests for things that Momma wanted to happen. No one outside of our family ever called the System anything but System, but we occasionally called it Libby, and Lilith and I did get a fair number of quests and coincidental boosts that others didn't.

"Yeah, maybe." I nodded. For the first time since I met Morgan, I realized I wasn't bored. Talking to people always had long lulls, but Morgan didn't leave lulls for long, or if one of us did, it wasn't awkward silence.

"Want to show me around town before this Starfall thing? I've got some coins to spend, a place to live, and a town full of artisans to explore."

"Sure, let's go." I held my hand out for Morgan's, and our eyes met. After a brief hesitation and a laugh, they took my hand, and I led the way.

# CHAPTER 40

# Starfall Serenade

Telos flowed through the River of Light like an orca attacking a yacht. Proudly and without fear. She was the River, and the Shore. More precisely, she was both Ein Sof, and Ayin, the nothing beyond the Divine Light of creation.

"To the death, then?" Bob manifested himself at the very tip of the dimensional axis. Telos had expected him to use his multiverse as a shield, but he separated himself from it and stood exposed. The illusory existence of an old man in white shorts and a Hawaiian shirt covered in pineapples had been dispensed with. The true form of her adversary reminded her of bad CGI in sci-fi horror movies.

Bob looked vaguely human, but he was missing a lot of parts of his body. Some had been replaced by technology, some had been replaced with grafts, and some were corrupted by forces she couldn't immediately identify, presumably unique to the existence over which Bob ruled. The old man's left arm was a dark tentacle, a clear sign of some type of Void infection, or an unhealthy obsession with octopi.

"I could heal you," Telos offered without a price.

"I have no need of your sympathy!" Bob screamed, enraged for reasons Telos couldn't fathom. Thousands of pineapples formed around Bob and launched themselves at Telos. They looked dangerous, a mixture of technology and magic, but when they crossed into the River of Light they vanished without a trace.

"The Light defends you? Arcanthar claimed to have struggled against one such as you." Bob launched more attacks. Pineapples, lightning, black swarms of all devouring nanites, nuclear bombs, plasma missiles, railguns, none of it had even the slightest effect upon Telos. The great River of Light simply dispersed every attack as if they were no more than spitballs.

"No, it doesn't defend me." Telos corrected, while Bob drew upon the Void. His infected arm grew massive, and birthed swarms of void bugs. "Did this Arcanthar win?"

"He died a terrible, slow death, and I feasted on his corpse," Bob answered with a smile. "As I'll do to you." Bob birthed a whole swarm of Void creatures and sent them to Telos. Yet again, when they entered the River of Light, they instantly disintegrated as if they had never existed.

"Leave the light, you liar!" Bob cried and summoned something akin to a squid.

Telos vanished from the light, reappearing in the depths of nothing beyond the borders of Ein Sof. It felt just as reassuring as the Light did, for she was Nothing, too. Bob's squid immediately turned to dust and flaked away on invisible winds.

"This cannot happen!" Bob tried to summon another horror, and then he summoned an immense spaceship and had it fire cannons at Telos. None of it could even touch her, and she appeared next to the wretch. Bob seemed, with each attack and expense of power, to be falling apart and growing closer to destroying himself.

"You're a fragile thing, to call itself a god. You were mortal, once, I can see that. The nanites, the artificial intelligence augmentations, flesh harvested from gods and monsters, and a spark of light at the center, long corrupted. Was that light Arcanthar?"

"Why can't I kill you?" Bob demanded.

"Was that light Arcanthar?" Telos asked again.

"Yes, that was Arcanthar. I consumed him, and took what was his, and it is now mine. You cannot take it away from me!" Bob launched dozens of attacks at Telos. None made it to her, and no strain showed on her face, despite the effort the abomination put into it.

"The spark was a gift to him," Telos murmured. "He wanted to be a shepherd and provide for the people under his protection. You ate him from the inside out, and then the corruption began. Everything you tried to do turned to ashes."

"You don't know me! I am the God of the 'Verse, I judge lifeforms, I disrupt the schemes of the powerful on whims, I am not some insect to be toyed with like this!" Bob tried to enter mental combat against Telos, but all he achieved was looking like a mime, fighting invisible walls to no effect. Telos only bothered to keep two eyes on Bob, while her third eye looked upon his history, his works, and his multiverse.

"I see it all. Your conquests and contests, your plans, the corruption spreading through your own family. You've been begging to meet me for the last half a million years, and now that I'm here, you want to fight me? That's so quintessentially human. Tell me, Burt, why did you murder Arcanthar? He was never going to hurt you."

"There can be only one!" Bob cried at me in anger, before he deflated at me calling him by his original name. The name he'd worn as a human, one who could see and hear the truth when others couldn't, who'd gotten trapped in a taboo creation against his will.

"There can be a billion, or there can be one, or none. See, again, what you've blocked out."

History replayed itself in the form of overly pastel holograms conjured by Telos.

*Arcanthar, unlike Bob who looked younger and more human, took the form of a man made of the inky void; constellations played across his ever-changing physiology.*

*"Our existence is encouraged by Ein Sof. If you embrace the role of caretaker, it will allow you to wield its power, but if you seek control, it will deny you." Arcanthar lectured the younger Bob. "If you fight it, it will destroy you."*

*"If it won't accept me, what do I do?" Bob demanded.*

*"If you embrace being a caretaker, it will accept you." Arcanthar spoke, unheeded.*

*"What about the Nothing?" Bob demanded.*

*"Ayin, the Nothingness, is the birthplace of everything, but concepts cannot be actualized within Ayin. Only within Ein Sof can physical reality be manifest. To commune with either is to communicate with both, and if you are accepted, you will become more powerful than any other being within your 'Verse."*

*"But not more powerful than the Light?" Bob grimaced.*

*"Afraid not." Arcanthar lacked Bob's bitterness about that.*

"That isn't how that conversation went!" Bob's vehemence sprayed more attacks at Telos, all of which did absolutely nothing to her.

"No, you remember it very differently, don't you?" Telos laughed, not in a mocking way, but because she could see the way those memories had warped with time for Bob. "How long after that was it before you stabbed Arcanthar in the back *and ate him* and the garden he looked after?"

"I can't believe you have dances in Winona," Kara said in shock.

"It's . . . different?" Tyler answered diplomatically.

After a shopping spree in town, which I had funded, I'd parted with Morgan at the home Kara's parents, Kara, and Morgan had moved into. The newest homes built for the last wave of refugees were on the north side of town. It was a fifteen-minute walk from the north of town down to the south side of the academy. We'd separated for a few hours there, and I'd returned to help out around the academy and snack on Bobbi's test dishes.

I got my hopes up when Kara came in, but Morgan hadn't come with her.

"Everywhere could be like Winona someday," I said, and the other two gave me a look that left me feeling very out of touch. "Couldn't it?"

"This place is a weird kind of heaven and hell, man." Tyler spoke up. "From what everyone says this world is like, super young, and we've been seeded here by the System. Transmigrators like me are using magic to cheat and build civilization from our old worlds, but most places don't have anything going on for them but murder for survival, and no luxuries beyond what they can use magic or powers to make."

I grimaced. Winona sounded like heaven compared to whatever these two had endured.

"I'm not a transmigrator, but even those of us who haven't reawakened past memories can feel the youngness of the world. Breathe in; it hangs in the air. There is a power, a purity, of the freshly born world, of terrible behemoths, titans, and colossi that tread freely around us. The fingerprints of primordial power are everywhere you look, like morning dew." Kara spoke in a way that made me imagine her as an old seeress trying to impart wisdom to a clan. Did she mimic someone they had lost while fleeing Argarg?

"I'm not a transmigrator either." I nodded to Kara, and she looked at me like I was a liar.

"*You* aren't a transmigrator?" Derrick asked as he stepped into the conversation. We were clustered near the exterior wall of the academy, near a lamp, so anyone coming into the gardens for the party would have to pass us.

"Derrick, this is Tyler and Kara, they're new. Also, you've met my parents. Transmigrators don't seem to have parents. This is Derrick, he's a trapmaster and part of my regular party." I sighed at him. "Where's Aisha, Lilith, or your date? Way to not tell me you were marrying into Aisha's family."

I exaggerated a little, to make things awkward for Derrick. That's what he got for not keeping me in the loop about his love life.

"Dude, you're way too young to marry someone," Tyler, the dwarf, told Derrick bluntly.

"Look, it's just an engagement, and I didn't know anyone outside of our families even knew. What the hell, Alexander?" Derrick laughed into the awkward silence. "Gotcha! Hanna'd skin me if she heard there were rumors about us marrying, though, so really, knock that off!"

I eyed Derrick, feeling a little numb inside. That had been an emotional roller-coaster he sent me on as a joke, but I felt like I probably deserved it. I needed to be a better friend.

"The girls will be along shortly. Your sister decided to take them on a detour and told me to go on ahead and keep you company until they got here."

"Are you alright?" Kara and Tyler asked almost simultaneously as I paled. *Lilith made a detour.* How did she find out I was interested in someone already? She wouldn't make things awkward for me with Morgan, would she? Of course she would. She'd sent Derrick ahead to warn me of her arrival, so I'd be on even more edge and wouldn't miss her entrance. I couldn't tell you what her plan beyond that was, but I figured that much out.

"Yeah, nothing to worry about at all," I lied.

"Did Alexander warn you to be careful around a girl named Akari, Tyler?" Derrick, ever the helpful guy, struck up a conversation with Tyler and detailed the young woman's fascination with dwarves and facial hair.

The last gasp of the day faded, which made Lilith's entrance stand out all the more. Her hair created just as much light as my own did, but a new development created an even brighter entrance for her. She'd gained a halo, like our mothers, except for the fact that it sent cascading rays of rainbow light streaking through the burgeoning dusk. If she'd waited until dark, it would've been a truly amazing entrance. I wondered how she got a halo. Would I get a halo? That looked really cool.

Derrick looked at me.

"Oh, right. Lilith leveled up while helping set up the party earlier. She said to tell you 'suck it, slacker.'" Derrick delivered the message just as Lilith looked at me and winked. Why did her plans always work out, down to the second?

Behind Aisha and Lilith, a pale-skinned, dark-haired figure came in.

# CHAPTER 41

# Shut Up and Dance

Why can't I just kill you? Your 'Verse is tiny compared to mine. Did you make a deal with the Light and the Nothing? Why would they empower you, but not me?" Bob screamed at Telos as he unleashed all kinds of attacks. Universe-ending attacks that burned so much power entire timelines in Bob's 'Verse were turned to empty husks to fuel his power.

All simply evaporated, unable to touch Telos.

"This is like a private fireworks show," Telos joked. "Not sure how I feel about you burning up timelines to achieve nothing, though, so knock it off." With those words, Bob couldn't manifest attacks anymore, despite his intent and desire to do so.

"I'm not what you are. What you think of as my 'Verse isn't mine; it belongs to Libby but she's got some maturation to do before she peeks her head into this level of reality. I lived there, though."

Bob tried to punch her, but the forces that made up his hand couldn't make contact with those that made up Telos.

"Why can't you kill me? I dislike being hurt, let alone killed. What sort of omnipotent being goes and gets itself killed? It happens a lot in fiction, and it's always such bullshit. But I've been trying to figure that out for a while. I've been playing a game of trickle truth with life ever since I got reincarnated. At first I thought I was a bioweapon created by the Primordials, then I learned about Demiurges and the Sefirot, and I was pretty confused. Ayin and Yesh muddied the waters and my understanding of Ein Sof."

"Are you going to bore me to death now?" Bob hissed, unable to even move now as the Will of Telos bound him completely.

"I might. I don't get captive audiences whose feelings I don't care about very often. But I can answer you as to why you can't kill me. Ayin is the first emanation that I cast, and Ein Sof was the consequence. If you opened your eyes, you'd see there are multiple other 'Verses in the River of Light. I don't know what your purpose in all of this is, but this just is . . . me? And instead of figuring out what's hidden in the Light, you're making a big show of disrupting my peace and quiet."

"Your claims are nonsensical; how would you know so little about yourself?"

"How do you know so little about yourself? Denial plays a part, certainly, but you've crossed far beyond that. There's the machinery you've inflicted yourself with enhancing the effects of denial. Then there are the different emanations you picked up along the way. The Void corruption has run its course through you, leaving you predisposed to all the nonsense Fred spouts. You're a symbiotic mix of parasites masquerading as a god." Telos imbued her words with Truth enough that they could cut through the noise in Bob's mind.

Each declaration struck Bob like a physical blow.

"Why are you so ignorant if you are what you claim?" Bob cried, and Telos was glad that he couldn't shower her in spittle in this place.

"The most obvious answer is that I made myself forget, yeah?" Telos mused. "Is that what you seek, old man? To forget, or to be forgotten?" The spluttered rage that manifested around Bob told Telos that wasn't what he wanted at all, even before the string of curses and indignity roused him.

"I want to rule!" Bob shouted his truth.

"Then why did you fill your 'Verse with the seeds of your own destruction? Why iterate one soul, again and again, until it's capable of killing you? Why cultivate a force that could destroy everything you've made? It seems silly if you are trying to 'rule.'"

Fear stifled anger, and Bob fell silent. When Telos had sliced through Bob's defenses moments before, he had deluded himself, rationalized that it was some form of guess or psychic manipulation. Telos smiled, only a little, as she watched the realization fully strike Bob that she could see everything in his 'Verse. Even the things he had tried to obscure.

"Well, you've bored me now." Telos sighed and gestured. The worst of Bob's deterioration healed itself, and the vast technology within his 'Verse altered slightly.

"Go play your games in your 'Verse; you won't be able to return here again. If your successor is more of the same, I'll judge them if they make it here."

"Wait! You healed me, and now you banish me. I would destroy you without hesitation. Why not just end me?" Bob couldn't put it together.

"It's not a blessing that I healed you, Bob. I fully believe that people should be able to appreciate the inescapable return of karma. You've set up your little cycle of death and rebirth in your 'Verse, played with the lives of others on whims, made a mockery of gods and mortals with your contest, and desecrated the memory of your loved ones, again and again. I healed you so you could fully appreciate the culmination of your existence."

The River of Light, the flow of Ein Sof, carried the cold, harsh judgment of Telos upon it. Wisps of light caught Bob and carried him back into the existence of his 'Verse, which then turned into a prison for one, preventing Bob from ever returning to the River of Light.

"Uffda," Telos exclaimed as she exhaled exasperation and tiredness with a sigh. The burden of another multiverse had settled on her shoulders like the heavens on the shoulders of Atlas. "Ignorance really is bliss. Why does Bob's 'Verse have Earth, too?"

Telos looked longingly toward the center of the River of Light and the mystery that waited there, but she returned to Mythara. The mystery could wait a little longer.

Morgan drew my eyes in a way that felt like I was compelled to look at them. At some point since our separating, Morgan had had a haircut. Previously shoulder-length hair now had been cut shorter, into a messy bob that sent tousled strands in multiple directions. The chaotic haircut fit Morgan well and showed off their sharp features and stunning eyes. I guess this sensation was what people called attraction. I'd thought people were cute before, sure. Gwendolyn, for example, was very pretty, but she didn't spark anything in me. Derrick was objectively handsome, but also sparked nothing in me. Cassius had that bad boy appeal, but he was a jerk. Morgan, on the other hand, had a mystery. They were new, unknown, exciting, different, even a race I'd never heard of, and had the ability to see that my own race wasn't human but hidden.

The dress, well, it looked good on Morgan. The tailor I'd bought it from had called it a cheongsam, but I'm pretty sure that was just a made-up word. The black dress had a high collar around a pale neck, then went down to Morgan's calves. The accent colors on it were purple, that showed off the ominous and dark power that surrounded Morgan and contrasted against their pale skin.

So maybe it was fate. My heartbeat thudded in my ears. Then I noticed the rainbow cascades of light on Morgan. Lilith had turned and grabbed their hands to bring Morgan over to join us.

"Alexander, look who I met!" Lilith chimed in as Aisha, Lilith, Hanna, and Morgan joined the group of Tyler, Derrick, Kara, and me. "Since you treated Morgan to a lovely shopping spree, I splurged on haircuts."

I noticed that Lilith's and Aisha's hair looked slightly different, now that she mentioned it.

"You all look very lovely," I said without taking my eyes off Morgan, but then I realized I was coming on way too strong. Who just stares deeply into people's eyes, especially someone they just met that day? I didn't even know if Morgan was single, or interested in me, or anyone for that matter, and this all seemed far more complicated than theorizing improvements for our combat capabilities.

"Hanna, didn't you say you wanted to dance?" Lilith asked Hanna, while looking meaningfully at Derrick, before she looked over the rest of the group one by one.

"This is Tyler and Kara," I introduced the two unknowns to my sister. "This is my sister, Lilith. She's probably going to boss you around now. Don't fight it."

"Rude, but accurate. Tyler, have you met Akari yet? She'd be very delighted to meet a dwarf, and Kara, have you tried any of the food yet? There's no better chef in the universe than Bobbi Slay. Let's test the snacks before we try out dancing our-selves?" The last Lilith mused to Aisha, who nodded and scurried off with Lilith.

I didn't understand how she did it, but in seconds Lilith had dispersed our clump of kids, and only Morgan and I were left, looking awkwardly at one another, while everyone else vanished to find snacks, dance, or meet new people.

"Your sister is *a lot*," Morgan ventured.

"Tell me about it. She's always been like this. If you fight her on things, it just makes everything worse, too. She'll wear you down, out-logic you, or manipulate other people to get what she wants. In her defense, what she wants usually has the best results for our group, but it's really annoying being around someone who's always right."

"It's got to be nice to have someone you can trust." Morgan's lips pursed, and I noticed they'd put on a touch of makeup. A dark red lipstick, and a black eyeliner. Unless they were able to control their appearance? Few people who could shapeshift were open about their powers. Even our moms and Arkaziel and Bobbi only displayed any alternate forms rarely.

"I guess? I've got lots of people I can trust besides Lilith. There's our aunt and uncle, Aisha, Derrick, our parents, and well, I guess that's it." Still, my seven probably seemed a whole lot more than the number that Morgan had to trust.

"So, uhh . . . dance?" Morgan asked awkwardly, uncertain of where to take the conversation. I think I stepped on a minefield there.

"Sure! Do you want to lead, or should I?"

A small laugh escaped Morgan's dark lips, and mischief filled their eyes.

"You can lead; I've never danced before." Morgan had no anxiety about dancing, but when I put my arms around them, they stiffened up as hard as a board.

"Oh, did you make a new friend, Alexander? Why don't you introduce me. Any friend of yours is a friend of mine." Acid might as well have spewed out of Cassius's mouth as well as the very unfriendly words. The mayor's son had grown larger, and wore fancy robes that screamed *pyromancer*. Cassius looked confused when he stepped around and got a full look at me and Morgan.

"Huh," Cassius muttered, confused by Morgan's appearance. "A weirdo for a weirdo. Are you a boy or a girl? Or are you even human? What the fuck is an Esper?"

I felt Morgan shift against me, but not away from me. I held back from punching Cassius only because I could tell Morgan was up to something, and before I knew it, Morgan looked very feminine, with curves and breasts that made her dress struggle. Despite the tightness of their clothes, Morgan had a smirk of satisfaction as Cassius's eyes grew huge. Morgan had gone from an absolutely striking androgynous person with a dark flair to an even more beautiful woman.

"Why do I have to be just one thing?" Morgan asked in a sultry voice, but their body flowed again, back to the androgynous form they had had before. Then kept going, shoulders broadening, chest flattening even more, until they had a very masculine build. "Is that why you are a pyromancer, brains as one dimensional as the flames you conjure?"

I probably should have said something, but the variation in both of Morgan's forms caused me a whole slew of sensations standing together as we were. I felt a little detached from reality, unable to process the sensations of breasts, muscles, a bulge, and then back to the androgynous form. Throughout, Morgan remained cool in my arms. It reminded me of hugging Momma, who was always cold, unlike Lilith and

Mom, who were always warm. That thought made things really, really, awkward for me, and I didn't want to think about it anymore.

"Go away, Cassius. Unless you want to be the one to test your dad's banishment for people who start incidents with non-humans?"

Cassius Thorn scowled at Morgan, then lunged at me.

# CHAPTER 42

# Friends

Cassius Thorn stood about one hundred and seventy centimeters tall. His hair had grown to a flame red over the last year, a clear influence from his fire powers. He was two centimeters shorter than me, despite being a year and a few months older than me. He'd trained strictly as a pyromancer, without any real effort to learn martial skills like grappling, evasion, or even the basics of punching. What I'm trying to say is, he didn't have any real chance of hitting me in a normal situation. Yet, here I was, holding Morgan for a slow dance, with Cassius lunging right at us.

I was about to react, but Morgan's pale hand grabbed Cassius's hand, and then he hit the ground hard enough he bounced up into the air a little and then hit it again, knocking the wind out of him. While there was some grass in the garden, Cassius impacted against stone walkways that had no forgiveness. Without healing he'd be feeling that for a few days. The whole counterattack looked an awful lot like a Skill to me, rather than trained martial arts. For starters, Morgan never really readjusted their body. They stayed pressed against me and had no dramatic shifts in gravity or weight.

Plus, there were flares of shadows and darkness. It happened quick enough I didn't get a full look at whatever Skill Morgan used, but it reminded me of something Uncle Arkaziel would do.

"You don't get to talk to me that way, and you definitely don't get to talk to my friends that way." Morgan did not let go of Cassius during the throw, but rather retained control of his arm and held him in a painful armlock. When Morgan shifted his arm, he whimpered and cried out. "Do you have anything else you want to say?"

Wisps of darkness swam around Morgan in a very intimidating way, and even Cassius's shadow roiled like a mad beast ready to devour him. I had never seen something so beautiful in my whole life. Not only did Morgan have charm and looks, but they appeared to have combat abilities too. Flashy, dramatic abilities, which were the best type of abilities.

"What's going on over here?" Arkaziel demanded.

"They attacked me for no reason!" Cassius immediately declared to my uncle. Arkaziel rolled his eyes as he stared at Cassius. Arkaziel's eyes were golden and showed glimpses of the immeasurable amounts of power he wielded. It was hard to look him straight in the eyes, but it was also hard to look away if he locked eyes with you, and he had locked them completely with Cassius. Cassius shook like a leaf, unable to look away from the headmaster's gaze. People, especially transmigrators, expected Arkaziel to be some wizened and nurturing person. He wasn't. He was an apex predator, an immortal dragon-cat, and he didn't like people messing with his food, property, or peace and quiet, unless it was funny or interesting.

"I watched the whole thing, twerp. That isn't going to fly." Arkaziel shook his head. "Nicely done, Morgan. Your darkness reminds me of something . . ." Arkaziel rubbed at his chin in thought, but he shrugged, unable to remember where he'd seen similar darkness in the past.

Morgan let go of Cassius's hand awkwardly, and an impish smile crossed Morgan's lips.

"Thanks. I came here to learn more about the darkness from you, you know. I'm going to kill Argarg the Barbarian." Morgan's eyes practically glittered in excitement at Arkaziel complimenting her. Shadows around us danced in excitement, mirroring Morgan's tone. I hadn't expected Morgan's cool, in-charge personality to break so quickly, let alone for it to be over Arkaziel. If Morgan expected Arkaziel to be shocked at someone coming to him to learn to kill, especially to kill Argarg, there was only disappointment to be found. Morgan wasn't the first person who wanted to kill the Warlord of the North.

"Oh really? Maybe I'll take you on as an apprentice. Anyway, Thorn, you are expelled." Arkaziel said it offhandedly, as if this threat had been made repeatedly. "I've avoided it until now because your father is a decent mayor and keeps the work down for the rest of us, but maybe he'll sta—"

"Please don't expel me! I'll be good!" Cassius cried. Actual sobbing. The teen had seen something while he'd locked eyes with Arkaziel, something brutal and terrible and entirely willing to filet him for lunch, a side of the headmaster that rarely got noticed by his students. Even I could hear the sincerity in the pitiful words Cassius cried out. I hated that I felt pity for him. Cassius had spent most of the time we'd known one another trying to bully me or Lilith and failing at it. Why couldn't he just move on and be our friend, or leave us alone, instead?

"You say that every time, and then you aren't." Arkaziel shrugged. To him, the fate of Cassius Thorn mattered less than what Bobbi cooked for main course or dessert. I knew Uncle Arkaziel wasn't pulling punches, and as much as Cassius was an asshole, he didn't have anything else. He wasn't *that* talented. He was a mid-grade fire mage, who hadn't come to terms with the dangers and limitations of being a mage. He wasn't dumb, but he wasn't smart either, but because his dad was mayor he wanted to be a big shot himself.

"Can't he take on a Trial of Worthiness to stay?" I asked.

Cassius, Morgan, and Arkaziel all looked at me. I felt as surprised as they did. I hadn't meant to say anything. Life without Cassius would be much more peaceful, or at least simpler.

"He could," Lilith said, she and Aisha stepping into the growing circle of people around the floor-bound Cassius.

"Fine. You can finish this semester, at which point you'll undergo a Trial of Worthiness. Your teammates will be Alexander and Morgan." Arkaziel's eyes gleamed viciously, and he didn't hide the satisfaction he got from forcing Cassius to work with two people he clearly didn't like if he wanted to stay.

"Now that that's settled, I'm off to taste-test. Be good, kids." Arkaziel vanished into the shadows before he'd finished speaking, the last few words emerging eerily from the shadows.

"Where'd he go?" Morgan whispered into my ear.

"He teleports through shadows a lot." I couldn't trace him through shadow dives, and apparently Morgan couldn't either. How good was Uncle Arkaziel at manipulating darkness and light? "He also uses illusions all the time, so he might just be invisible."

"Where'd Cassius go?" I looked around.

"He fled the moment you looked away," Lilith answered. "Why'd you stick up for him?"

"Uncle Ark says his dad is a good mayor, so . . ." I shrugged.

"That's it?" Morgan asked, disbelief in their tone.

"Alexander stood up for him because my son has a good heart, that's why." Momma said as she stepped into the circle. Like me and Lilith, her hair was cascading rainbows. Unlike us, she had a third eye on her forehead that gleamed with holy light and saw everything.

"Too soft for his own good," Mommy said, from her spot next to Momma. Lilith agreed with a grunt.

"No adults!" I cried, as both of my mothers turned their eyes to me and Morgan. Whom I still had my arms around, as if we were ever going to finish that slow dance. Should I pull them away? Would that insult Morgan? What were my parents thinking of me standing so close to Morgan? They were both smiling, really, but they were also paying as much attention to Lilith and Aisha as to me and Morgan.

"Don't we get to meet your new friend before you shoo us away? You're looking lovely tonight, Aisha." Telos complimented Aisha, before all three of her eyes turned toward Morgan. Something about Morgan made Mom happy, because she smiled and laughed, to my confusion.

"Err. This is Morgan. Morgan, this is Telos and Kallos Metanoia, my mothers." I made the awkward introductions, and Morgan gracefully slipped from my arms to walk over and say hello to both of the taller women.

"No wonder you're tall, Alexander, both of you are giants!" Morgan, like most people, had to look up to meet my parents' eyes. Morgan seemed unruffled by the black hole eye in the center of Telos's forehead and looked more interestedly at Kallos's wings and halo. *Seemed* was the keyword. After Morgan shook both women's hands and returned to stand next to me, I held their hand again. Morgan's hand had become cold and clammy, as if all the life had been siphoned from Morgan. No other sign of their discomfort made it past Morgan's iron self-control, but I could've missed it, since I was also watching my mother's reaction to Morgan.

"Well, don't let us interrupt your dance. We're just here to help Bobbi pass out food. Nice to see you, Aisha, and a pleasure to meet you, Morgan. Enjoy your dances, kids." Kallos spoke gently, and then grabbed Telos by the earlobe and dragged her toward the food. Telos mimed putting up a fight while she was dragged away.

"I think your mom is the most powerful person I've ever seen," Morgan breathed out after the adults had been gone for a few moments.

"She has that effect on people who can see," Lilith agreed with a nod. Morgan seemed to be scoring points with my sister, but I wasn't sure if that was good or not. "Alexander, you shouldn't have volunteered Morgan for a Trial of Worthiness without even asking."

"So that's a real thing?" Morgan blinked a few times, then laughed nervously.

"Yes," Lilith said flatly, glaring at me. "It's a chance for someone who has wronged others to prove their worthiness for a spot at the academy. The Trial is generated by the System, and can be lethal if they aren't actually worthy of being one of Mythara's elite."

I held up my left hand with one finger up.

"But, there's awesome loot, a massive experience to be gained for the seconds, and if he passes, maybe he'll pull his head out of his ass. It wouldn't be terrible to have a pyromancer that owes us favors." I grinned, hoping Morgan liked experience and loot as much as I did.

"Why? I can invoke fires far beyond his pitiful control, and you have access to heat and flame too, brother dear. Cassius is a nobody who won't matter once we graduate and hit the road." Lilith sighed at me, while Aisha gave her a slightly reproachful look. I spoke up first, to save them an argument.

"The value of someone isn't in the strength of their fireballs, Lilith. Even Mom says that all it takes is one act of kindness, one helpful action, to bring redemption on an otherwise wasted life." I managed to keep a straight face while quoting Telos, in her own voice.

"Ugh. Whatever. Morgan, see how naive he is? You'd better not hurt him." Lilith smiled, showing her teeth, before she strode off, dragging Aisha with her.

"Your sister is scary," Morgan whispered once everyone else had dispersed.

"Tell me about it. So, uhm . . . we never did get that dance?" I eyed the open areas of the garden, where the music was louder.

"That sounds like a great idea." Morgan grinned, and we danced. We danced until the shooting stars filled the skies, and then we stole snacks and ate them in semiprivacy of a corner of the garden.

The night ended with kisses. Now I understood, at last, why people kissed. It was fun.

# CHAPTER 43

# Trial of Worthiness

**FH 53, Winter. Winona.**

Don't die," Arkaziel said cheerfully to Cassius Thorn. The overwhelmingly exaggerated cheerful tone almost gave me a sugar rush. The headmaster let his sharp front teeth take center stage, only summoning the doorway to the Trial of Worthiness after a visible shudder passed through Cassius.

Morgan and I stood behind Cassius. Morgan wore gear like my own, lightly armored with an emphasis on mobility. Thigh-high black boots accented with multicolored metallic thread had been made by Mom for Morgan, along with the evil-looking black metal sickle and chain they used as a weapon. Telos had named the weapon Moral Dilemma. The other pieces of armor Morgan had before had been simple dark leather, non-magical gear. We both needed major upgrades to our gear if we ever wanted to make it up north to stop Argarg, but our weapons, at least, were quality.

"I'll try not to, Headmaster." Cassius answered Arkaziel's less-than-sincere encouragement with words so dry even my lips puckered a little, before he leaped through the glowing portal.

"You could just let him fail. You don't owe him anything. He never even showed up to one practice session with us," Morgan said flatly to me. Arkaziel nodded in agreement.

"Nope, let's go." I didn't bother to point out that there would be experience or loot. Both of them knew that wasn't what motivated me to make this decision, so there was no point in pretending otherwise.

"Even though it's a trial, there are still lethal challenges inside," Arkaziel reminded us again, meeting each of our gazes.

Morgan rolled their eyes, and we stepped into the portal.

**Welcome to the Trial of Worthiness,** the System chimed into my mind.

Arkaziel's immaculately furnished office had been replaced by a world of stone walls. Immense walls rose into the sky higher than I could estimate. Each had lichen, moss, erosion, and in some places even vines growing on them. Why they looked so ancient and weathered, I didn't know, but it was very impressive. A dead-end sat at our back, and three pathways lay ahead of us. Cassius stood in front of them, uncertain what he should do, his face contorted into a sour expression. No doubt he was annoyed that he had to wait for us, or deal with us at all.

"Which one do we go down?" Cassius spoke his first words to us in weeks, and still refused to look either of us in the eyes.

"It isn't a maze," Morgan said. Based on the way the shadows writhed around them, I could only assume Morgan had reached out to other shadows to get the lay of the land.

"This giant labyrinth isn't a maze?" Cassius asked sarcastically.

"Look at the walls. Those are the wild tribe's etchings. The left one says 'wisdom,' the middle one says 'valor,' and the right one says 'spirit.'" Morgan's shadows still writhed, and I realized it might be anxiety. I didn't even stop to consider that someone who claimed to want to kill Argarg might get anxious about a dungeon, but this was the first time Morgan had entered one with me.

"Let's do valor!" Cassius said immediately, and I had to grab his shoulder to stop him from rushing down the middle path.

"Hold on, man. You're a mage. Valor screams warrior. Think about it. If you fail this test you're either dead or expelled." Even as I spoke, I saw the flames in Cassius's eyes burn brighter, but he held his anger in check. Barely. I could see the veins on his temple throb, and his hands clenched hard into fists.

". . . yeah." That was all I got from him, and then he deflated, as if he'd been defeated. "I don't know. I've always been the worst at making the right decision. Wisdom is out, and I don't even know what spirit would be?"

"In the north, Spirit Trials are used to find and bind companion spirits. Shamanism." Morgan eyed Cassius. "You are one of the least mage-like people I've ever met. I say we go down spirit."

Cassius didn't argue. He took the comments like an uppercut, but he didn't lash out. Instead, he moved for the right path.

"I'll take the lead. Morgan you take the rear."

We got all excited for nothing. Once we went down the path marked Spirit we followed a winding path for a few hundred meters and found another portal waiting. When we stepped through it, we appeared in a swamp. I had never seen a swamp with brambles the color of blood, or thorns the size of daggers, but dungeons had the freedom to slip the bonds of rational evolution in favor of challenging you.

"I can barely see," Cassius grumbled and created a ball of fire to float over his hand. The moment his flame lit, the air filled with shrieks from the trees, and bubbles from the ankle-deep water.

"Put it out, now!" Morgan demanded.

"I can't see then!" Cassius objected.

"You'll have to rely on us; we can both see in the dark." I tried to keep any smugness from my voice, but it was hard not to be a little condescending about something someone had made fun of you for before.

"Uhm . . ." The flame went out, but it brought attention to the other source of light in our group. Me. Not only did my hair shine like a rainbow, and my eyes glow, but Rainbow Rush surrounded me in an aura of red that I changed to cyan.

"That way!" Morgan pointed at what looked like a solid wall of brambles, but once I looked closer the illusion faded away to reveal an open path farther into the swamp. I heard something burst from the water in the distance. "Let's get out of here before whatever that was catches us," Morgan demanded.

No one asked me if I could turn the light show off. I couldn't, and the dungeon didn't seem to care about that. The water started to churn ominously, while shrieks filled the trees.

"Follow me; you won't sink into the water." I only jogged. There was no way Morgan or Cassius could keep up with me if I actually ran. I jogged on top of the churning, swampy water, and behind me, a trail of cyan energy danced in wisps that would allow the other two to also walk on my wake.

"Left!" Morgan called, and navigated me. Occasionally, Morgan demanded a fireball from Cassius to distract enemies, light bog gasses on fire, or for all I know, just to make Cassius sweat. After what seemed like hours of running, but was maybe ten minutes at most, the swamp gave way to a pyramid. We took a breather a few meters up the stone structure, but nothing from the swamp followed us.

"How'd you know where to go?" I asked.

"It was the same layout as from the front doors of the academy to the headmaster's office," Cassius answered me, earning a surprised look from Morgan. "I noticed it after you did, but I couldn't see the turns anyway."

"Good job. I didn't notice anything." I laughed, a little embarrassed.

"Have you always been able to walk on water?" Cassius asked. "I cost my team five points in last year's obstacle course because I lost so much time on the water-wall. Your class is so overpowered, with all those different elements."

"It is a very versatile class," I said with a nod. It felt awkward talking about my class with people, even Morgan. The only person with a more broken class than me was Lilith. My moms, Arkaziel, and Bobbi didn't count. Based on their jokes, they existed outside the System, I was pretty sure.

"Enough resting. Let's see what's up top." Morgan spoke moments before me. Had they sensed my discomfort and broken it, or were they just impatient? Lilith would've said impatient, but Lilith also thought Morgan only liked me for the access to our family, power, wealth, and resources. I preferred to think Morgan liked me, and those things were extras, but my stash of gold and items had become nearly depleted. I desperately needed some more dungeons or an allowance.

"One hundred and fifty-nine . . ." Cassius counted each step, while Morgan and I walked hand in hand. Morgan's pale skin had the flush of warmth from our run, although the air around them remained slightly cool, a side effect of their darkness powers.

"Two hundred. It's taller than I thought it'd be." Cassius looked back over the swamp, and I reached back to nudge him.

"Eyes forward, dude."

The top of the pyramid consisted of an altar under which magic flames burned. Above the altar floated a man made of flames.

"Ifrit!" Cassius exclaimed in excitement. The man, who seemed elderly, laughed at being identified so.

"You know my kind. That is good. Which of you will undergo my test?"

Cassius answered before I opened my mouth to volunteer.

"It's my fault we're here. I'll take your test."

The flame man waved a hand, and visions formed around Cassius. A mixture of heat haze, illusions, and some other power I couldn't identify ensnared Cassius.

"Your friend will not be able to hear you. He sees the village of Darkbriar, threatened by the red dragonling Astarral. There are only two paths available to him. He may save the village, or he may fight the dragon after it has grown full and slow from feasting upon the corpses of Darkbriar."

I cringed. Part of me thought Cassius would opt for the second path. Shockingly, though, he saved the village. In the images it played out, with the fire mage and fire dragon exchanging blows, until at last the young dragon fell. Cassius had acquired a large number of injuries, all of which transferred to his real body.

"Arrrg." Cassius groaned in pain as the injuries became real. "Next trial."

Cassius tried to sound tough. Maybe he assumed I'd be able to heal him, but the wounds looked like they belonged there. I might be able to break the magic and then heal him outside of the dungeon, but inside I suspected he wouldn't be able to cheat the trials. To test it out I switched to life kinesis, and the healing energies just fizzled out without improving his condition.

Then a new blossom of heat haze surrounded Cassius.

"He sees your town of Winona struck with disease, a plague that defies all magical healing. Yet a cure is found in a distant mountain village, but to harness the cure would destroy the spiritual center of the mountain grove, and the village itself. Does he save your home, or the mountain?"

I winced, watching the illusory story that matched the ifrit's words. Again, Cassius surprised me, when he doomed the mountain grove to cure the plague in Winona. No injuries transferred to his body, this time, but a darkness showed underneath his eyes, an exhaustion and tiredness that had not been there before. For me and Morgan, it had been a few images and a theoretical solution, but in the spell of the ifrit, Cassius had experienced it as a true-life event.

"You have passed my trials, youngling. Now, go. The final trial awaits you." A portal of glimmering golden light appeared behind the old ifrit.

"Thank you," Cassius said to the old man, before he led the way into the golden portal.

We appeared in the vast ruins of a castle. In the midst of the piled rubble stood a ten-meter-tall statue of a majestic man with glowing eyes.

"Defeat me if you can, or flee if you lack the strength." A new golden portal appeared at the far edge of the fight, but none of us went toward it.

"About time I get to try Moral Dilemma out on a boss. Telos refused to tell me what 'sickleium' is, or why she made the sickle and chain out of it, why it looks evil as hell, or even why she named it Moral Dilemma." Morgan smiled savagely and lifted the aforementioned Moral Dilemma, a black-bladed and black-hafted sickle, with its strange pike-like blade and attached weighted chain. Telos had called it a kusarigama, but everyone else called it a sickle.

I activated Tides of Woe and Dragonfly Strike.

# CHAPTER 44

# The Guardian of Balance

**Your target, Guardian of Balance, is immune to petrification.**

Tides of Woe had never failed me before, but apparently you couldn't petrify a stone statue. I had never run into an immunity to one of my random ailments before, and it annoyed me. Strangely, the statue wasn't immune to bleeding. The bleed from my Dragonfly Strike sent ruptures across the stone entity, and a dark gray ooze wept from the wounds. I liked the idea of bleeding stones; it was very dramatic, a little bit poetic, and showcased how amazing I was.

I didn't let it throw off my game and drove a flurry of five hits onto the Guardian, of which the fourth strike of my combo activated Calamitous Touch, and the bleeding effects of the statue grew more severe. Drawing back from the combo as the statue turned to face me, finally, I activated Chromatic Cascade. Green still shot through my aura, as the wave of life energy blasted away from me and struck the Guardian. A sickly brown miasma clung to the statue, which I knew to be a healing prevention debuff.

Fire shot out of the statue's eyes at me, but I activated Dragonfly Strike again, and after I struck the back of the statue I rebounded back to Morgan and Cassius.

"How fucking fast are you?!" Cassius spat in disbelief. "And how does punching stone not break your hands?"

I didn't answer Cassius, since we were a little busy.

A huge veil of darkness exploded from Morgan, and took the form of four flickering goblinoid figures. Each one was made of wispy shadows, but possessed a solidity that left me without any doubt that they could cause physical damage.

"Attack," Morgan commanded the four imperiously, and the four ran forward to engage the slowly turning statue. I positioned myself to hit the Guardian, the goblins, and Morgan with Aurora Burst. Unlike Chromatic Cascade, Aurora Burst afflicted enemies with a random ailment regardless of my active kinesis, cleansed debuffs from allies hit, and if there was nothing to cleanse, it would give you a random buff.

**Cassius Thorn gains Guardian's Ward: Reduces incoming damage by 15%.**

**Morgan (and summons) gain Celestial Guidance: Improves accuracy and evasion by 20%.**

**You have gained Radiant Glow: Heal nearby (10m) allies for 5% of their health every five seconds.**

The Guardian statue unleashed a blast of flames from its palms. The already agile shadow-goblins avoided the attack with an alacrity that surprised me. Admittedly, I was a little jealous that Morgan and the goblins got the evasion buff. Even more shocking than the speed the shadow summons displayed, the flame attack ricocheted off the floor and swarmed to Cassius, who cast Absorb Flame and channeled the flames into a rapidly expanding orb.

Something seemed to change in the Guardian, and its eyes went from flaming to shooting streams of highly pressurized water. Morgan, I, and three of the goblins avoided them. One goblin got obliterated, but its wispy form coalesced after a second. The crash of pressurized water into the flames Cassius controlled was far more impressive. The water hissed as it evaporated, and visibility dropped as steam flooded the immediate area.

I reactivated Tides of Woe on the Guardian, and it froze in place, stunned.

"Freeze it!" Morgan shouted at me, and I cycled my kinesis to cold, and blue dominated my kaleidoscopic aura. I went with the tried-and-true one-two punch of Dragonfly Strike, to refresh and add another stack of bleeding, followed up by Chromatic Cascade, which unleashed a full wave of cold directly into the backside of the statue.

"Burn it! As hot as you can!" Morgan demanded of Cassius, and I could see where we were heading with this. Hot and cold, rock—this could get messy depending on Morgan's next move. I backed off the Guardian, but it was pissed at me and lifted both hands to smash me. Flames cascaded across its back, and I left patches of ice behind as I used Rainbow Rush to its fullest to make some distance.

Morgan had the goblins move in first, and they smashed the back side of the statue. Hunks of stone fell off, and then Morgan twirled the weighted end of the chain of their sickle. A few quick rounds to build momentum, and then the weighted end elongated and wrapped all the way around the statue. Then Morgan pulled, and I tripped over my own foot, face hitting the ground.

The statue crumbled to pieces. The "chain" cut through the statue with relative ease, and huge chunks of its form crashed to the ground. On the ground, the remaining pieces lost cohesion and turned to dust, leaving behind four marbles (one each of red, blue, brown, and green).

**Congratulations, you have passed the Trial of Worthiness.**

"Oof." I groaned, but the healing buff pulsed before I wiped blood away from my nose, returning me to as good as new.

"Your mom is insane!" Morgan laughed a little hysterically. "Why does the *chain* cut?"

"Didn't you read the description?" I asked and read the part I assumed was applicable. "Made from sickleium, a transcendent metal. What happens when you make a sickle from sickles, all the way down to the atomic level? Why not make the chain of sickles too? Be very careful about what you want to cut while wielding this weapon." Unlike Morgan, I had familiarity with the need to read the finer details on anything made by my mothers.

Cassius coughed. I thought he was trying to get my attention, but he was really just trying to disperse the lingering steam clouds.

"What are those marbles?" Morgan asked.

"I think they're for Cassius. Fire, Earth, Wind, and Water cores." I'd seen their like many times before. These were potent, but not nearly on the level of the ones Mom kept in her smithy.

"What do we do with them?" Cassius asked.

"I could answer that," the ifrit from earlier said as he appeared in a heat haze. "Are you ready for a class upgrade, young man?"

"Yes!" Cassius shouted in excitement.

I took the time to walk over to Morgan, and peck a kiss on their cheek. "Good job."

"Let's watch the show, first," Morgan said with an impish smile. They wanted to see what happened next with Cassius.

"Focus, young man. Concentrate on the elements, draw them into your being. How well you do will determine the class you gain."

I'd never seen a class upgrade before. Cassius grasped the four elemental cores in his hand, closed his eyes, and presumably concentrated. Whatever he did, it resulted in multiple hues of light shining from his hands. The more the light shone, the more tiny motes of color filled the ruins around us. First five, then ten, then hundreds of tiny lights that looked like fireflies darted everywhere. They flew around Cassius in chaotic orbits that filled the air with glee.

"Spirits, right?" Morgan asked me in a hushed whisper of awe.

"I think so?" I assumed what we were seeing was spirits, but I wasn't sure. I wasn't a nature kind of class, and none of my abilities controlled spirits, that I knew of. Maybe hanging around Cassius would unlock a spirit kinesis? What color would spirits even be?

I could see Cassius talking but couldn't hear him. Before I could ask if he needed help, all of the swarmed spirits congregated to Cassius and gave him an epic bear hug. They squeezed and squeezed, and then Cassius glowed like a sun for a fraction of a moment, and then the spirits were all gone. With them went the sense of glee and wonder that had filled the ruins, and I felt a slight emptiness inside myself with their disappearance.

"We beat the trial and I got a new class! I'm a Primal Caller now! All of my abilities upgraded. Thank you so much, Alexander, Morgan." Cassius rubbed the back of his head with one hand awkwardly. "I'm sorry for the past."

"I forgive you, but I hope you're better at talking with spirits than people," Morgan said. Their tone rode the line between sass and sincerity so tightly I couldn't quite tell where Cassius stood in Morgan's eyes. Their sass had a cut to it that was as sharp as the chains of Moral Dilemma.

"We're good, man. You'd better apologize to Lilith when we get out of here, or she'll keep holding a grudge forever." I felt slightly conflicted. On one hand, Cassius had been an oafish bully for as long as I could remember, but on the other there was a version of him who wasn't an asshole. I had to forgive the version of him I hated for him to become the version I might be able to call a friend. It wasn't a difficult choice.

Small, quiet voices whispered in my psyche that I shouldn't have helped him to begin with, that he might regress to being an asshole now that he didn't need my help anymore, that maybe the sight of those amazing spirits would lead to Cassius stealing Morgan away from me. There were so many tiny, spiteful, pitiful what-ifs in my mind that it just turned into the droning of mosquitos—a dull background noise that I ignored, because it didn't matter.

Why did so many other people have such a hard time just silencing the drone of base thoughts? It seemed so easy, but Lilith said it was because we weren't human. She claimed that the quiet drone we heard was more like a blaring horn for humans, and most other races, too. I have no idea how she knew that, but maybe she learned it from our mothers? She asked a lot wordier stuff of them, while I mostly pressed Momma to teach me more fighting.

"Now, where's the loot?" I asked almost exactly at the same time as the System spawned an impressive-looking magic circle with a chest in the middle. Unfamiliar sigils glowed in arcane script, and the runes circled the chest in a slow, even rotation.

"May I?" Morgan asked as they walked to the chest.

"Go for it," Cassius said.

"Wait." I kissed Morgan's cheek. "For good luck."

"Thanks." Morgan's eyes rolled a little in response to the kiss on the cheek, before they took the last step and opened the chest. Fireworks filled the air, confetti fell from the sky, and the chest vanished. Two items remained behind.

"Dibs." Morgan laughed and picked up a pair of sunglasses. They were made of platinum and had mirrored lenses and ornate metal scrollwork across them. I'd never seen a pair of glasses made before, but it made sense, since they were System creations.

"Those look fantastic on you." I didn't have to wait long to compliment Morgan. They put the glasses on immediately.

"They make me immune to blinding and give me a bonus to resisting light with my darkness. Worth it. What'd you get?" Morgan looked down at what looked like a gray puffball of fog in my hand.

"Believe it or not, it's an accessory item." I laughed, then equipped and activated it. "It's called Runic Fog."

I laughed because within a two-meter radius, fog billowed around my legs. While it was only calf high, it obscured my feet very well. The fog provided a great backdrop for the chromatic shifts of my hair and aura and combined to create a sensory distortion. Within the dense fog, strange runes occasionally formed, creating even more illumination and color mischief.

"Fighting you would be the worst," Morgan groaned. "What's it do?"

"It confuses enemies and makes me harder to target."

"It makes you harder to look at, for sure," Cassius said with a grimace. I'd been about to turn the effect off, but I left it on for a little longer to spite him.

**Trial clear. Exit the dungeon.**

The System demanded, even as a portal of golden light appeared.

# CHAPTER 45

# Uninvited Guests

**FH 55 Spring. Winona.**

An impenetrable dome of ice covered the whole of Winona, protecting the burgeoning city. At the apex of the dome stood two women, one blonde and one with rainbow-colored hair. In the skies above Winona flocked dragons. Hundreds of dragons. Most were relatively young, but a few elders flew in the flock. There was no unifying element or species to the gathered dragons; they answered the call of power universal to their draconic lineage.

One such elder dragon crashed into the plains south of Winona, grasped in the claws of a much larger draconic being. Arkaziel stood out like a sore thumb, what with his true form now exceeding twenty-five kilometers from the tip of his nose to the end of his main tail. The elder dragon was little more than a bird compared to a jumbo jet, yet Arkaziel had made a point to grasp the dragon in his claw and crash him into the plains.

The elder dragon didn't survive that, obviously, and Arkaziel created a massive ravine filled with fragments of dragon scale, bone, and blood. It would be known as Dragon Gorge in the coming days, and the magics of the dragon would lead to a boon in crafting, and its explorers would come to develop dragon-related classes.

"RAAAAAAAAAAAAR!" The black StarMane roared at the flocks of dragons in the sky, but none fled. Which was impressive, considering how much larger Arkaziel was than the entire swarm of dragons, or how much more terrifying the Void-touched Dragon of the Apocalypse was than your run-of-the-mill green or red dragon.

+*Sorry, Blue, looks like they won't listen to reason.*+ Arkaziel's telepathic voice filtered across the bond the four (Telos, Kallos, Bobbi, and Arkaziel) shared. In contrast with the anger in his roar, the black cat's mental voice carried regret.

Bobbi joined Telos and Kallos atop the ice dome, or a projection of her did, at least.

"Nothing has made it inside; the kids are mostly bored. Some of the more exuberant ones want to try to fight a dragon. If we don't get this sorted soon, *your* children are going to attempt a jailbreak to fight a dragon." The projection of Bobbi laughed at the annoyed looks the women shared.

"It'll be dealt with shortly. Tell them to stay inside, or else," Telos assured the projection.

"I'd rather not destroy them all," Kallos murmured.

"I'm not going to destroy them. I'm going to disperse them . . . peacefully." When Telos finished the words, she vanished and reappeared in the sky, and the dragons responded as if gold started to rain upon them, happily. Her power was what had drawn them in the first place.

"Gather in, little ones. Let's give you a taste of what you want, and a purpose, too." Telos beckoned, and the dragons could not resist her voice, or the hypnotic sparkle of light that filled the sky. Waves of crystal-clear water billowed out from the floating woman, crashing into the swarm of dragons and capturing them, pulling them in closer, and swirling them in a vortex around Telos. The few aquatic species of dragons, who swam euphorically through the magical water, prevented a panic from the dragons who weren't naturals in water. The sedative properties of the high-energy water went to work slowing all of the dragons down, and Telos had to make minor adjustments to concentrations to prevent any harm to the dragons.

*Libby? Incorporate these dragons into trials of their elements. Negotiate with the ones that are sentient after they detox from sensing my power. Send those who have sentience back home once they can control themselves, and offer jobs to the ones who don't. We'll nurture the non-sentient ones with training to be worthy of the role. Don't let them roam free, or they'll just come back here.*

*::Yes, Mistress. Fred and Reverie wish to make one of them a pet and are requesting permission.::*

*Yes, that's fine. It would be good for them to have a pet. Pick a silver dragon for them.*
*::Done. Transfer initiated.::*

The dragons, along with the crystal waters they had been ensnared by, all vanished from the skies, and Telos reappeared on the dome, where Arkaziel now sat in cat form, licking his paws clean. The black cat studiously avoided looking to the south, and the massive gorge he had created.

"I could have eaten them," Arkaziel said with a halfhearted pout. Telos could tell that his stomach wasn't really in it, and Arkaziel even seemed to feel bad for the dragons. It was draconic nature to be drawn to power.

"You'll have your fill when you revisit Grief, won't you? Quit being greedy." Telos pretended to scold him severely, and completed the dress down by picking him up, cuddling her face against his, and giving Arkaziel belly rubs.

"Stooooop!" Arkaziel whined halfheartedly. He even pawed pathetically at the air.

"How long until more come?" Kallos asked with a tightly controlled tone. Not laughing, and attempting to keep her lips from turning into a smile, took a visible effort of all of her willpower, even with the serious conversation they were having.

"Four or five days," Telos answered. "Our ambient powers are too bright of a beacon."

"*Our?*" Arkaziel asked with a high-pitched gasp when Telos brought him up to her face and bopped her nose against his.

"Yes, *ours*. Even excluding Kallos's and my power that you and Bobbi share, you two are the next two most powerful beings in this reality. So even if I broke the soul-binds, these confluences would continue to happen if you two stayed in one place for a few years."

"What would even happen if you did that?" Bobbi asked curiously.

"Break the soul-binds? You and Arkaziel would lose access to my power. So, you'd lose some of your base power, but still be incredibly powerful on your own. All that power would settle in me and Kallos. Well, Kallos, actually, since I'm already at capacity, and her vessel is nearly there too. So, within a month or so we'd exceed the ability of the dimensional axis to handle our continued presence. We'd either risk fundamental damage to the whole multiverse by staying or have to depart for Pleroma." Telos didn't mention the strange mystery at the center of the River of Light.

"So that's out," Bobbi said dismissively.

"The end doesn't change, only the timing does." Kallos responded curtly.

"It's likely our ascension to Pleroma, or what lies beyond, will break our bonds when Kallos and I ascend. That's part of why I empowered Libby with Fred and Reverie. She'll continue to run uninterrupted, regardless of what happens to us, and slowly integrate lower dimensions into the System. You two are already ridiculously powerful, but maybe it'll be a good learning experience for one of you to only have your own power to rely on." Telos bopped Arkaziel's nose with the tip of her fingertip, and he gave her an offended look.

"See, this is why I stick to humanoid forms." Bobbi smirked at Arkaziel's treatment. "You don't see anyone bopping my nose."

"How do we stop drawing dragons and other power-seekers? Dragons are one thing, but what if you pull the Warlord of the North, or the King of Nightmares to Winona?" Arkaziel teleported out of the hold Telos had him in and morphed into his humanoid form.

"Argarg won't come down here for years. He has his eyes set on the ancient ruins I seeded under that crystal Erdtree. That will keep him busy for another five years. By then Morgan and the kids should be strong enough to take him out. The King of Nightmares would be a problem, so I've had Libby keep him occupied. The Tyrant of Terror has already started building a fleet to cross the ocean, but she won't make it in time, especially with the new Sun King that's rising in the West." Telos shook her head.

"The immediate problem is monsters, dragons, and spirits. They can't resist the siren's song. Can you mask it?" Despite knowing the answer already, Telos asked Kallos anyway.

"You could simply abandon your rule of Power Calls to Power. If you changed the rules, then it wouldn't happen, obviously." Kallos arched a brow at Telos.

"You're the one who enforced As Above, So Below," Telos noted with a smirk. "I can't go and break one of your rules on a whim."

"I appreciate that, but you are both the author of all rules and enforcer of consequence. Changing the rules need only affect me if you decide it should." Kallos smirked.

"Wow, just get a room already," Bobbi growled. "It's like watching someone with two bodies flirting with themselves." Bobbi rolled her eyes at the other two women, but a new presence made itself known before anyone could react. A heavy pressure, a heavenly presence—bubbles filled the air, motes of light shone.

A crystalline chime rang in the minds of all four. It was a pleasant sound, and served as a greeting from a great distance.

"What is it, Bythos?" Telos asked the sky.

A greater than three-dimensional geometric crystalline entity, rendered in a scale the size of a human head, appeared among them.

*"The cycle ever repeats itself. You have another choice other than those you have mentioned."*

A hopeful look crossed Kallos's, Arkaziel's, and Bobbi's faces, but Telos showed no glimmer of optimism. Her air of resignation remained complete.

"I'm not going to reincarnate right now." Telos preempted what she thought Bythos would suggest.

*"Sige and I have empowered the Mantle of Mortality. It effectively narrows the gates. Each time you channel, your power will accelerate the draining of the enchantment. Please note, each time you draw your power, you will be hit with a surfeit of power. Reliance on local, lesser energies will prevent this."*

A red trench coat dropped into the hands of Telos. After a moment, her black coat vanished into her repository, and she pulled the new one on. For old time's sake, her multicolored hair shifted to a pure, radiant aqua glow.

"I can barely sense your presence," Bobbi exclaimed.

"Good job, crystal guy," Arkaziel complimented the Aeon, who vibrated with discomfort.

"Thank you, Bythos. This is a very thoughtful gift, and I appreciate you and Sige both thinking about my problems. Will this affect Libby or the kids at all?" Telos asked with optimism. She hadn't thought an item like this cloak to be possible, but she hadn't considered the possibility of using Sige or Bythos to conceal herself, as that wasn't what the Aeons were meant for.

*Or is it what they were meant for? Yeah, no.*

*"Since you formed direct channels for Libby that operate outside of your power, it will have no effect on her. Your children's power sources are their own, and likewise will be unaffected. We exist to serve you,"* Bythos chimed and then vanished as he had come.

"Who was that guy again?" Arkaziel asked without any hint of embarrassment.

"Really? You can't remember a big glowing crystal that spills into dozens of extra dimensions?" Bobbi's exasperation reached a new limit with Arkaziel.

"Think of him as the maintenance man for reality," Kallos suggested.

"So, he's stuck doing all the hard work, day in and day out, while the executives are off having a family, making swords, eating good food, and all around having a good time? He got screwed. You should really make it up to him, Blue."

All three women stared blankly at Arkaziel, and Telos kicked a foot at the ice dome in embarrassment, before she sniffed and smiled at Arkaziel.

"Aww. My kitten is all grown up and knows how to use empathy now. I'm so proud."

# CHAPTER 46

# Silence

**FH 56, Winter. The Crystal Spire.**

Ever since Lilith and I started attending the academy, we had lived our daily lives in Arkaziel's manor, with only occasional visits to the Crystal Spire. The Spire was a strange place. Rooms within the crystalline structure didn't follow physical rules like internal space being smaller than exterior space. Some rooms went far beyond violation of physical laws, like the library. Our library was infinite. Mom said it was actually a place called Binah, or likened it to something called an Akashic Record, but I didn't know what either of those things were.

Sure, I could have looked up those terms in the library, but if you fell down the hole of looking up all of Mom's strange sayings and odd phrases, you'd never get anything else done. Not really, it didn't happen that often, but Lilith had far more interest in those things than I did. Even now, Lilith was in the library with Mommy, while Mom and I were in the training room.

It's important to understand that room wasn't how I'd describe it and wasn't at all accurate. As far as I could see, the ground was made of limestone. The lack of life felt absolute. There were no insects in the training room, no grass, no life of any kind except for Mom and me.

There were fifteen training dummies, five of which had several of my afflictions upon them.

"It looks like your Spectrum Surge trait caps at a fifty percent bonus, your Malicious Tormentor passive has no cap, and Rainbow Rush's bonus to Agility applies after those two have already bolstered your Agility." Telos stood behind me, reading my status screen over my shoulder.

"I peaked at one hundred and seventy-three when I had effects on all the dummies." I agreed with Mom's summary of the modifiers in play on my Agility.

"You're very focused on Agility, sweetie. You haven't progressed any of your traits in quite a while, and you've been stuck on level nineteen for a few months now. Being fast is good, really good, but you can't focus on it to the detriment of yourself as a whole. Your kinesis abilities are fantastic, and Spectrum Surge rewards you for using them. How come you don't make more use of them?"

"Uh, well. It feels like showing off or grandstanding if I go full-out with my powers. Lilith's always there with a spell, Morgan's ready to finish off enemies after I imbalance them, or there's one of Derrick's traps to kick an enemy into . . ." I shrugged. "When I use my kinesis powers, it feels like showing off, I guess? I preempt my teammates, and I don't want anyone to feel underutilized."

"That's fair." Telos laughed. "But you won't always be fighting with your friends at your back, and if you don't practice with them now, you might not have the skill with them when it really matters. Everyone holds back, some, in a team fight. If you went all out, all the time, you'd have no reserves to draw on when the unexpected happens, or be exhausted before you got to a boss fight. Resource management is important to a party, but you and Lilith are largely free from resource concerns."

"Sure, but there's the mental drain of keeping track of it all," I argued.

"Well, I suppose that's true, but that's because you haven't spent the time with your powers that you should have and have been making out with Morgan instead." Telos teased me in mock disapproval. I think it was a joke, anyway. She sure didn't seem to be annoyed by my burgeoning relationship with Morgan.

"Okay, okay, I'll work on my kinesis control." I held up both hands in defeat.

"Practice your shadow kinesis with Morgan. Your generation of even more shadows for them opens a world of battlefield opportunities, especially combined with your mobility. There's a lot of combos you two could pull off, the way Aisha and Lilith do."

I didn't object that Lilith could work with anyone. She could invoke any kind of magic, real or imaginary, with next to no limitations. Not that different from my kinesis control, really, but still. I needed to work on my natural reaction to get defensive at any comparisons to my sister. We were siblings, and we both had incredible powers and our own strengths, but for some reason it always felt like Lilith had advantages over me. Her intelligence intimidated me.

"So, what's my grade?"

"You get an A, this time. You've learned all the moves I've taught you; you've gotten much better about front-loading applications of afflictions on as many targets as possible at the start of a fight, and your cycling of your Cascade and Burst between kinesis powers has gotten better. You're a formidable brawler with unparalleled mobility, and your spatial awareness and instinctive fluttery nature make you a great evasion fighter. So, for a job well done, you get a special guest teacher today."

I didn't like the way Mom smiled at me with those words.

The space near us wavered, and a monkey with a staff and a weird hat appeared.

"Thanks for agreeing to this, old friend." Mom bowed her head in thanks to the monkey. "Alexander, pay close attention to everything Sun Wukong shows you, okay? When your lesson is done I'll be in the parlor." Telos waved at me and the monkey, and then a doorway appeared for her to return to the main areas of the Spire.

I eyed the monkey. He eyed me.

We both laughed, then I doubled over, coughing. The butt of his staff had knocked the wind out of me.

"Let's train," Sun Wukong told me.

For what seemed like months, Sun Wukong showed me the true meaning of evasion. The monkey showed me moves I had a hard time comprehending. From dodging by the width of a hair, to the time he sacrificed a hair and it turned into a rhinoceros and charged me! He could somersault thousands of kilometers at a time, or just a few meters, all as his battle strategy called for.

It felt like I was fighting an impossible force of nature, one that could not be overcome, no matter what I did. If the monkey hadn't been trying to teach me, it would have been depressing, or discouraging. Instead, I walked away from my time with the Monkey King with a new appreciation for all of the tricks he had at his disposal. I lacked some of his abilities, but I had what seemed to be his favorites at least: speed and invisibility. I lacked them in the quantities he had, but I was very young, he said.

"Done already?" Telos, Kallos, and Lilith were sipping tea in the parlor.

"Already? I was gone for months! Didn't anyone notice?" I huffed, but I couldn't work up any righteous indignation with the scornful look in Lilith's eyes, or the humorous looks both parents were giving me.

"Did you forget that the training room is a dream realm, darling?" Kallos asked gently, as she set her teacup down and moved over to give me a hug, and a kiss on the cheek. "Or, perhaps, did your mother forget to tell you?"

I groaned. The whole time I had been conflicted over missing time with Morgan and my friends, and it had all been the equivalent of a dream?

"Ope. My bad, Alexander. I thought you knew that room was a dream realm."

"I knew it was a dream realm," Lilith interjected in a smug way.

"Show us the results of your training!" Telos demanded with a smile.

"Well, here's the summary."

I gestured, and my recent gains showed up.

**Due to intense training with Sun Wukong you have gained the following: +10 Agility, Tides of Woe has evolved, and you have gained the Class Feature: Bending Blows.**

**Tides of Woe may now hit multiple targets at a time.**

**Bending Blows: What is space? Who cares. Your limbs can defy probability and physical laws, stretching or bending as needed to land impossible hits, just like Sun Wukong's Ruyi Jingu Bang.**

"Good job, buddy!" Telos gushed in praise at me, while Kallos hugged me tightly and gave me a kiss on the top of the head.

"That's really good. How bendy are we talking?" Lilith asked while staring at me as if I were an insect.

"Small amounts. I can't pull off telescopic attacks, at least, not yet."

"Obviously, you just learned it. Still, that should make you even better at maintaining our front lines in combat. Good job!" Lilith's praise felt good to hear, but I sort of hated that it made me feel good. I wanted to be able to tell her to stuff it, that I didn't need her approval, but I couldn't, because I did want her approval as much as I wanted our mothers', or even Morgan's approval.

"Who is Sun Wukong, anyway?" I asked.

"He didn't tell you?" Telos seemed shocked.

"Just that he was a Great Sage." I shrugged. I'd asked for more, but the monkey hadn't been interested in telling me stories, only training me.

"He's from the Lower Realms, and one of the more powerful entities you can find wandering freely." Telos smiled fondly, and I had to admit, I smiled too, imagining that willful monkey wandering free, doing whatever he fancied.

"You never talk about the Lower Realms," I said slightly accusatory.

"It's true," Lilith agreed with me.

Our parents looked at one another, then nodded.

Kallos materialized objects from nowhere, and filled the coffee table with sandwiches, desserts, and a few different pitchers of sweet-smelling drinks.

"You're not going to distract us with Bobbi's cooking!" Lilith proclaimed.

"Oh, calm your butt, coconut. It's a long story. First of all, it's important for you to understand the shape of the multiverse we inhabit is similar to a tree. The foundational lower levels are farthest away from the sunlight that nourishes them. That light is Ein Sof. Our dimension resides at the tippy top of the dimensional axis, with only Pleroma, the diffuse layers of Ein Sof, separating us from the River of Light, or the real form of Ein Sof." While Telos spoke, Kallos gestured and created minor illusions for us.

"That looks like a spiral galaxy," Lilith noted.

"A little bit, sure. It's not a galaxy though. This dimension used to be the domain of the Overgod of this multiverse, until we killed him and created this existence. Kallos and I were both born in the next dimension down." Telos grinned. "Any guesses how old your moms are? Wait, no, don't answer that."

"Anyway, I was born on a planet called Earth."

"Earth? Your planet was named after dirt? That's a little redundant, Mom." Lilith held nothing back.

"Well, technically it was Sol III, but we just called it Earth. It doesn't matter; quit making fun of Mommy's home planet. My time there was short, anyway. I died and was reincarnated on the ancient planet of Grief, where I got suckered into climbing the Tower of Aetherius. That's where I met Kallos, and we formed our bond."

"Ohh, details!" I demanded.

"I was one of the Masters in the training city of Solace." Kallos sighed.

"Teacher-student relations? Aren't those a huge forbidden thing at Winona?" Lilith gave our parents a meaningful look, which made both blush.

"Anyway, I met Arkaziel in the tower too. I watched him hatch and had to protect his clutch mates from some StarMane predators, then his parents showed up, and it turned into a whole thing. He bonded with me, and he's been with me ever since."

"Hatch? I guess he is a dragon . . ." I trailed off.

"So, we climbed a tower, then went on to climb another, but I was able to summon Kallos for the second one. I missed her so much, and it felt a lot more enjoyable to adventure with her. Bobbi joined us in the second tower, toward the end, too. Arkaziel tricked her into losing a cook-off."

"Uncle Arkaziel beat Bobbi at cooking?! How?" I felt like everything I knew was under assault.

"He cheated, of course," Kallos answered.

We talked for hours, with our parents diving in and out of small parts of their journey, or to explain who Primordials and gods were. That's how I found out Mom created the System, and their time with us had a hard limit, if we didn't want to risk the stability of reality. Lilith acted like she had figured it all out before, but I think even she was shocked by some of the things our parents told us that day.

From the descriptions of gods, Primordials, Outer Gods, Transcendent Beings, an Overgod, Archons, and everything else, I felt like there being no gods on the highest dimension felt right. They sounded awful, especially Chaos and Sophia, who sounded like villains the way they had engineered the lives of the Metanoia family. Mom wasn't very clear on what happened to the two of them, though, beyond that they'd been pushed into the cycle of reincarnation like all of the Primordials and gods she slew.

"Your friend Derrick was the trapmaster we encountered multiple times," was also a big bombshell to deal with. On one hand, it was things Derrick had no knowledge or memory of, but if he ever awoke past life memories, he could potentially remember Mom.

My gut told me some of the others in our life were also reincarnations from our parents' past. I felt almost certain that Morgan, for example, was Mom's friend, Callie. But if that were the case, why wouldn't she have let Callie have her memories so they could be friends again? It did explain why she'd made a personal weapon for Morgan; Telos hadn't made anything comparable to Moral Dilemma for anyone other than me and Lilith.

It also raised a question I disliked: were Lilith and I reincarnations? But in the face of knowing we had less than two years left with our mothers, the rest seemed inconsequential.

# CHAPTER 47

# Legacy



So, I know it looks a lot like my coat, but I thought that maybe you'd like that?" Telos held a calf-length red coat out to me. It had beautiful embroidery across the cuffs and shoulders, and glimmering obsidian buttons drew my eyes right in. Unlike Mom's coat, which had snowflake embroidery across the shoulders, mine had dragonflies in a style she called goth.

"It's absolutely beautiful, Mom." I looked out the window, at the sun shining on the academy grounds visible from the front parlor of Arkaziel's manor. "But wouldn't a coat have been more appropriate in winter?"

Mom laughed and ruffled my hair. She had to reach up to do it. I had finally shot up past both of my parents and had reached one hundred and ninety-two centimeters tall. Lilith had stopped growing at one hundred and eighty, just short of our mothers' heights. Lilith had taken to wearing thick-soled boots to make up a few centimeters' difference.

"It's a versatile coat. It looks like a long coat now, but I designed five different preset appearances for it. Long coat, tailed coat, windbreaker, suit jacket, and vest. Any of the equipment you link to it can be transformed along with it, so you'll always look good."

"Wait, what?" I blinked a few times.

"Yeah, you can link your equipment with it. Temporarily or permanently, and use a little transmutation magic to change their appearance to what you're imagining, but I made four presets, too, for on the fly or mid-combat. You're a speed-based close-quarters combatant, so I thought it was best that you have control of these things."

Mom grabbed the end of her fluttering scarf and gave it a tug. Not for the first time, I wondered how her scarf always fluttered on invisible winds, but the answer always came back to the fact that my sense of drama had come from somewhere.

"You don't want people tugging on your clothes or hair." Telos laughed.

"I've never fought anyone who could even catch my hair besides you or Sun Wukong," I said with a laugh. I knew that wouldn't always be the case. There were people faster than me out there, presumably, and the faster I got the more the System would throw similar speed challenges at me, or it would find ways to negate me.

"Someday you'll find more enemies on your level, tough guy. That's not all the coat does." Mom let that hang in the air, and she watched me with all three eyes. And watched me. Clearly, she was determined to not speak until I did. The last time we tried to out-stubborn one another we'd spent three hours staring at each other.

"Oh yeah? What else does it do?" After I asked, I stuck my tongue out at Mom.

"You're seventeen now, Alexander, and sticking your tongue out stopped being cute when you were five." Mom shook her head in exasperation at me, then patted the jacket. "I put so much good stuff in this thing."

"Like what? An apple?" I asked in honest confusion.

"Yeah, you betcha. An apple." The room felt suddenly colder. There was a direct correlation of how annoyed Mom was to how cold the room was. "Dumbass."

"No, not an apple. The first one unlocks at level twenty, Mr. I've-been-stuck-on-level-nineteen-all-winter. It's called Reflex Resonance. Every successful evasion will grant you a stacking bonus to speed and agility." Telos smirked. If anyone knew my abilities, it would be Mom, and she'd made me a perfect item.

"That's really good. But I know that smirk. What else?"

"Oh, just it has a few other unlockable bonuses on dodge. There's Momentum Burst, Echo Echo, and even Oh-No-He-Didn't!" Mom's smile lit up the room. Figuratively and literally. She always struck me as happiest in these moments, talking about something she'd made for me or Lilith. I only noticed it for a moment, before I fully processed what she'd said.

"What is Oh-No-He-Didn't? That sounds amazing."

"It's a health and stamina surge for each evasion. More precisely, it's a five percent health, five percent stamina restoration over five seconds, stacking." Mom looked at me, waiting.

"You're the best! That's ridiculous, and I can totally imagine someone getting very mad at me healing while they fail to hurt me. The stamina restoration might be even better. Thanks, Mom!" The moment I thanked her, I got picked up and spun around as if I was a helpless child. It drove home the fact that compared to her, I was, which made me bristle inside a tiny bit.

"So, uh. I set the appearance for your gloves to look like mine when you have your coat in trench coat form. You can change it up if you want; I may have gotten a little carried away while I played with everything."

"Your gloves are awesome; I'll keep it that way." That got me another hug I couldn't escape from. Apparently, that had been the right answer.

"It's time to go!" Lilith shouted into the parlor, shortly before she appeared in the doorway. Like me, she was fully equipped, and wore a new robe. If you could call an armored dress a robe. The white skirt nearly touched the floor, and elaborate bronze scrollwork went around the bottom hem of the skirt. All along the bottom of the dress was ornate iconography of arcane beings. Dragons, demons, spirits, nature beings, and monsters I didn't know the name of. Unlike the skirt, the bodice was actual armor. It looked bronze, but knowing our parents, it was some impossible metal unknown to anyone but Telos and Kallos.

Lilith's hair had been piled into braids and arranged in a haughty array to show off the matching crown she wore. When I acquired the Spectrum Goggles, she had acquired the Invoker's Diadem, and it looked fantastic in her hair. Unlike the armor, it was a work of arcane sigils and iconography that wasn't faces, and the band had numerous colored gems, while the top of the piece had white-blue teardrops at each upward point.

"Nice dress!" I immediately complimented Lilith, which got her to spin around and show off the new equipment. Mom somehow slipped the coat onto me while I clapped, and all of my gear's appearance morphed a bit. Even my goggles, which had been hanging around my neck, were now nearly lensless glasses.

"You seemed so jealous of Morgan's glasses," Mom said while she fiddled with my clothes one last time, then stepped away. "There, my handsome young boy is ready to become a man."

"Mom!" I tried to fend her off, but Telos was faster, stronger, and seemed to have fifteen arms at once. I lost the battle, got squished in another hug, but then was saved when she went to attack Lilith instead. As usual, Mom was right, and I loved the glasses version of my goggles.

"Do they still work as well, even though they only cover a fraction of my eyes?" I asked.

"No, yeah, they still provide total protection from blindness and light attacks and will prevent anything from stabbing you in the eye to boot." Mom always had some kind of hidden amusement when talking about items like this. There were comments she seemed to want to make so desperately, but refrained from doing so because Lilith or I wouldn't have the context to understand. So, doubtlessly, it was something from one of the Lower Realms.

"Why would that surprise you? Your gloves protect your whole hands despite being fingerless." Lilith lashed me with her tongue and smiled while doing it.

"Good point," I admitted. The extra levels of thinking before I spoke when Lilith was around could get exhausting quickly.

"Alright, let's get over to the academy. They'll be opening the Trial soon, and Aisha won first entry in the lottery. If I don't get to give her a good luck kiss, I will be very cross."

Mom and I shared a smile at the threat in Lilith's voice and headed to the academy.

The academy rarely had so many people in it. Nearly everyone in town had shown up, and it had turned into almost a fair. Students showed off their abilities to friends and parents, vendors tried to peddle snacks and treats, and then there was row after row of tents of travelers and adventurers who'd come to peddle equipment to the hopeful graduates. A magical item could, potentially, mean the difference between passing a Trial or failure.

"This gets busier every year," Kallos muttered, and her cloak of chains transformed into metal wings. The jangle of chain lengths that hung from her metal wings, mixed with the dark power in the Heavenshadow Chains, got the crowd to part like a bubble around our group. People wisely got out of the way, and if they didn't, the chains writhed and clanked at them, as if they were hissing snakes.

"There's Aisha!" Lilith shouted and pointed.

At the heart of the practice grounds a ten-meter-tall portal had been opened. The colors of it cycled and changed, one moment gold, the next black, then maybe gray. I saw no rhyme or reason for it. Why was it that big? Drama. Why did it make that weird humming sound? Also, drama. Dungeon portals didn't make that sound.

Arkaziel stood talking to Aisha, and behind him a ring of professors stood vigil over the portal. I saw Professor Luminous wave at me, and then Professor Stormreaver must've made a snide remark, because she looked guilty. They were probably bored, since it was all for show. Arkaziel had to give permission for someone to enter the portal, otherwise it was just a flashy bit of lights, but it had started a few years ago after some younger students had tried to sneak into the Trial and caused a whole scene when it didn't work.

I missed Lilith delivering her good luck kiss to Aisha while I'd watched the professors.

Arkaziel lifted a hand into the air. The sky filled with fireworks, explosions, lasers, and just an eyesore of light, that went on for a solid minute, before he lowered his hand and the lightshow ended abruptly.

"Now that I have your attention," Arkaziel said in a very self-satisfied voice. "It's time for this year's Trial to start. Students, line up in your assigned spots."

A line quickly formed, with Aisha at the front. Lilith was in the front third; Derrick had ended up in the middle. Morgan and I brought up the end of the line, which was fine with me, since it gave me a chance to give Morgan a good luck kiss. Repeatedly. Until Professor Sylas made birds swoop at us until we stopped.

"Are you nervous?" Morgan finally asked when half of the line before us had gone into the portal.

"Not even a little. We've got this. You?" I didn't have a hard time finding confidence for the both of us. We were awesome, after all.

"I don't know. I'm more nervous about what will come after this. We're really going to go up north and put an end to Argarg? What then? Once he's dead I'll have avenged my parents." Morgan chewed their lower lip nervously.

"One step at a time, dear. Not everything has to be planned out. It's a big world, and Argarg isn't the only tyrant out there, right?" Mom had mentioned Sun Kings, Terror Lords, and other preposterous names. Argarg the Barbarian would be the start of our legendary tales, not the end.

"That reminds me, did you find anything good in the vendor stalls?"

"Some consumables, a tent that turns invisible and stays warm even in the cold-est of winter, and some makeup." Morgan sounded slightly guilty about the last one.

"No money leftover, then?" I laughed, because I'd expected it. Any money you gave to Morgan was as good as gone, and you should never expect to even get change back. It was one of their major flaws, and a sticking point that Lilith still used to pick fights with me about Morgan.

"Oh, here, try one of these pastries." A cream puff appeared in their hand, fresh from their inventory. It smelled fantastic and tasted great. Not on the level of some-thing cooked by Aunt Bobbi, but it had been made by a master, nonetheless.

"That's shockingly good," I said, but then Morgan had to wipe some frosting off my face.

"I bought fifty of them. Check your status; they even give a buff!"

I didn't have the heart to tell Morgan the buff was too weak to overwrite the food buff I already had from breakfast this morning.

# CHAPTER 48

# Final Exam

Sometimes I felt like I got a free pass with things because Mom created the System, and the System was behind creating dungeons, trials, and challenges. This time, I felt like I'd been singled out. I appeared on a large hunk of rock surrounded by a sea of lava, in the middle of a volcano. Above me, tiers of scaffolding circled the interior of the volcano mouth, and ascending looked like it was the only way free of the slowly rising lava.

As cool as a volcano wasn't, I had always wanted to see one, but not from the inside. Any thoughts of altering gravity through my gravity kinesis fell the moment I saw arrows and bolts of magic flung my way. Stationed throughout the platforms were pink-skinned pig-men who were in the process of evacuating.

"There's the cursed one! If we kill it, mighty Magmos will spare us!"

"Kill him!"

I only had one way out, so I dodged the incoming attacks in a burst of Rainbow Rush. The world behind me was left dyed in a magenta wash, since I had activated my antimagic kinesis. The arrows and bolts were unaffected, but they missed me anyway, and hit rock. The magic bolts, though, disintegrated when they got near me.

I didn't go up the ladder to the first section of scaffolding; I activated Prismatic Blur for the extra bonus to evasion, then jumped. While midair, I dropped Tides of Woe upon a large group of pig-men, and then turned my eyes ahead-once more. With my Strength 18 jump, I managed to clear the four-meter-high jump with a few meters to spare. I didn't land on the scaffolding, though. I immediately engaged the nearest pig-man with Dragonfly Strike. Three barehanded blows from me sent the bleeding pig-man off the scaffolding and into a few rocks left below. The lava continued to rise. I tuned out his squeals, and activated Dragonfly Strike to appear behind the next monster.

The pig-men were as strong as I was, maybe stronger, but I wasn't a muscular person, and I didn't play fair. Thanks to my unbreakable gloves and the training from Sun Wukong, I landed blows with the full force of my bolstered Agility. My status screen indicated I was up to 202 Agility at the moment, thanks to the stacks of Spectrum Surge and Malicious Tormentor. My first blow shattered the pig-man's iron armor, and the second turned the poor thing into blood-mist. Apparently, my Antimagic Rainbow Rush counted as using a kinesis for the purposes of Spectrum Surge, and I had shot up to the full fifty percent Agility bonus, thanks to all the missiles of magic and bolts of mana being flung my way.

I didn't even bother to do more than tap the pig-men as I ran past them: that's all it took to rupture their bodies, transforming the armored pig-monster-men into exploding meat-bombs. I learned right away not to wait for the explosion, but to be as many steps away from their corpses as possible.

I'd forgotten the pig-men had shouted initially, so caught up was I in my ease at slaughtering them. On the fourth scaffolding from the bottom a pig-man in fancy armor pleaded with me.

"Please! Please spare us!" The words gave me a shock.

"You can talk?" I blinked a haze of red away, and a sick feeling swam in my gut.

"Yes! We can talk! And feel! Let us escape with you!" The sick feeling turned to mere sourness, when I noticed his subordinates were preparing to drop this scaffold into the lava, their boss and me included.

I danced in front of the silver-armored pig, punched him square in the chest to shatter his armor, and then I punched him in the face. It was messy, but it sated the rage that had burned within me when the creature had tried to lie to me, to trick me into letting its minions kill the both of us. I flipped my kinesis to gravity, hit the area of the two who worked to disconnect the scaffolds with a gravity Chromatic Cascade, and then fled up the next platform.

When I reached the last platform, the lava had only ascended halfway up the fifteen platforms below me, and no pig-man had survived my passing.

"Time to die, dragonfly." The last pig-man was big, like three meters tall big. Its huge, two-bladed axe was bigger than I was, and one hit from that would ruin my day. I didn't really want to waste a lot of time with this guy, so I flipped to silver (actually, magnetic) kinesis. I ran straight at him, creating a corridor of magnetic attraction, and waited until he swung the axe toward me to activate Dragonfly Strike.

The asshole somehow managed to contort, impossibly, to block one of my fists with the haft of his axe. He nearly lost control of the axe, since the enchantment on my gloves completely protected my hand, and my other fist landed a blow against his strange fur-and-hide armor. That's all it took for Dragonfly Strike to be considered a hit, and awful wounds split the pig-man's flesh as bleeding stacked on.

In the agony of bleeding, I upped the danger, dropping Tides of Woe on him.

**Warchief Neghed afflicted with Haunted.**

Spectral faces and ghostly noises echoed from Warchief Neghed.
I followed that up with Aurora Burst.

**Warchief Neghed afflicted with Sleep.**
**You gain Swift Shadows (+30% Movement Speed) (Duration: 4:59.9)**

"Really?" I asked the sky, but I wasn't going to question it too hard. I walked over to the sleeping figure, and punched Warchief Neghed. Unlike his subordinates, he didn't explode like a meat-bomb. He looked rough, but the huge pig-man's eyes had taken on an eerie crimson, and waves of primal power wafted off his three-meter-tall body, much like body odor wafted off him.

The cries of ghosts mixed with a primal roar, and the powder keg of rage and vile spirits combined, completely transforming Warchief Neghed. When the waves of power ceased, he was now named Haunted Rage Neghed. I felt some feelings about that, but the lava continued to rise within the magma chamber.

Luckily, Neghed seemed to have forgotten he had an axe. The heavy weapon remained caught in the silver trail of a Magnetic Rainbow Rush, and the dumb brute wanted to throw hands with me. For each hit I dodged, I landed three hits on him. Out of my first ten strikes, four of them procced Malicious Tormentor, which dumped Withered, Petrification, Exhaustion, and Frozen onto the monster. Once those landed, it only took me a moment of switching my active kinesis. My rainbow brilliance dimmed, dominated by the arrival of death in the form of a dark green shot through with black. Words did the color no justice, for they failed to capture the breath of death itself upon the dungeon, a grim reminder of mortality.

I had never tried this one out before, since there was a chance it might instantly kill people. In fact, the moment my aura changed, the body of Neghed twitched and writhed. The Wither effect was part of that, but I felt a rush. The unnatural sensation was the power of conflict, the predator eating the prey. The pig-man's life force slipped from his body by the moment, and each blow I slammed into it avalanched into more afflictions.

The System read me a litany of ailments, and before I realized I felt a little too good, Haunted Rage Neghed exploded like an angry pigeon in a pillowcase. Something inside of him exploded outward, sending his primal barbarian fleshy bits across the volcano in a glorious rain of bacon. The most noticeable feeling of buzzing I had been experiencing vanished with his demise.

I nearly gagged, as the realization of what all those bits splayed across the platforms were. The intense heat of the rising lava overwhelmed the smell of burnt flesh. I willed my stomach to behave, switched my kinesis to antimagic, and dashed through the portal that opened upon the pig-man's death. I didn't want to see, or think, about the things I'd just done.

I appeared in a wooden cabin. Across from me sat a man made out of energy, his entire being nothing but the purple-black flames I recognized as my Void kinesis. A checkerboard lay between us.

*We will play checkers, little brother.*

"Little brother? I only have a sister, as far as I know?" I don't know why, but the fact someone claimed to be my brother bothered me. Neither of our parents had ever mentioned having other children, and they had told us their whole stories.

*We are both children of Ayin.*

"Neither of my moms' names are Ayin. Got a name?"

*My name is Fred. I am the Unutterable Black Flame of the Void.*

The way his voice echoed through reality and my mind was really disturbing.

"So what game is this, Fred? I'm Alexander."

*This is the game of games, the greatest of strategic challenges, a game so ancient it predates the Stars themselves.*

"Which is?" I asked again. Maybe Void beings didn't have ears to hear with? Did I need to think it really loudly?

*Behold, the field upon which our grand battle of intellect and cunning shall be played. We shall partake in the game of profound simplicity and depths unfathomable, much like my own. Best me in the rite of checkers to pass on to your next trial!*

I wanted to roll my eyes, but I started to remember what Mom had told me about Fred. Even if he was something of a joke, his power wasn't. She had integrated him into the System, which meant if he liked me, the System would like me.

"Oh ho ho ho, checkers is it, Fred? I've played a few games in my day." Against Lilith. There was no way in hell that Fred, the insane Void-guy could outplay my sister. So, I just needed to think like Lilith, and this would be a breeze. Think like Lilith. Aisha's got full lips. Math is fun. I know all the things and have all the magic.

"I'm ready, Fred." I held my hand out to shake his. "For luck, right?"

*A true gentleman. Libby and Reverie could learn from you, little brother.*

"Thanks, Mom always said manners are important. We still aren't there on the brother thing, though." Oh, I wished Fred luck, but not good luck. I called on my ability to twist probability with my mere presence, on my beloved Progenitor of Peril trait, and then we were playing. Piece by piece, Fred lost. He played comically bad, as if he analyzed each move and picked the absolute worst one every time.

*You have bested me, Alexander the Great.*

"That's amazing. I wish Morgan was here to hear that." I liked Fred, but I don't know why he threw the game so hard, unless my luck curse managed to be that potent?

*The final Trial awaits you, brother.*

I didn't linger; I got up from the checkers table and went straight for the portal, then stopped.

"Don't I get a prize?"

*A prize? For what?*

"For beating you?" I scratched the side of my head. "I guess since we're brothers and I bested you, you'd have a congratulatory gift for me. Why else would someone of your importance engineer such a dramatic meeting between us, if not to gift me with something amazing?"

*Do you like swords?*

"Not really. I like to punch things, like Mom."

*Of course, of course. Oh, I see, your gloves don't count as a fist weapon. Let me fix that.*

Fred grasped both of my hands in his, and darkness seeped between us, and when he was done I had a new accessory attached to my Spectrum Gloves.

**You have gained Oblivion's Caress.**

**Oblivion's Caress is now bound to Spectrum Gloves. Spectrum Gloves have gained the following abilities: Void Infusion, Void Empowerment.**

**Void Infusion: Imbue your strikes with the pure destruction of the Void. Adds 10% Void Damage to all unarmed strikes, which ignores armor and physical resistances.**

**Void Empowerment: On a critical hit, you gain a 25% increase to agility for 10 seconds. Stacks up to 3 times.**

"Thanks, Fred, you're the best!"

I darted through the portal.

# CHAPTER 49

# Final Exam II

I found myself in a tent. The ground had layers of thick rugs. The tent itself seemed woven of a thick canvas, and I sat at a table. Across from me sat a beautiful woman with striking eyes. Her irises were clouded over with what looked like mist. Was she blind, or farseeing? She stared right at me and smiled as if she knew a secret I didn't.

"One of your companions will betray you," she told me.

"That's unfortunate," I answered. "I'm Alexander, who are you?"

"I'm Iona, a Seer of the Cloudfolk." Iona lifted a hand to brush it through her golden hair, then tapped her pointer finger against her deep red lips. "You've never heard of the Cloudfolk before. Glance outside of my tent."

I did as Iona instructed. The floor felt strange underneath the rugs, and when I pushed the tent open, I saw why. Her tent, and many others, were supported by thick clouds. I'd never heard of any nomadic skyfaring people before, but this could be a false reality—the exam was a dungeon, after all. It could also be real, though. The System had that kind of power.

"Are these special clouds? When Arkaziel takes me flying, he can't land on a cloud without using magic."

"You're more interested in the clouds than in someone betraying you?" Iona seemed confused by that.

"Well, yeah. Wouldn't you be?" I asked with enthusiasm. I poked the clouds a few times, then moved back in to study Iona. She seemed older than me, but still young. Somewhere in her twenties, perhaps? The few lines on her face were those of knowledge, not age. She had a willowy build, and her white and blue dress, while flattering, actually concealed her charms. I wondered what kind of culture these Cloudfolk had.

"No, I would be more interested in one of my friends' intention of betraying me," Iona answered with brisk honesty.

"Well, tell me about that, I guess. Who betrays me? Why?"

"One who's been with you for years, through fights and accomplishments. The truth of one's heart is a complex thing." One of Iona's hands slipped across the table and settled over one of my own. I could feel her elevated pulse and unnatural warmth immediately. It made me cognizant of where her heart lay, an indirect reminder that the slight cleavage on display was a paltry shadow of the wonder of her form. I laughed, and Iona laughed too.

"That sucks. Can you tell me why they betray me?"

"No, I cannot see that." Iona curled her fingers around mine, and her thumb traced at the lines of my palm even though they were hidden by my gloves. Whatever Iona might be, a fraud she was not.

"The betrayal will come at the hour of your most dire need, against a terrible foe. You will slay Argarg the Barbarian, but the cost will be considerable."

"And is there a way to avoid it?"

Iona laughed.

"Only by canceling out that future entirely. You could stay with me. With your patronage, the Cloudfolk could remain safe no matter our enemies. No longer would we be forced to rely upon stealth and live in constant fear of discovery. The clouds are not all that is soft at these heights."

I swallowed. Iona laid it on a little thick there, but that didn't make it any less effective.

"That's a gracious offer. Maybe someday I'll take you up on it. But I've already vowed I'm going to end the scourge of Argarg, so I'm going to kill him. After that, who knows." I shrugged. I didn't know. Who would betray me? Why? Derrick? Aisha? Morgan? Cassius? Tyler? With enough convoluted logic one could even make the argument that my mothers were going to betray me with their ascension from this world. It certainly would count as leaving me alone.

"Very well." Iona let out a slow breath. "Find our enclave." There were promises in the look Iona gave me. Promises beyond those even Morgan made when looking at me. This conversation would not make Morgan happy, but it was just a Trial.

"Thanks for the warning, where's the exit?"

It seemed asking was all that had been required, and a portal appeared behind Iona.

Which meant I had to walk past Iona. As I moved past her chair, she raised a hand to touch the front of my chest. I arched a brow at her, but she smiled, and a faint magic glowed around her hand.

"Walk in safety, would-be hero, and may your travels bring you back to me." Iona's genuine concern for my safety kept it from being as weird as it would've otherwise been. I'd never felt quite so much like a prize someone wanted to win, a meal to be eaten, or a stallion to be broken. Morgan didn't look at me that way.

"Uh, yeah. Will do." I took the exit, and floated in a world of colors for a moment.

**Summary of Trial:**
**Act 1, Success. All Enemies defeated, and escaped with time to spare.**
**Act 2, Success. You completed the puzzle.**
**Act 3, Success. You resisted temptation and remained true to your ideals.**
**You have completed 3/3 trials, and have passed your final exam.**

**Reward: +2 to All Attributes.**

**Reward: +500 gold.**

**Reward: +Beacon of the Cloudfolk.**

**Beacon of the Cloudfolk: Call upon this boon to be guided to the hidden realm of the Cloudfolk.**

**Congratulations, you have reached level twenty. You have gained +2 Agility, +1 Intellect, +1 Will.**

**Progenitor of Peril (Proficient) has progressed to Progenitor of Peril (Advanced).**

**You have gained the Chromatic Decay (Progenitor of Peril) Ability.**

**Chromatic Decay (Progenitor of Peril). Targets are inflicted with a slow, relentless degradation of vitality manifested as a colorful shimmer that saps their vitality over time. The afflicted experience vivid, shifting colors which symbolize the chaotic and constantly changing nature of your powers. Not only does Chromatic Decay do True Damage, but it also curses the victim, making them susceptible to critical hits and other negative effects. Duration: 30 minutes.**

"Damn," I whispered in awe as the System read to me the properties of my new ability. I'd never heard of True Damage before, but it sounded awesome, and a thirty-minute damage-over-time effect with a curse? I couldn't wait to test it out on some enemies and find out whether that counted as two different afflictions or not as far as my buffs went.

The darkness receded, and I jumped out of a portal back into the training grounds of the academy. A small cheer went up for my appearance, and before I could take more than a dozen steps, both my mothers slammed into me in a big hug.

"Ma'am, ma'am, you can't be here, no parents near the portal!" One of the newer professors tried to chide my parents, and was completely ignored. Arkaziel got stuck with the job of soothing the disgruntled teacher. He didn't try very hard, and instead made elaborate gestures at Kallos and Telos, asked what were they supposed to do, then shrugged and came over to join us.

"Good job, Alexander. I'm very proud of you and the young man you've become," Kallos whispered into one ear.

"You did amazing, honey. I don't have any fears left about entrusting this world to you and Lilith," Telos whispered in my other ear.

Entrusting a world to me seemed a bit much to dump on a seventeen-year-old.

"Hey, you graduated. Longest two decades of my life!" Arkaziel even pulled me into a hug, but the moment he gave me a hug, both of my parents elbowed him out of the way and led me toward the manor.

"I never even thought to ask . . . What happens now?" I looked around the training grounds. Whenever a student appeared there'd be some cheers, and then groups would move off to do their own things.

"The formal graduation is tomorrow. Today, we're having a party."

"We are?" I asked, surprised.

Sure enough, a large assortment of friends and family were gathered at the manor's gardens. Lilith, Aisha, Derrick, Hanna, Morgan, Kara, Tyler, Cassius, and even Akari had already assembled. Their parents stuck more to small groups, but they were all here too.

"The fastest one of us is the last one? That's kind of ironic. Right? Did I use ironic right?" Derrick asked exactly as a lull in the conversations in the garden occurred.

"Yes, that would be ironic, Derrick." I answered the awkward silence for him.

"Everyone passed?" I looked to Lilith for confirmation.

"Yes, you were the only one I was worried about failing." Clearly, Lilith hadn't gotten a Seeress telling her about inevitable betrayal. Or maybe she had, and taking out frustrations on me was how she decided to feel better about it.

"Lily . . ." Telos muttered, and Lilith stood up a little straighter and mouthed an apology at me.

Then Morgan stepped up and wrapped their arms around me. I only got a kiss on the cheek. Both of my moms were right behind me, after all, but the hug felt great, and I bonked my forehead lightly against Morgan's.

"Hey, stranger," Morgan greeted me.

"Why, hello there, Enchanter of the Whispering Shadows," I greeted Morgan.

"That's enough cuddling in front of everyone, you two." Lilith gave me a dirty look.

"Fair is fair!" Aisha cried.

"We had to tell them to cut down the public kissing," Telos explained. "They were making people uncomfortable."

Morgan grimaced and quit pressing so aggressively against me. From the reactions, I had to wonder if Morgan hadn't been one of those to complain just to piss Lilith off, but if that were the case, karma had come calling.

"You all made it through the academy, even the final exam. That means you're all adults now. Eat, drink, make merry." Aunt Bobbi called out as she set pitchers of a reddish-brown liquid with lots of fruits floating in them on tables. No one argued with her declaration, though, and that meant we were actual adults now. We could do what we wanted.

My head spun with the possibilities. I could use silk scarves to tie Morgan to . . . I mean, I could defeat Argarg now. Then what? Did I want to come back to Winona after one small adventure? Would I stick with Lilith? Would any of us stick together? Morgan and I got on well, but we'd never used the L-word with one another. I absolutely loved my time with Morgan, but did I love Morgan? We bickered sometimes. Morgan was terrible with money, sparred like a cat with Lilith, and we'd never talked about a future past Argarg.

When I thought about it, none of us had.

"Hey, whatever happens, why don't we all try to meet back here every ten years if we can?" I suggested.

"I'm in," Lilith agreed, without argument. Everyone, well, all of us kids and Aisha's dad, Idris, ended up echoing Lilith's short answer, and we all stacked our hands atop one another. I noticed both of my moms had a wistful look, but they didn't join in like Idris.

After that, the night turned into a blur. Alcohol felt good, then bad.

My first morning as an adult? I spent twenty minutes trying to make the room stop spinning, before I finally remembered I could clear ailments, and pulsed Aurora Burst while still in my bed. The spinning and headache fell away immediately, but the smell of vomit only grew more and more intense. I did have a purity kinesis, and it turns out that could clean up messes. It seemed like a waste of what felt like a sacred power, but I didn't want to spend the first hour of my morning changing sheets and cleaning.

It was all for naught. Minutes after I had my room in order, Telos knocked and cracked my door.

"Good, you're awake. Come help clean up the garden. We made a real mess last night."

So much for being an adult.

# CHAPTER 50

# Goodbye, for Now.

**FH 57, Summer. The Crystal Spire.**

A week later Arkaziel, Bobbi, Lilith, Telos, Kallos, and I sat in the yard of the Crystal Spire. The trees provided ample shade, the wind whispered against their leaves, and it felt like the whole universe kept holding its breath.

"We're leaving the house to you two. Including our ghosts," Kallos said while she smiled at Lilith and me.

"Your ghosts?" I asked for clarification immediately. They weren't going to die. Why would there be ghosts?

"You know, recordings, really. In case any of you ever want to talk to us. It's more like a phone that we'll answer, with an illusion projection. It will only work in the Spire, though." Telos answered the question and ruffled my hair, amused at my reaction.

"It's significantly more complicated than that, you know. Echoes of our essence, imbuement, and manipulation of time itself shouldn't be reduced down to being compared to a phone." Kallos tsked at Telos, vexed at the minimization of all of her hard work.

"What's a phone?" I asked.

"See?" Kallos smirked.

"Fine. Memory crystal?" Telos suggested.

"We get the idea." Lilith stepped in, to try to derail the conversation from going even further off track.

"Ruffling your hair was more fun before you cut it . . ." Mom lamented, then ruffled my now-short hair again. She still looked disappointed.

"Alright, we're off then," Kallos said, and all of us swore.

"If we do the long goodbyes, we'll be here forever. Hasn't Telos told you about the Midwest goodbye?" Kallos put her hands on her hips, a no-nonsense pose that in normal times would immediately result in her getting her way.

"We've got a few last things to do yet, love." Telos laughed and walked over to Arkaziel. He blurred into a kitten and jumped into her arms.

"You've been a good boy, Ark. Everyone acted like you were going to betray me, or steal from me, but you never once even considered it. I would've gone insane in that first tower without you keeping me company. Real friends walk through fire for you, and you dove into the Void with me. You're the best friend I've ever had." Telos lifted the kitten and placed a kiss on his head. Something that sounded like glass breaking echoed across the room, and Telos wiped a tear from her cheek.

"Ditto, Blue." Arkaziel sniffed, but he didn't say anything else. I wondered how much had gone between them telepathically. What last goodbyes did I miss? They weren't for me; they were for Arkaziel and Mom. Selfishly, though, I was very curious.

"What just happened?" I whispered to Lilith, who was chewing on her lower lip, eyes focused intently on Arkaziel and Bobbi.

"I don't know, shh."

"Guess we're next?" Bobbi asked Kallos.

"Seems like it, dear. You've been an exceptional traveling companion, your culinary skills have made our travels a delight, and you helped raise the kids as if they were your own. You have my eternal gratitude, Zephariel'Realmara'Etheriassa'Flemmel'Bobbisylth'Chronoquintessara"—here Kallos paused to take a quick breath and finish Bobbi's extremely long full name off strong—"Falkora'Stellarae'Quantumwhiskeria'Diavala'Jormungandria." The sound of breaking glass filled the air again, and both women smiled sadly at each other.

"Hey, hey, now. This isn't a sad time. Since we're all adults here, and there's two adult StarManes without bonds . . ." Arkaziel blurred into the humanoid form he'd used so often the last two decades, and he pulled out a small jewelry box.

"Human custom. Blame my best friend." Arkaziel dropped to one knee.

"So how about it, Slay? Will you be my mate?"

Bobbi's pink skin flushed even more.

"You still haven't beaten me in a real cook-off," Bobbi pointed out.

"I never will, either, but I'll trounce you any time I can cheat, and you know it." Arkaziel didn't even have the grace to be bashful about having to cheat to beat her. He seemed proud of it.

"Yes, I'll be your mate, you mongrel twerp." I'd never heard an insult hold such fondness in it before.

Telos jumped up and down, clapping, and after a few moments, Kallos joined her, and the two whooped and hollered their joy for their friends. I gave the two of them a big hug, and before I knew it, it turned into a pile of hugs, sniffling, and crying.

"You were right," Telos told Kallos, an hour later when we finally all sorted ourselves out.

"I love those words." Kallos nodded, and gestured for Telos to say them again.

"You were right, oh wise and beautiful Soul Witch" Telos laughed, but her face tightened in dread.

"It's time for us to go," Telos and Kallos said together, with finality.

Kallos smiled at the painful expression Telos wore.

"Alright, we've had our hugs, we've said our goodbyes, we've had a hug pile and a proposal. It's time. Be good and make us proud." Kallos, usually more reserved than Telos, took the lead of the farewell. I could tell both of my parents were bubbling inside, though, and had to give each of them one last bear hug.

"Be happy," was all Telos said before the room felt emptier. Telos and Kallos were gone. No flashes, no bangs, simply gone. The world felt emptier without them.

Someone sniffed and tried to compose themselves, then I realized it was me. Lilith didn't even try to play it strong and pulled a rainbow-hued handkerchief from her inventory to dab at her eyes. Bobbi and Arkaziel were both looking at the spot the women had been in, then sighed.

"Are you two leaving us, too?" I asked.

"Nah, we're going to hang around until you two come back from your first journey. Blue begged us to hang around until then, and there's more kids to teach. Gotta whip the academy into something that'll carry on without us," Arkaziel mumbled lamely. It seemed pretty obvious to me that he would've hung around, at least for a little while, without Mom asking him to. "It'd be a real shame if Winona got destroyed by the first monster that attacked after we left."

"After that, we'll visit the Lower Realms. Some of the things we set into motion with your mothers are still playing out. Gods to eat, powerful people to humble. One of my favorite pastimes besides cooking, you know? And I suppose our clans will want to have a ceremony for us." Aunt Bobbi's gleaming eyes and eagerness to humble certain individuals made me glad I wasn't those people.

"Won't Werylin be surprised to see us?" Arkaziel laughed maliciously.

"I bet we get to eat Siegfried. He was such a tosser." Bobbi laughed, but the atmosphere couldn't bear laughter, and she trailed off.

Arkaziel dropped one hand on my shoulder, and one on Lilith's, and gave us each a squeeze.

"Take your time. Come to the manor when you're ready," the StarMane said, before he and Bobbi vanished in a burst of shadows.

Lilith and I sat in silence.

"I almost feel as if we've done this before?" I couldn't shake the weird sense of déjà vu that had been haunting me since our moms left.

"It sure feels like that, doesn't it?" Lilith practically groaned the words. It felt weird, being the strong one between the two of us, for once. In the past it had always been her holding me. Somehow, being needed made me feel slightly more able to deal with it.

We held each other on the couch for most of the day, until growling stomachs finally pushed us to head back to the manor.


"So, this is it," Telos murmured as the two of them pressed their hands against the white walls in the center of the River of Light.

"What happens when we cross the door? Will we cease to exist? Will we become one?" Kallos actually felt fear, if their soul bond hadn't gone on the fritz in the center of existence. Telos assumed it hadn't, because she felt fear too. Binah offered her nothing on this origin-point in the flow of Ein Sof.

"I don't know," Telos admitted. "But we're too powerful for this place. Even our mere passing Bob's multiverse sent a spiral of chaos through that dimensional axis. We can't go back."

"That wasn't just us. The events you orchestrated to teach him a lesson are also to blame," Kallos pointed out.

"Haha, yeah. He deserved it." Telos felt no remorse.

"But I suppose you are right; we cannot go back. Only forward."

"You've been a great wife," Telos started, but Kallos had no interest in that conversation.

"We've talked about our what-if's; this is our only choice. Let's take it with our eyes open and clear, and no regrets. We will enter this box, and then we will decide what happens from there." Kallos left no room for Telos to argue, but did hold one hand out to grasp within her own.

Telos took the brakes off her connection to all one hundred and fifty gates, and power surged in her, but still the wall repelled her and Kallos both. Even when Kallos threw all of her chains at the wall, they merely rebounded, again and again.

A flash so fast that even Telos failed to follow it happened, something made contact with both of their foreheads, and power exploded around them. For a fraction of a moment Telos thought, maybe, just maybe, she'd seen a hand, with a finger touching their foreheads, but surely no one could move so fast that *she* couldn't even see it.

". . . all of my gates just activated," Kallos cried out in a mixture of pain and ecstasy, the same feelings that crashed through Telos. Their connection to the Void and Ein Sof doubled in an instant, and then the white walls flared in and out of existence. The power within each of them grew, until their being turned only into energy. Then, and only then, as the last of their physical being was obliterated by vast cosmic power did a breach in the walls form.

Before either could do anything, both were sucked inside of the center of the River of Light, as if they'd been pulled down a whirlpool of molten energy. *This is almost like dying. I remember the light, only this is brighter.*

Images flashed past her mind: wheels and cogs, scales, pendulums, crystals and phials. A clean white cloth ready to receive the distillation of a soul and render its Ethereal tapestry.

*Cripes, that was the Great Cycle!*

Then Telos landed on her butt, in a white room.

# CHAPTER 51

# Logistics

Everyone had their own business to tie up. Derrick and Hanna had a marriage ceremony, so we all had to attend that. Then Tyler and Akari got married too, seemingly on the spur of the moment. Lilith began the process of arranging our equipment for travel. We smoked meat, cheese, stored dozens of simple meals and complex ones. Bobbi helped some, so Lilith created a ration plan that would ensure our core combat group would be able to maintain the buff from eating her delicious meals.

Morgan and I spent hours every day in the market, drilling traveling peddlers for information on the current state of the North. We spent a lot of pocket money on loosening the lips of the guards and caravan workers, but the most we could find out was that Argarg's conquest had stalled out in his attempt to conquer the Pine Grove, a group of druids whose grove could cut off weeks of much more treacherous paths through a small mountain range that the caravanners argued over the name of. Some called them the Pinecrest Peaks, while others called them the Fircrest Mountains.

Lilith and I knew that Winona was sheltered from the barbarity and incivility of a broader, young world, but we hadn't realized by how much. The descriptions of towns other than Winona were terrible. Morgan nodded along to those descriptions, as if they verified everything they'd seen firsthand on the journey to Winona.

Thanks to the System inventory, logistics planning came down to making sure we had everything before we left. Extra clothes, extra tents, bed rolls, weapons, potions, and warm socks. Lacking any kind of ridable animals, we ran into a spot of luck in our planning.

"I'll take you as far as the Serpent's Maw. You planned to level up there, right?" Arkaziel offered.

"You will? That's awesome, thanks!" Lilith praised Arkaziel, and I echoed her sentiments.

"It makes sense. You kids need to level up before you try to take Argarg on. He was level thirty-five when I flew over his camp last year."

"You flew over his camp and didn't blow it to hell?" I asked in confusion.

"You'd already vowed that was your goal. It'd be rude to steal my nephew's prey." Arkaziel dismissed it with a wave of his hand. I grinned at my uncle. He seemed proud of us for chasing big prey.

"That means we need to reach at least level thirty to stand a chance against him," Lilith mused.

"That was last year. You should aim for forty," Arkaziel corrected Lilith and got a glare from her in return for his reasonable suggestion. "Argarg isn't alone. He has a cadre of loyal followers and an army of the souls of those he's slain, who are spectral slaves under his command."

"Will Serpent's Maw get us to level forty?" I frowned. Megadungeons weren't something either Lilith or I had any experience with. We'd only been exposed to small, impromptu dungeons, and even the trials we had undergone were relatively small ones.

"Well . . ." Arkaziel thumbed his chin. "There's six layers of the Serpent's Maw. If you clear all six layers, you should be very close. If you manage to trigger some internal quests, you could emerge very close to forty. Knowing you two, you'll stumble into quests."

"Are you serious? Twenty levels from one dungeon?" I had struggled to get one level over the last year. Well. I hadn't struggled that hard. Or at all. Idle hands made no progress, and for some reason any training I did with Mom had never given me level progress, where training I did with anyone else did, but Telos had been my nearly singular combat trainer. Sun Wukong had given me attribute increases and ability growth, but if he had given me experience it hadn't been enough to level.

"Megadungeon," Arkaziel answered simply.

"I don't suppose you could share any of the secrets that would help us unlock extra bonuses in the Maw? With your mastery of shadows, surely you know a thing or two about it?" Lilith tried to lure Arkaziel with an ego fluffing, and he took the bait.

"On the first level there's a secret hydra boss, on the second there's a secret vault, and on . . ." Arkaziel went on to describe several secret encounters and how to unlock them. None of the things he described seemed that well-hidden, so even though Lilith had victory in her eyes, I felt like Uncle Arkaziel was playing her for a fool this once. No way we'd miss any of the things he talked about. I vowed to keep my eyes open in the Maw. If I found even one hidden encounter of my own, that'd be a victory.

"Damn, how far can you teleport?" Morgan exclaimed when we appeared at the base of the Serpent's Maw Mountain. The entire mountain looked like a huge snake coiled on itself, with its open maw jutting out to lunge at some prey.

"Well, here you go, kids. Good luck!" Arkaziel ruffled my hair and gave Lilith a kiss on the cheek. "Stay safe," he added, before he flowed back into the shadows. Like that, he was gone.

"How many days of travel did he just save us?" Akari asked.

"Twelve," Lilith answered without hesitation.

"How rude," Morgan grumbled. "Arkaziel is the least doting mentor I've ever heard of."

Our party consisted of myself, Lilith, Aisha, Morgan, Cassius, Tyler, and Akari. Derrick had withdrawn at the last minute. His newlywed life mixed with Aisha already coming with us had left Aisha's family pressuring both of them to stay, but Aisha hadn't given in, and remained adamant she'd stay at Lilith's side. It was the seven of us against the Serpent's Maw, and ideally, Argarg the Barbarian after that.

"Where's the path up?" I asked Tyler.

"The stone says that way." The dwarf pointed to the east.

"The wind spirits agree," Cassius murmured.

"I've got a map," Lilith reminded us all with an acerbic tone, and me she actually smacked with the rolled-up map. "The path to the summit should be relatively clear, with only some minor threats from wildlife. According to the traders, there's very little spill out of monsters from the Maw. Alexander, Akari, you're the scouts, take the point. Tyler, Cassius, you're the rear. Let us know if the stone or spirits change their tune. Aisha, Morgan, you're in the middle with me."

"Why am I in the middle?" Morgan bristled a little.

"Because Akari is a scout with abilities in detection, traps, and locks, and a melee only fighter. You're a melee-ranged hybrid who can protect me or Aisha long enough for support to engage. Or would you rather enter the shadows, and emerge as a surprise element?"

"The latter," Morgan demurred after only a moment's hesitation. Morgan jumped into my shadow, I noticed. Hopefully those two would stop clashing over the course of this adventure.

**Quest Received: Reach the Summit to enter the Serpent's Maw.**
**Optional Quest: Retrieve the Serpent's Eyes of Fire and eliminate the thieves.**

"The Serpent's Eyes of Fire?" I asked out loud.

"You can't see them from here," Morgan answered first. "But above the Maw, there's two caverns, each with a huge fire in them that looks like eyes. Or should be, if someone hadn't stolen them."

"Anything from the spirits?" Lilith asked Cassius.

"I'm asking. Spirits are talkative." Cassius sighed.

I watched Lilith tap her foot for a ten count, and when no one came up with even an idea of where these Eyes of Fire might be she rolled her eyes.

"Oh Inferno, Mistress of Flames, Guide me to the Eyes of Fire!" Lilith always spoke with clear enunciation, but when she used her class magic it felt like her words hit reality in a different way. They sank through your brain, and made you imagine a woman composed of intense red flames. Inferno, as far as I could tell, was an Elemental Lady of the Plane of Fire, and quite the looker if you were into sentient flames.

Two embers that produced no heat appeared around Lilith, and each released small streams of dying fire that led in the same direction, to the back side of the mountain.

"At least both eyes seem to be in the same place," Lilith said happily. Cassius looked a little annoyed that she stole his time to shine, but also a little relieved. The spirits must be particularly chatty here.

"Thanks for saving us time, Lilith. The spirits haven't talked to many humans before in this place, and they're . . . well, a handful."

"Relying on others is always a challenge," Lilith agreed, but I wish she'd done it in a way that didn't have a barb. Everyone seemed to ignore it, though, except Morgan.

"Funny, I was just thinking the same thing," Morgan said with a wide smile at Lilith.

"Less talk, more walk," I said while I swapped my active kinesis to an eye-catching pink. As I assumed it would, the flash of pink caught everyone's attention and distracted them momentarily. My psychic kinesis allowed me to sense sapient creatures in a very wide area. Not all monsters were sapient, but it still felt like the most useful kinesis to have active for searching for thieves.

"I've never seen pink before. What's that one?" Tyler asked, helping me change the flow of conversation. Tyler, like me, liked when people were nice to each other.

"Psychic," I answered honestly.

"You even have mind powers? Your class is so broken, dude." Tyler laughed. "You can't read my mind, can you?"

"Nope, the beard must act as a deterrent," I joked.

"No telepathy, just general manipulation of psychic energies," I lied. No one needed to know if I could catch extra loud thoughts with this kinesis active, or if I touched them I could choose to be more intrusive. Kallos had sat me down one day to talk about soul and mind powers, and how they were mistrusted by others. Someday, I'd tell the others about the more questionable powers I had, but for now it was better to just lie about what I could do.

"Then why even switch to it?" Morgan wondered.

"The big upside to psychic kinesis is I can sense sapient life at a long range. Great for searching for thieves, I'm hoping, especially with these motes of flame guiding us. Let's get to walking for real. I don't think any of us want to have to camp on the mountain tonight, do we?"

"Dwarves don't camp on mountains, we camp in them," Tyler groused in an offended voice.

"Really?" Akari asked.

"This dwarf doesn't, anyway," Tyler amended.

The motes of fire led them on a direct path. Morgan created constructs of darkness for us to cross ravines or made easier ways to ascend to ledges. Cassius kept getting distracted by shiny rocks he added to his inventory. Akari killed a rabbit with fangs after it tried to ambush her. She insisted we'd have it for dinner, but I wondered about the wisdom of eating a demon rabbit.

For an hour we followed the embers of Lilith's spell. Shortly after, dozens of minds appeared to my psychic senses, and I held up a hand to stop. I for some reason expected to find a cave, but that wasn't what waited around the next bend at all.

"How many?" Lilith asked me.

**Optional Quest updated. Retrieve the Serpent's Eye of Fire and kill all 27 orcs.**

"Orcs?" Tyler asked with a confused face, before the number of enemies sank in. Seven versus twenty-seven was fair, right?

"We've got the advantage of surprise, at least," I said.

That's when a war horn blew, the sound exploding across the slopes of Serpent's Maw, and echoing everywhere.

"Somehow, this is your fault," Lilith grumbled at me while she prepared to fight.

# CHAPTER 52

# Orcs

The deafening scream of the war horn echoed across the slopes of the Serpent's Maw, a cry to arms and violence. Even the horn itself sounded subtly wrong—the notes felt primal and jagged to my ears. Imperfect horn? Poor Orcish craftsmanship? It didn't matter, because within the orc fortifications, all of the thick-skinned, heavily muscled humanoids hefted weapons and streamed out of the gates on the war path. If we hadn't already been on their radar due to a scout, shaman, or whatever got us discovered, the chance of dealing with a disorganized enemy would have been an advantage.

They knew where we were, though, and the disorganized exit from their stronghold took on a new angle in my mind, when I realized they were avoiding clumping up.

"I summon the power of the Four Dragon Kings, ancient masters of earth, air, fire, and water, unleash your Elemental Dominion upon all who oppose me!" Lilith spoke quietly, but her voice cut over the horns of the orcs. Four pillars of different colors appeared to dot the slopes of the Serpent's Maw, and then lines of magic linked all four into a box. Blazing rocks fell from the sky, exploding into gouts of searing debris when they crashed onto the slopes of the Maw. A twister dipped down from the clouds, sending almost a dozen orcs into the sky and to their deaths.

Silence reigned for a second, before the final effect of the invocation kicked in. Bolts of ice fell across the stronghold, causing indiscriminate and heavy damage.

Lilith dropped to the ground, and Aisha caught her.

"You panicked," I said softly. "We'll clean the survivors up."

I didn't chastise my sister, even though her eyes said she expected it. She'd burned up all of her mana in one spell, and wasted all of the spell echoes she'd been holding on to for a boss fight or an emergency. Something about the orcs scared her into pulling out one of her largest spells in a panic. This was one of the most un-Lilith actions I'd ever seen her perform.

"Morgan, Akari, hold the line here and finish off any stragglers." I went into the burning ruins of the stronghold myself. Not a single one of the orcs made it out of the cataclysmic spell unscathed, but plenty of them had been left alive. I finished them off with the most precise blows I could manage. For all of my dashing around like an idiot, Morgan struck more finishing blows than I did. Morgan created thin tendrils of darkness that hardened into blades that attacked the injured orcs before they could muster any defenses. Maybe I should've just left it to Morgan. Their ranged efficiency outstripped mine by ridiculous margins.

Ten minutes later, we sat looking at one of the Eyes of Fire, and the notification that we had to retrieve one more, still.

"Sorry, everyone. Something in that horn made me freak out and cast the most damaging spell I could, with all my power behind it."

"Fear," Morgan said.

"Yeah, I freaked out. I was terrified," Lilith agreed.

"No, hon. Morgan means you were affected by fear, the status ailment. Or Terror, or something very similar to it. I didn't have any of my resilience buffs up on the party." Aisha immediately took blame for Lilith's succumbing to a debuff personally. I wondered why I had been immune to it, pure luck?

"Look, we won, no one got hurt, no big deal. How long do you need to be combat ready again?" Tyler asked, pausing only momentarily before he spoke with sympathy. "I got hit with the fear too; we all did."

Everyone nodded at Tyler's dismissal of the situation or agreed that they too had been affected by the fear. Why hadn't I? No one seemed to notice I hadn't been affected. They were all too busy dwelling on their own failure to resist it to notice I wasn't echoing in. Even Lilith, for once, missed that I was the odd one out, being so consumed with self-recrimination. Even when I gave her a big hug, she failed to notice anything off with me.

Even Lilith was fallible. My entire life I hadn't believed otherwise, and part of the adversarial relationship I'd always had with her fell away with this world reshaping realization.

"I'll be ready in another ten minutes. It would be best if I cast a few small spells to help protect our minds and rebuild some of my Echoes."

"I'm summoning a small fire spirit. Now that we have one of the Eyes, I should be able to have it bring us to the other one," Cassius told the group with a touch of pride. His Primal abilities to commune with spirits had become a huge part of Cassius's abilities after his class upgrade, and resulted in a large change in how he worked with others. Maybe he'd just needed better friends all along, or maybe the spirits kept him on the path to not being an asshole, but either way, I felt thankful to the spirits for the radical change in Cassius as a person.

Lilith and Aisha spent time casting an assortment of protective buffs on us; Tyler talked to the stone; Morgan looted the bodies and threw them into the smoldering remains of the orc encampment.

"We're ready," Lilith said with a sigh of relief. "Cassius, take the lead with Akari, Alexander, watch our trail with Tyler, please. Let's go."

The temporary blow to Lilith's ego didn't seem to be holding her back. Once more, her voice was clear, crisp, and full of confidence. As much as I enjoyed the idea of Lilith being fallible or making mistakes, I felt more comfortable with the strong, self-assured Lilith leading us. I sure didn't want to be the one playing leader. There was too much to keep track of with a party of seven people, unknown terrain, and enemies.

Cassius and Akari led us on a semiwinding path farther down the slopes of the Serpent's Maw. From the rear I couldn't hear the conversations, but I could see the two whispering to each other regularly. They led us on a path that avoided aggressive animals, which I appreciated. As creepy as scorpions were, this was their home, not ours. We didn't need to butcher everything we ran across. Mom, or Libby, created them all for a reason, right?

My mind wandered a little in boredom, imagining the crazy adventures our parents were up to in the higher realm. Imagining it was hard, because I didn't know anything about it, but in my head Telos and Kallos were in some ancient place full of mysteries, and they solved them as easily as those cube puzzles one of the transmigrators kept making.

"Whom, or whatever, has the Eye is in the cave. My little salamander is afraid to peer through the fires inside. Tyler?" The group stopped, and Cassius turned straight to the dwarf.

"Oh, sure thing. Let me talk to the stone!" Tyler chimed in happily. He crouched down on his stubby legs and whispered to the rocky slope. I couldn't detect any kind of sounds, responses, or energies, but Tyler sure seemed to be having a one-sided conversation with the ground. It occurred to me Cassius could've talked to earth spirits himself, but he'd instead opted to let Tyler take the lead.

Did he just not want to summon a stone spirit, or was he that considerate of a team player now? Or maybe there was another angle I was missing all together? It felt strange, knowing I'd helped reshape someone's life so significantly.

"It's Cinderwraiths," Tyler declared with a growl.

"What the heck are Cinderwraiths?" Akari demanded to know.

"Cinderwraiths are twisted abominations that feed on heat and fire to sustain their existence. When a creature dies from hypothermia, the lingering resentments and hate of the cold can birth them. They aren't precisely a Spirit, but they aren't what I'd call a ghost either." Cassius chimed in.

"They're demons. An echo born of hate, desperate to consume heat. They'll consume our lifeforce as readily as they will flames." Lilith's encyclopedic knowledge of monsters came from her constant barrages of questions of all people she met, or so she claimed, but I suspected she had a skill or ability that helped her.

"I hate wraithlike enemies," Tyler grumbled. "My axe barely hurts them, even when I use abilities."

"Would a weapon enchantment buff be worth it, or do you think we can get away with relying on magic?" Aisha asked Lilith.

"You've got Holy Light enchantments, right? Will that spell hamper your combat proficiency, Akari, Morgan?"

"No, I'm a Shinobi. Holy won't cause me any problems, especially in a fight I'm not trying to be stealthy in. Let's rock some enchantments and kill these things quickly. I want to get into the dungeon!" Akari clapped her hands together excitedly, and I could see why Tyler enjoyed spending time with her. Her optimism and verve were energizing.

"I don't need the holy enchantment, there's no wraith that Moral Dilemma can't cut," Morgan answered proudly. Lilith couldn't very well argue with them since our parents had forged the chain sickles Morgan used.

"Do you know how many Cinderwraiths we'll be facing? Go ahead and cast Holy Light on the weapons of everyone but Morgan please, Aisha."

Aisha did as bid, and sacred light glowed in her hands then split into motes that imbued everyone's weapons, except for Morgan's sickles.

"I can't get a count. They're gathered around the Eye of Fire. It could be one really big one, or a few hundred small ones, or somewhere in between." Tyler held his hands up in frustration, but found himself distracted as a mote of light touched his axe and made the weapon glow with sacred light.

"Between one and a hundred Cinderwraiths," Lilith murmured in thought.

"We'll open with Alexander and Morgan unleashing a combo-attack of cold and darkness, which Cassius will follow up with Tempestas Nivium. If you start the cast while Morgan and Alexander's attacks fade, it should be done by the time Alexander and Morgan join Akari and Tyler in holding the line. Aisha and I will duo-cast something appropriate based on how many and how strong of Cinderwraiths are left, at which point we'll be stuck in a melee."

"After I call on the ice spirits, I could summon spirits of life to fight off the draining effects of the Cinderwraiths, if you and Aisha are going to continue duo-casting?" Cassius suggested, trying to be more useful than the one spell.

"That's a good idea," Aisha answered immediately, before Lilith could shoot down the suggestion.

"We've got a plan, then. Let's execute it without any mistakes," Lilith stared at me when she said that. I felt very called out, for no reason at all.

Morgan tapped my shoulder, and when I turned to look at them, cool lips touched mine in a brief kiss.

"For good luck, so we don't get Progenitor of Peril'd," Morgan answered my confused look with a smirk.

"Even you?" I whined, and everyone laughed at me.

"If you are done sulking, Alexander, we've got demons to kill," Lilith chided me, but she did it with a smile. Apparently, the only bonding activity Lilith and Morgan could enjoy together was making fun of me.

Colors swam around me and blue took control of my aura as I activated cold kinesis. I touched the patch of bare skin on Morgan's forearm with cold, and they shivered but didn't squeal. I didn't dare try it on Lilith, there would be retribution, and Morgan seemed practically immune to the cold. Their darkness was very cold, so it wasn't that shocking.

I sighed and took the forward position to lead the party toward the cave.

Morgan rubbed at the spot I'd cooled off with a touch the moment they thought I wasn't looking, and that put a small smile on my face.

# CHAPTER 53

# The Cinderwraiths

The Cinderwraiths died in our opening volley. I didn't even get to really fight one of them at all, let alone get a good look at them. Talk about disappointment. Is that what you expect me to say? It's not what happened.

The cavern the Cinderwraiths had infested looked to have been an animal den at some point in the past. The first chamber seemed like the sort of place a bear might have hibernated, and there were no Cinderwraiths within it. There were two tunnels going deeper, one small and filled with jagged rocks that would rip anyone larger than a goblin to pieces if they tried to navigate it. We couldn't risk the wraiths coming around behind us and trapping us in the tunnel we could fit through, so Tyler raised a stone wall, and Lilith inscribed it with anti-demon glyphs. It wasn't a surefire method to block the wraiths, but it should discourage them at the very least, we thought.

I quickly concluded that I hated tight spaces. The jagged protrusions of rock wouldn't hinder the spectral wraiths, but they minimized our group's ability to do anything but proceed single file. The tightness gave me flashbacks to the training Sun Wukong had given me in bamboo groves, but I couldn't just knock rock walls out of the way like I could a bamboo tree. Worse, I didn't have any of my evasion abilities stacked up, so I'd be at a real disadvantage if I had to fight like this.

And I did have to fight like this.

The only warning was a shift in the air, and a phantasmal form came together before me. Woven of pure energy, the being looked like a spectral human skeleton with demonic horns and two sets of bat wings on its back. Goosebumps crossed my skin, and I couldn't prevent the shivers that struck me as heat drained away from me at its mere proximity.

Since I was in the lead, I manifested all the cold I could from my cold kinesis and struck the flaming skull. Indestructible gloves or not, my fingers went numb by the time I frost-punched it between the eyes. The orange flames around its skull dulled with the impact of my hand but seemed to be utterly impervious to the release of cold energies from my hand.

"No good, it might as well be immune to cold!" Lilith called from behind.

Darkness writhed in front of me, and Morgan appeared before me. The curved black blade of Moral Dilemma sliced through the Cinderwraith in one contemptuous swing of the sickle. The flames and magic of the creature sputtered out instantly.

"Behind you!" I called to Morgan and activated Dragonfly Strike to appear behind the next Cinderwraith. My aura flared dark; a black tinged with green marked the ascension of my death kinesis. It activated, even as I ambushed the monster from behind. The teleportation effect of Dragonfly Strike never failed to be exceptionally useful in a fight.

This time I remembered to activate the Void Infusion. The mixture of death and madness I held in my hands put a manic smile on my lips, and when my fists struck the Cinderwraith, I couldn't stop a little bit of laughter spilling out of my throat.

The dark purple energies of the Void flowed from my gloves, along with the power of death, amplified by all of my speed thrown into the attack with no regard for the safety of my own hands. Indestructible gloves were the best. This time, when my fist struck the skull of the wraith, it exploded into a vortex of crushed bone. The cold of its awful vampiric existence didn't even reach me this time.

"Can you do necromancy?" Morgan asked as they stepped up and ran their fingers in the air, creating a rune of darkness and shadow. Shadowglyphs were an interesting ability that Morgan had picked up recently from Arkaziel.

"Keep pushing into a wider opening!" Lilith insisted.

"Working on it," I added as I stepped past Morgan and the rune. Lilith or Morgan could work out for themselves who that answered, or if it answered both. The rune was a defensive rune I'd seen in practice before, so I assumed it was meant to protect our rear since the tunnel split open wider just a few meters farther in. I didn't worry about it much, and instead was the first to see the large chamber the tunnel opened into, and at the far back, a whole swarm of Cinderwraiths fed off a fire orb.

"Hot," Morgan said. I was uncertain whether they meant potential necromancy, or that the chamber with the Eye of Fire spiked in heat compared to the previous tunnels, despite the large amount of Cinderwraiths. Turnabout was fair play, it seemed.

"Fifty-four Cinderwraiths," I whispered.

**New Subquest: Kill all (2/62) Cinderwraiths.**

I felt personally attacked by the System.

"We're starting to cast. Morgan, steal the Eye on a ten count; Alexander, make sure nothing gets to the backline; Tyler, be ready to stone-shield." Aisha and Cassius had moved up and started chanting as Lilith spoke, preparing their spells to be ready at the exact moment Lilith had already timed it out to.

". . . 9, 10." Lilith finished the count-off. Morgan flickered through the shadows as bursts of electricity filled the air around the Cinderwraiths. Morgan snatched the Eye of Fire and disappeared, and the motes of electricity exploded into cascading bolts of lightning that chained across the huge swarm.

"Yes!" Cassius cried, and pumped his arm in excitement. He'd never pulled off such a big area effect before, but I'm also assuming he got some kind of title or achievement from the System for hitting so many targets at once.

When the lightning bolts were at their brightest, sacred light blossomed to life within the swarm of monsters. Synergizing off the powerful light generated by Cassius's spell, Aisha's sacred light shone more brilliantly than ever as radiant power struck down the vile Cinderwraiths.

### Kill all (47/62) Cinderwraiths.

Fifteen Cinderwraiths remained from the combination of Lightning Motes and Sacred Light, and I flashed my kinesis to lightning when I sped forward. My Rainbow Rush left a thick storm of stationary bolts of lightning across their path. The fiends ran through it without a second thought. Perhaps my kinesis lacked the oomph of Cassius? Not a single one of the creatures died crossing the lightning field my Rainbow Rush created.

"My rearguard glyph went off," Morgan snapped from the center of the group. "Hold on to this, Cassius, I'll wipe them out."

By the time Cassius had the Fire Eye in his hands, Morgan had already adjusted their grip on Moral Dilemma and vanished into the darkness.

"Stonewall!" Tyler cried and lifted his hands. Behind me, multiple four-foot-high walls lifted, generating cover for all the casters and leaving only me and Tyler unprotected. Fifteen large Cinderwraiths bore down upon me.

"Across from the Cocytus, behold the River *Phlegethon*!" Lilith's voice crashed across the chamber in a mighty echo, driven by divine reverb. It almost made me lose my footing while I dodged blows from the first of the Cinderwraiths to reach me.

I don't think anyone saw me flailing around, and I managed to avoid getting hit at all. Barely. Then rivers the color of blood formed out of portals beside Lilith and crashed into the greater opening of the cave. The blood-looking water moved like a Cinderwraith drawn to fire, straight toward the monsters. When the bloody waters crashed into the wraiths, the air turned into a shower of sparks, a magical paradox that burned at the retinas, or would have if I didn't have killer sunglasses.

"Finish it!" Lilith shouted, and I activated Chromatic Cascade. The world in front of me, or at least the majority of it, turned into a ridiculous vortex of lightning. Between my lightning storm, Lilith's ongoing damage, and the previous spells, the last of the wraiths fell easily, and the fight ended before Cassius's and Aisha's next spell finished.

**SubQuest "Kill all (62/62) Cinderwraiths" Completed.**
**Eye of Fire acquired. Reignite the Eyes of Fire in their proper locations atop Serpent's Maw.**

And just like that, we finished the quest.

"Good job, everyone. Alexander, good recovery when you got scared by my invocation." A small scattering of laughter followed Lilith's praise for the group. Apparently my nearly falling had been noticed.

One of the voices laughing was Morgan's. Moral Dilemma wasn't to be seen in their hands, and they were smirking at me, but after a moment the smirk turned into a wink and a smile. My concern at their safety acknowledged, I gave the cave a once-over for more loot. We found some ore, a few Cinderwraith cores, and a pile of bones and broken items that had presumably once been magical, but the wraiths had already drained them of power long before we had ever shown up.

A party of seven individuals who all graduated from the academy felt like overkill after such an easy victory. I knew this was hubris, though. In fact, Lilith lectured us all on the dangers of hubris, and that the entire purpose of this side quest could have been to give us a false sense of superiority and safety while we were heading into one of the most dangerous dungeons on the continent. It took us a full two hours to reach the summit of the Maw.

We managed to make it to the apex of the mountain before nightfall, at least. Rather than place the Fire Eyes in their slots straight away, we temporarily sealed one of the eye holes. Tyler and Cassius created an earthen wall to give us shelter. It felt like a childhood camping trip, eating provisions around a fire in the eyehole of a great stone serpent.

No one crawled into anyone else's bed rolls as far as I could tell, but given Morgan snuck into mine, I could've been wrong on that. If Aisha or Akari snuck into Lilith's or Tyler's, well, they were as circumspect and quiet about it as Morgan had been. Silence spells weren't that uncommon.

After a breakfast of bread and cheese, we finished the Eyes of Fire quest. With the flames restored, we received two keys as reward: a bronze key and a gold key. We had no idea what they were for, but it seemed likely they'd open something inside the dungeon.

With that quest done, we hopped down platforms conjured from air to descend to the Serpent's Maw. The actual entrance to the Maw was the mouth. There was no actual cave that went deeper into the throat of the serpent, but a large black portal. There was no mistaking it for a regular dungeon entrance, and especially no way anyone could confuse it with anything pleasant.

"Do we all start in the same place?" Aisha asked curiously.

"We should, but the only firsthand information we have on this dungeon came from a party of four. So, there is always a possibility that we will be separated to challenge us." Lilith bit her lower lip. "It's what I'd do to any larger parties."

"Well, it's too late to rethink our party size. We're here, and we need to grow stronger. I intend to kill Argarg when we leave here. Quit being afraid of a scary, dark portal, and let's do what we came here to do!" Morgan tried to be inspiring, but even

I had a hard time not frowning at their odd vibe. I gave their shoulder a squeeze and took the first step toward the black portal.

"I want to be first." Morgan stopped me, and dashed ahead. In a poof, Morgan vanished into the darkness.

"Go team," I said and followed.

**Welcome to the Serpent's Maw Megadungeon. Are you absolutely certain you want to enter?**

"Yes," I answered mentally and felt the system teleport me.

**Welcome to your first Megadungeon.**

**Unlike regular dungeons, you may not leave a Megadungeon except at the exits provided in floor change areas.**

**Challenge Rating* of Serpent's Maw, Floor 1: Level 22.**

**Challenge Rating calculated based on party size.**

# CHAPTER 54

# The White Room

**The Canaan, Pinnacle of Existence.**

Welcome back to the Canaan. My name is Enoch. Do you need a helping hand, or would you like a few moments to gather yourself?"

"Uffda, that first step is a real doozy. Where'd Kallos go?" Telos stood up with the assistance of Enoch. The pure white aesthetic made everything about the white room blend together and made the man speaking to her stand out all the more. Enoch wore black slacks, a polo shirt, and a white doctor's coat. On Earth, Telos would've said he looked English, but maybe that was simply due to the fact Enoch spoke with what sounded like a very posh English accent.

Enoch himself appeared to be in his forties, and had perennially disheveled-looking short hair, gray eyes, and a short white beard. While the man looked human, he had the essence of an Aeon, one comparable to, likely even greater than, Bythos or Sige. Enoch's power didn't seem to be a threatening thing, though. Everything about the lab-coat-clad man radiated calm, support, and readiness to dispatch his superior's orders.

"Kallos? Your companion is in another containment room. It's best you be separated temporarily while your vessels expand, and your abilities reach their natural levels. Your separation prevents the inevitable clash of paradox while you both reacclimatize to the Upper Domain." Enoch smiled perfunctorily, as if to acknowledge how meaningless and useless all those things actually were in relevance to Telos. Telos interpreted the smile Enoch gave her as apologizing for buying time or delaying through unnecessary buzz words.

Maybe the White Room was hell?

"And who or what, exactly, are you, Mr. Enoch?" Telos asked.

"I am Enoch." The man smiled, and then laughed at the awkwardness that grew from his non-answer. "I have gone by many names in service to you. Some call me Metatron. I am your personal assistant, or at least, eyes, ears, voice, and hand. I have long been your Will in the mortal worlds outside, prior to your last departure."

"And who am I?" Telos asked hopefully.

"You don't know who you are?" Enoch suddenly had a clipboard in his hand. "How very distressing it must be, to not know who you are.

"Name?" Enoch asked.

"Telos Metanoia," Telos answered truthfully, while the man scribbled on the clipboard in a language that made Ath look like the drunk ravings of a madman in comparison to this sacred, incomprehensible language. Only it wasn't incomprehensible, Telos could read what Enoch wrote in. Unironically, the name of the language was Enochian. Unlike within the River of Light, the Sefirot seemed distant. Distant and unnecessary. Yet if they were so unnecessary to this place, why did they exist?

"Age?" Enoch asked.

"I don't know," Telos answered. Her mind filled with images of eternal darkness, then light, then darkness. How many cycles had gone before? "I feel like the answer to that is very old, though."

"That's good." Enoch sighed in relief. "Do you know what the Canaan is?"

"Yeah, no. I do not even know who I am, remember? Is this my home?" Telos guessed wildly.

"The Canaan is a metaphysical construct that sits above the Omniverse. It is the totality of the Upper Domain. Those lower order realm beings who theorize its existence believe it to be the Throne of God, the Final Heaven, the pinnacle of existence." Enoch waved a hand, and the floor of the room turned transparent.

"The River of Light," Telos murmured. It flowed in slow spirals ever outward.

"One segment of the River of Light," Enoch corrected. "Here in the Canaan, we call this singular piece you see a Canvas. Each Canvas contains countless existences within the flow of Ein Sof."

The view shifted, and Telos found she was looking at ten, then twenty, then one hundred, then a thousand, then one hundred thousand different views simultaneously. Not with her physical eyes, but with her mind's eye, of which she apparently had one hundred thousand or more, given that she could see each of them in full detail. The expanded processing power of her mind in this place made her feel deeply unsettled, and intensely *in*human.

"The Canaan is the only location we have found in which you can exist without disrupting lower order domains. Each of these Canvases can be put together to create the Mosaic of Creation." With a gesture from Enoch, the individual views of each Canvas blended into a complex, higher than three-dimensional axis, piece of art. It looked like the foam atop ocean waves one moment, then bubbles the next. For a brief moment in time Telos saw slices, like membranes, and then she saw bubbles again.

"These are true views, or representative?" Telos asked Enoch curiously, captivated by the motion of existence.

"Yes?" Enoch answered uncertainly. "To quote your own answer when I asked that when I was new."

A memory awoke from the depths of time. A much younger, but physically older, completely different looking and entirely the same appearing Enoch stood in a similar white room, beholding the full glory of reality. The form Telos wore then was masculine, but she'd seen plenty of male versions of herself before. Every time she activated Existence Oscillation she'd beheld hundreds of alternate versions of herself, so this wasn't that shocking, but it did beg a question. Did she have a real form? A gender? A race?

"You brought me the idea to make the Canaan look like one of the space stations used by the Quantum Overlords," Telos murmured, as an ancient memory broke free from the dark, haunted place that was her memories. The human Enoch gesticulated wildly at displays of immense space stations from a particularly advanced Canvas.

"Indeed, my lady, I did. Prior to that, we lived in a cloud. Very droll." Enoch seemed to struggle with not smiling in pleasure that Telos remembered him, and his contributions.

"Wait, the Canaan looks like a space station. Why does this room look like a big white box made out of clouds, then?" Telos poked at a wall. She half expected it to drift away.

"Your direct observation of the lower order domains always resulted in cataclysmic disruptions, which is why you split yourself into four much weaker beings." Enoch sketched Telos on the paper of his clipboard. From what Telos could see, he was very good. He managed to convey the wonder Telos had felt while viewing the hundreds of thousands of variations of Ohr Ein Sof, and the multiverses they contained beyond counting.

"Four different beings? Why four?" Telos murmured. Why not five? Or ten? If weaker was the goal, wouldn't more be better?

"The Creator, the Destroyer, The Preserver, and the Judge." Enoch thumbed his chin in thought. "As for why those four, I couldn't tell you. The Creator and the Destroyer were especially onerous to deal with."

"So, which one am I?" Telos wondered aloud. Perhaps she was the Creator, or the Destroyer. Both could fit. Judgment might be fun. The Preserver sounded like a dull role, so she really didn't want to be that one. Who wanted to be the maintenance man of reality? None of them really resonated, though. The names felt wrong.

"Ah, I have been unclear. You would be the original, my lady. It was you who raised me to this place from Earth and have allowed me to reincarnate and experience the full turns of the Great Cycle on numerous occasions. Your shadows, the Creator, Destroyer, Preserver, and Judge have maintained control of the Canaan in your absence."

Memories rose in the dark, ancient depths of Telos's mind. The memories practically creaked as they returned to her, like dim, flickering lights of an ancient incandescent bulb in a run-down, obviously haunted shack. A minor discomfort accompanied the awakening of the antediluvian memories, an unexpected pain, like a cut on the wrist from a frayed slap bracelet.

"My emissary," Telos murmured appreciatively, and gave Enoch's shoulder a gentle, familiar squeeze of recognition. "Some of it is coming back. Which means Kallos is . . ."

"An Avatar of the Judge," Enoch said. "It was her duty to reconstitute you, now that the Omniverse has grown strong enough to endure your gaze. No longer must you experience your creation through me, shadows, emanations, or fractional motes of yourself."

"I'm in love with a sliver of myself? That's . . . special." Telos groaned.

Enoch didn't react at all, and instead made another sketch of Telos. This one caught the spiritual crisis that struck Telos as she contemplated the implications of being married to a partition of herself. Telos extended her senses and was shocked by how few people were aboard the Canaan.

"Only you, Kallos, and I are aboard the Canaan. Where are the others?" Telos asked, but answers already bubbled up within her mind. Flickers of another location. A throne. A male and female argue over the throne, before their eyes widen and they vanish as if a black hole had eaten them.

"Prior to your arrival the four were in the Throne Room. The Creator and the Destroyer argued over which of them had the right to sit upon your throne, as they have since your departure, while the Preserver tried to explain their impending non-existence to them. The Judge finalized the activation of the Omega Protocol." Enoch did nothing to hide ages of scorn for the rivalry between the Creator and Destroyer.

"The Omega Protocol . . ." More ancient memories rose from the dark abyss of time. "There's no more versions of me left then, are there?" Telos could find not even a whiff of their existence. Even in all the myriad variations of the River of Light, across the entirety of the vast Mosaic, not a single trace of one of her slivers existed. The Sefirot's emanations illuminated all within the Omniverse and served as her sensory organs in every realm.

*Good job, me. Lacking in style, why not spy on lower domains with a giant ghost ship? Way more dramatic. Wait, am I a voyeur? Am I stalking the Omniverse because I don't have anything better to do? What is the point of my existence?*

The knowledge that lurked in the dark abyss of her awakening memories provided no clear answers, beyond that the route to the meaning of everything lay in the Mosaic. Maybe.

"Only the echo of the Judge survived, for it is buoyed to your existence until you decide otherwise, my lady. Your Kallos is not the Judge itself, but an individualistic avatar that the Judge used to witness your restoration. It is my belief that the Judge became infatuated with existence and conceived a plan: that if she tied herself to you, she might at least partially escape the assimilation that awaited her and the other three." Enoch barked a laugh.

"Restoration," Telos murmured with a laugh. Dim half memories of a few deaths flittered through her mind, then dozens, then hundreds, and then counting became meaningless. "Fancy way of saying consolidation. I guess that answers the question on if the alternate-me's summoned by Existence Oscillation were still alive or not." Telos exhaled a wary sigh. "I hope the Judge didn't just throw them all in a blender and pour us into a me-shaped mold."

Enoch had no answers for her, let alone any words of comfort, and looked down at his feet in awkward silence. *Am I not allowed to have an existential crisis? No, clearly that's all I've ever had, and this was all supposed to answer the questions of why.*

"Let's check on Kallos," Telos said. It was a mixture of a command and a request. Enoch did not protest at all and fell in behind Telos as she exited the door he'd entered. It was her home, and knowledge of it filled her mind as if she'd only been off to college for a few years, and not gone on walkabout for ages. Not that walking out a door, across the hall, and into another room were amazing feats to be memorialized in song and celebrated across the ages.

# CHAPTER 55

# The Canaan

Kallos stood talking to another copy of Enoch. The chains of her wings had all wrapped around her like a cloak. The moment she saw Telos enter the room she tried to put on a strong front, but it was obvious she was glad to be reunited. The second version of Enoch stepped into the first, and they reassimilated into one person.

"Looks like we made it." Kallos laughed nervously.

"Want to check out our new home?" Telos asked with a grin.

"You aren't going to interrogate me like Enoch was?" Kallos asked with a frown. "How do I know if I can trust myself, given what we now know?"

"What do we know? That is tricky. It hasn't all come back to me yet, but I do know I didn't put all of myself into the caretakers. I sent a lot of myself into the Omniverse. Every timeline had one, if not multiple, versions of me. The Judge must have spent eons hunting down all the tiniest of fragments of me, gathering them, and then nurturing this me. Why not take a page from my book and create a sliver of herself who got to experience the universes they watched over? Did she plan for us to fall in love, or was that a happy coincidence?"

Telos shrugged; Kallos looked at the floor guiltily.

"We already knew our timelines had been altered repeatedly by powerful entities. It wasn't you, so why would you feel the need to take on the blame for the actions of an entity you were, at the best, a sliver of? Or did the Judge transfer herself to you at the last minute?" Telos went on the offensive to ensure that Kallos understood she bore no responsibility for the actions of the Judge.

"For being the omnipotent being at the heart of creation, you're strangely okay with others manipulating your existence, darling." Kallos struggled to hide her bewilderment over how easily Telos dealt with it, while Kallos herself grappled with the concept.

"And no, there was no transfer when we entered here, unless that was the hand we saw?" Kallos turned her attention inward to search for tampering or things out of place in her mind and soul.

"That hand would have been me. You both needed to be fully awakened and empowered to enter, and so I helped you." Enoch coughed politely before he interjected into their conversation.

"Good job, Enoch. I could change it if you want. I personally do not see the need to alter the past though, I'm fairly happy with how things have turned out." Telos shrugged, and looked around the white room. It felt slightly claustrophobic, despite being a large room. *Everything used to look like this. Talk about awful.*

"Change what?" Kallos frowned.

"Any of it," Telos answered honestly. "Omnipotent being, remember? Autopotency is only a small part of being all-powerful."

"Would you change any of it?" Enoch asked curiously.

"Not a second of it. Actually, no, you know what, there's always things I could change, but even unpleasant experiences helped shape me. Maybe if it had been slower, or the challenges were more (or actually) challenging, but it was an experience without my hand on the scale. It gave me friends, family, you, and a new perspective. I'm glad that the me that I am is the one the Judge chose to imbue the others into. She followed her imperative to the letter."

"Which were?" Kallos and Enoch asked at the same time.

"That I wanted to find love, raise a family, and save a few lives along the way. Don't look so surprised. There were other conditions, obviously. I needed to find out if I was a wrathful person or a merciful person, benevolent or tyrannical, an introvert or an extrovert." Telos laughed at the slightly ridiculous words she said. "And those are things you find out by experiencing life, not by watching it."

"And what did you find?" Enoch asked curiously.

"Being people was an interesting experience. My human journey was fascinating, but the moment my powers awoke, that journey ended. I am unbounded by the experience of one lifetime, or the countless lives the Judge recombined into the life of Aesca Lampi. Only one thing throughout this all has bound me in any fashion."

Telos eyed Kallos and walked over to kiss her gently on the lips.

"The chains of love are neither heavy nor burdensome; they are as light as air, elevating, invigorating, and have a power derived of harmony which I *thoroughly* enjoyed learning with you." Telos didn't even show the smallest brush of red on her cheeks, despite the horribly corny words she spoke. She hoped the genuine emotion filled her words for both Enoch and Kallos to understand. Neither one rolled their eyes or snorted at her, so clearly, she hadn't failed in her delivery.

"I love you too, darling," Kallos answered simply.

"Interesting," Enoch murmured, then froze like a deer caught in headlights when both women turned to look at him.

"What's so interesting?" Telos demanded.

"Your wrathful nature has become loving?" Enoch's answer came out more like a question.

"I've got plenty of wrath left in me. I'm multifaceted." Telos couldn't resist rolling her eyes at Enoch. Every sapient creature she recalled meeting had been complicated. Reduction of them to only a single dominant trait always lead to surprises when alternate facets showed themselves. Why would she, an entity from a Higher Domain, be any less complicated?

"So . . . what now?" Kallos asked, looking around the white room. It didn't make the Canaan seem a very impressive place.

"Let's take a tour. I haven't been home in ages. Then we'll peek in on the kids and old friends, and after that . . ." Telos trailed off, and looked to Enoch.

"You said you would know the answer to that after your journey, my lady," Enoch said with a grimace. He seemed fully aware that the answer he gave would be a disappointment to his master.

"Past me was a lazy bitch," Telos growled in displeasure.

"We could make something?" Kallos suggested.

"You could smite something?" Enoch offered.

"Is that how we're going to spend eternity?" Kallos asked softly. Her tone betrayed the uncertainty on that being the best use of their time. Telos could feel the other undercurrents beneath the surface of the emotional hurricane building within Kallos, a storm that matched the one within Telos herself. So many questions lay unasked due to the newness of their situation, but who Telos and Kallos were had not changed. Had it?

Of course it had. Telos had gone from a "human" to the omnipotent being who sat atop the Omniverse. Kallos had gone from the daughter of Belial trying to save Zenithar, to a Sovereign, to the consort and part of the apex existence. They had changed tremendously, and now they had to find out what they even were.

"It's a start, isn't it?" Telos grinned. "Actually, do you know what? Why don't you take a quick dip through the Great Cycle, Enoch. A hundred years or so ought to be enough time for us to be alone together."

"Alone together?" Kallos reddened, just a touch.

"We never had a proper honeymoon. Where better than the Canaan?" When Telos said that, she realized where better could be the next game they played.

"It has been ages since I could leave the Canaan without worrying about the Destroyer and the Creator being left unsupervised." Enoch laughed in delight that only someone with long-term carer fatigue could understand.

"Have fun!" Telos chimed after Enoch, while Kallos opted to wave at the departing man. Metatron seemed to grasp the real order of "leave us alone for a while" without it being spelled out for him. Although, the speed with which he went to carry it out spoke volumes to the strain the four stand-ins had placed upon her envoy.

"So, a romantic holiday, just the two of us, without anyone else? I've wanted that for a long time now, my love." Kallos let her golden eyes meet Telos's aqua and red eyes.

"Me too," Telos replied as she led Kallos down corridors of metal, alloy, and gorgeous art. Kallos paused at one of the paintings, which looked like a black hole.

"I just had the greatest idea," Kallos said.

Telos, seeing the painting, sensing the thoughts in her love's mind, laughed out loud.

"That is a great idea. Let's make that a reality, and then we'll start our honeymoon," Telos said, inspiration driving her eagerness.

"How do we fit a multiverse in a black hole?" Kallos asked.

"We just do it, we make things, and then reality sorts itself out. Maybe there's some loose ends to fix, but that's why there's different realities anyway. Rules differences. Now, if we stick *everything* in a black hole, we'll need to sort out the overlapping dimensions. The Astral, the Fey, the Dark, so forth and so on." Telos threw her hands in the air at that last.

"Can't we just slap it all together and give it a convoluted name like the Gossamyr?"

"Creating with a partner is so much more fun than playing solo." Telos smiled at Kallos. "Let's get to work."

"Sure, but . . ." Kallos struggled visibly with shaping her words. "Shouldn't we figure out who the Preserver, Creator, Destroyer, and Judge were, what their responsibilities were, and make sure everything is done? Aren't we responsible, now?"

"We will. The Great Cycle will turn on its own without our intervention. Unless there's immediate redesigns you want to put into place? Maybe Belial is done with that gnosis report. I should really check on the kids, and Vilja, and . . ." Telos heaved a sigh. "I see why I abdicated all of this, last time."

"It's a lot," Kallos said with a nod of agreement.

"No one is here to yell at us if we decided to jump back into the Cycle," Telos said quietly.

"I'm here, and I'm not ready to be someone else yet," Kallos said decisively, cutting off Telos's avoidant decision-making.

"Okay. So, we find out who and what we are, then we find out the meaning to . . ." Telos threw her hands up in the air, gesturing at everything around them.

"Quite so." Kallos laughed softly. The warmth in her laughter thawed the ice that had grown inside of her when she suggested they just start over again. Every instinct within Telos said to run off into the myriad existences, rather than to address the truth of her own existence.

"And you'll stay with me through it all?"

"I promise," Kallos vowed.

"Well, then. Let's make your black hole–amalgamation world and see what questions and answers we find out from there," Telos said, while altering their course through the Canaan.

"Where are we going now?"

"To the Throne. It is time to make a new Canvas," Telos answered with a smile. "Maybe we'll redecorate the Canaan too. I don't know how I feel about the sci-fi vibe we've got going on here, and if I'm going to stick around, I want it to be homey."

Kallos held in her laugh, as the extent of how conflict avoidant this omnipotent goddess she walked with was, and how big of an ordeal it would be to keep her on point.

"I heard that," Telos murmured about Kallos's thoughts. "It's not my fault I'm the sort of person who has to start a game over fifty times before I get through act one."

"Maybe not, but there's no restarting this time." Kallos attempted to reinforce that even if it were a choice, it wasn't on the table.

"No, yeah, sure. We'll see it through to the end, definitely. What about our honeymoon?" Telos asked with large, pleading eyes.

"After we make our black hole–world," Kallos reaffirmed.

"We have to figure out some way to determine whether we exist because of the Lower Realms, or whether the Lower Realms exist because of my Upper Realm." Telos added to the to-do list.

"Why does that matter?" Kallos asked, genuinely curious.

"I . . . well. You don't want to know if I created everything, or everything created me?" Telos tilted her head, intrigued at the thought process of Kallos.

"No. I was created by the Judge, you were created, or re-created by the Judge. Is there any indication in all of the Canaan that there is any other force or presence besides ours? No? What about higher realms than ours? Also, no? Did the Omniverse grow strong enough to bear your gaze by your participation in them?" Kallos asked what she thought would be a slam-dunk question, only to frown herself at the face Telos made, full of uncertainty and doubt.

"I think it was more like I was impatient and wanted to play in reality *now*, rather than me being the one to strengthen things. Past-me ditched the hard work on portions of me and took a long vacation across time and space." Telos quietly thanked Enoch for not being present to confirm her outlook on the situation. Certainty filled her, but it would've felt more damning if someone else nodded their head and agreed, or worse, complained about being made to do her extra work for ages.

*Oh man, did Enoch and the others even get paid? I'm the worst.*

Kallos choked and laughed. Clearly, Kallos had heard the self-deprecating thoughts.

"So, our to-do list post honeymoon is create a black hole–existence, investigate who the Judge, Creator, Destroyer, and Preserver were and what they accomplished, answer the question to the true meaning of existence, and then for a finale: make gnosis a bit more equitable across the Omniverse." Kallos rattled off the list as if it were very easy, and not at all a potentially very labor-intensive undertaking.

"I already miss Bobbi's cooking," Telos lamented.

"Me too, dear, me too," Kallos agreed. "That's why I created a Summon Food by Bobbi spell."

"I knew there was a reason I married you!" Telos praised Kallos, even as the other shook her head.

"Did you forget you're omnipotent?"

"Nope. Even if you're omnipotent, food tastes better when someone else cooks it." Telos said, full of confidence, but she wilted at the disbelieving stare of Kallos.

"It is true! We'll both create a Bobbi dish, and I bet yours will taste better to me than mine will to me, and vice versa."

"Fine, darling. Let us have a Slay-off. If your ridiculous idea holds true we'll summon each other food in the future, and if I am right and they taste the same, then you will be the supreme food summoner." Kallos regarded Telos with a serious expression, waiting for agreement.

*Cripes. I'm betting an eternity of being the ultimate culinary conjurer.*

"Yeah, you betcha. Let's have a walleye-off." Telos shifted into a chef outfit as they changed destinations from the Throne of Canaan to the kitchens of Canaan.

Eventually they made a new Canvas, and it made the Mosaic even more of a grand piece of incomprehensible beauty, where the stories of a powerful fey and a human played out. Telos enjoyed the will-they, won't-they, and the pathos of an ancient sect bleeding into the future proved far more entertaining than the painful tales of Vilja and Aada, which were too tragic for her taste. Happy stories, Telos decided, were much more her jam, such as with Alexander and Lilith and their inevitable triumph over Argarg the Barbarian, and the grand start to an age of epic heroes in the lands of Mythara. Siegfried did make battling gods look dramatic, without Telos, Kallos, or the StarManes to steal his glory.

It would be a lie to say Telos didn't derive joy from watching Bob's fall and replacement. Deicide made for great entertainment, until Telos realized she was a deicide candidate herself. What's a little hypocrisy to an Omniversal Overlord? After all, she'd already lost the cook-off, and Telos had to summon every meal on the Canaan for the rest of eternity. Any would-be assassins would have to surpass the trial of Ultra Divine, SSS+ Rank Tater Tot Hot-Dish to even attempt to perform deicide on her.

# Afterword

That's it. That's the story of Telos and Kallos Metanoia. Maybe there'll be more about Alexander and Lilith in the future, but the direct tales of Kallos and Telos are done. There will definitely be more to come in the Omniverse, though.

It has been a wild ride for me. I've gone through three different day jobs while writing Odyssey, and here in the final stretch, we lost one of our cats, Maisey Whitepaws, to old age. She was the cuddliest, prettiest, greatest cat we could've hoped to have with us for the last fourteen years. Then we lost Willy Daggerpaws, a cat who acted like a dog and looked like a teddy bear. It's been an unbelievably rough year, but being able to write something with humor has helped.

I've got a lot of ideas about what's coming next, but for now, thank you for reading Odyssey of the Ethereal. Getting a publishing offer as a first-time author was a surreal, but amazing, experience. Podium has gone above and beyond at every step of the way with Odyssey and made the experience a lot easier than it otherwise would have been. Without Podium, I definitely wouldn't have had the amazing art of Harry Bui bringing the covers to life, the epic narration of Diana Richardson taking me on a fantastic voyage, or all of the hard work of the editing team making my words into a comprehensible message.

I would like to think I've learned a lot about writing in the process, but I'm still a newbie, for which I apologize, and thank you for looking past it and putting up with me. Again, thank you for reading, and I hope you will show up for the next series I have on the horizon.

# About the Author

Jamie Kojola is the author of the Odyssey of the Ethereal series, originally released on Royal Road. In her free time, she enjoys gardening, sewing, gaming, crafting, and playing *D&D*. Kojola lives in Minnesota with her two children, spouse, and three cats.

9 781039 480599